MARIANNE A. SCOTT

OF
FIRE
AND
SACRIFICE

A FAE ROMANCE NOVEL

Editor: Roxana Coumans

Cover Design: Moonlit Town End Art & Design

Fantasy Map: Eternal Geekery

For Amanda,
who once said, "I want to be a fairy in one of your books."
It only took me three years, but this one is yours.

Content Warning

Your mental health is important! Please be aware of the following situations in this book:

Alzheimer's/Dementia in a Parent

Death of a Parent

Recreational Drug and Alcohol Use

Explicit Sex (MF)

Torture

Battles, Violence, Blood

Talk of Addiction (not the main characters)

Author's Note

Of Fire and Sacrifice is the third installment in the Fae Romance Series. Each book in this series features a new couple, has a HEA, and can be read independently of the other books in the series. However, this book contains heavy spoilers for the first two books.

If you would like to read the timeline in order, *Of Ice and Heartbreak* and *Of Vines and Rivals* can be found in paperback, ebook, and on Kindle-Unlimited.

Happy Reading!
—Marianne

Chapter One
Devorah

A Short While Ago

"We need to *take care* of the queen."

My head snapped up. The thousands of thoughts that constantly vied for supremacy paused their chatter, and my mind went still, focused solely on the words of my advisor.

"I'm sorry," I said, trying to keep the blatant shock from my face. "Can you run that by me one more time?"

For as long as I was alive, Hershel served as my mother's advisor. He was a constant in my life and the closest thing I had to a father figure. It was only natural for him to aid me when I began running the Summer Court.

Hershel was a broad male, so broad that he made the large wingback chair in my office look tiny. His chocolate-brown hair was buzzed down to stubble, the same faint growth tracing his jawline and standing out sharply against his pale skin.

"She's sick," he sighed.

"I'm aware," I said through clenched teeth. Like I needed the reminder that my mother—an immortal Fae and the Queen of the Summer Court—was *fading*. It was an awful disease that ate at the mind,
attacking the memories and personality. Not even humans in the mortal
realm had a cure for this kind of disease. It was an illness that took my
mother and left me carrying a weight of responsibility I wasn't ready for.

"And since she won't step down, we need to do something dras-
tic." His brown eyes were soft and pitying. He dared to look upset by
this proclamation—the suggestion that we kill my mother, the fucking
queen!

It was true that we were in a predicament. My mother could have
abdicated the throne to me; it would have made our lives much easier.
But on the days she was lucid, she believed she could handle it. On the
days she wasn't...

There was only so much I could do without being handed the literal
keys to the kingdom. I forged her signature on some documents, excused
her absence at missed events, and kept the secret of her decline confined
to the staff in the palace—who were bound by a magical oath that spelled
death if they divulged her condition to anyone. But the court was floundering without a true leader, and soon, others would notice.

Still, killing her wasn't the answer.

I steepled my hands in front of my mouth, trying to remember the
polite way to tell someone to get fucked, when a shift at the back of the
room drew my eye. Hershel's son leaned against the overstuffed bookshelf beside the closed door. He only looked vaguely like his father—the
pale coloring was the same—but his hair was black and was kept slightly
longer, and his eyes were a brilliant blue that bordered on purple. His
muscular arms were folded over a broad chest, sleeves rolled to his elbows
in a way that showed ridiculously corded forearms. He was normally

so still that I forgot he was there, so the fact that he moved at all was intentional.

He trained under his father for a long time, preparing to take over once Hershel decided to retire. But since Fae were immortal, I didn't see that happening anytime soon. Unless something tragic happened and Hershel's life was cut short for suggesting to off my mother.

"You," I said, my eyes connecting with his. He straightened and dropped his arms to his side, a soldier ready for battle. "Little Hershel—"

"It's Ari, Your Highness," he said, his voice deep and silky, conjuring images of slipping into a warm bath. I knew his name, of course—I'd known Ari forever—but we rarely interacted. Now that I had to, calling him Little Hershel would allow me to detach, to remind myself exactly who I was talking to, and help me ignore the the part of me that noticed his *ridiculously corded forearms* and likened his voice to *slipping into a warm bath.*

"Right," I said, affecting an air of indifference. "What do you think of this plan?"

He swallowed, his Adam's apple bobbing beneath dark stubble, and glanced between me and his father. His tongue slicked his bottom lip.

By the fucking goddess, Devorah. *Stop looking at his damn mouth.*

"What will it be, Little Hershel?" I asked, my voice sharp as a blade.

He gave me a small smirk that said he wasn't impressed. "I think there's no way in all the realms that you would take that suggestion seriously."

"Why's that?" I leaned back as if the office chair was my future throne. "I could very well be power-hungry and ready for the change. At the least, I'd appreciate the bigger office—I've outgrown this one."

My office was small and cramped, barely large enough for the giant desk and three chairs. It didn't help that I was an utter slob, and every surface, including the built-in bookshelves, was covered in papers that I had no intention of organizing. Add that to the lack of windows, and the tiny office was oppressive, unlike the rest of the airy palace.

"You value family, Your Highness."

I arched an eyebrow. It wasn't something I broadcasted; Fae had a reputation for attacking the things you care about. Ari must have been paying attention all these years.

"And..." he glanced at his father. "It's a shit plan."

"Why?"

"Someone would realize the order came from you, and there would be backlash. You would be accused of treason and killed."

I nodded and turned back to my advisor, who had gone still as a statue. His eyes were completely devoid of emotion, like he had locked them behind a wall of iron. "Your Highness—" he started, but I held up a hand to silence him.

"Hershel, you're fired." Both males' mouths dropped open in identical expressions. "Little Hershel, congratulations. You've been promoted."

"You can't fire me," Hershel said, some anger creeping into his impassive expression.

"I can, actually," I said, running my fingers through my dark brown hair. "It's amazing what one can do when they run a court."

"I could tell everyone," he mused. "Tell them all about the queen and what you're doing here."

I could have answered, but instead, I glanced at Ari. It was probably cruel of me to make him go toe-to-toe with his father, but if he was going to be my advisor, it would be the least I asked of him.

"You took a magically binding oath," Ari said. He moved away from the door, rounding the desk to my side. The way he stood, slightly in front of me as if to protect me if his father got violent, shouldn't have been so sexy—but it gave me a clear view of his ass in his tight, black pants.

I'm only female; anyone would have looked.

They probably wouldn't have ogled, though. And when Ari turned back to me and caught me red-handed, the smirk he gave me probably should have made me blush. Instead, I lifted my chin and motioned for him to proceed.

"In fact," he continued, "you're lucky Her Highness is only firing you and not hanging you for treason."

"Beautifully said."

"Thank you."

Hershel flushed red, the color tinting his cheeks, his neck, and up to the top of his head.

"You have a choice," I said, examining my nails. "I can call for your head on a spike, or you can go quietly. I'll even swear an oath never to speak of this meeting so you can find work elsewhere. Though you swore a non-compete oath when you took the job, so you can't work in the other courts—but I'm sure my brother has some openings in the army."

There was a moment of utter stillness, and then Hershel chuckled and ran his hand over his head. "You're going to make a great queen, Devorah."

I blinked. I expected him to lose his mind, to flip out and set my office on fire. Instead, he was...complimenting me?

He extended his hand across the desk. I eyed it with trepidation, still expecting some kind of attack. Slowly, I shook it.

Ari cleared his throat. "You will say nothing about this meeting, about the queen's illness, and about anything pertaining to the private dealings of the court."

"I agree," Hershel said. I felt the binding seal of Ari's magic solidifying the oath.

"And, as a thank you," I added, "I will say that you stepped down to make way for your son and will mention nothing of this meeting to those not in this room or the royal family."

He nodded, grimacing a little at the added addendum, but I kept nothing from my twin brother, and he knew that. My magic rolled over us, heat blooming over my hand until Hershel released it and stood.

"It's been an honor," he said, bowing at the waist before leaving and shutting the door behind him.

As soon as he was gone, I flopped onto my desk with a whimper. My head throbbed, pulsing right behind my eyes. Now, not only was I in charge of the entire court, but I'd need to do it without my trusted advisor. Not that I didn't trust Ari, but I barely knew him. Not in the way that mattered.

A warm hand touched my arm, and I jerked up to find Ari with a small vial of tonic—the very one I hid behind a false book on my shelves. Fae weren't supposed to have persistent ailments, but I was under more stress than most Fae experienced in their lifetimes, so I had a secret stash of tonics that helped with the headaches.

"How did you know?" I asked, taking the vial and downing the contents, the taste of rosemary washing over my tongue.

"I know more than you think." He banished the vial into thin air on my behalf and sat opposite of me.

"Watching that closely?"

My teasing was rewarded by a smile that revealed a dimple on his right side. "It's my job, Your Highness."

"You can call me Devorah."

"Devorah," he said like he was tasting the word, savoring it.

Fucking hell, I could not be attracted to my advisor. Very bad idea. We were going to spend countless hours together, not to mention that it was a gross abuse of power.

"So, what do you think we should do about..." I waved my hand in a gesture that encompassed everything.

He sighed. "Honestly? You need allies."

"I have the Seelie Courts."

The Seelie Courts were comprised of Summer, Day, and Spring Courts and had been aligned for centuries. Similarly, the Unseelie Courts—Winter, Autumn, and Night—were aligned just as long. All the courts had a tentative truce at the moment, but I feared that the second the others heard of our predicament, they would seize the opportunity to attack. I couldn't order the movement of troops to fend off a large-scale invasion without my mother's stamp of approval.

"I didn't mean them," Ari said, fixing me with an intense stare. "You need a...stronger ally."

Oh fuck no.

He meant Winter Court, our neighbor to the east. Specifically their queen, Gwyneira. She was the undisputed strongest Fae alive, and because of it, her court was impenetrable. She was the sole reason the Seelie Courts needed to unite our armies into one large force.

An alliance with her would send a clear statement to the others. Unfortunately, because of a past altercation that resulted in a very bloody war, our courts had a tenuous relationship. We weren't unfriendly, but there was some frostiness—pun intended.

"How do you suggest I convince her to align with us?"

He grimaced. "You're not going to like it."

"I don't like any of this," I laughed bitterly. Honestly, on any given day, it felt like I was thirty seconds away from bursting into tears.

Ari reached for me like he wanted to take my hand but thought better of it. "Marriage. You can get her help through an alliance by marriage."

"Pretty sure I'm not her type," I deadpanned. Gwyneira had seven husbands and made it very clear that she was madly in love with each of them.

"Not you," he whispered. His purple eyes locked with mine, almost unblinking until his meaning sunk in.

"What is with your family today?" I breathed. "Your father wants to kill my mother, and now you want to pimp out my brother?"

"It's a good plan."

"No. It's the literal opposite of a good plan. She'll never go for it."

"She would if you tell her about our problem with those rogue Fae. You know she'll want to be involved in their apprehension, and then we'll have an alliance for both reasons."

"You want me to *lie* to the strongest Fae in the realm and trick her into a political marriage?" I asked, dropping my voice as if she would hear me despite the distance between our courts and the shields surrounding my office that mute sound.

"I prefer *withhold the truth*." Goddess, that smile should be criminal. It's the kind of smile that's just mischievous enough that it looks dirty. "And you wouldn't lie, your brother would."

"So, I throw Eldoris to the wolves?" I groaned and flopped onto the desk again, my head hitting with an unsettling thud. Ari made a concerned sound but didn't move to help me.

Deep down, I knew his plan would work. Eldoris often reminded me he wanted to help. But the thought of doing this made me feel slimy. He had a hard life; I shouldn't ask him to enter into a loveless marriage for the sake of our court.

Unfortunately, I didn't have any other ideas.

"You can't tell him you're my advisor," I said into the wood of my desk. "My brother will agree because he's selfless to a fault, but he won't think it's a good idea unless it comes from me—and Hershel."

"You'll have to tell Eldoris eventually."

I tilted my head up just enough to level him with a glare. "Don't tell me how to handle my twin."

Ari held his hands up in supplication. "I won't tell him until you do," he agreed, and the magic of our agreement slid into place. His magic was warm—not hot like mine—and it had the gentle caress of water.

A knock on the door drew our attention, and a female healer came in, her hair in disarray. "Your Highness..." She didn't need to continue. I knew her presence in my office had something to do with my mother, and her haggard appearance didn't bode well.

"She's asking for you," the healer said. "She appears lucid and is asking why she's not permitted to leave her rooms."

"Have you sent for my brother?" She nodded. "Thank you. I'll be up in a minute."

As soon as the healer left, tears sprang to my eyes. It wasn't that I wasn't happy my mother was lucid, but sometimes those brief glimmers of the female who had raised me were harder than the days when she was gone. It was a tease, a splash of hope in a desolate ocean.

"You should—" Ari started.

"Try to get her to abdicate the throne, I know."

This time, his smile had none of that roguish charm. Instead, it was soft with a touch of pity that made me want to throw things. "I was going to say you should spend as much time with her as you can."

I bit the inside of my lip so hard it bled. I wouldn't cry in front of this male, not on his first day. I needed to be strong, to be the princess I was raised to be. The one capable of running an entire court.

I couldn't fall apart.

The threat of my voice coming out choked was enough to keep me silent. So, I stood and left the office to head to my mother's chambers.

Chapter Two
Devorah

Present

"WHAT DO YOU THINK?" I ask, leaning back in my chair and returning my advisor's challenging stare. He's preternaturally still, his only movement that of his eyes. They scan my face like they're cataloging every blink, every twitch of my lips. It feels like he's stripping me bare, delving beneath my flesh and seeing the most intimate parts of me.

Servants surround us, traipsing through my room in a frenzy of activity. The thudding steps of Melia—the best seamstress in the realm—make the pale oak wood floors tremble, and my lady's maid, Kalinda, sighs. I can see her slump against one of the robin's egg blue walls in my periphery, running her fingers over the white wainscotting. They're all waiting for me, but I can't bring myself to care.

"What. Do. You. Think?" I repeat.

"I think," Ari starts slowly, licking his lips. He breaks my stare and rolls his shirtsleeves up to his elbows. When he finds me staring, his face transforms into a smug smile that reveals one dimple. "I think you're bluffing."

"Try me," I shrug, using a bit of magic to let the ripped neckline of my oversized shirt slip down my shoulder. He latches onto the bit of exposed skin, and now it's my turn to smile smugly.

"Fine." He reaches into his pocket, withdraws a pack of cookies—specialties from the mortal realm—and tosses them on the coffee table between us. "I call. Show me what you've got, Your Highness."

"You first, Little Hershel."

His lips purse at the nickname, but he flips over his cards.

"Damn," I swear, dragging my hand through my long, brown hair. He chuckles and reaches for the pot in the center of the table. "Wait." I place my hand atop his. A little zing travels up my arm from the feel of his skin against mine. As if in sync, we both stare at the point of contact before our eyes lift—his purple connecting with my ocean blue.

"Remind me," I whisper, breathily. "Does a straight beat two pair?"

He blinks.

I flip over my cards—ace to five, all in hearts.

"Fucking hell." Ari flops back in his oversized white armchair. My laughter breaks the tension that—while completely real and always present—I used to my advantage. With a playful shimmy, I slide the winnings toward me.

"You should know better. I never bluff," I say in faux innocence. Ari glares.

I open the coveted packet of cookies, twisting the halves apart and popping the cream-less half into my mouth. "That was my last pack," he grumbles and grabs the cards to reshuffle. "Now I need to wait until Edina goes back to the mortal realm."

"Poor baby." I lick the cream from the other half in a way that's only ninety percent suggestive. "We can play another hand for the remainder of the pack..."

"Don't you have to get ready?" He gestures to everyone waiting for us. Melia has abandoned my sitting room—clearly over my bullshit and off to serve one of the other royals she's fitting for the coronation today—but Kalinda is waiting patiently.

"Who says I'm not already dressed?" I gesture to the T-shirt I wear to bed that's long enough to hit me mid-thigh. It's so faded you can't see the original design, and there's a small hole under the arm, but it's so soft. I'd live in it if I could.

"My mistake, Your Highness," he smirks.

"I have time for one more game, right, Kalinda?" I ask, looking over my shoulder to where my lady's maid has abandoned the wall and is sitting in a round chair tucked into a nook with a view of the ocean.

"Sure. It's not like today is important." She flips through my sketchbook with deliberate curiosity. Normally I would ask her not to look; my art isn't anything special. It's just something I do to quiet my mind when I can't sleep. But she's going to be in a hurry to get me ready, so I let it slide.

Ari laughs and deals out five cards each.

As much as they give me a hard time, they know how much I need this little moment of normalcy. Large events never used to give me anxiety, but since Mother's illness, I can barely breathe throughout them.

And today is going to be a long day.

It's not just a ball where I can excuse her absence if she's starting to show signs of memory loss. It's an entire day. As Queen of the Summer Court, my mother needs to participate in the ceremony crowning the new queen of the Spring Court. Then we have the celebratory dinner and a ball after that. An entire day of making sure she knows what's happening and is behaving appropriately without anyone suspecting she's sick.

I barely slept last night, worrying about all the ways things could go wrong, and when I did wake, it was because of a nightmare in which she went into a fit of rage and burnt down Spring Court's palace. Irrational since the entire thing is made of stone, but my subconscious didn't seem to know that.

Ari came in to ask a few questions about some little squabble between two villages in the Wyld Jungle when he found me curled in a ball on the bathroom floor, trying to even out my breathing. He didn't pause; he just sat beside me and then suggested a game of cards for his last pack of cookies.

It was exactly what I needed. A break from the reality that is my life.

"We should go over a few things for today," he says as I peek at my cards. "How many?"

I have nothing, but I keep my face impassive. "Two." I slide two of the worst cards to him, and he deals me two more before discarding one card himself. "What are we going over?"

"You remember your code word?" The word I'll say if I need him to get my mother out of there. As our advisor, it would be a lot less inconspicuous if he claimed there was a problem than if I suggested she return home. It's not a perfect solution, but it's better than nothing.

"It's a...fruit or something?" He glares over his cards. Needling him is too much fun. "Elderberry."

"Good girl."

By the fucking goddess.

How am I supposed to focus on anything when he's calling me a good girl? And judging by his satisfied expression, he knows exactly what he did. I guess I deserve it after my tactics of the previous hand.

Ignoring the way my core tightens, I drop my cards. Pair of threes. Pathetic.

"You win." He tosses his cards face down atop the others.

"Bullshit." I reach for them. He hastily snags my hand.

"I don't want your pity win, Little Hershel."

"I had absolutely nothing."

"You're a shit liar." I use my free hand to turn over his cards, revealing three of a kind. "Why would you pretend to lose?"

"Maybe I just want to watch you lick the cream again," he winks.

"Cad." I toss one of the remaining treats at him, and he catches it before shoving the whole thing in his mouth. I stare in horror. "Who eats Oreos like that?"

"Me."

"Pretty sure you'd get sent to jail if you did that in the mortal realm."

As he puts the cards back into the pack, all traces of humor and flirting turn to dread that settles over me like an anvil, the weight compressing my chest. I slide the last cookie toward him, my stomach twisting at the thought of eating.

"Hey." Ari crosses to my couch and squeezes his large body next to mine until I'm forced to scoot over. He takes both of my hands in his, their size dwarfing mine. "You can handle this day." I look up to see the earnestness in his eyes. "You are one of the strongest females I have ever met. And I'll be beside you the whole way."

Swallowing down the tears threatening to spill, I nod. But I don't lean into him like I want to, keeping that very thin line of decorum between us.

"You go above and beyond, you know that?" I choke out. "You going for employee of the century or something?"

He flinches at the word *employee* but covers it quickly. "Or something."

His thigh presses against mine, the heat warming my bare legs. My heart flutters wildly in my ribcage, my mouth has gone completely dry—and not from anxiety.

I've done a really good job of ignoring my attraction to Ari. Sure, we flirt, but it's mainly just playful banter. It's become natural, the way we interact with each other.

Today feels different. Charged. It's only been like this one other time since he became my advisor. The time I refuse to think about except for a few weak moments when I'm alone in my room at night.

Kalinda clears her throat. I completely forgot she was here. "Shall we get you ready, Your Highness?" The amusement in her voice is barely concealed.

"Right," Ari says, releasing me and running his hands through his hair as he stands. "I'll be back to escort you and your mother in an hour."

"Thanks, Little Hershel," I say, trying to keep my tone light.

He doesn't even scowl or berate me on the use of his nickname; he just nods and runs out of the room.

I turn and find Kalinda grinning at me from her spot in my chair. "Oh, shut up."

She breaks out into raucous laughter. "You could do worse, Princess," she teases, guiding me to the vanity in my bedroom.

The room is painted in a soft sherbet and is offset by cream trim and furniture. My bed takes up most of the space—I insisted on it being so large that I could spread out like a starfish—and is adorned with piles of pillows in every shade of the sunset. Spotted throughout are little hints of the Summer Court's three different terrains: a red-clay pot from the base of the Orasite Mountains that's inlaid with turquoise rocks, a mural made from pearlescent seashells from the beach of the island Pa Ferie, and vases of tiger lilies and birds of paradise from the Wyld Jungle.

The double doors to my balcony are thrown open, the sun so bright that no magical lights are needed to show the depth of the bags beneath my eyes. Thank the goddess for Kalinda and her makeup skills. If she wasn't here, I'd have to resort to using glamour to conceal my exhaustion.

"He's my advisor, nothing more," I respond. Even *I* don't believe the line.

But the truth is, Ari *is* only my advisor. I'm aware of our mutual attraction, but if we were to start anything and it went sour, it would be catastrophic. Having an advisor you trust is essential in a realm where everyone is out for themselves. Ari has been goddess-sent, especially since his father was such a colossal disaster at the end. I can't afford to lose him because I want to fuck him.

Even if it would be amazing.

"You're overthinking it," Kalinda says as she styles my hair. She usually does it by hand since I love having my hair played with, but we're short on time, so today, she uses her magic. Two strands of my long, brown hair are pulled off my face and fastened behind my head—which will help secure my tiara—while the rest is tamed into a sleek sheet down my back.

"I have too much on my plate to think about it at all." She moves on to my makeup, her magic painting my face in record time—though she handles my eyeliner and mascara by hand since that makes me nervous.

"That's exactly why you could use a bit of fun." She motions for me to stand, and I strip out of my shirt. "No underwear in this dress."

The dress Melia made for me is a satin that will indeed hug every curve and show every line. It has a modest neckline but dips down in the back and is held together only by a thin tie across the shoulders. It's a beautiful dress, and the aquamarine will highlight my eyes perfectly, but I was hoping to have a little more maneuverability today.

Kalinda barely has me in the dress when someone comes charging into my suite. "Princess Devorah?"

"In here," I call, knowing that if they got through the wards on my suite, they mean me no harm.

A healer enters, the female a petite Fae that I think is part pixie with the way her teeth are pointed. Her delicate features are set in a hard line.

"What is it?" I ask, stepping toward her.

"It's your mother."

Chapter Three
Devorah

The vase clatters to the ground, beautifully crafted blue and green sea glass coating the brown sandstone floors in an ocean of shards.

"Get back," my mother screams, backing herself into a corner of her office. Her ocean eyes—the ones my brother and I both inherited—are wild and unfocused, bouncing between me and the healers surrounding her. Her coffee-colored hair, which she always took such pride in keeping sleek and shiny, is a rat's nest of tangles. She tugs at the errant strands that have escaped her hair tie while brandishing a letter opener as a weapon.

Thank the goddess she doesn't seem to remember that she has fire magic. There have been episodes like this when she calls on her element, and this room—with its books and papers and precious tomes—would be kindling.

"Who are you?" she hisses like an alley cat.

"I'm Devorah," I say softly, reaching toward her. She shrinks back further, using her free arm to cover herself, as if she just now realized she's only in a pale nightgown. "You know me."

"No." Her head shakes wildly.

It's not the first time she hasn't recognized me. It's not the first time she's mistaken me for a maid, or her sister, or literally anyone else. And it's not the first time she's looked at me with fear—like I'm the enemy.

It still hurts.

No. Hurts isn't a strong enough word. It feels like someone has reached down my throat and latched onto my stomach, dragging the organ up while the leaking acid scorches my esophagus.

"I'm your daughter," I continue, keeping my voice calm, not letting her see one ounce of that excruciating pain.

For a brief moment, it looks like the fog is clearing. She lingers over my eyes before looking at the rest of me, parsing the statement for any truth. Unlike my brother, who takes after our human father, my features are all hers. I smile encouragingly, silently praying to the goddess to let this go our way.

I know the second she stops believing me. Her eyes shutter. The hand holding the letter opener shakes as she clenches around it. Then, she exhales derisively.

"Your Highness," the healer hedges, eyeing the letter opener. My mother is holding it so tight that the dull edge looks like it's about to pierce her skin.

I motion for them to wait. If they sedate her, like they want, there's no way she'll be able to attend the coronation. Normally, I wouldn't hesitate to leave her home in their care. However, each monarch from the different courts has specific duties for the ceremony, so her attendance is mandatory.

One more tactic. I can try one more thing.

I transform my smile into one that conveys ease and respect. "Queen Talia." I bow low, keeping my eyes on my mother even as I drop close to the floor. The healers follow suit.

My mother blinks. "That's right," she mutters and stands tall, squaring her shoulders and lifting her head as if she can sense the weight of her crown.

I wait until she motions for me to stand. "Your Majesty, we have a coronation to attend. Will you allow us to assist you in getting ready?"

"A coronation?" she sniffs. "No, that's not possible. Did someone die?"

I inwardly swear.

I'm better than this. I know to wait until my mother reveals what period she thinks she's in before giving any concrete details. But the clock is ticking, and it's made me sloppy.

I take a deep breath and go over my options. If I tell her Titania—the now-deceased Queen of the Spring Court—has a daughter who is taking her throne, she'll think I'm lying. Goddess, *none* of us knew Lysandra existed until a short while ago when she revealed she'd been hiding in the mortal realm. The problem is, I'm not even sure if she knows who *Titania* is.

"The coronation," I begin very slowly, "is in Spring Court."

"Liar," she scoffs. "The goddess herself couldn't pry Titania off her throne, and that bitch will never die."

Well, at least she remembers that much. "She is dead, M—Majesty." I opt not to tell her that Titania was murdered; there's only so much I can expect her to handle well.

Just as I think she's about to comply, one of the healers shifts. It's the slightest movement, adjusting their stance in case they need to run, but it's enough to set off her hackles.

"Guards!" she screams. "Get these imposters out of here."

The letter opener falls to her feet, and a small flame blooms in her palm.

"Mom, please," I beg, but it doubles to the size of a grapefruit, and even from a distance, I can tell it's hotter than a typical fire.

"Your Highness..." the healer beside me says, watching the flame as it gets dangerously close to the curtains. My mother's eyes lock on mine, and she cocks her hand back to throw the fireball.

"Do it," I command.

The three of them surge forward. The two with light magic—the magic most healers have—call brilliantly blinding light, taking my mother's focus off me and distracting her from the third healer—a siren male in his land-dwelling form. He partially shifts, his hands becoming webbed and his fingernails growing into barbed points that drip with venom. He jabs one directly into my mother's arm, and the fire immediately winks out as the venom suppresses her magic. She shrieks, and he takes the advantage to slip a tonic into her mouth and forces her to swallow. When she flops forward, all three healers are there, catching her as she falls into their arms.

"We'll take her back to her room," they say, loading her onto a canvas stretcher that two more healers bring in.

I take her limp hand in mine. She's warm from the fire buzzing in her veins, but her skin is like paper. She's so frail that I'm afraid if I squeeze, I'll break a bone. "Make sure she gets an extra nutritional potion today," I instruct.

"Yes, Your Highness."

They leave as soon as I release her, closing the door to the office behind them. Breathing in through my nose and out through my mouth, I wrap my arms around my stomach, my satin gown wrinkling as I fist my hands into the fabric. I want to sink to my knees in a puddle, but if I do that, I'll never get up. A pounding that mimics my heartbeat thuds right between my eyes, and I pinch the bridge of my nose, willing it away.

For the millionth time in recent history, I curse the goddess. I curse her for making my twin's ears rounded and making mine pointed—which, in the minds of prejudiced Fae, makes me more eligible for the throne. I curse her for making this coronation today, of all days.

Most of all, I curse her for giving my mother this illness that steals her away from me, bit by bit, moment by moment.

"Your Highness?"

The sound of Ari's voice nearly shatters the fragile hold I have on my composure, but I manage to rein it in. I keep my back to him, swiping away the one errant, escaped tear.

"Yes?" I ask, clearing my throat.

"Eldoris and Edina are here," he says, referring to my brother and his betrothed. When Ari suggested that Eldoris marry the Winter Court Queen for an alliance, she instead offered her daughter. Against all odds, they fell in love and formed one of the strongest bonds I've seen between two Fae who aren't fated mates. After everything my brother went through—losing his mate when she was so young—it warms my heart to see him get a happy ending.

"Okay," I murmur distractedly. How the hell am I going to get through this day? I know the monarchs suspect something is wrong with my mother, but no one has confronted me. If she doesn't show up today...

There's no way I can excuse her absence without telling them the full story.

And if I tell them we're vulnerable.

I can't count on the alliance with Winter Court—and Queen Gwyneira's considerable power—until Edina and Eldoris are married. She may step in to help us because they're betrothed, but it's a long shot.

I'm not even sure the Seelie Courts would be able to resist the thought of conquering a weakened Summer Court.

"What is it?" Ari asks when I don't move.

I'm backed into a corner, no worse than my mother was backed into one a moment ago. But there's no way out for me. No sedative that can make this go away.

My breath comes in faster. I can't control it. It feels like I'm burning up from the inside out as my magic tries to rally around me, but it's not strong enough to combat this feeling.

"Devorah." I blink, and Ari is in front of me, face full of concern. He reaches for me.

"Don't," I breathe. He halts. "Don't touch me."

"Okay." He steps back.

"If you touch me, I'll fall apart. And I don't have time to fall apart."

"Okay. I'm not going to touch you, but I'm right here." He takes a large inhale, and I find myself mimicking the movement. "That's right, breathe with me."

I don't know how long we stand there, just breathing. Whenever mine hitches, he gently murmurs praise and reminds me to take it one breath at a time. My eyes are magnetized to his, letting him anchor me, guiding me through my riptide of emotions.

Slowly, my heart rate returns to normal, leaving only a fuzzy feeling in my head. "Thanks," I say on another exhale, taking his hand and squeezing it once in thanks.

Taking that as permission, he steps closer. "What can I do?" he asks. I feel the kiss of his magic against my skin, the scent of citrus wrapping around me like a warm embrace, and I know he's shielded us so that none of the nosy servants can hear our conversation.

At this angle, I have to crane my neck to see him. I'm not a small female, but he easily has six inches on me. I become hyperaware of the fact that he's still holding my hand, his thumb rhythmically brushing over my knuckles.

"I don't know," I laugh mirthlessly. "My mother can't go today."

"I know."

"I can't tell them she's sick; I need to mobilize the military first." Why haven't I done that? Why haven't I pulled our troops from the Seelie Army and brought them to our borders?

"Breathe," Ari gently reminds me. I want to lean my head against his chest and bask in his warmth, but there's only so much I can blur these lines. Flirting is one thing; leaning on him to help with political decisions is fine. But this? Leaning on him while I'm mentally crumbling? I can't do that.

Releasing him, I give myself an inch of space to think clearly. I shove down every insecurity, every doubt, and every fear and try to look at this pragmatically. I'm a strong female, I've been training to rule an entire court. I can solve this.

"Okay." I pace the length of the room, and Ari extends the shield to cover the entire office. "We need it to look like my mother is there."

"Correct."

"If we wake her and keep her sedated, she won't be able to perform her part in the coronation."

"Right."

I swipe my hand down my face, grateful Kalinda magically set my makeup.

The makeup she did so I wouldn't have to glamour myself.

A plan takes form in my mind. A fucking crazy plan that won't work. Shouldn't work.

Could maybe work.

"You're going to hate this." I stop in my tracks and look back at my advisor. He's in a full tuxedo and by the fucking goddess, he looks mouthwateringly good. He shaved away the stubble from this morning, and his black hair is swooped back for a clean-cut look that's as attractive as the rugged handsomeness he typically embodies.

It's a shame I'm going to make him change.

"What am I going to hate?"

"I'm going to glamour myself to look like her." His brow furrows, but he doesn't outright oppose the idea, so I keep going. "I'll style my hair the way she wears it and change into the dress Melia made her, so I only need to modify a few features."

"That's not—" Ari rubs his jaw. "You need to be there too. You can't be two people at once."

"That's the part you're going to hate." I sway my hips a little as I approach him, hoping to distract him from the truly outrageous task I'm about to ask of him. He doesn't fall for it. "You're going to be me."

His mouth parts.

"Just listen," I rush. "You know me. You know my mannerisms. All you'd have to do is sit in the audience, keep a glamour up, and try not to talk to anyone."

He swallows, and I follow the bob of his throat. "Your brother will figure it out in seconds."

"We'll tell him and Edina. That way, they can run interference." I grab his hands in mine, letting the desperation I often hide surface. "Please, Ari."

Yeah, I broke out the use of his real name. I'm that desperate.

"Fuck," he swears, tilting his head back to stare at the ceiling. "Fine. But only for the coronation. I'm not glamouring myself for the damn ball."

I throw my arms around his neck, pulling him into a tight hug. He goes still for a moment before relaxing into the hold and wrapping his large arms around me. I linger a little too long—when was the last time I was hugged by someone other than my damn brother?—but he doesn't pull away either.

"Thank you," I whisper.

"I want two packs of your cookies," he grumbles.

"Deal." I pull away and kiss his cheek. "You should have asked for more. I would have done pretty much anything to get you to say yes."

With one last smirk in his direction, I turn to head to my room to change.

Chapter Four
Devorah

The Day I Emerged

I SPRINTED DOWN THE hall from my brother's suite, where he promised to wait. We were supposed to do this together, to endure emerging beside one another, just as we did everything else.

Emerging marked the moment when Fae became...well, Fae. It signaled that we were fully grown, and our aging slowed to a snail's pace as our immortality kicked in. It was also when our features became distinct. For elemental Fae like the two of us, our ears would grow into points, we'd sprout wings or horns, and our magic would amplify.

Where are you? I shouted down our mental link. Instead of the open line of communication we usually had, a wall of fire blocked me. That asshole. Did he not realize what day it was? Did he not realize what *time* it was?

As I ran down the hallway, bowling over several servants and palace guards in my haste, I cursed him out—even though I knew he wouldn't hear the creative expletives. There were three places my brother might be, and of course, all of them were in opposite fucking directions.

"I'm going to fucking kill him," I growled, scaring a poor maid as I skidded around a corner of the sandstone hallway. If I'd known I'd be running, I wouldn't have worn my damn pajamas and socks, but I expected to go to the room next door, not the other end of the palace.

Or should I go to the beach?

Goddess-damnit, Eldoris.

I raced down the stairs that led to the first floor. Okay, decision time. I didn't think he'd be in the basement training; he wouldn't have closed his mind off if he was exercising. Which meant he was either in the kitchens or at the beach. And I had to decide when I reached the bottom of these steps. Right to the kitchen, left to the beach.

Right or left.

Right or—

I collided with a male's chest. It would have hurt less if I hit a damn wall.

"Woah," the deep voice said, reaching out arms to steady me as I stumbled back, a little dazed.

I latched onto his arms. "Sorry," I muttered, blinking up to see purple eyes and a wide smile.

"You alright?"

My post-collision brain fog cleared enough to take in the Fae before me. We only met once, when he was much smaller than the mountain of a male before me, but the face was unmistakable.

"Oh, hey. Hershel's son, right?" I asked.

"Ari," he supplied, grin not slipping at all.

"Right, sorry," I said again. "Listen, I don't mean to be rude, but I need to find my brother. We're supposed to emerge in about five minutes."

"He was headed toward the kitchens a few minutes ago," Ari said, and the breath whooshed from my lungs. The kitchen. Which meant he was with Arella, my best friend and the female my brother had been in love with since we were children.

"Thank you!" I reached up on my tiptoes and kissed his cheek before sliding around him.

"See you at the ball tonight," he called, and I waved over my shoulder as I ran down the halls that led to the kitchen and the servants' rooms in the same corridor. I ignored the workers who wished me a Happy Emergence until I finally reached a small door that was hand-painted with little flowers—a project Arella and I did one rainy day when we were bored.

"By the fucking goddess," I screamed as I entered the small bedroom and found Arella riding my twin's cock—her head thrown back so her braids fell low enough that they covered her bare ass.

Eldoris growled, pulling Arella down and flinging the covers over them both while she giggled into the crook of his neck. "You could knock," he barked.

"We're about to emerge, dumbass." I knew my voice was bordering on shrill, but I thought it was warranted. "It's not like you can be inside Arella when that happens."

Again, my friend laughed. She dismounted and stood to grab her clothes, not a care in the realm that she was naked as the day she was born. We grew up together, so I had seen her naked, but with her ebony skin all dewy and the scent of arousal in the air, it was a little much for me. I covered my eyes.

"Stay here, I'll go," she offered, and I heard the rustle of fabric as she and my brother got dressed. Arella patted my shoulder when she was done. "I'll see you after, my darling," she said to my brother.

"Then you'll be able to call me your mate," Eldoris called after her. His eyes—the only feature we shared—glistened. He had no way of knowing if Arella was his mate, but I knew they both suspected and wished for it. Since she already emerged, the mate bond—if it existed—would snap into place once Eldoris emerged.

I'll see you at the ball tonight. Ari's sentiment echoed in my mind. Royals always had a ball the night they emerged to see if their mate was alive. He could very well be my mate. Anyone could be. Suddenly, the memory of his hands on my shoulders took on a new feeling, and I shivered in anticipation.

"From your lips to the goddess' ears," Arella said and blew him a kiss.

As soon as she was gone, I leveled Eldoris with a glare. He smirked and rubbed his jaw, probably savoring the scruff Mother would make him shave. He performed a cleansing spell on the sheets and patted the mattress beside him.

Arella was the daughter of one of the chefs, so her room was tiny. It was certainly not the opulence we planned on emerging in, but it didn't matter. Just me and my twin taking the next step of our lives. That was all that mattered.

"You ready?" he asked, sitting cross-legged by the head of the bed. I mimicked his position on the foot of the bed, reaching across so we could link our hands together.

"It's going to hurt," I said.

"Probably. But I'll go first," he teased. Eldoris was born one minute before me, which, in his mind, gave him the liberty to treat me like a little sister. It was also the reason why he was the future king, and I got to enjoy my coveted position as *the spare*.

Unless something terrible happened.

Neither of us ever acknowledged the fact that we might take after our human father, that our magic may never magnify, or that we might not develop horns or wings. Every half-human we knew emerged without fail; there was no reason to worry.

Eldoris extracted his fingers from mine and smacked the tops of my hands, challenging me to a game we played. It was the distraction I needed for these last few seconds. "Has your head been hurting?" he asked as I jerked away from his slap.

"My back." I did a little jig as I landed a blow. "Which means I'm getting wings."

"Maybe you'll develop a hump."

"Asshole."

He hissed and pulled away. "Fuck, here we go."

My breath caught as he gripped his temples. He gritted his teeth in an attempt to be stoic but then gave up and howled. It was an awful sound, one of pure pain that I'd never heard from my twin. He was impenetrable, so strong. Goddess, if he's screaming like that—

My back exploded in agony. I didn't even try to hold back my screams as bones snapped and skin tore open. I couldn't stay sitting, but I also couldn't go very far, which resulted in me hunching over the bedframe as my spine rounded as if anything could help this torment.

"Fuck, fuck, fuck," Eldoris swore, and I joined his swearing as my blood erupted like a volcano. *My fire magic.* I knew it would enhance, but I had no idea it would boil my insides.

Then, at the pinnacle of pain, a sharp sting pierced my ears, the force of it popping the cartilage and making my mouth drop open even farther.

"Almost done," Eldoris said after what felt like an eternity. His voice was ragged, but it sounded like he'd ridden out the worst of it.

I inhaled sharply, and when I released it, it was over.

In the silence that followed, only the soft flutter of wings broke through. I stood tall and rushed to the full-length mirror, spinning to the side to catch a glimpse of my profile.

My wings were gorgeous.

They were a gauzy material that was iridescent except when they caught the light, and then they shone with red and orange hues. They looked like burning embers—like I was a phoenix. I pushed my hair behind my ears, reveling at the sharp points. I poked them and found they didn't feel any different.

"El!" I turned to him to find him smiling widely, content not to look at himself but to admire me. Two large, curved horns the same color as his umber skin extended from his black curls. He reached up tentatively to touch them and then gasped like he was burned. "Sensitive?" I asked.

"Damn," he whistled. "One more second touching them, and I'd need to call Arella back in here."

"Disgusting." I wrinkled my nose.

We both cackled, and when he tilted his head back and the tips of his horns got stuck in the wall, I roared.

Then I saw his ears.

His still-rounded ears.

"No," I breathed, but Eldoris was still laughing and dislodging himself, so he didn't hear me.

"Do you feel powerful?" he asked. "I feel like I could take down the fucking realm."

Well, that was something. My magic felt like it was enhanced a little, but not nearly that powerful. Maybe it would be fine. It was only one feature that didn't change. *It would be fine.*

"El..." I said, but before I could complete the thought, the door burst open.

"Why in the goddess' name did you emerge down here?" My mother barged into Arella's small room, filling the space with her presence. "We had a whole crowd waiting in the hall outside your suites. If Ari hadn't told us that he bumped into you, I still—"

She broke off, her hand flying to her mouth when she saw him. "Mother," I pleaded. Eldoris still hadn't looked into the mirror, and I didn't want her to hurt him. Her attention switched to me as she scanned my body, taking in my wings and my pointed ears.

"What's wrong?" Eldoris asked.

"You—" my mother choked, her ocean eyes wide and filling with tears.

He clambered off the bed and ran to the mirror. I watched him admire his horns, only for his attention to lower. His jaw tightened, and his shoulders rose.

"This changes nothing," he said calmly, with all the grace a future king should possess. But I knew my twin. He was scared and trying not to spook her. "I can feel my power; it's immense. And my horns are—"

My mother averted her gaze.

Eldoris swallowed.

"They're just his ears," I insisted. "It's nothing."

"No, sweetheart," she said with a sigh. "It's not nothing." She pushed past me to stand by his side, cupping his face. "I'm sorry."

"No. Mother, you can't," I begged.

"Devorah will henceforth be heir to the throne."

Eldoris' calm mask shattered, hurt replacing the otherwise unflappable exterior. My heart ached. Not only did I bear the pain of his crushed expectations, but the weight of my new responsibilities threatened to topple me to the floor.

"I'll get you some jewelry to affix to your ears," she said, and he nodded, not bothering to argue with her decision. When my mother turned to me, she squared her shoulders, all traces of the caring mother gone—a queen left standing in her wake.

"Tomorrow, we'll begin your training. I'll see you both at the ball tonight."

She left, shutting the door behind her, and I launched myself at my twin. "I can't take this from you," I cried into his shoulder. "I'll abdicate. I'll become a priestess or something."

"No," Eldoris said, brushing away my tears. "No, you won't."

"I don't want to be queen."

"I know." He wrapped me back in his arms. "But you'll be amazing, Dev. And it will be my honor to serve you when you're my queen."

We stayed like that for a long time, the two of us sobbing in each other's arms as our worlds forever shifted.

EMERGENCE BALLS WERE, TO put it charitably, the worst fucking things ever created. They were long—because everyone in the realm needed to make an appearance to see if the emerged royal had a mate—they were full of courtly mind games, and on top of all that, I was the center of attention. Eldoris was excused from the evening because, as expected, he and Arella were mates.

While it was true that El and Arella would be tangled up in the 'magic that is mating,' my mother excused him because she wanted to introduce me as her new heir apparent before revealing Eldoris' human-esque features.

Which meant all eyes were on me. All courtiers vied for my attention, for the opportunity to dance, to kiss my ass, and to probe for questions as to why my twin was really absent. I stuck to the script, all the while counting down the seconds until I could leave the dance floor.

"Devorah?" Zahir, the prince of the Night Court and another future heir, broke me from my daydreams of setting fire to the silks decorating the ballroom. I shook off the sense of impending doom and blinked up at his concerned face. His white hair was stark across his rich, beige skin, and tonight, his curved, ram-like horns were on display. "Are you alright?"

It was then I realized that the song we were dancing to had ended, and everyone was clapping for the orchestra.

"Sorry," I muttered and pasted on my best faux smile. "I was..." There was no good way to answer, so I let the sentence trail off. "I think I need a drink." Zahir's mouth opened, and I could already hear the question before he asked. "I'm fine, truly."

He nodded. "If you ever need anything..."

I patted his chest before stepping from his grasp. Zahir was a good friend and someone I'd no doubt turn to in the future since our situations were now similar. But I wasn't ready to discuss my feelings yet; I barely knew them myself.

I excused myself and made my way across the ballroom to the small bar set up in the corner where Hershel—my mother's advisor—was waiting with an outstretched glass of water. "Thank you." I took a greedy gulp before signaling to the siren behind the bar for something stronger. He placed a deep purple drink, whose smoke smelled like honey, in front of me.

"Watch those," Hershel warned. "They're deadly."

I tipped the entire thing down my throat. Hershel clicked his tongue. "You'll regret that in the morning."

"I plan on doing at least one more thing I'll regret by morning," I said under my breath, not caring if he heard me. It wasn't that I was rebellious; it was that everything in my life suddenly felt out of control. I had no autonomy anymore. The least I could do was drink alcohol and pick a partner to fall into bed with.

"Ari," Hershel waved over my shoulder, and, like a damn wraith, Ari appeared, making me jump. He looked even better tonight than he did in the hall this morning. His hair was slicked back in a fashionable wave, and the suit he wore highlighted every cut of his muscular frame.

"Since you're asking to be treated like a child, Ari will be your chaperone," Hershel said. Then, to his son, "She's the future queen. Don't let her do anything stupid."

I fought the urge to roll my eyes at Hershel's back as he left. Ari took his spot in front of me.

"You don't need to watch me," I said, taking the glass of water once again. "I'm pretty sure there wasn't even alcohol in that drink."

"There wasn't," the bartender confirmed with a shrug. "Your mother's orders."

I gestured to emphasize the point. "See? No babysitting required."

Ari chuckled. "I was going to ask if you wanted to dance." He held his hand out, giving me a small bow in the process. The motion was large enough that others around us took notice, making it impossible for me to say no even if I wanted to.

Not that I did. There were worse partners.

I let him lead me to the dance floor in time for the next song—a slow waltz.

"How are you feeling?" Ari asked once we'd fallen into the easy steps, our bodies rising and falling with the cadence of the music.

"Why does everyone keep asking me that?" I barely knew Ari, but something about him made me feel comfortable, like I could share all my concerns and frustrations without judgment. His purple eyes were almost hypnotic in their intensity, and an overwhelming sense of trust suffused my body.

"When I emerged, it felt like I was too big for my body." His voice has dipped low, so it's almost a caress across my skin. "My skin felt too tight, too hot. I needed...release."

"Excuse me?" I breathed. I'm not sure if he meant it to sound suggestive, but—

"From the excess of magic, of course," he said with a smirk that said he absolutely knew of the innuendo.

Two can play that game.

I leaned in close, pressing up on my toes so I could whisper in his ear. "It's so bad," I added a little moan to my words. "I can't wait until I get out of this dress and expel some energy." Ari coughed. "Some magic, I mean."

"Obviously," he rasped.

Satisfied, I returned to my position, encouraging him to take up the dance again and spin me out in a wide arc.

When he reeled me back in, he pulled me closer than was appropriate. "Well, it suits you."

"The dress?"

"Emergence." His gaze raked over me so intensely that goosebumps rose on my skin. "You're luminous tonight."

It was my turn to swallow hard. There was something potent between us, here on this dance floor. Something electric and charged that I couldn't begin to name. It wasn't a mating bond, just intense attraction.

"So, are you meant to be my advisor now that I'm the heir apparent?" I asked, bypassing his compliment. The question seemed innocent enough, but there were ulterior motives.

Ari, being a smart male capable of reading subtext, said, "I'm training to be an advisor—I actually leave to train tomorrow so I can be a bodyguard as well."

"A male of all trades."

He maneuvered me away from a couple that careened across the dance floor in a haphazard assimilation of dance moves. "But you need to trust your advisor implicitly," he continued. "I'd never presume to be your choice, though I'd be honored if you decide to choose me."

Translation: tread carefully.

Ari would be in my life for the foreseeable future. Not a passing acquaintance or someone who could be easily avoided. At the minimum, he'd be a guard or—goddess forbid—an advisor in a rival court.

This was not someone to have a passing fling with—no matter the chemistry.

Our eyes met, and I lost track of all the completely valid reasons I had for wanting to stay away.

"Though." Ari wet his lips, drawing my attention straight to them. "You have ages to make that decision."

"Lifetimes," I agreed.

"Something we shouldn't worry about right now."

"Exactly."

"Exactly."

The music ended, but we stayed locked together, trapped in a bubble of our own making. His scent, citrus of some sort, was intoxicating, and I wanted to lean forward and—

"Princess."

I jumped at the sound of the voice over my shoulder. The male behind me was tall and pale, with subtle fangs that poked into his bottom lip. I vaguely recognized him as the human who was turned by one of our vampyres, creating a whole new creature.

"Vladimir Orlov," he said with a bow. "Would you do me the honor of this next dance?"

I wanted to tell him to fuck off so Ari and I could plan an escape, but there was a dangerous air about him, something I didn't want to get on the wrong side of.

Ari tugged my hand, pulling my focus back to him. "It's been a pleasure." Once again, he bent to kiss my knuckles. This time, it felt like liquid magma traveling up my arm from where his lips touched. "Perhaps when I return from training, we can pick up where we left off."

"Not tonight?" I winced at how desperate I sounded.

"You have guests to greet and a potential mate to find," he said regretfully. "And I have to leave in a few hours."

I nodded. "When you get back, then."

Before letting me go, Ari pulled me in close enough to whisper in my ear. "Looking forward to it, beautiful." Then, as if the advisor instinct took over, "Don't make any deals with the vampire."

With the buzz of his nickname in my ear, he departed, leaving me in anticipation of our next meeting.

Chapter Five
Ari

Present

WHAT THE HELL WAS I thinking?

Right. I wasn't.

Devorah blinked those beautiful eyes up at me, and I lost my mind. I want to say that I'm just serving her the way any loyal advisor would, but I know that's bullshit.

She was right earlier when she said I go above and beyond. Since that first moment in her office, the moment she let her guard down around me in a way she never did with my father, I lost the plot. I knew she needed someone to be more than an advisor, more than a confidant and friend. And when she refused to hire a personal bodyguard, I became that too.

If I'm honest with myself, I've wanted to be close to her ever since her emergence ball—maybe even before that. I wanted nothing more than to go home with her that night, but I held back. And then, life got in the way. I left to train, and when I got back, she was seeing someone. By the time she was available, I was headed to the mortal realm for a bit, and then I was seeing someone. When we were both single, I was training to be her advisor, and it felt inappropriate.

It's never been the right time.

It's *still* not the right time.

Every day, I tell myself I should put more distance between us, but I'm a moth to a flame. And it's not only about the intense physical attraction—which is a whole other issue. I'm addicted to the banter we share, the easy conversation, and the elation that comes when I can make her smile, especially on days like today, when it seems impossible.

There's this deep part of me that hates seeing her sad and wants to fix it.

Even if it means pretending to be her for a whole fucking coronation.

After a quick stop in Queen Talia's room so Devorah can grab her mother's dress, we head back to her suite so we can begin this insane transformation. Devorah's brother, Eldoris, and his betrothed, Edina, are lounging on a couch with her legs draped over his lap as he idly draws circles on her ankle and calf.

Eldoris and Devorah—considering they're twins—couldn't look more different. While her skin is barely a sun-kissed bronze, his is a deep umber. His hair is several shades darker than her coffee brown, and his is curly and cropped short, whereas hers is straight and sleek. In short, Devorah takes after their mother, and Eldoris takes after their human father—right down to his ears, which are currently affixed with golden jewelry to hide their rounded edges.

"Why do you look like you saw a ghost?" Eldoris asks Devorah, jerking his bearded chin at me by way of greeting.

"Mother isn't well today," she says simply and walks straight into her bedroom. Eldoris upends Edina's legs and charges after his sister, leaving the two of us in the sitting room.

Edina is the type of female who could be a supermodel if she lived in the mortal realm. She's tall and lithe without very many curves, but she's classically stunning. Her blonde hair is long with a slight wave, and her eyes are a brilliant shade of sapphire that's only intensified by the dress she wears, of the same color.

Not that she's to be underestimated. The pretty package masks incredibly powerful magic—second only to that of her mother's.

"Hi, Little Hershel," she says, flashing me a wide grin.

I roll my eyes emphatically. "Glad that's catching on."

Edina laughs melodically, and I fight the grin that threatens to tug at my lips. "I think you secretly love it." Her tone and the simple shrug of her shoulder scream nonchalance, but I can hear what she's inferring and I wasn't born yesterday. I'm not going to aid the already abundant rumors surrounding Devorah and me, even if Edina wouldn't say a word.

"Are you out of your damn mind?" Eldoris bellows, saving me from the knowing stare of his betrothed.

Devorah enters the sitting room, ignoring his outburst. She's changed into a ballgown, one that has skirts of soft, billowy fabric in brilliant turquoise color and a sweetheart neckline that sags a bit from the ill fit.

"That's cute," Edina says. "Not really your style, though. That looks like something your mom—"

Devorah casts a glamour over her features, becoming her mother in one fluid motion. She sets a crown inlaid with pearls atop her head, using her magic to curl her hair around it seamlessly.

"Shit," Edina breathes, looking between the three of us.

"Yeah, shit," Devorah agrees, her voice magically lowered to sound like her mom. She turns to me, and the way she matches her mother's stern expression is terrifying.

"This is insane," Eldoris asserts. "Can you even hold the glamour that long?"

Devorah inhales like she's been punched, and Edina snaps, "El!"

When I became her advisor, Devorah admitted that she hadn't used her magic nearly as much as other Fae. Magic is like a muscle: the more you use it, the stronger it gets. Devorah is proficient when it comes to enchantments and simpler spells, but when it comes to her fire—her raw element—the magic has atrophied. It was one of the reasons I insisted she get a bodyguard.

But glamour is one of those enchantments you set and—barring any intense emotional response that would cause a flicker in your magic—stays.

It's bad enough for her brother to question her at all, but especially about something like this.

"Do you have any other ideas?" Devorah seethes. Eldoris has the good sense to look apologetic, even though he doesn't respond. "Exactly what I thought."

"I'm sorry," he says, taking her face—their mother's face—between his hands and kissing her brow.

"You're a dick."

"Also true."

She smacks his chest but nods, accepting his apology. I've been around long enough to see them get into worse fights—and to say worse things about each other. At the end of the day, their bond is unshakeable.

"You're up, Little Hershel," Devorah says, turning back to me. "The dress is on the bed. Don't put it on until you glamour yourself; you're too big."

I can't help myself, and I toss her a wink. Which is weird when she's disguised as her mother—but it makes her smile.

Closing the door behind me, I stare at the scrap of satin Devorah was wearing earlier, contemplating the life decisions that brought me to this point. I could glamour a dress onto my body as I change my features, but if the seamstress is in attendance—which she will be; coronations are a big deal—she'll notice. And, if we're being honest, Melia scares the shit out of me.

I close my eyes and picture Devorah, every minute detail I can conjure. My magic surges forth, and slowly, I start to change. I shrink first, then my shoulders narrow and my pecs shift and mold into breasts that I do a damn good job not looking at. My hair lightens and lengthens, forming the style she wore before, two braids tied back as the rest cascades into a waterfall down my back. The easiest transformation is my eyes—I've spent too many hours staring into Devorah's ocean depths to not know every fleck of cobalt amidst the turquoise.

When I'm completely changed, I shuck off my tuxedo and slip into the dress. The satin is cool against my skin and surprisingly comfortable, considering how tight it is.

I'm assessing myself in the mirror, changing a few things, when I notice the faint line where my boxers lie. I groan and shuck them off.

And then I realize Devorah must not have been wearing anything underneath, and I groan for a whole other reason.

Plopping the tiara laid out for me on my head, I head back into the sitting room. "You could have warned me that I can't wear underwear," I say, but my voice is still my own, which sends Edina into a bout of hysterical laughter.

"But it's so much more fun this way," Devorah teases. I take the opportunity to give her one of the glares she is so good at.

"Oh my goddess," Edina wheezes. "That was perfect."

"Not bad," Devorah agrees.

"Thanks." I glamour my voice so it sounds like hers, but the inflection is off. "Thanks?" I try again, and this time, Eldoris gives me a nod of approval.

"Right, let's go over how this is going to work." Eldoris sticks a finger out at me. "You're going to talk as little as possible and sit between me and Edina."

"He can't sit between us," Edina says with an exasperated sigh. "He'll sit to your left on the aisle; I'll be on your right next to Puck."

"Puck is going?" I ask, and Edina nods grimly. Puck is the male who killed Queen Titania, the former Spring Court Queen. He was magically enslaved by her for centuries, and she made him do truly despicable things in her name, including rejecting his fated mate. He was set to become the king until Lysandra—Titania's daughter—arrived in Faerie. They competed in a trial to see who would rule, and Lysandra won.

"We need to go," Devorah says, worrying her bottom lip.

Without thinking, I reach forward and free the flesh from her teeth. Her glamour shutters for a minute, revealing her true self, before it snaps back into place.

"Don't do that," I murmur, dropping my hand.

"Right." She shakes her head as if clearing away the slip-up. "Mom does this." She clasps her hands together in a move that looks regal and practiced, but there's a slight wringing motion that speaks to her nerves. It is indeed something Queen Talia does.

"This is going to be a disaster," Eldoris says, swiping his hand down his face.

"It's gonna be so much fun," Edina says and links arms with Eldoris, who gives her a soft but exasperated smile before kissing her temple.

"I'll go first," Devorah says. "Ari, you're behind me to my right."

I fall into step, walking the way I've observed her do countless times. Devorah glides from the room, head held high.

"They're good," I hear Edina whisper as she and Eldoris follow.

I turn and offer them one of Devorah's playful smirks, which makes Edina dissolve into another fit of giggles.

The halls are relatively empty, most of the palace staff having already left for the coronation. The few we see look confused, knowing Queen Talia is asleep in her rooms, but they don't say anything.

Two doors past Devorah's office is an entrance to a portal—one only members of the royal family and workers of the palace know exists. Today, a pack of six guards waits outside the door, wearing ceremonial white uniforms with the wave insignia of the Summer Court woven in gold on their chests. They bow deeply when they see Devorah and me and then straighten and salute Eldoris—the general of their army. At his signal, they fall into formation, two in the front, one beside Devorah and me respectively, and two at the back.

The guards in front open the door, a periwinkle mist leaking into the sandstone hallway. As a pack, we step through and onto the ley line—a magical stream that the Fae use to travel between courts and even realms. We hurtle through space, passing by doorways in the mist that lead to different locations.

When our exit approaches, the guard beside me takes my arm. I shake him off. "Your Highness?" he asks, his face a mask of confusion. *Shit.* Devorah would allow him to help her out of the portal.

"Sorry," I murmur. "You startled me."

"By the goddess," Eldoris groans.

This time, I allow the guard to take my arm, and together, we jump off the ley line and through the mist toward the coronation.

Chapter Six
Ari

You know what's really fucking weird? Walking in heels. In the grass. While also trying not to flash too much skin despite the thigh-high slit in your tight-fitting satin gown.

I'm a progressive male, but that's a sentence I never thought I'd say.

The portal exit is on the edge of the Varesen Forest. The enchanted wood seems brighter today. The greens are more vibrant, and the flowers are unfurled without a petal out of place as if they're welcoming their new queen. Leaves rustle on a non-existent breeze, their magical laughter mixing with the buzz and chirp of forest life.

Fae of all species exit the portal, chatting animatedly as they take the short walk to the Etherealia Meadow, where the coronation ceremony will take place. The entire realm is coming to celebrate. Because Fae lifespans are so long, coronations don't happen often. It's not an event that one misses.

Devorah keeps her head high, strolling through the forest like she owns every blade of grass. "Tone it down a bit," I murmur. Her head snaps to mine as if in warning. "Your mother is softer now that she's sick. You don't want it to look like she reverted to her healthy attitude."

She nods once before relaxing her shoulders and lowering the angle of her chin.

I step into a divot in the grass, rolling my ankle and stumbling into the guard beside me. And, because the goddess has a sick sense of humor, I land in a way that puts my boob in his hand. "I'm so sorry, Your Highness!"

I have no idea how Devorah would react to her breast in a guard's hand, so I fumble through a combination of apology and reassurance while righting myself. Edina casts an enchantment at my heels, and I suddenly rise out of the soft earth. When I take another step, it's as if I'm walking on an even surface. "You're welcome," she singsongs.

Luckily, none of the Fae around us seem bothered or suspicious of my little display. They separate to allow our group to pass and bow respectfully to the royalty in their midst.

The guards lead us out of the forest and into the idyllic meadow. Dew dots the freshly cut grass, winking in the sunlight. It never absorbs into the fabric of my dress but rather remains in perfect droplets. The sky is powder blue with fluffy clouds drifting by often enough to give a reprieve from the sun without cooling the balmy temperature. Clusters of white daisies line a path toward a stone dais that's draped in garlands of flowers in every color.

Two sections of chairs that extend as far as the eye can see bracket an aisle that Princess Lysandra will take toward her dais. Courtiers, advisors, and other high-ranking members of each court are seated toward the front. Taller races—like trolls—line up along the tree line, large tanks housing the races of Fae that need water to survive—like the water sprites and kelpies—are wheeled in and angled so they don't refract the sunlight, and some of the winged races—including pixies, dragons and even some elemental Fae—take to the skies for a better vantage point.

Atop the dais, the four remaining monarchs speak to the priestess who's presiding over the coronation. She has skin as dark as the night sky and wears a robe with embroidered symbols of all six of the elements—earth, water, fire, air, light, and dark.

As if sensing our presence, their attention lifts to Devorah as we enter the clearing and make our way to the front. King Zahir of the Night Court's eyes narrow, and his jaw tightens so visibly we can see it from our position halfway to the dais. He wears an impeccably tailored tuxedo over his broad frame, and his horns—large and curved like those of a ram—jut out proudly from his thick white hair. Zahir is the most recently crowned monarch; he only became king after his parents both passed from a magical accident. I don't know if it's because he feels he has a lot to prove, or if he's always been an asshole, but he's been nothing but antagonistic, especially to Summer Court.

Beside him is King Oakley of Autumn Court. Oakley is the only monarch who isn't an elemental Fae; he's a brownie—a race of Fae known for their short stature and their predisposition for cleanliness. He's got a quiet sort of strength, like an immovable rock in a stream. He gives Devorah a nod in hello, though his greeting isn't nearly as warm as King Simi of the Day Court, who beams at our entrance. His russet skin is a warm contrast to the long white hair and beard that reaches his belly button.

But all of them pale in comparison to the fourth monarch. I feel her gaze on us like a laser, as if she can strip away our glamour with only her eyes.

Queen Gwyneira of Winter Court. The ice queen herself.

It's remarkable how much she and Edina look alike. They have that same long, lean body type and the same cornsilk blonde hair—though Gwyneira's is piled on top of her head in elaborate curls and surrounded by a silver crown that looks like ice. But their eyes are different. Where Edina's are sapphire and sparkle with mischief, Gwyneira's are so pale they're almost white and are harder than stone.

"Talia," she greets. I follow Edina and Eldoris' lead and bow to the other monarchs as one of the guards escorts Devorah onto the platform.

"Gwyn," Devorah says before greeting the others. I hold my breath, waiting for one of them to discover our ruse.

When we rise, Gwyneira's attention turns to our trio. Her eyes scan me momentarily before immediately addressing Edina. "What happened to the dress Melia made for you?" she asks, her tone even despite the tic in her jaw.

"You mean the velvet one with the long sleeves?" Edina scoffs. "Sorry, I'm not interested in boiling alive." Gwyneira arches an eyebrow but doesn't comment further on her daughter's fashion choices.

"You may join the others," Zahir says with a dismissive wave of his hand.

I narrow my eyes at the slight. "Douche," Edina coughs under her breath. Eldoris hastily guides me and Edina away, across the front of the dais to the first row of chairs on the opposite side of the center aisle.

"'Bout time you lot got here." Radley, prince of the Autumn Court, appears in front of us, blocking the way to our seats. He runs his hand through his shoulder-length brown hair. He has his father's sienna skin tone, but since he's half elemental Fae, he is closer to Devorah's height—still short compared to elemental Fae males but taller than a typical brownie.

He stands and claps hands with Eldoris, then places a smacking wet kiss on Edina's cheek. She grimaces, making an un-princessly sound before returning the gesture on the bare inch of skin between his beard and eyes. His booming laugh echoes, drawing the attention of several courtiers in the front rows of Fae.

"Dev," he says suggestively, turning to me with a roguish smirk. Something so simple as a look shouldn't put me on edge—Radley flirts with everyone—but the way he scans Devorah's body makes my blood boil.

"Looking gorgeous as always," he purrs and leans in. I catch Edina's eye over his shoulder, and she makes a smacking motion. My brow furrows, and she mouths something I can't read as Radley places a much tamer kiss on my cheek than the one he did for Edina.

After a moment, he pulls away, and his head cants to the side, but he says nothing. Unlike Edina, who dramatically puts her head in her hands.

What did I miss? There's no way I did anything wrong; I didn't say a word.

We greet the other princes and princesses—the second generation, they call themselves. Izar, prince of the Night Court, and his mate Baxter separate just long enough to say hi before snuggling back into each other, Izar wrapping his lanky form over his mate's shorter, softer body.

"Where's Hades?" Edina asks, referencing the Princess of the Night Court. The nickname was given to her ages ago because she runs a section of Faerie called the Underground—which is just as salacious as it sounds.

"Here," the short female pops up behind Edina, making her squeal and Hades' red lips tilt up into a sinister smirk.

I'm not sure if Devorah and Hades get along, so I don't know how to act around the princess. Hades notoriously avoids the mandatory "royal" events that Devorah has to go to, and the ones she hosts in the underground, Devorah often skips.

Except one.

One that I certainly shouldn't think about in public.

I opt for a warm nod, and Eldoris practically drags me into my seat before we can greet Larisa—Princess of the Day Court. Which is fine; she and Devorah don't get along, so the snub would be expected.

Once we sit, the rest of the second generation and their significant others take their seats.

"Where's Ari?" Izar asks, leaning over the aisle between us, where the Unseelie Courts—minus Edina—are seated. Izar is one of the kinder royals. As the middle child in a family with three siblings—a rarity amongst elemental Fae families—he's adopted an easygoing air that makes him a darling amongst the citizens. Zahir and Hades are both ambitious, but Izar seems content to run his court's modest navy and spend time with his mate, Baxter.

I shrug one shoulder. "Somewhere."

"I'm surprised he left your side," he chuckles and gives me a wink.

"Seriously," Baxter chimes in, leaning over Izar. "It's like you have a tall, dark, and sexy shadow."

"Hey."

"Oh please, you could be brothers."

Appeased, Izar and Baxter turn to engage Hades in conversation. I suppose Izar and I do look similar—we both have a paler complexion with dark hair, but he's much lankier than I am, and he's covered in tattoos, whereas mine are hidden.

I wonder if Devorah is hiding any tattoos.

Since I don't know what Devorah looks like naked, they wouldn't be on my glamoured form, but the thought is...

By the goddess, this is not something I should focus on. I need to worry about my disguise and getting through this day. And I won't fool anyone if I'm sporting a semi in this tight dress.

"Hey," Radley says over my shoulder, making me jump. The female sitting behind me looks aghast that he's sandwiched himself between her and the back of my chair, but gets over herself in favor of checking out Radley's ass.

"Hi," I mutter, trying to keep my eyes forward.

"So, I was thinking," his voice dips, and a finger brushes a strand of hair off my shoulder, lingering to draw lines on my skin. "The other night was fun."

The other night? What other night?

As much as the others may think I'm Devorah's shadow, I don't monitor her when she's at home or in one of the other courts' palaces. In outside events—like Hades' club opening—of course, I'm with her. She's the future queen. If something happened to her, it would be chaos. But since we spend most of our time in the security of the palaces, I have no idea what Radley is talking about. I wrack my brain, trying to figure out where Devorah was over the past few days. It could have been anywhere.

Did she spend a night with him? I know they're friends, but I didn't think she was sleeping with him.

Acid churns in my gut as he chuckles, low and deep and full of suggestion. "How would you feel about a repeat?"

I don't know how to answer. I look over at Eldoris, but he's not paying attention. Even Devorah on the dais is preoccupied, deep in conversation with Simi.

"Um—" I fight the instinct to tell him to fuck off and never touch me—Devorah—again.

"But this time, maybe we could do a role reversal."

"Hmm?"

"You take the reins."

I'm not submissive by nature—quite the opposite, in fact—but the image of Devorah on top of me, using me for her pleasure, floods my mind and is impossible to ignore. My breath comes in faster, and I feel the blood rise in my cheeks.

Radley takes my physical response as a sign to continue. "Off the top of my head," he hums. "Maybe you could be a sexy teacher, and I'll be the student." My eyes bug out of my head, and I turn to finally face Radley, who is grinning like a cat who got the cream. "We don't have to, though. We can do the whole 'princess and her advisor' thing again. The forbidden relationship kink was hot as fuck."

The words sit between us for a moment before they register.

Princess and her advisor.

Did...did they role-play about Devorah and *me*?

Radley's suggestive chuckle turns into full-blown, unchecked laughter. "You should see your face," he gasps, clutching his stomach.

A confirming glance at Eldoris and Edina, their eyes bright with amusement, tells me all I need to know. Radley was fucking with me. *Son of a bitch.* "I hate you all," I grouse, which only sends them all into another round of hysterics.

"Oh, don't be like that, *Dev*," Radley drawls, wrapping his arms around me from behind.

"How long have you known?"

"Since you walked in." He kisses my cheek again and whispers, "Your girl would have smacked me upside the head if I kissed her cheek."

That's what Edina was pantomiming.

"By the fucking goddess," I swear and smack his arms until he lets me go. "Listen, Radley—"

"I won't say anything," he says, sobering. "But is she okay?"

Does he mean Devorah or Talia? Does he realize it's the queen who's absent today?

"She's good," I say, leaving it vague. Then I put my hand over his face and shove him away. "But I'm gonna get you back for this."

"Looking forward to it, lover." He blows me a kiss and retreats to his seat beside Izar just as the processional music for the coronation starts.

Chapter Seven
Ari

The Night of the Club Opening

By the goddess, she's insufferable.

Ninety percent of the time, Devorah was calm, collected, rational.

The other ten made me want to tear my hair out.

"You cannot go to this party," I said, for the fifteenth time. I lingered in the doorway of her bedroom while she sat at the vanity. Her suite was located on the side of the palace that bordered the ocean, and the open windows allowed in a cool sea breeze and the sounds of waves crashing against the sandy shore.

Devorah fluffed her hair, gathering it over one shoulder. Her dress was no more than a scrap of silver material that had one long sleeve while the other was bare, and while the neckline was straight across, there was a large cutout below her ribs on the same side as the sleeve.

In short, she was a fucking wet dream.

"You keep saying that, and yet I'm going." She stood and shimmied down the bottom of the dress so it covered her ass, but just barely.

After slipping her feet into uncomfortable-looking heels, she turned and placed her hands on her hips.

Fuck, she's gorgeous.

She did something with her makeup that made the ocean blue of her irises pop even more than usual. My attention drifted to her lips, pink and pouty, as she swiped her tongue along the plump flesh.

She could *not* go out like this.

"It's dangerous," I said, my voice low and rougher than intended.

"Wrong." The challenge made her eyes sparkle. "Hades' clubs are monitored extensively, and the opening night will be even safer. Plus, the entire second generation will be there."

Not that I trust those fuckers.

The pampered princesses and princes—and Puck, whom they'd adopted—would be more concerned with chasing their pleasure than ensuring the safety of their friends.

"You're not like the rest of them," I said, but my argument was losing steam.

I didn't know why the thought of Devorah at Faerie's most exclusive club opening made my throat close, but it did. I went through centuries of training as a bodyguard, and something about this night was triggering alarm bells.

It had absolutely nothing to do with the thought of her writhing on a dance floor with some other male.

"No," she agreed. "I need this more than they do. My life is..." She broke off with a thick swallow, and I hated that the earlier light in her eyes dimmed. "I need to blow off steam. I want to dance and drink with my friends."

She jabbed a finger into my chest. "And you, Little Hershel, are my *advisor*. You're not my boyfriend or my brother or my dad, so you have no say in what I do with my spare time."

That hurt.

Even though she was my princess, I began to view Devorah as a friend. A friend I enjoyed flirting with, but that was neither here nor there. To hear her reduce me to only an employee...

I shoved down the feeling—I could deal with that later.

From a purely *professional* standpoint, if something happened to her, the court would be in shambles. It would never recover. I was about to say as much when her face fell. "Fine," she sighed, turning away from me and stepping out of her heels. "I'll stay home." The dejection in her voice physically hurt, like I took her one form of happiness and crushed it in my palm.

"Fuck," I swore, running my hands through my hair. "I'm coming with you."

"Like fuck you are," she whirled on me, all traces of that sadness gone. *She played me.* That little minx.

"Like fuck I am," I countered. "You're right. We've been working hard; I need to blow off some steam, too."

"You weren't invited."

I pulled out a black envelope with my name in swirling red ink. "Hades delivered it personally." Hades was a menace and thrived on chaos. No doubt she had ulterior motives for inviting me, but I didn't care. Even if Devorah snuck off and tried to go without me, I'd be able to follow her in and make sure she stayed safe.

"I don't need a babysitter."

"Who said anything about a babysitter? I'm just going to a club to spend time with my very dear friends."

"You hate my friends," she sniped.

No, I was jealous of them. It didn't matter that I was the one she saw daily, the one who held her secrets and whom she turned to for help. They were the ones who knew what it looked like when she let loose and laughed and had fun. I craved that part of her.

But there was a line drawn between us, one that, no matter how close we toed it, we never crossed.

Devorah groaned dramatically. "Fine." She scanned my body. "Change, and we can go."

I DIDN'T MISS THE way Devorah ogled me when I came to collect her. I wasn't in anything special, just a pair of dark denim jeans I brought from the mortal realm and a black button-down. Though I did roll up my sleeves to the elbows, which seemed to captivate her.

She held onto her anger the entire trip, through the portal, to the Underground, and through the labyrinth of tunnels that eventually led us to Hades' new nightclub—Tartarus. Hades was anything but subtle in her branding.

The club was dark with flashing, multicolored magical lights that hovered over writhing bodies on the dance floor. As soon as we entered, a waif of a Fae in a skimpy black outfit approached us, holding test tubes of brightly colored Faerie dust.

"No," I growled, grabbing Devorah's hand and tugging her away from the female.

"I wasn't going to take Faerie dust," she shouted over the music, jerking out of my hold. "I don't have a death wish." Before I could respond, she stalked off toward the back of the club.

A wave of magic pulsed through the crowd, hitting me like a shot of the strongest whiskey. My shoulders relaxed, and the tension around my chest began to ease. The movements of the Fae around me grew languid, more sensual.

Hades hired sirens to control the moods of her patrons. *Great.*

I reinforced my mental shields to keep out their influence, but by that time, I'd lost Devorah in the crowd. I swore and picked my way through the mass of bodies that reached for me, and attempted to entice me to dance.

When I found her, she was standing in front of a circular booth beside Lysandra—the newly discovered princess of Spring Court—and Hades. Larisa, Princess of the Day Court, was drunk off her ass, judging by the haphazard state of her honey-colored hair or the misaligned neckline of her dress; she flopped into the booth beside Puck, who was seated beside Radley.

I pushed out of the remaining throng and came up beside Devorah.

"This is my babysitter," she waved over her shoulder. "Because, you know, Hades' security team isn't enough."

Hades, thankfully, didn't react to her jab.

"I'm Ari," I said to Lysandra, as we hadn't been formally introduced. "Devorah's advisor. And the deal was that she could come here with me or not at all."

"I'm a grown-ass female."

I took a seat beside Radley, shaking hands with the males and smiling brightly at Larisa, who coquettishly pushed a strand of hair behind her pointed ear, revealing a golden butterfly tattoo on her temple. Devorah sat opposite me, quietly seething. The rest of the group chatted and laughed, but I kept my eyes on her, returning her challenging stare.

Hades bid us farewell, and Lysandra followed shortly after.

"She shouldn't be going off on her own," Puck muttered, drawing my attention away from Devorah to the brooding male in the back of the booth. Puck was a tall, thin male with auburn hair and pale skin dotted with freckles. Tonight, his emerald green eyes almost glowed, as if his earth magic was ready to bubble over and spill out.

"Then you should go after her," Radley winked, but Puck just clenched his glass of whiskey until his knuckles turned white.

"I'm on it!" Larisa screamed—too loudly, even with the music.

She stood and climbed over Devorah, who let out an *oomph* as she kneed her in the chest in her bid to get out of the booth. When it looked like she was going to fall flat on her face, I sprinted up and caught her. "Oh," she breathed, running her hands over my chest as she regained her footing.

"You alright there?" I could feel Devorah's gaze like a physical brand.

"Yeah." Larisa's voice was breathy, and her amber eyes were dilated when she looked up at me. "You're like my hero or something." Her hands floated up to my shoulders. I could have pushed her away, but one glance at Devorah in my peripheral vision made me linger.

She was fuming, and it had nothing to do with her long-standing feud with Larisa. I knew that look all too well.

She was jealous.

"Aren't you in a monogamous relationship?" Devorah snapped, and Larisa blinked as if clearing away a fog.

"Right," she slurred. "Yeah, I am." She pushed out of my arms and staggered toward the hall where Lysandra and Hades disappeared.

I stood, watching to make sure she didn't fall over again, but when I turned back to Devorah, her glower was near comical. It must have looked like I was checking out Larisa's ass.

Radley leaned forward, his head ping-ponging between the two of us like we were his favorite form of entertainment. Until he got distracted by a trio of Fae making eyes at him. Puck was still staring off in the direction of Lysandra.

"I need a fucking drink," Devorah said, standing from the booth. This time, she didn't fix the hem of her dress, so I caught the barest glimpse of her ass as she pushed past me.

I followed as she made her way to the bar serving free drinks. She ordered two, and when I reached to take one, she grabbed them both, downing one in a large gulp before sipping at the second.

"Fuck," she breathed, and I watched as the magical drink flooded her system at the same time as the siren pumped another wave of emotion at the crowd. It wasn't lust exactly; it felt like a lowering of inhibitions.

"I want to dance," Devorah proclaimed, and proceeded to slip into the swarm of dancers.

"This female is going to be the death of me," I muttered under my breath. The bartender, who I didn't realize was right behind me, chuckled as he gave me my drink.

"Here," he said, adding another measure of the whiskey to the glass so it was filled to the top. "Seems like you need it. But if I can offer some advice?"

"Nothing I love more than unsolicited advice," I grumbled, but he smiled and continued.

"Don't hold on too tight." He jerked his head toward the crowd. Devorah's silver dress was like a beacon under the flashing lights. She was dancing in a crowd of females, head tilted back in laughter. "Give her another minute."

I waited the length of a song. Then two. She ignored the passes of two males, continuing to dance with her new friends, and even though it tore me up inside, I kept waiting.

When she finally looked at me, the anger and resentment were gone, replaced by something that looked an awful lot like want.

"See?" the bartender remarked, and I turned to find him smiling like an idiot. "Go on, then. Minute's over."

I tipped my glass to him in thanks and slid through the crowd. The alcohol must have been infused with extra magic because it made my body feel loose and warm in a way normal whiskey didn't. My mental shields slipped, and the siren's magic slid in just as the music slowed, the bass throbbing like a heartbeat.

Devorah danced with her back to me, the swaying of her hips magic all of its own. Several males and some females around were watching her, but they kept their distance.

All I could think of was feeling her hips swivel like that against my body. All other rational thought abandoned me, and I stepped in behind her until we molded together. She didn't turn around, but instead asked, "Don't you want to be dancing with Larisa?" Jealousy bled into her tone.

"I'm right where I want to be," I said into her ear before leaning down and skimming my nose along the slope of her neck.

"Yeah?" she breathed. Her head landed on my chest, giving me access.

"Yeah." I brushed my fingers against the bare skin below her ribs, and despite the loud music and the sounds of the crowd, her gasp reached my ears. My cock hardened in my pants. I know she felt it because she stilled momentarily, before pushing her ass further against me and making me groan.

She felt so good against me, her body fitting with mine like she was meant to be there.

A server came around and took our empty glasses, allowing me to place one hand on her hip while the other slid possessively around her stomach. I didn't care that in the light of day, she couldn't be mine. Right here, in the darkness of the club, she belonged to me. And I belonged to her.

The club faded around us as we danced until we were the only two people in the realm. We danced until Devorah's skin grew dewy with sweat and our breaths quickened and shallowed. I was so fucking hard my cock ached.

"Ari," she gasped, spinning around. The gorgeous ocean blue of her eyes was almost completely eclipsed by her pupils. Her arms wound around my neck while mine splayed across her back.

"Yeah, beautiful?" I asked, the nickname slipping from my lips. At its sound, she let loose a small moan.

"I need..." She shifted, pressing up so her lips were inches from mine. She smelled sweet, alcohol mixed with the jasmine of her perfume. It was heady, intoxicating, and I wanted to sink into it, to smell that same concoction on my sheets in the morning.

"I know." I moved so my leg was between hers and tugged her impossibly closer. Her body stuttered at the feeling, and her mouth popped into a perfect O. I gripped her ass, encouraging her to ride my thigh while I continued to sway so it looked like we were only dancing.

"This is the kind of release you need, isn't it?" I whispered in her ear before taking her lobe between my teeth. She shivered and made a sound that could have been an agreement, could have been a moan.

I switched to placing hot, open-mouthed kisses along her neck and shoulder, pausing only to suck on her pulse point. "Goddess, yes," she sighed. "Mark me."

"Fuck," I growled against her skin, and bit down before soothing the hurt with my tongue. She bucked and writhed against me, quickly approaching an orgasm as she rode my thigh.

"Are you going to come all over me? In front of all these Fae?" Her obscene moan was lost to the crowd. "You're so fucking wet, I can feel your arousal seeping through my jeans."

"It's too good for me to care," she laughed breathlessly.

"Good." My grip must have been bruising, but if she didn't care if I marked her neck, I can't imagine she'd mind my fingerprints on her hips.

"I'm so close," she whimpered, her movements turning jerky and erratic. Watching her lose control had my cock straining at my pants, desperately trying to escape its denim prison.

"Come for me, beautiful."

"Ari," she screamed as she came. I wanted to kiss her, to swallow those moans so no one else could hear them but me. But I didn't want to kiss her for the first time in a crowd of people while we were both drunk.

She buried her head in my chest as she shuddered out the remains of her orgasm, and when she pulled back, her eyes were glazed, and there was a sleepy smile on her face. "You're so sexy when you come," I smiled.

She chuckled, snuggling into my arms as I slid my leg into a normal position for us to dance. The damp spot on my pants made me fucking preen. I did that; I made this powerhouse of a female so out of her mind with pleasure that she came on my damn thigh.

How perfect will she look when she's coming on my cock?

A scream of delight had us both craning our necks up. Lysandra, green wings out, was hanging upside down on one of the cages suspended from the ceiling, her purple hair falling over her face and her large breasts threatening to spill from her little black dress.

The sight of one of her friends shattered the little bubble we encased ourselves in, and Devorah took a step back. "I—" she stammered, smoothing her mussed hair. "Ari, that can't happen again."

The sentence made my cock deflate instantly. The way Devorah looked at me...there were no traces of her previous pleasure. She looked ashamed.

"I mean..." she stuttered, grabbing my arm.

"I got it."

"No," she insisted, turning me with surprising force. "No, you don't get it."

She wrapped her arms around my neck again so she could whisper in my ear. "If you weren't...if I wasn't...but we can't."

I pulled away. "I know." I tucked a piece of hair behind her ear.

"You're my advisor."

"Believe me, I know."

"Which means we can't. Fae would have a field day with that."

"I know."

She tugged her bottom lip between her teeth, and without thinking, I brushed my thumb along the flesh, freeing it. Devorah whimpered.

"This never happened," I said sadly, even though I knew I'd never be able to forget the way she writhed against me, the way her arousal smelled so sweet it made me ache. I'd never forget the way she screamed my name when she came, like a mixture between a prayer and a damnation.

"It never happened," she agreed, wrapping her arms around her middle. "I'd like to go home now."

I nodded and gestured for her to exit, following closely as she once again slipped from my grasp.

Chapter Eight
Devorah

Present

ARI HAS BEEN TALKING to Radley for entirely too long. The plan was to ignore everyone, not to have hour-long conversations with my friend. Okay, it's been five minutes, but Radley is like another brother to me. There's no way he won't detect our ruse. It's not that I don't trust my friend, but the fewer people who know Ari is glamoured to be me, the better.

"Are you all right, Talia?" King Simi asks, concern creasing his brow. Simi reminds me of those human cartoons of crazy old wizards with all their white hair and long beards. In actuality, his hair is its natural color, and if he shaved it all, he wouldn't look older than thirty mortal years.

"Fine, fine," I say.

"Are you certain?" He steps in closer. "It's been a while since we—" his hand skims down my outer arm, "—had a night together."

Oh fuck no.

I struggle to control the urge to vomit at the thought of my mother and King Simi in a fuck buddy relationship. There are things a child just shouldn't have to know about their parent.

He waggles his bushy eyebrows suggestively. I have no idea how much time passes as I gape at him in horror—because there's no way I'm controlling my facial expressions—but he doesn't seem to mind. He licks his lips; I pray to the goddess to blind me.

Luckily, I'm saved by the sound of Lysandra's procession entering the meadow. Simi winks and retreats to his position between Gwyneira and me, who has been watching the entire exchange.

Goddess, this was a terrible idea. How did so many people agree to let me do this?

Lysandra makes her way down the center aisle. Her dress is a beautiful blush tulle that's adorned with real, multicolored flowers that perfectly highlight her curvy figure. She's shorter than most of the elemental Fae—her stature inherited from her late mother—but today, with her head held high and her shoulders back, she looks commanding, regal.

When she reaches the end of the aisle, the priestess steps forward and begins the ceremony. Lysandra dips her head to the floor so her plum hair covers her face, and we all close our eyes in prayer to the goddess to bless her reign.

The ceremony takes ages. Even with the lightweight material of my dress, I'm sweating. I can't imagine how Gwyneira, in her satin gown with endless layers and long sleeves, isn't about to pass out.

After too long, we get to the part where I'm needed. Simi and I present Lysandra her ceremonial scepter and crystal ball, while Oakley, Gwyneira, and Zahir fasten a cape to her shoulders. Then, finally, the priestess proclaims Lysandra as queen.

For a moment, I set my worries aside to celebrate. It's a big moment for all of the second generation. Technically, Zahir was the first of our group to ascend to the throne, and technically, we didn't know Lysandra until recently, since her mother hid her away in the mortal realm, but it's still momentous. One of our own has replaced the previous regime.

That will be me soon.

The thought settles like a stone in my stomach.

Even if my mother doesn't give me the throne, she's fading, dying. I'll soon be standing before the realm, making my vows to the goddess and my court. I'll be solely responsible for countless lives.

I wonder if Lysandra is quietly panicking at the weight of this responsibility.

"I am dissolving the monarchy."

"What did she just say?" I blurt, forgetting myself completely and using an inflection that is very unlike my mother. Gwyneira looks directly at me, her blue eyes like dry ice—cold enough to burn through your skin. But after a moment of scrutiny, she returns her attention to Lysandra, who invites Puck to rule alongside her.

While not related to royalty, Puck was inducted into our little group ages ago, when he and Larisa of the Day Court became friends. Puck is a lot of fun, but I never thought of him as a ruler until recently, when he acted as an interim king.

He straightens his tuxedo jacket as he ascends the steps, his auburn hair appearing red under the bright Spring sunshine. When he reaches Lysandra, a shield is erected around them, muting their conversation. I watch his freckled nose scrunch before his features break into a smile. Then he's kissing Lysandra—it's about time, the tension between them has been palpable—and the crowd applauds.

Finally, when the shield disappears, Puck accepts his appointment to rule alongside Lysandra.

And then, because the goddess has a sick sense of humor, we start the coronation ceremony all over again.

What must be eighteen hours later, the ceremony is over, and the entire realm gathered in the meadow erupts into cheers. I clap politely until the newly coronated king and queen teleport away, leaving the rest of us to disperse.

I catch Ari's eye and do my best to subtly signal for him to come get me.

"So," Simi says, approaching me again. Fucking hell, I thought I was done with this.

"So," I respond, frantically tracking Ari as he moves through the aisle between the dais and the front row of chairs. Just when he's about to get to the steps, he gets snagged by Zahir, who somehow made it off the dais and is talking to Ari, with very little space between them.

Shit.

"Talia?" Simi is frowning, and I realize I cursed aloud. "Is everything alright?"

"Yes, Talia," Gwyneira's cool voice slices through the air like a whip cracking. "You seem out of sorts today."

Simi, to his credit, bristles on my behalf—probably assuming Gwyneira is trying to exploit a weakness, whereas he was genuinely concerned.

Doesn't make the fact that Simi and my mom were screwing any more palatable.

"It's fine," I say, attempting aloofness. Gwyneira's lips purse.

"Mom!"

I have never loved the sound of my voice more than I do right now. Ari reaches me and gently takes my elbow, then leans in to whisper in my ear. "Say whatever you need to let me teleport you out of here."

I release an exaggerated sigh. "Apologies," I say, switching from faux frustration to faux politeness. "There's something I need to see to at home. I'll see you both tonight."

Before either can object or question my flimsy lie, Ari takes my arm and teleports us to the nearest portal.

WE SPILL INTO MY suite, and I slam the door behind us. There's one second of silence, only our panting breaths filling the sitting room, and then we both break into uncontrollable giggles. Ari's glamour dissolves, the seams of my dress snapping as his shoulders broaden. He rushes and scoops me into his arms, twirling us around as I let my glamour fade.

"I can't believe we got away with it," I say, throwing my head back and laughing until Ari sets me back on my feet.

He cups my face. "You're brilliant." His praise washes over me like warm honey, and I sigh into his touch, leaning in and letting my eyes drift closed. He feels so good against me, his arms strong, his chest solid.

The easy amusement feels comforting, like sinking into a soft mattress after a long day, yet it still makes my heart flutter. "Thank you," I whisper, covering his hand with my own and meeting his fathomless purple irises.

He smiles softly. Then he coughs, "Um, Dev—" His gaze flits pointedly to my chest before he looks up at the ceiling. My mother's dress, which was designed for her larger chest, has slipped down, and my breasts are close to spilling out, the fabric barely high enough to cover my nipples.

"Oh," I chuckle breathlessly, tugging up the neckline.

Then, I notice Ari is still wearing my dress. And, well, the tight-fitting satin means I can see a very clear outline of his dick. "Oh," I repeat. I try not to stare, but by the goddess, he's huge. *He's not even hard.* And is that—is that a piercing?

"Shit," he mutters, shifting the dress so the head of his cock isn't poking out of the thigh slit. Our eyes meet, and we descend into laughter again. "I'll just change." Not releasing his grip on the dress, he summons some clothes.

"Probably a good idea."

I excuse myself to my room, throw on a simple pair of leggings and a crop top, and meet Ari back in the sitting room. "I feel like I need to do something," I announce. I'm practically vibrating with adrenaline, riding the high of pulling one over on the entire realm. I don't want to go back to the monotony of paperwork or dealing with healers yet. I want to celebrate. "Something fun."

Ari nods thoughtfully. Then, with a devious smirk, says, "Have you ever been swinging?"

"I'm gonna need some context."

He chuckles and holds out his hand. "Come with me." The mirth in his eyes is enough to override my skepticism, and I take it.

His magic envelops me, squeezing as we teleport from the comfort of my breezy room into the humid jungle. The sun is high enough in the sky that it breaks through the thick canopy, giving everything a hazy kind of glow.

"I don't think I've been to this area," I say, looking for familiar landmarks. We're somewhere deep in the vegetation with no villages to be seen, but the trees here grow in remarkably straight rows, which suggests someone planted them deliberately. The vegetation on the floor is made of thick plants with frond-like leaves that overlap so closely they're almost thatched together. Thick green vines drip from branches so wide we could stand comfortably front to back.

"There was a battle here a while back that led to the trees being cut down. So, when the earth elementals regrew them for us, they did so with this in mind." Ari touches the trunk of the tree closest to us. The tree shivers, as if waking from a long slumber, and a vine lowers to the ground. It rounds out until it forms a perfect swing. Ari sits in the cradle of the vine and gestures for me to sit beside him. I regard him warily. "Come on, beautiful."

I take a step closer, and Ari snatches me around the waist. With a laugh, he tugs me into his lap, and the vine rises.

"Was this your angle?" I ask, throwing my arm around his neck. "To get me in your lap?"

"I swear it wasn't, but I'm not complaining."

The smile he gives me should be illegal.

I bite my lower lip, shifting slightly so I'm balanced on his thigh. It sends a flood of memories—delicious memories that I've done a terrible job at suppressing—and liquid heat pools in my core. Ari inhales deeply, then makes a sound low in his throat that's close to a purr, and I know he can smell my arousal. His citrus scent permeates the air, eclipsing the eucalyptus and jasmine of the Wyld Jungle.

It's hard to get a breath with the heat between us and the thick, wet air.

"Ari," I murmur, sounding all too desperate.

He nuzzles my neck, breathing me in deeper. My head tilts back, granting him access. He's bolder here, tucked into the canopy where no one can see us. It's just like that night when we were in the club, when it felt like everything and everyone disappeared.

By the goddess, I want him.

The vine abruptly dumps us on a branch, and we land with an *oomph*.

"Thanks," Ari grumbles at the vegetation. The vine swats him on the ass, and I have to cover my mouth to keep from laughing.

"So, swinging," Ari says with one final glare at the vine. "Do you see the vines hanging just there?" Sure enough, two long, looping vines flutter in a humid breeze. The flutter grows until they're swinging in a pendulum motion.

Ari passes me a vine from our tree. "Take a running start, and...well, swing. When the vines cross, you want to switch hands and grab the other."

My heart thrums in anticipation. This sounds so colossally stupid, so reckless.

It's exactly what I wanted.

Ari continues, "After every two vines, there will be a branch to perch on." He gestures to a tree not too far from ours. "But, eventually, the distance between the vines will grow until you need to let go entirely and jump."

I make a show of consideration. "Are we racing?" He smiles wickedly and nods. "What are the rules, then?"

"No wings unless you're actually falling to your death. No sabotage, just focus on your own swinging."

"Got it," I chuckle.

"Winner is the first one to land in the lake at the end of the path. You'll know it when you see it."

"And what are we playing for? We're out of cookies," I tease.

Ari glances at my lips. "Winner's choice."

How is it that two completely unerotic words have the power to have my core clenching? There's not even an abundance of suggestion in his tone, it's just where my mind goes because every day is harder to ignore my attraction to Ari.

"Deal." I stick out my hand to shake his, but before he can take it and magically bind our wager, I snag the vine and take a running leap off the tree branch. Ari's laughter is drowned out by my squeal of delight as I soar through the air, unceremoniously flapping like an untethered flag. The green landscape blurs around me, the muted light disorienting everything so I can't tell right from left, up from down.

I reach the pinnacle of my swing and float weightless for a moment before I remember what I'm supposed to be doing. I grasp at empty air for a few moments as I start to swing backward. Out of the corner of my eye, I see Ari swinging on his vines, reaching for his connection. Shit, I'm gonna lose before we even start.

A thick, spongy rope lands in my outstretched hand, and without time to second-guess, I grab it. I get a better handle on this one, tucking myself around the vine as I hurtle toward the branch of the next tree. I drop onto the branch in a heap, landing on my ass hard enough to smart.

Ari is already there, propped against the trunk. "That was just the warm-up," he says, passing me the next vine. It's noticeably shorter, and the next vine is roughly the same distance as the first. This is what Ari meant when he said the jumps will get harder.

"On your mark," I say, stepping back as far as I can on the branch.

"Get set..." Ari stands beside me, leaning so his body is practically hanging off.

"Go!" We shout in unison and take off for the edge.

I wrap my arms and legs around the vine as it swings me over the greenery of the jungle floor. This time, rather than flailing about, I pivot my body so I approach the next vine at an angle. Even with my fingertips extended fully, I barely manage to grab it without jumping. I hang, one-handed, as I hurtle toward the next tree, whose branch is thinner than the last, adding an extra level of difficulty.

This is more of a leap than a jump off onto the branch, and I use the momentum to run forward and grab the next vine.

Ari whoops somewhere close behind me, but I don't focus on him as I jump from vine to vine, feeling like a monkey. The wind of my own making stirs my hair, fluttering behind me despite being tied up.

Three branches and six vines later, the lake—and our finish line—is in sight. But the gap between these vines is a chasm. The little jumps I've made so far have been thrilling, exhilarating. This is...this is jumping off a building with my wings tied.

I'm overwhelmed, paralyzed, and I swing back and forth enough times that I need to return to the branch so I don't end up hanging suspended over the jungle.

The branch jolts as Ari lands beside me. "Come on, beautiful, don't give up on me now," he says. I think he means for it to be a taunt, but it comes out as gentle encouragement. He's covered in a thin sheen of sweat, and his hair is tousled from the swinging.

He makes no move to go, even though he can use my hesitation to win. Together. The unvoiced agreement rings between us. We'll do this last bit together—the way we do everything.

I flash him a smile, and then we're off. I swing on the short vine as far as I can and then let go.

For a moment, there's nothing but weightlessness as my momentum lobs me up and over, so high I skim the leaves above me. Then I start to plummet.

It takes everything in me not to unfurl my wings. I give in to the freefall and reach out, groping the air until I find the vine. I latch onto it like a buoy in the middle of an ocean and tuck myself in tight so I fly faster.

There's no tree at the end of this vine, no branch waiting as a stopping point, and no other vines ready for me to grab onto. Instead, below is the dark waters of a large lake.

I made it.

Waiting until I'm squarely over the center of the water, I release my hold and drop feet first toward the water with a shriek. "Open your eyes!" Ari's voice carries over the wind rushing around me, and I open in time to see him in the same position as me, a few feet away. The sight of him, even with me after all these obstacles, has me laughing as I plunge into the warm water.

When I pop up, Ari is there, crystalline blue droplets clinging to his lashes. He snags me around the waist, and my legs wind around him.

"That was amazing," I pant.

"Was that the kind of fun you wanted?" He smooths my wet hair from my face, and his palm lingers against my cheek.

"It was perfect," I whisper. I focus on fiddling with a piece of fabric on his shirt, knowing that if I meet his eyes right now, I'll kiss him and possibly never stop. "But who won?"

"Ari did," a cool voice says from the direction of the shoreline. We both turn frantically, Ari clutching me to him protectively.

Gwyneira sits perched on a rock, making the moss-covered boulder look like a throne.

"When you're done with your swim," Gwyneira says, "perhaps we could discuss why you felt the need to impersonate your mother at the coronation today."

"Fuck," Ari breathes. Without waiting for me to dislodge myself, he swims to the shoreline, depositing me on the silt banks. I summon towels for us, prolonging the inevitable.

"Anytime now," she drawls.

There's no way around this conversation, so I have two options. Another lie—though I'm not sure I can come up with something convincing enough under pressure—or I can tell her the truth. Putting my faith in another monarch goes against everything I've been taught, but my gut is telling me I can trust Gwyneira.

I give Ari a nod, letting him take this part. "We need you to take a vow," he says. Gwyneira cocks her head to the side. "The information we divulge here will not be spoken to anyone unless explicit permission is given by Princess Devorah of the Summer Court."

Magic stirs at the words, waiting for Gwyneira to solidify the agreement. "I agree to those terms." We shake hands, and the citrus scent of Ari's magic swirls around us as the deal locks into place. As soon as it's done, Gwyneira softens, her expression thawing slightly. "Now, what's the problem, Devorah?"

Right. Here we go. "My mother is fading."

She nods. "I had a feeling."

Of course, she did.

"That's why she wasn't there today. She...she couldn't..." I clear my throat. Ari's fingers twitch at his side, as if he'll reach for me, but thinks the better of it.

"How bad is it?" Gwyneira asks.

"Bad," I whisper, choking up. "She has very few lucid days."

"And the events she's attended?"

"We've had her sedated. It's why she's so quiet. She's there, but she's foggy."

Gwyneira purses her lips. "And you've been running the court since this has started?"

I nod. "I've done what I can."

"You've done well."

I know I shouldn't need it, but hearing I've done a good job from Gwyneira—a truly powerful queen—makes me feel lighter than a cloud.

"She won't agree to step down," I continue. "When she's lucid, she thinks she's fine and can handle it. And when she doesn't remember—"

"She thinks she's in her prime," she surmises. "Well, it sounds like we need to solidify our alliance."

My mouth parts; Ari stands at attention.

"I'd have to ask Edina and Eldoris if they're ready to be married—"

"Not necessary at the moment," she says with a wave of her hand. "We'll begin planning the wedding, but we can drag our feet. Royal weddings take time to plan.

"In the meantime, we will support Summer Court."

"How?" Ari asks, his voice still skeptical even though Gwyneira is offering us a golden ticket.

"We will send troops to your borders to keep others from getting ideas."

"Has there been talk?" I ask.

"Some," she says nonchalantly. I've never wanted to shake the information out of someone so badly.

"Night Court," Ari guesses. "He insinuated something at the coronation earlier." She remains completely still. It's proof enough.

Fucking Night Court. Fucking Zahir.

Faerie has been in a tentative period of peace for the first time in ages. Of course, he's the one who wants to break it. He's desperate to prove himself as a monarch. Summer and Night Court have been in wars before—the most recent of which claimed the life of my best friend and Eldoris' mate—but I never understood it. There's an entire court between us that's comprised of desert and mountains, not exactly easy terrain to march an army through or maintain control over.

"We need to bring Eldoris in on this," I say. My brother is the general of the Seelie Army and has a much better head for battle tactics than I do.

"My generals will confer with him, but I believe stationing our troops on the Padauk River will be best," Gwyneira says. I nod. That's how they attacked the last time. "And, to make our alliance clear, we'll enter the dinner tonight together. I also suggest you tell Zahir more directly."

"Me?" I ask.

"No, me," Ari says. "I'm friends with Zahir's advisor. I'll tell him the extent of our relationship with Winter Court tonight, make it seem like I'm accidentally revealing court secrets."

"Good," Gwyneira agrees. "As for your mother..." She trails off.

"With all due respect, Your Majesty, if you say I should end her life—"

"I see that avenue has been suggested," she says. "No. I think she should take an extended vacation. Tonight."

"You want me to ship her off somewhere?"

"You have that large house on Pa Ferie. An island retreat sounds lovely."

"I still don't have her seal of approval to run the court." Not only does my mother need to sign a document saying I can run the court, but I need her magical signature. It's not something that can be forged.

"There's no doubt this is a temporary solution, but I will ensure no one questions you. Delegate as much as you can to your military and keep up the work you've been doing."

I sigh heavily and look to Ari for his opinion. I don't love the idea of sending my mother to Pa Ferie. If she becomes lucid while there, it'll take me that much longer to get to her, and I need to be able to convince her to sign over the court. But it would give a much-needed excuse as to why she can't attend events.

"It's the lesser of two evils," Ari says.

I coalesce. "We'll leave tonight."

With that, Gwyneira stands and extracts her wings. They're delicate, with sharp edges that look like they're tipped with icicles. "Now, if you will, I'm melting."

She takes off, leaving us to process the weight of that conversation.

Chapter Nine
Devorah

PA FERIE IS AN island just a short boat ride from our shore. Despite being separated from the mainland, it's one of the most populated areas of the Summer Court and is a hub of tourism.

Our sprawling estate is in a private cove on the water, the white façade starkly contrasting with the black sand beach. In addition to the main house, there are servants' quarters—including the modest house that belongs to Hershel and Ari—a fresh-water pool, and stables. It's the perfect place to get away.

A contingent of staff left ahead of us to prepare the house, while another group—including my mother's healers—helped me ready her for the ride across the channel. Mother's sedative has mostly worn off, but thankfully, she's in much better spirits than this morning. She's present, if not a little groggy, and is engaged as we tell her about the coronation.

But then she calls Eldoris by our human father's name and thinks I'm her dead sister.

We go along with it as best we can—it's better to accept her distorted reality than correct her—but I can't deny that it stings. I know it's worse for her, that she knows something is off and is scared.

By the time we have her settled in a rocking chair on the patio that faces the ocean, the sun is setting, and we need to leave for the dinner and subsequent ball in the Spring Court. It's the last thing I want to do tonight. I want to stay here and soak up one more evening with my mother before I'm laden with even more responsibility.

When we can't put it off any longer, Eldoris kisses my mother's cheek. "Love you," he says. She smiles sleepily. He steps away for me to say goodbye.

Something about this is incredibly sad. It feels...final. I know there's a good chance she'll never return to the palace—at least not permanently.

But this can't be goodbye. I refuse to believe it.

I lean down to kiss her cheek, but she grabs my arm, halting me in my tracks.

"Devorah?" she whispers. "Eldoris?"

I inhale sharply. I fall to my knees. Eldoris rushes to my side.

"Hi, Mom," I squeak, tears filling my eyes until my vision is completely blurred. I furiously blink them away, refusing to let them obstruct my view of her while she's lucid.

"What's wrong?" she asks, looking between us. The soft, sleepy voice is replaced by her typical hardened tone, the way it was when we were growing up. The voice of the Summer Court Queen. It's such a shock that it makes me laugh in relief.

She's here.

She's really here.

"Nothing's wrong," I say. "We just don't want to go to a ball tonight."

She huffs a sigh. "You're royalty. Which means—"

"We have responsibilities we must adhere to," Eldoris and I finish in tandem.

She smirks, but then it slips. "Why are we in Pa Ferie if there's a ball?"

"It's for the second generation and some officials," Eldoris answers smoothly.

She regards us carefully. Her ocean eyes, the ones she passed on to us both, scan us with intense scrutiny. "You're lying," she murmurs, brow creased.

"We're not—"

"You know better, daughter of mine," she says, but there's no edge to it, no sign that she's angry. She looks down at her hands, which are shaking slightly, at the blanket tucked around her legs, at the tray beside her with a bowl of her favorite pudding.

I hold my breath, waiting, unsure of what to say. Nothing could prepare me for her quietly saying, "I'm sick, aren't I?"

I want to deny it. I want to let her stay unburdened. But Eldoris touches my shoulder. We don't speak telepathically, there's no need when a thousand words pass between us with a simple look.

"Yes," I say.

"I'm fading?" We nod. Her head bobs up and down in understanding. "Have I signed over control of the court to you?"

"Not yet."

She removes her hands from ours. "Can I have some paper?"

I summon the paper and a pen from thin air and pass them to her. I wait for a moment as she scribbles something on the page. Then, she releases a breath, and a soft glow emanates from her hands. The scent of fire is so strong that I'm worried she's set the paper alight, but it's just the signature of her magic.

When she's done, she passes the paper back to me. It's just a statement indefinitely naming me the interim queen, but it's enough to let me run the court completely. It's a huge weight lifted off my shoulders.

"Tell me what's been happening," she demands, once again taking our hands. "Give me an update on your lives."

Eldoris tells her of his betrothal, of his new home with Edina, and the state of the army. I realize I don't have much to share. So much of my life has centered around my mother and the court that I have no news. I briefly think about telling her about Ari, but then I'd have to explain that Hershel wanted to kill her, so I opt to catch her up on some court gossip instead.

When we're done, and we've lapsed into a brief silence, Mother whispers, "When I'm... When I—" a tear brims on her lashes. Eldoris leans forward and swipes it away. "Do I remember you?"

"Sometimes," he says. Now, a tear slips down my cheek.

"Well," she says, her voice wobbling, all trace of that commanding presence gone. "In case...just in case..." She clears her throat. "I love you both with all my heart."

She reaches for us, "You are the best thing I've ever done. And..." Another hard swallow. "And, if I've ever made you think otherwise, if I've ever been too hard on you...just know...just know..."

She blinks, and her eyes go unfocused.

"Mom?" I tighten my grip on her hand. She looks at the point of contact with a furrowed brow.

"Please," Eldoris begs. "Please stay with us."

When she looks up, there's no recognition.

She jerks out of hold and wraps her arms around her middle. "Who are you?"

"No," he whispers.

My mind goes blank. It feels like someone has encased me in concrete, and I can only watch the scene play out in front of me. Eldoris turns abruptly and doubles over. He makes a strangled sound, slams a shield around himself, and fire explodes within it as he loses control of his magic.

My mother screams and fire blooms in her hands. I summon the strength to put a shield around her so she can't hurt anyone.

"I need a healer," I say, using an amplification spell because I can't speak louder than a broken whisper. Something makes it hard to see, and when I touch my cheeks, my fingers come back wet. I'm crying. It's an odd sensation, knowing you're sobbing to the point where you can barely breathe while also feeling numb.

My mother thrashes within the confines of her shield, my brother rages behind me, cursing the goddess and fate and whoever else he can think of.

The healers arrive with a sedative. Just after they administer it, my mother's gaze meets mine.

"We love you, too," I whisper.

I PULL MYSELF TOGETHER until I reach my guest suite in the Spring Court palace. I promptly dismiss Kalinda, assuring her I can get dressed myself. I just need five minutes alone. Five minutes where I can feel everything before I shove it all down and get back to work.

Her departure, signaled by the click of the door, releases the flood-gates.

I sink to the floor in a heap, wrapping my arms around my stomach as if I can staunch the hemorrhage of emotions. The motion reminds me of my mother, how she did the same thing when she slipped away from me, and I release a keening wail.

I love you both with all my heart.

How is it that the one moment of clarity hurts more than a thousand moments of confusion? It was a taste, a glimpse of the way life used to be, a tease.

It wasn't enough.

You are the best thing I've ever done.

Five minutes turn to ten; ten turns to fifteen. I can't stop crying. A slideshow of every moment from today bombards me, refusing to let me get myself together.

I should go home. I'm useless here today. There's no way I can pretend everything is fine.

You're royalty. Which means you have responsibilities you must adhere to.

How many times did my mother drill that into my head? How many times did she tell me to swallow my tears and go to an event? It didn't matter if I broke up with a boyfriend, or that my best friend died, or that my brother was so depressed I was afraid he'd kill himself to join his deceased mate. I had to paste on a smile, or at least a mask of indifference, and go to the party, or the luncheon, or visit the army base.

Such is the life of a queen, she'd say.

She wouldn't want me to stay here in a puddle.

After twenty minutes, I get off the floor and don my armor—a buttercup, A-line dress, and a gold tiara with a lapis lazuli gem in its center. I curl my hair and glamour my face to hide my puffy, red eyes.

By the time Ari knocks on the door to escort me to the grand hall, I'm the polished princess everyone expects me to be.

We reach the door and Gwyneira, Eldoris, and Edina are waiting for me. Entering alongside Gwyneira declares to the entire realm that Winter and Summer Courts are officially aligned. Ari disappears, slipping into the hall through a side entrance—only royalty get an entrance through the main doors—and the rest of us fall into formation.

"Head high," Gwyneira whispers. I didn't even realize I'd dropped my gaze until she points it out, but I follow her instructions and raise my chin. Standing directly behind me, Eldoris' hand grazes mine in silent support.

A few hours; that's all I need to get through, and then I can sleep. Or drink myself into a stupor. Or find some...other distraction. Maybe all three.

The grand hall—like so much of the rest of the palace—is teeming with plant life. Each table boasts a large floral centerpiece with plum-colored flowers and thick green leaves. Rose petals are sprinkled on the floor, and garlands of hydrangeas hang from the high, wooden rafters. At the front of the room, a large tree has grown into the wall so its branches hang over two crystal thrones carved with vines and other symbols of the Spring Court.

There's no fanfare tonight, no separate entrances for each monarch, since tonight is all about the new King and Queen. So, when Gwyneira and I enter side by side, arms linked, a hush falls over the entire room.

My eyes zero in on Zahir. Steam practically rises from his reddened ears, and his reaction gives me a small flicker of satisfaction, just enough to dull the edge of my sadness. Let him fume. Let him realize that his potential war will be harder than he thought. Let him see what disrupting the peace of our realm means.

Gwyneira splits off, joining the table with the monarchs and their spouses, while Edina, Eldoris, and I join the rest of the second generation. My brother holds out my chair for me before he does the same for Edina, and then takes the seat between us.

Izar, who sits on my other side, leans in. "Are you alright?" he whispers, his gray eyes creased with concern.

"Fine," I say, forcing a smile.

In the past, I would have been tempted to confide in him. Even when our courts were at odds, our group tried not to let it affect our friendship. But we were younger then, and Izar is still Zahir's brother—even if they notoriously don't get along. I need to be wary around my Unseelie friends, excluding Edina.

He doesn't seem entirely convinced, but we're interrupted as guards announce the arrival of King Puck and Queen Lysandra.

They beam as they enter, their hands clasped in a way that feels like they're entering their wedding reception rather than their coronation ball. Lysandra completely bucks the tradition of wearing a ball gown, instead opting for a tight-fitting corset dress in gold that complements her pale skin and plum hair. It clings to every inch of her ample curves, and while some of the stuffier courtiers turn their noses up at it, she looks gorgeous as she owns her body. Puck, on the other hand, goes with the full regalia—velvet cape and all.

Together, they take their thrones for the first time, sitting on the elaborate crystal that's been carved by the earth elementals that populate their court. The ballroom erupts in applause, and it brings a genuine smile to my face. For all they've been through, they deserve nothing but happiness.

When the ovation dies down, Puck and Lysandra make a short speech, and then plates magically appear. A salad with dried cranberries, some sort of soft cheese, and drizzled in a fragrant vinaigrette sits before us. Everyone turns their attention back to their tables and their first course.

"It's odd, isn't it?" Larisa asks, ignoring her salad in favor of playing with her boyfriend Behar's hair. Behar seems unfazed, content to eat his food with the gusto I'd expect of a Seelie Court soldier. When he senses my attention, he looks up and arches a questioning eyebrow. The expression is so similar to Arella's—his late sister—that I smile, even as it makes me miss my friend.

"What is?" Baxter, Izar's mate, asks when no one responds to Larisa.

"They're not sitting with us anymore," she says, referring to Puck and Lysandra. They remain on their thrones since someone summoned a small table for them to eat on the dais. "After tonight, they'll move to the monarchs' table."

"We're growing up," Eldoris says.

That earns a contemplative silence before Radley excitedly asks, "Who do you think will be next?"

"Not me," Izar teases. Zahir was the oldest of his siblings, so unless something tragic happens before he has children, Izar and Hades will never see the throne.

"Sound a little more upset about it," I quip.

"I'm perfectly happy commanding our navy."

Oh. My. Goddess.

Izar runs the navy. The same one that would sail up the river to attack us.

Does he know his brother is having thoughts of war? Has he been sitting beside us, joking and fucking around all while planning an attack?

Get that look off your face, Eldoris says in my head, while aloud, he asks, "Where's Hades?"

Gwyneira said Night Court is on the move against us, I respond. I planned on telling Eldoris the extent of my conversation with Gwyneira earlier, but then everything with my mother happened, and I decided it would be best left for tomorrow when we could discover more.

I'll look into it.

How am I supposed to sit here if he's planning on attacking?

We've done it before.

I miss Izar's answer to Hades' location, but tune back into the conversation to hear Edina say, "My mother is going to rule forever, so it won't be me."

"Facts," Radley agrees. "I think it'll be me."

"Dear old dad still riding your ass about getting married?" Eldoris asks. Radley groans emphatically and recounts all the times his father suggested he find a female to marry and start producing heirs with.

No one suggests that I'll be the next to ascend to the throne, but I know they're all thinking it. Even if they don't know the details of my mother's illness, they're not stupid. They see that she's been to increasingly fewer functions. They may assume she's just going to step down, but either way, they know it'll be soon for me.

Very soon.

Too soon.

Chapter Ten
Devorah

WHEN DINNER IS FINISHED, an orchestra plays and we're expected to dance. Puck and Lysandra take the floor first, spinning in an elaborate waltz. They glide so well together like they were made to be partners.

Watching them leaves me with a hollow feeling, which isn't helped when other couples, including Edina and Eldoris, join them on the dance floor. I know I'll be asked to dance soon, but it's not the same. Dancing with someone for political gain isn't the same as having a partner.

"Dance with me," a raspy, feminine voice says in my ear, and I spin to find Hades hovering over me. She's in a form-fitting red dress that matches her brightly painted lips. Her hair is cut short at a hard angle at her just as-sharp chin, and her eyes, such a dark blue that they're almost black, sparkle with mischief.

"When did you get here?" I tease, placing my hand in hers, my pale skin standing out against her warm beige. I'm taller than her, but you wouldn't know it by the way she escorts me to the dance floor.

"You know I have a one-hour tolerance for court bullshit."

She leads, moving in a simple box step that tells me she's more interested in talking than dancing. "Why do you look like you swallowed a lemon?" she asks.

"Such a charmer," I deadpan, earning me a chuckle. "It's a marvel so many Fae throw themselves at you."

"That has nothing to do with tact and everything to do with—"

"Yeah, yeah, I've been to *Cerberus*."

In addition to running the Underground, Hades owns three clubs in her subterranean kingdom. *Tartarus*—her newest, and the one where Ari and I, well—is a dance club. *Styx* is a strip club, and the other—*Cerberus*—is a sex club. In addition to the private rooms, there's a main stage where she puts on sex shows—many of which Hades presides over from a throne.

"How is Minthe?" I ask, referring to her newest submissive. Hades has plenty of partners, but this one seems different. Since they've been together, I haven't heard of her publicly playing with others.

"Don't change the subject," she says, narrowing her eyes in challenge. "What's wrong with you?"

"I actually did swallow a lemon."

"Try again." I feel her magic surround us so our conversation is muted to the nearby couples. "Are you concerned about someone in my court?"

"Who would I be concerned about?"

"Someone in power. Who's related to me. Who isn't Izar." As if her meaning wasn't clear enough, her gaze flits to where Zahir is dancing with his wife, looking like he'd rather be anywhere else, even though Haiza is one of the most stunning females in the realm.

"Not concerned," I answer, my voice light and carefree even though my mind is whirring.

"Well, if you were to *become* concerned—" She pronounces every word with explicit care. "—You should know he doesn't speak for me. *Or* the Underground."

I can feel the sincerity in her words. It feels like the stirrings of hope. I may have another ally, one with access to some of the deadliest materials and weapons in the realm.

"And if I were concerned about the other male in your family?" I hedge.

"I can't speak for him," she says on a sigh. Then, after a glance around the room to make sure no one was reading our lips, "You can use the Underground as you see fit. Say the word, and I'll have my ears to the ground and the tunnels cleared enough to house an army."

So not only is she offering me the use of the tunnels themselves, but she's offering access to her network of spies—and potentially the mercenaries. While they're technically independent contractors, nothing happens in the Underground without Hades' knowledge, and most are too afraid to lose their connection to her to act without her approval.

But I don't for one second think she's giving me permission out of the goodness of her heart. "And what would I need to exchange for these services?"

"I'll let you know."

"Do I look like I was born yesterday? You think I'm going to make a deal without knowing the terms?"

"You're not looking for anything at this moment, so when you are, we can discuss terms."

I want to protest, to know what I should *expect* to offer, but the song ends, and Eldoris and Edina approach. Hades swiftly drops the shield around us and smiles a wolf's smile at the couple approaching.

"May I cut in?" Eldoris asks, offering a hand to me.

"Does that mean I can dance with your betrothed?" Hades says with a wink to Edina, and, to my surprise, her cheeks pink.

"By all means," Eldoris says, trying to hide his smirk.

The two females whirl off, and Eldoris watches them with heat in his eyes. "Ew." I smack him on the chest before getting into formation. "Do not dance with me if you're turned on. I can't handle it."

He pulls his attention from Edina and Hades and we start to dance. "Edina has a little crush on Hades."

I choke on air. "Goddess," I swear once I can breathe again. "And by the look on your face, you wouldn't mind that pairing at all."

He shrugs. "I don't think Hades is playing with other couples right now, but no, I wouldn't mind."

"You're remarkably unpossessive."

"I'm an evolved male." He glances over my shoulder. "Speaking of possessive, do you want to tell me what's going on with you and Ari?"

"Nothing." Not technically a lie. Unless you count riding someone's thigh in the middle of a club, or almost-kisses in jungle canopies, something. We spin until I can see Ari over Eldoris' shoulder. He's just chatting with one of the advisors—the one from Night Court, I believe—but when he catches me watching, the smile he gives me is positively criminal.

I sigh, looking away. "Nothing can happen."

"Why?" Eldoris asks, tilting his head to the side.

"You know what everyone will think."

"So? When I was falling for Edina, and was afraid of what people would say, what did you tell me?"

"While I'm sure it was a groundbreaking moment for you, I have many moments of brilliance. You'll have to remind me."

He rolls his eyes in a way that's entirely too similar to his betrothed.

"You said—" he clears his throat, and in a high-pitched voice, says, "—*who gives a shit what they say if you have the chance to be happy.*"

"Was that supposed to be me?"

"There was also a bit about me letting down my walls, do you remember that?"

"Vaguely," I mutter, even though I remember that conversation very clearly. Eldoris was refusing to let himself fall out of loyalty to Arella, even though we both knew she would have wanted him to be happy. Once he let go of that notion, he and Edina were blissfully happy.

He gives me a knowing smile. "He's a good male."

"I know." My voice is small, barely a whisper. I'm having trouble reconciling that fact with the excuses I've concocted to keep Ari out.

Was that all they were? Excuses and walls I've hidden myself behind?

If I just got out of my own way, could I be happy?

Well, probably not happy given the current circumstances, but I could have a partner. Someone to lean on when all the shit that's coming our way hits the fan.

"You have so much pressure," Eldoris says. "Take the happiness where you can."

I swallow around the lump in my throat and nod tightly. Then, because I've had enough seriousness today to last several lifetimes, I smile and whisper, "Did you know Mom and Simi were fucking?"

His eyes bulge. "No, shut up."

"It's true, he propositioned me at the coronation."

"Stop."

"He licked his lips, El!" And I'm enough of an asshole that I send the memory down our mental connection so he can see the moment play out.

"Why?" he groans.

"Because if I needed to see it, so did you."

We dissolve into laughter as the song ends.

"Princess, may I?" Ayelet—advisor for the Day Court, and the foulest male in existence—asks. He was possibly handsome once, but years baking in the constant sun of Day Court have turned his skin leathery and orange and have dried his blonde hair to straw.

And he's a lech. He hits on every female at every party, even those who are clearly uninterested.

"No," Eldoris answers for me and drags me off the dance floor with him and back to the table.

"My hero." I feign swooning.

"You're welcome."

ARI

Tonight has been an exercise in my willpower, and I'm failing miserably.

I've been trying not to look at Devorah, to not salivate after her like she's a fucking steak, but I've been wildly unsuccessful. It's unfair how stunning she is.

More than that, I can see how tense she is tonight, how she's only partially here in this room. And because I'm watching obsessively, I can feel her concern. The way she interacts with everyone is like they're out to get her. I want to go to her, to hold her and provide her a safe harbor.

But she's made it clear we can't be together, so I keep my distance. I don't ask her to dance, even if I do steal glances at her as she dances with Hades, then her brother.

"You alright?" my friend Tarek—the advisor of the Night Court—asks. He's equally distracted by the females in the room, but unlike me, his gaze roams over many.

"Good," I say, lifting my glass of whiskey in salute.

"How are things with the princess?" he asks, sipping his drink. "You're serving her, not her mother, right?"

It doesn't matter that we've been friends for centuries, or that we trained to be bodyguards together. At this moment, we're loyal to our courts, and he's fishing for information the same way I am.

"Both," I say. The whiskey is smooth and smoky as it slides down my throat. "But since Her Majesty has signed over control to Princess Devorah while she's on vacation, I'm at the princess's beck and call for a bit."

"Vacation?" he scoffs. "Come on, brother. You expect me to believe that?"

"Does a queen who has ruled for centuries not deserve a vacation now that she has a capable interim queen?"

He flashes a smug smile that says he sees right through me. "Of course, she does."

"The alliance helps," I add. This is my job tonight. To leave no doubt that Gwyneira is aligned with us, in case her entrance with Devorah left some questions.

"That's not in effect until the marriage is solidified."

I take another long gulp, so it looks like I'm spilling secrets rather than carefully placing information. "Edina and Eldoris have started planning, so Gwyneira is moving troops to our borders while they do."

He nods slowly, digesting. "Is that so?"

I shrug, like it's of no consequence, keeping my face as relaxed as I can while I wait to hear what he has to say on the matter. I expect him to ask about our intel and why we feel the need to have soldiers at our borders during a time of "peace," but Tarek gets distracted again. I follow his gaze to the queen of his court, who is no longer with Zahir. Her eyes meet his and go hooded.

I chuckle under my breath. "Dangerous game you're playing."

"I have it under control."

I hum around the rim of my glass, and he flicks me with a cloth napkin. "Like you're one to talk." We're back in friendlier territory, ribbing each other over romantic partners rather than sifting for political facts, but I still file away the tidbit for later use.

"I have no idea what you're talking about." But even as I say it, I glance across the room to where Devorah is now chatting with Lysandra and Puck. Her head tilts back in laughter, the sound bright and full. It tugs on my heartstrings, making my chest feel like an inflated balloon untethered by a string.

"Sure."

"At least my inappropriate crush isn't married," I joke, but he only smiles wider.

"Who said mine's just a crush?"

Oh shit.

I lean forward, failing in all attempts at subtlety. "You're sleeping with Haiza?" He gives me a cheeky smile. "How is that even possible?"

Marriages in Faerie are a magically binding ceremony. Once the Fae—be it a couple or multiple partners—agree on the terms, it's impossible to disobey them. It's why so few Fae are actually married, and those who are, marry their fated mates.

"There's a clause," he says, excitedly. "As long as Zahir keeps being a philandering douchebag, I have Haiza."

I let out a low, drawn-out whistle. I don't think he realizes just how much he gave away in that little exchange. Not just his queen's infidelity, my dear friend revealed he isn't so happy with his king. And if Zahir's trusted advisor isn't loyal, we have a much easier task in front of us. Their court is a house of cards; one strong gust of wind—or blast of fire in the case of Summer Court—can take the whole thing down.

That's probably why Zahir has his sights on us. If he can take on a territory, he'll appear stronger than he is.

Very interesting.

"Tarek, it's good to see you," Devorah says, approaching us with a gracious smile. My friend jumps to his feet before bowing at the waist and kissing her knuckles. I growl a soft warning, and he gives me a cheeky smile.

"Princess," he coos, not letting go. "How are you this evening? You look beautiful."

She's not just beautiful, it's too mundane a word for Devorah. She's radiant, stunning, magnetic. No one should be this devastating.

But I can't say that like Tarek can. He says it, and it's just a compliment. I say it, and it'll be gossip fodder for days. Devorah doesn't need a scandal right now, not when she already has so much on her plate.

"I'm well, thank you." She not-so-subtly removes her hand from his. "But I'm actually going to retire for the evening, and I figured if I didn't tell Little Hershel, he'd send out a search party."

Tarek finds that hysterical, and his laugh draws attention to our little trio. I glower at Devorah, who gives me a challenging smile. I'm glad her playful side is coming out; she was so serious and dejected before.

"Would you like me to escort you back to your suite?" I ask.

"No," she says, but her eyes widen slightly like she's trying to tell me something. "Have a good night."

She leans forward to air kiss Tarek's cheek. He's too professional to react, but I can tell he's taken aback. Typically, a member of a higher station wouldn't give that kind of farewell to someone beneath them.

With a meaningful glance, she leans over to do the same to me. Her sweet scent envelops me, and I fight the impulse to draw her closer. "Come to me later," she whispers, her breath hot against my cheek.

My mind runs wild. She probably just wants to talk about the things she's discovered this evening, but it doesn't stop my cock from hardening at the implication.

All too soon, she pulls away, taking the warmth of her body away. With one final smile, she leaves.

Now it's my friend's turn to whistle. "Little Hershel. That has to make you feel about this big." He holds his fingers up in a very small pinching motion.

"Fuck off," I grumble.

"I didn't realize how one-sided your crush was. I figured you had a bit of a chance, but if she calls you Little Hershel..."

If I were a lesser male, I'd tell him I know exactly what she sounds like when she's screaming my real name. And maybe in the past, I would have, but not with Devorah. She's not some random female I want to fuck. She's...important. Special.

Instead, I sucker punch him in the gut

"On that note, I'm going to bed," I say, as Tarek doubles over. He's hamming it up; I didn't hit him that hard.

"All alone?" he sputters. "There are plenty of other Fae here."

"Are you offering?" I tease, holding my hand out for him to shake. He bats me away before taking it and bidding me farewell.

Chapter Eleven
Devorah

I PACE THE LENGTH of the sitting room, Eldoris' words echoing in my mind over and over again.

You have so much pressure. Take the happiness where you can.

Having happiness in my life shouldn't make me feel guilty. Eldoris and Edina have found something great despite everything, and it doesn't make them any less devoted to their courts. It doesn't mean Eldoris isn't also mourning. Logically, I know this. In reality...

I haven't wanted anything for myself in so long. I've gone with the flow, a leaf caught in a hurricane being blown this way and that to avoid being sucked into the churning water. After all that, can I choose something that's just for me?

Take the happiness where you can.

A knock on my suite door pulls me to the present. "Come in," I call, my voice hoarse.

Ari enters, face hard as he scans my body for signs of anything amiss, as if I could have been injured in the five minutes since I last saw him.

He's more disheveled now than he was when we left for dinner, but fuck if that doesn't make him sexier. His hair looks like he ran his fingers through it repeatedly, and his tie is loosened. "Everything okay?" he asks, not commenting on my blatant ogling.

"Yes." As soon as I say the word aloud, I realize what it is. A decision; a promise.

I can do this. I can choose something for myself. I can take this happiness.

I motion for Ari to follow me into my room. His brow scrunches, but he doesn't argue.

My bedroom in the Spring Court is simple, done in pastel blues that contrast with rich, oak flooring. I left the windows open so the sweet scent of night-blooming roses trickles in on the soft breeze.

As soon as we're inside, I close the door and put up a shield to keep our conversation silent.

"What did Hades have to say?" Ari asks, making himself comfortable and sitting on the edge of my bed.

"I don't want to talk about her." I walk forward until I'm right in front of him, standing between his legs.

He swallows. "Devorah..." I brush a piece of his black hair off his forehead, running my fingers through the strands. His eyes close, and he hums, leaning into the contact. "What are you doing?"

"Aren't you tired of fighting this?" I ask.

As if he can't control himself, his hands find my waist, toying with the material of my dress. "More than you could ever know, beautiful." I smile at that, warmth coursing through my blood, blooming in my chest, and settling in my core. "But you're going through a lot—"

"I am," I agree. I grab onto his tie and slowly undo the knot. "But I'm not making this decision out of grief. I'm not using this to hide from my problems. I'm doing this because I want you."

I pause, staring intently into Ari's eyes. "Fae will talk; they're assholes who live for scandal. I don't care what they say, but if you do—"

"I don't." His voice is a deep rumble that has everything in me tightening.

"Then..." I lightly drag my nails down his chest, and he inhales sharply. "We don't have anything holding us back, do we?"

He stands abruptly, but when I try to step back, he keeps me close, grabbing my hips. Even through the layers separating us, I can feel how hard he is. All for me.

"You want this?" he asks, leaning in until our foreheads touch. It's amazing how he can make me feel so comfortable, so safe, even when I'm desperate with need.

"Yes."

"Really think about that answer." His hands drift up my ribcage, pausing underneath my breasts. "Because I won't be satisfied with a quick fling, Devorah. I won't be able to have you for just the night and then let you go. If we do this..."

"I want it," I assure him. My breath is so ragged that my chest brushes against his, and my nipples are so hard that when his fingers brush against them, he can feel the stiff peaks beneath my clothing. "I want it all."

"Thank fuck."

The kiss is searing, the culmination of so much time wanting. It's frantic but tender, desperate but sweet, soft but demanding. It's the perfect dichotomy that has my toes curling while making my heart soar. This isn't just a kiss. This is...fuck this is everything.

Ari drinks me in like fine wine. I can't touch enough of him, my hands roving over his muscled arms and broad chest while his sink into my hair and tug until I'm exactly where he wants me. When I moan into his lips, he takes advantage of the opening and slides his tongue inside my mouth. He kisses me like he wants to fuse us. Like he never wants to let me go.

"Goddess," I breathe when he uses the grip on my hair to tilt my head to the side so he has access to my neck.

"She's not here," he says, nipping my skin a little too hard. I love it though, fuck do I love that little burst of pain with that pleasure. "The only name you're allowed to call out is mine."

Oh, my damn.

Why is that so hot?

"Say it," he growls, moving to the hollow of my neck, my collarbone. His scruff has grown back since this morning, and it scrapes against my sensitive flesh, creating the most delicious friction. "I've been dreaming of the way you screamed my name when you came. I want to hear it without the sound of the bass drowning you out."

"Ari," I gasp, and he rewards me by yanking the neckline of my dress down so my breasts spring free.

"Louder," he says, gripping himself through his pants while his tongue draws a line of fire down my breast, around the areola, but not where I need him.

"Make me then," I huff.

In a whir, he wraps one hand around my jaw. His eyes are dark and filled with promise. "Oh, beautiful," he chuckles. The fingers that rest against my pulse press down ever so slightly. Not enough to hurt, but enough that I feel it. "You're going to regret that."

He tosses me on the bed, and I barely have time to bounce before he covers my body with his, his leg slotted between mine. I writhe against him as he kisses me again, his fingers expertly teasing my breasts, but still not giving me enough. He's got me so wound up that by the time he touches my nipples, I think I'll combust.

"I'm going to make you come so hard, you'll feel me for days," he growls, grinding his thigh against me. "I'm going to erase the memory of everyone who's ever touched you until all you know is me."

"Yes," I plead. Finally, he drops his head and grazes my nipple with his teeth before sucking it into his mouth. My back bows off the bed, arching into the pleasure.

"I need a taste." His voice is soft enough that I'm not sure he's talking to me.

"Lift," he orders, and I lift my hips so he can push my skirt up around my waist. "By the goddess, Devorah. Where are your panties?"

I took them off when I got back to the room, but I don't say that. Instead, I blink innocently. "Did I forget them?"

"You better have done this for me and not for some other male."

I hesitate the slightest amount, and he sinks his teeth into my thigh. I yelp. "It's all for you!"

"Good girl."

If the praise wasn't enough to drive me insane, his tongue draws a line from my entrance to my clit. My eyes roll to the back of my head when he groans like the taste of me is the best thing he's ever had.

He doesn't waste any more time.

Ari *devours* me.

He switches between licking and sucking, between long luxurious strokes of his tongue and little flicks against my clit. When I dig my nails into his soft hair and hold him close to me, he chuckles, sending vibrations up my body so I feel them everywhere.

"Ride my face," he commands, the sound muffled because I won't let him up. "Take what you need."

You don't have to tell me twice.

I grind into him like my life depends on it. I've never built to an orgasm so quickly, never have been on the edge with barely a touch.

When Ari slips a finger inside me, I lose it.

Like he asked, I scream his name loud enough that my voice breaks with the force of it. My vision goes hazy around the edges, the world narrowing to his purple eyes locked on mine as I ride out my orgasm. He doesn't stop when I release his hair, instead slowing his ministrations until he's wrung every last drop of pleasure from me.

And when I'm done, he crawls back up my body and kisses me deeply. The taste of me on his lips makes me moan again. "I could live off the taste of you," he says, fumbling for the button of his pants as he continues to kiss me. "I need to be inside you. Is that okay, beautiful? Can I fuck you?"

Goddess, I need that more than I need air. More than I need food or water. "Yes."

Ari groans and kisses me again. He runs his cock down the length of my slit, and I jump at the feel of something cold. I push up on my elbows and get the barest glint of metal before he pushes me back down with a firm hand on my chest. "Shh," he murmurs, and repeats the motion, and the sensation goes from foreign to oh so good.

"Please," I whimper. Ari notches the head of his cock at my entrance.

And then, because the goddess is a cold-hearted bitch, someone knocks on the door.

He jumps enough that his dick is away from me but he doesn't go far.

Another knock comes, this one more insistent. "Get rid of them," Ari says, moving to kiss my breasts again.

I modify the shield around the room to let sound out. "Fuck off," I shout, and Ari laughs against my skin.

"Dev—"

I was expecting Kalinda or another servant. I wasn't expecting Eldoris. I sit straight up, knocking Ari off me with the abruptness of my movement.

"I need you to open the door." His voice breaks on the last word.

All arousal is gone; any remaining embers of heat are effectively doused. Because I know exactly what he's here to say. I can see the whole scene play out in my mind as if I'm a clairvoyant. I can feel the truth of it like a tidal wave that's ready to sweep me away as soon as I open the door.

"Shit," Ari swears, shoving his cock back in his pants. He never even got his jacket off; that's how frantic we were.

He helps me stand and smooths my hair while I fix my dress.

At the handle of the door, I hesitate. If I can stop this, hover in this moment, then I won't have to deal with what comes next. I can stay here, suspended in time with Ari, and never have to hear the words I know Eldoris will say.

Ari's hand lands on top of mine, and I meet his gaze. He knows, too—or at least he expects. And this, his warm hand atop mine, is his way of telling me he meant what he said earlier. He wants more. All of it.

Even this.

I drop the shield completely and Ari and I twist the knob together and open the door.

Eldoris has removed his tie and left his shirt collar open so I can see the beginnings of the tribal tattoos that cover his torso. His eyes are bloodshot, still fresh with tears. Behind him, Edina is standing with her hand on the center of his back, a frozen tear beading on her eyelashes and her mouth set in a grim line.

I shake my head, blinking back tears that I refuse to let fall.

"Say it," I insist.

He pulls me into his arms. "Mother's dead."

I crumble. His strong grip enveloping me is the only thing keeping me upright as I sob into his shirt. His chin rests against my chin, and his chest heaves as he cries.

"When?" I croak out, staying buried in the safety of my twin.

"About an hour ago."

We should have stayed. We should have ditched the ball tonight and stayed with her in the summer house. She shouldn't have been alone.

I can't breathe, guilt clogging my throat and stealing oxygen from my lungs. My mother is dead. The woman I looked up to my entire life is gone. I still have so much to learn from her, so many stories I haven't heard, so many milestones she'll never get to witness.

She's just *gone*.

Ari comfortingly rubs the space between my shoulder blades, much like Edina's was on Eldoris, but that makes me cry even harder. Not because I don't want him here, but something about the extra layer of comfort makes this more real.

"She's at peace," Eldoris says, still making no move to let me go from the cage of his arms. And I know that. Logically, I know she was confused and hurting. I know she was miserable and felt helpless.

But it doesn't help.

It doesn't make the giant chasm in my chest shrink. It doesn't keep me from missing her.

Just when I think I can't shed another tear, the weight of what this truly means settles heavily on my shoulders. My mother is dead, and now

I'll be queen. The entire court will rely on me. I know I've done the job for a while now, but the pressure of expectations wraps around me like a vice and squeezes out more tears.

When I finally pull away and swipe at my eyes, Eldoris' shirt is soaked, and my hair is damp from where he cried into me. I shake my head, shoving down the pain and crushing anxiety into a pit in my stomach.

"We need..." I clear my throat. Ari's heat disappears from my back only to appear a moment later with a glass of water for me and one for Eldoris and Edina. I thank him and take a large drink.

"We need to call a priestess," I say, glancing at Ari. He opens his mouth like he wants to protest, but closes it and nods. "And we need to find Mother's will. It should have the official statement naming me queen. The interim notice will be fine for now, but we need to get this official—"

"Dev," Eldoris says sternly enough that I'm forced to look at him. "You don't have to be the one to do this."

"I do, though," I say, my lower lip wobbling again. "There's no one else now. It's me."

"I'm here," he insists. "I'm right here, and I'll be here through all of this. But tonight...tonight let's mourn our mother."

I want to tell him it's a terrible idea, that I need to do all this and keep busy so I don't completely fall apart. But tears clog my throat again.

"Beautiful," Ari says, stepping up beside me. Eldoris lets me go to him, and he cups my face in his palms. "What do you need? Would you like me to handle everything for you, or do you want me to stay?"

He reads the answer from my face. "I'll take care of everything."

I reach up and kiss him softly. He doesn't try to deepen the kiss; he just repeats the motion twice more before backing up.

"Well, that explains why it smells like sex in here," Edina mutters, and a watery laugh bubbles from my throat. My future sister comes forward then and hugs me tightly enough to crush my bones.

"I suggest you all return to Summer Court immediately," Ari says, snapping back into his authoritative advisor mode.

We all nod. While everyone will understand that we're in mourning, we can't appear too weak in front of others. The Fae are wicked creatures when they want to be. The freak out I had can't happen again unless I'm in the privacy of my suite—and only in front of my brother, Ari, and Edina.

"Give me a minute," I say, and run into the bathroom to splash cold water on my face. Once I look somewhat presentable, I return to the sitting room. Edina is tucked under Eldoris' arm, and she's got her arms wrapped around his waist. When they see me, they straighten, and I watch as their faces shift, their features becoming fixed in a solemn mask.

Together, the four of us walk out of the palace with our heads held high. No one stops us as we teleport back to the palace.

But the moment we're back in the familiar sandstone halls, we fall apart all over again.

I STAND IN THE foyer of the palace facing a crowd of all the servants, palace guards, and other personnel stationed at the palace. Eldoris said I should have this meeting in the throne room or the ballroom, but I'm not ready to hold an audience in either location yet. It's bad enough that I'll have to host some kind of event after the funeral.

True to his word, Ari left to deal with some of the logistics, but I insisted on doing this. The staff are part of our family; they deserve to hear of my mother's death from me.

Eldoris grabs my hand in silent support as I clear my throat and amplify my voice. Everyone quiets.

"I have some bad news," I start. Someone gasps, preemptively guessing my announcement. I continue. "The Queen is dead."

It might seem blunt, but if I say any more, I'll start crying, and I don't want to do that in front of a crowd. There are more gasps, some muttered prayers, and a few tears from the staff.

"I wanted you to be the first to hear the news," I continue. "We'll be hosting the royal families in the next few days for the funeral. Narolie?"

The palace event planner steps forward, chin lifted. "I'll take care of everything, Your Highness."

"Thank you." I don't know what else to say. Do I provide comfort? Condolences? In all my training, I never prepared to announce my mother's death to a group of people who served and cared for her.

"We appreciate your prayers and condolences," Eldoris steps in. "Please take the rest of the evening off to grieve."

He gently guides me down the hall, leaving the staff behind and absolving me from any further remarks.

He and Edina stay with me in my suite, refusing to leave no matter how much I insist I'm okay. We talk and cry until my head throbs in my skull, and I finally insist they go to bed. Even then, they take one of my guest rooms rather than return to Eldoris' suite.

In the early hours of the morning, just as I'm about to give up on sleep and head to the living room to sketch, Ari quietly slips into my room.

He's traded his suit for sweatpants and a T-shirt. Without saying a word, he climbs into bed and pulls me into his arms.

"I didn't think you'd come back," I whisper, burying my nose into him, soaking in his citrus scent.

"I'll always come back," he murmurs, kissing the top of my head. "Sleep, Devorah. I'm not going anywhere."

Against all odds, I do.

Chapter Twelve
Ari

DEVORAH SITS A FEW rows ahead of me in the small temple, dressed in the customary mourning black of Summer Court. Located on the beach at the farthest corner of our court, the temple of the goddess is comprised of white wooden walls and driftwood pews. It's a simple space—unadorned and undecorated—save for the ceiling, which is crystalline glass. At night, when the stars are out, it's a tapestry of celestial majesty. But today, with the sun high and unrelenting, it's hotter than hell.

Atop the polished rose quartz altar is the queen's modest wooden coffin. The priestess presiding over the funeral today is a pixie—a Fae the size of a dragonfly, with gossamer-like wings, delicate features, and razor-sharp teeth—who wears black robes, the symbols of the six elements etched in gold. She hovers above the coffin, chanting in the ancient Fae language and occasionally bowing her head to the floor or lifting it to the sky.

The service in the temple is only the first part of the funeral—the private portion specifically designed for royalty, their advisors, and a handful of courtiers who were deemed high enough in society. The rest of the public will pay their respects at one of the many subsequent events happening throughout the day.

I use the handkerchief that was given for tears to dab my brow, wiping away some of the sweat. The sun wouldn't be nearly as unbearable if there were windows in this temple. Or even if the door was left open. Instead, the room bakes, and the longer we sit here, the harder it is to breathe.

Mercifully, a gust of air whips through the enclosed room, providing momentary relief until King Oakley smacks his son on the arm. Radley tilts his head to the sky with a silent groan that I internally echo. Edina glances over her shoulder at the Autumn Court prince, and seeing this exchange, sends an ice cube into his open palms.

"Thank the goddess," he breathes—loud enough to get him a glare from the pixie priestess. A second later, frost creeps up the back of my neck, acting like a cold compress. Edina turns forward again before I can thank her.

"As we lay Queen Talia of the Summer Court to rest," the priestess says in English since she's finished with the old Fae portion of the service. "We remember the magnificent life she led and her amazing contributions to her court and the entire realm. She was truly goddess blessed, as evident by the birth of her twins, Devorah and Eldoris."

All Fae have some sort of fertility issue, but elemental Fae—who make up the majority of royalty—are notoriously infertile. It's why they began coupling with humans and other races of Fae. Having one child is considered a miracle, so twins are practically divine.

"Before she is ready for her final resting place," the priestess continues, "we will bring Queen Talia's body to the far reaches of the court so that all her citizens may say goodbye and so she can get one final glimpse of her home."

She gestures to the coffin, and the princes and princesses from the other courts approach the altar. Radley and Izar take the back two corners, while Edina, Hades, and Larisa take the front. Slowly, they lift the coffin and walk up the aisle of the temple, Devorah and Eldoris following close behind. Devorah has been composed all morning, solemn but stoic. There's been no sign of the full-body sobs or keening wails of the night her mother died.

Since that night, I've spent every night in her bed, holding her as she cried softly in my arms. All I want to do today is to support her, to show her she has someone to lean on. But we decided not to publicize our relationship, agreeing it would be in poor taste to be open and affectionate while she's in mourning.

So, I wait dutifully until the monarchs follow behind the family, and fall in with the rest of the advisors as we exit the temple. The procession will travel through the Wyld Jungle and along the bank of the Padauk River before we skirt the edges of the Orasite Mountains on our way back to the ocean. While we don't cut through the center of the court, following the edges will allow for citizens to meet us along the way. As we pass, village elders and leaders are allowed to join our procession to witness the final burial at sea.

It's a beautiful tradition, full of history that dates back to the very first monarchs of the realm. When the priestess suggested it, Devorah got teary-eyed and instantly agreed. It's a ceremony befitting of a great queen.

The pixie failed to mention that navigating a coffin through a fucking jungle is damn near impossible.

Sure, they're using magic to do the majority of the heavy lifting, but getting it through the thick vegetation requires careful work. Puck and Lysandra—newly crowned King and Queen of the Spring Court—help by using their earth magic to bend the trees, flatten shrubbery, and push aside vines. It's still very slow going.

The first village we come upon is virtually hidden unless you know where to look. The houses are thatched from the same dark wood as the trees, and many of them use leaves and branches atop their roofs to camouflage their outpost. The jungle is quieter here as if the birds and insects don't dare approach this area.

Hades is pointing out the outlines of the houses to Edina when a group of cloaked Fae appear in the path before the casket. Edina shrieks and looks like she's about to drop her corner, but her magic snaps out and holds it aloft.

Necromancers have that kind of effect.

They're lovely Fae once you get to know them...if you can get past the scent of decay that accompanies their magic.

The leader, a tall, imposing figure in a black cloak, steps away from the rest of the group. She inhales deeply as if breathing in the death surrounding our little party before she bows low to Devorah and Eldoris. "On behalf of the Fatum Village, we express our condolences."

Devorah extends her hand for the necromancer to kiss before the female leans close, whispering something. She nods and tells the second generation to set the casket on the ground.

The necromancers surround the coffin, joining hands and bowing their heads deeply. A sickly-sweet scent that reminds me of rotted fruit permeates the air as the leader withdraws from the circle and lifts the coffin's lid. There's a pulse of magic that sends a shiver rolling through the crowd. Even the plants shrink away.

When they withdraw, and the coffin is closed, the necromancer once again whispers something to Devorah and Eldoris, and they smile and thank her profusely. The necromancers melt back into the trees, and we resume the processional, the leader joining at the end of the line.

The rest of the trek through the jungle goes much of the same way. Sometimes, entire villages wish to hug or shake hands with Eldoris and Devorah, sometimes, they'll stand off to the side and let their elders speak for them. Occasionally, villages from the center of the territory intercept us on our path. Regardless of the time spent, no matter how much I know her heart is breaking, Devorah is gracious and kind.

She looks like a queen.

When we reach the sandy shores of the Padauk River, we're greeted with the sight of Fae from other courts. Spring Court citizens stand on the opposite bank, throwing flowers that Autumn Court citizens then float on balmy breezes across the water. Centaurs shoot arrows, werewolves howl, and winged Fae—including a family of harpies—swoop down, murmuring their condolences before swooping back into the skies.

The river stretches to the Orasite Mountains, where we find Day Court citizens in the hills. They light the path in brilliant white light, shooting beams of it up to the sky. Healers pass out potions to stave off dehydration, while others simply send their healing energy to revitalize us on the final leg of our journey.

The different terrains are one of the things that make our court so special. This part, the section closest to Day Court and the base of the mountain range, is comprised of hard-packed earth that bakes in the sun until it's dry and cracked. Dust kicks up around our group as we pass by several caves filled with Fae, only pausing when we reach the mouth of the largest cave.

A broad male wearing an open shirt approaches the group. His chest is obscured by piles and piles of gold chains. In fact, almost every inch of him is covered in jewelry, from his earrings to the cuffs snaking up his arms and the golden sandals winding around his ankles and calves.

A dragon shifter, the leader of this hoard.

"Your Highnesses," he says, walking right over and clasping Eldoris by the forearm before kissing Devorah's cheek.

"Shesha," she greets, smiling warmly at him before a female shrouded in equal amounts of jewelry replaces him. Despite the condolences she whispers, she has a predatory glint in her eyes. This is Shesha's mate, and I'm sure even his kissing Devorah's cheek in greeting was enough to set off her compulsion to protect her treasure.

"Who's that?" Tarek—who has been walking beside me—asks, as another large, stocky male comes up beside the couple, greeting Devorah and Eldoris as well.

"Kai. Shesha and Agni's youngest." Their eldest son, Ormr, is in the mortal realm visiting the hoards there.

"*That's* Kai?" he asks, whistling low. "He certainly grew up well."

I roll my eyes. "Don't you have enough entanglements?"

"Never." He winks.

To the dismay of the other advisors, Shesha and his mate settle into the spots directly behind the other monarchs. The dragons make up one of the largest populations of Fae in Summer Court, and their leaders are the highest-ranking members of our society, even if they choose not to attend many of the society gatherings.

"Little Hershel," Shesha greets, grasping my forearm in the same way he did Eldoris'.

Tarek snickers.

"Great to see you," I deadpan, earning a rare smirk from the dragon.

We cut inland, stopping by the queen's favorite lake so the selkies can wave their goodbyes from the water before we reach the palace. Straddling the two terrains, the Summer Court palace's sandstone exterior is like a beacon amidst the greenery of the jungle. We condense our line until we're two-by-two within the torch-lined path that leads to the palace grounds, where the entire staff is waiting. Guards hang in the trees overhead, missing nothing from their high vantage point. The brownies have polished the bricks until they gleam, with not an errant vine or leaf in sight. Smaller winged Fae—pixies mostly—sit atop the terracotta tiled roof, while elemental Fae crowd every balcony along the rounded towers.

We circle the palace until the moist jungle ground turns to sand, and the vegetation thins until there are only a few palm trees. Waiting on the shore is a line of priestesses. They guide the second generation to set the coffin down on the sand at the edge of the water. Waves lap up the sides, turning the wood dark as the salty spray kisses the edges.

"It is now that we say goodbye to our dearly departed queen," the pixie priestess who led the ceremony announces. "We call upon the goddess to take Talia into her loving arms. May she find peace in the beyond, and may she watch over us all."

"May she watch over us all," everyone repeats.

Devorah's posture is rigid as the waves continue to cascade around the side of the casket. The sand beneath it slips, and it slowly gets dragged out to sea.

I move in close to her, an inch closer than is appropriate. Subtly, she reaches back, and her fingers brush mine in silent confirmation—she's happy I'm here.

We all watch as the azure sea takes Queen Talia further out. When it reaches the open water, Devorah and Eldoris step forward together.

"Love you, Mom," Devorah whispers.

They each conjure a ball of fire, though Eldoris' is much larger and appears to be burning hotter. With a look, they launch their magic in a long arc. Eldoris' connects to the far end of the casket, while Devorah's reaches the closest. Everyone is silent as the wood goes up in flames, a bright spot of orange amidst the blue. After a few moments, the priestesses dismiss everyone, inviting them into the palace for dinner.

When it's only us, Edina and Eldoris, I walk up behind Devorah and place my hands on her shoulders. She sighs into me and pulls me closer so her back is against my front.

We don't speak, we just watch until the fire is nothing more than a trickle of white ash in the dusk sky.

Chapter Thirteen
Devorah

FATIGUE CLINGS TO ME like a second skin as I battle through the post-funeral dinner. The 'celebration of life.' Such bullshit if you ask me. It's an excuse for the vultures to circle, to suss out any gaps in our defenses, to see if our grief has made us vulnerable. And, in turn, it's our chance to prove to the others that we're fine...missing our mother, but ready to rule the court.

Since it's a smaller gathering, we're seated at one long table in the dining room, one of my favorite places in the palace. It's the perfect blend of everything our court has to offer. The floors are made of burnt sienna rock that was mined from the Orasite Mountains, the walls are mostly windows made from sea glass—some clear and others mosaics in green and blue tones—and accented with driftwood, and everywhere you look, there are flowers from the jungle.

Since Eldoris and I are the only royalty of the court, we're seated at opposite ends of the table. Gwyneira sits to my right in the position of honor—in case anyone has missed that we're aligned. But putting Zahir on Eldoris' right was a stroke of genius on Ari's part. Zahir can't possibly try to scheme when my brother is watching his every move, and he wouldn't be stupid enough to try, not in front of the general of the Seelie Army.

The first course is one of my mother's favorites—a salad filled with tropical fruits in a light vinaigrette. I always found it too sweet for an appetizer, but tonight is all about her and the things she loved the most. It's also why the place settings are in shades of turquoise instead of traditional mourning black.

"Have you spoken with the record keeper yet, Devorah?" King Simi asks, his white beard resting on his plate and soaking up the salad dressing. He's directly on my left, with King Oakley beside him, although I would have much rather been beside Puck and Lysandra, who are joking and laughing with my brother at the other end.

"We've arranged a meeting for tomorrow." I move my salad around with my fork, taking only one bite before setting it back down.

When we contacted the record keeper, she insisted we bury my mother before we dealt with any other legal matters—namely, her official decree that I would be the next queen. Her tone left little to be argued with.

"Such an unusual situation," Oakley remarks, neatly dabbing the corners of his mouth with his napkin. "I'm not sure there has ever been a set of twins in a royal family. What say you, Gwyneira?"

"None in my recollection," she says.

"Wouldn't it be a hoot if Talia named Eldoris her heir after all that?" Simi snorts.

My fork clatters against my plate.

And it's not just because of Simi's musings, but because of what they reminded me of.

THE HEAD OF THE *necromancer village, Desdemona, took my hand in hers. Her skin was paper-thin with almost no fat, making it feel like I touched a skeleton.*

"My deepest condolences, Your Highnesses," she crooned. Her voice was both young and old, one and many. A master of death. It was impossible to see her features beneath the thick, black cloak obscuring her face, save for a scrap of straw-blonde hair that escaped its confines.

"It would be our honor to perform a final rite for our queen. To ensure her soul has moved on. And..." She let the word hang there as she looked between me and Eldoris. "Some souls leave traces...a memory or a message for those of us who remain."

Do you think we should? *I asked Eldoris through our mental channel. He worked with necromancers in the army, so I trusted his judgement.*

It won't hurt, *he responded.*

We agreed and instructed the second generation carrying my mother's casket to set it down and step aside.

Desdemona's group formed a circle with my mother's remains at the heart and began a low, very rhythmic chanting in the old Fae language. Their magic wasn't visible like the elemental Faes', but I was instantly aware when they began using it to aid their ritual. It was almost calming, but there was the barest hint of something amiss.

Desdemona stepped into the circle, prying open the lid to the casket. I shut my eyes. No, watch, *Eldoris urged.*

When I gathered my courage, I realized I couldn't see my mother's remains, but there was a bright yellow spark of magic. Desdemona cupped it in her palm, raising it to her ear before standing back and opening her arms, releasing the spark into the sky where it quickly disappeared.

I turned to look behind us, but no one reacted. The other necromancers must have blocked their view.

The chanting slowed, and Desdemona covered the casket again before returning to me and my brother. "Her soul is at rest," she said. I blinked away the tear that threatened to fall.

"And..." again, she held onto the word. "Her message was for you, Princess. She said, 'Tomorrow will hold a surprise, but I've done everything for a reason. Trust me.'"

"A surprise?" I asked, and the necromancer nodded.

"Leave it to the dead to be cryptic," Eldoris grumbled.

"The dead often are," Desdemona said, and I swore I caught a glimpse of a smile beneath that cloak.

Tomorrow will hold a surprise.

My mother was adamant that I take the throne. She insisted Eldoris looked 'too human' to command the court's respect, saying the Fae would never follow someone like him and that it had to be me.

But...what if she changed her mind?

What if everything I went through was all for nothing?

I know Simi is just curious. He's an academic, the kind of Fae who finds interest in irony and likes to think of every possibility.

But what if he's right? What if this is what the necromancers meant?

"What would happen to your alliance, Gwyn?" he goes on. "Edina is the only heir to the Winter Court throne. If Eldoris becomes king here, they would have to end the betrothal, correct?"

Oh my fucking fuck.

I didn't even think of that kind of fallout. If Edina and Eldoris can't get married, not only would they be devastated, but Gwyneira would pull her support. We'd be fucked. We'd have a war on our doorstep in thirty seconds.

Judging by the gleam in Oakley's eyes, he would join Zahir's quest to take us over in a second.

I want to punch Simi in the face for even mentioning this. As if my anxiety wasn't bad enough, thinking I'd have to take over the throne, now I'm anxious about *not* taking over the throne.

But my mother trained me well. So instead of yanking his stupid beard off one strand at a time, I smile and say, "I'm sure that won't be the case."

He nods and gnaws on another chunk of fruit.

From the middle of the table, Ari catches my eye. I give him what I hope is a reassuring nod, and it must translate because he turns back to his conversation with the advisor from the Day Court.

I convince the monarchs to share stories of my mother from before my brother and I were born, and that, thankfully, keeps me distracted from the worry surrounding tomorrow's meeting. And it keeps Simi from speculating on any other aspects regarding my ascension.

Four excruciating courses later, in the safety of my room, I can finally breathe again. I deserve a fucking medal for getting through that. Through the whole damn day.

I've just changed into an old t-shirt when there's a tap on my balcony door, with a familiar silhouette backlit by the moonlight.

"I thought you were staying away tonight," I say, opening the glass wide enough for Ari to come in. He scans my body, hovering on my bare legs beyond the hem of the tee before rising to meet my gaze.

"I'm not sure I said that," he smirks, closing the distance between us. His hands naturally fall to my hips.

"We said we'd be discreet." All the monarchs are staying at the palace tonight, and there's no way someone wouldn't notice if Ari came to my room and didn't leave until the morning.

"Which is why I came in through the balcony." He sighs, pulling me a little closer. "I wanted to make sure you're okay. I'll go if you want me to."

Now it's my turn to smirk, and I press up on my toes. "I'm not sure I said that," I echo, and brush my lips against his. The kiss is light, sweet. It's the kind of kiss that makes you go weak in the knees. There's no way something so simple, so deceptively chaste, should be able to make me feel this much.

Too soon, Ari pulls away and grips the hem of my shirt. "Off," he rasps.

"I—" I brace my hands against his chest. "Ari, I'm not...I can't tonight."

"I know," he says before taking his shirt off and giving me a glimpse of all his muscles. By the goddess, I didn't know it was possible to have that many. I've felt most of them, but to see...

And what's even sexier is the fact that the Summer Court's crest—my crest—is inked right over his heart.

Well, that and the faint line of hair starting on his lower abdomen and trailing south...

"You can't look at me that way." His voice draws my attention back to his eyes, which are dancing with amusement. "I have a very thin line of control when it comes to you, beautiful. And if you keep looking at me like that, I'm going to bury myself so far inside you that you won't be able to walk for a week."

"Promise?" I breathe, and he releases this pained, guttural sound. "Why do you want me to take my shirt off if you're not—"

"Because..." He finds the hem again, and this time, I lift my arms so he can toss it over my head. "If you're going to wear a male's shirt, you're wearing mine."

I'm only bare for a moment before the warm, soft cotton of his t-shirt slides onto my skin. It's bigger than mine, hanging down just above my knees, and it smells like him. Fuck, I want to bury my nose in the collar and soak up his scent.

"Better," he says, and settles us both in bed, pulling me against him. I wriggle closer, my back to his front, and become very aware of what seeing me in his shirt did to him.

"I hate to tell you this," I murmur as I extinguish the magical lights. "But that shirt was never another male's. I summoned one a few sizes too big on purpose."

"I hate to tell *you* this," he kisses the juncture of my neck and shoulder. "But I don't give a shit. I like seeing you in my clothes."

"Possessive."

"You like it."

"Maybe," I chuckle, which feels like a miracle. I never thought, on this day, I'd be able to laugh.

I roll over, slotting my legs between Ari's, and run my fingers along his stubbled jaw. For a long moment, we lie like this, tangled up in each other, close enough to breathe in each other's air but not kissing. A sense of calm I've never experienced washes over me.

It feels too good to be true. Like there's an anvil hovering over the delicate peace we've found.

Tomorrow will hold a surprise.

As if he senses the turn of my thoughts, Ari tips my chin up and places a feather-light kiss on my lips. "Tomorrow," he whispers. Another kiss.

"Tomorrow?"

"Whatever pulled you away from me?" Another kiss. "We'll deal with it tomorrow."

I respond with another, longer kiss.

He's right. The surprise—good or bad—will come tomorrow, whether I obsess over it or not. So, for now, while this amazing male is in my bed, I'm going to be present.

Chapter Fourteen
Devorah

"YOU HAVE TO STOP," Eldoris says. I shoot him a glare and go right back to my pacing.

The record keeper couldn't meet us in the morning like I requested, so I spent the better part of today pacing. First my bedroom, then my office, and now here, in the throne room. I keep trying to rationalize the necromancer's warning. A surprise could be anything. I was surprised the chef served breakfast after noon. I was surprised Kalinda suggested I wear pants and a blouse instead of a dress. I was surprised when Ari joined me in the shower, and even more surprised when he didn't do anything besides kiss me underneath the spray.

No matter how hard I try to convince myself that there's no reason for my doom and gloom attitude, I can't expel my nervous energy. So, I pace.

"You're going to wear a hole right through the runner." My brother, annoyingly, appears perfectly calm. He lounges on the dais in a position better suited to the beach, one arm keeping him propped up while his long legs stretch down the steps.

I toe the aforementioned runner that spans the length of the room, from the arched glass doors to the white and gold cushioned throne. I always hated that throne—it's so outdated and clunky compared to the rest of the palace. Maybe I'll have the earth elementals that designed Puck and Lysandra's new thrones make me one.

If this surprise doesn't come back to bite me in the ass.

"You're not worried?" I ask.

"Of course, I am," he says, like it's that simple. "But what will be will be."

"Helpful," I deadpan. I glance out the windows, toward the setting sun. "Where is she?"

The record keeper lives in the Seelie Army Base—a small city between Day, Spring, and Summer Courts—where there is a record hall for all Seelie Fae. In addition to their jobs organizing, cataloguing, and writing our history, record keepers handle legal matters and any long-term agreements that aren't sealed by magic.

While I know she must be busy, there's no reason for her to be hours late. Even if she walked from the city, it wouldn't take that long.

"So, what's happening with you and Ari?" Eldoris asks.

I roll my eyes, completely aware of his attempt to distract me. But still, I say, "We're...waiting. To announce things."

"Until you're queen?"

I shrug. "Possibly. Probably not." My lips turn up. "I don't think we'd make it that long, honestly."

"Please spare me the details."

"He's a little...territorial. But not in the 'No one else can look at you' type of way. More like, 'I want everyone to know you're mine.'"

"Is that why you have a hickey?"

"What?" I summon a mirror and crane my neck this way and that, finding a very small purpling mark under my ear. I want to be mad about it, but a little thrill goes through me at the sight of it. I don't glamour it away.

Eldoris chuckles, standing and coming over to me. "I think he's good for you." He adjusts my hair so it lies over the hickey.

"I agree."

Something about Ari makes me feel grounded. When I'm with him, I'm not always worried about the next moment. And when I am anxious, he stays with me, not pressuring me to calm down but helping me find my way there myself. It's different than any relationship I've ever had.

He makes me excited for the future.

The doors open, revealing the record keeper. The centaur—a type of Fae that has the body of a horse and the torso of a Fae—has a coat that's speckled gray and leads to snow-white skin with hair that matches her raven-black tail. Her hooves clack on the stone until they reach the soft carpet of the runner.

"Nava," my brother says warmly, gesturing for her to join us at the front of the room. She walks past one of the stained-glass mosaics, the teal, aquamarine, and the occasional cobalt blue drifting over her skin and making it look like she's underwater. "It's good to see you."

She trots over to him first. "We've missed you in the jousting ring." My brother laughs fully. Jousting in Faerie is done on the back of centaurs, and though they rarely perform anymore, Eldoris and his friend Philippe are a spectacular team.

Nava bows to me and engages us both in light conversation. Normally, I can play the game, schmooze with the best of them, but all I can think about is what my mother's directive says. My gaze is lasered in on the leather-bound folder tucked under Nava's arm. That folder holds my entire future.

And Eldoris keeps talking about a fucking joust.

"Well," Nava sighs, the laughter from my brother's joke still coloring her words. "I suppose we should get to it."

She conjures a tall table out of thin air, the kind you'd find in a bar. With a sharp thud, she drops the file onto it, the leather cover smacking against the wood.

It's going to be okay, Eldoris says in my mind. *Everything will go as planned, and we'll start planning your coronation.*

You don't know that.

He doesn't answer, just reaches out and squeezes my hand.

"Let me start by expressing my deepest condolences," Nava says. "I don't know much about the circumstances surrounding her death, but Talia was a dear friend, and she will be missed."

"Thank you," we mutter in unison.

She opens the folder and starts sorting through papers that have yellowed with age. "Most of this is straightforward." She procures three pens, one for each of us, and begins setting the papers into piles for us to sign.

"All assets pertaining to the court, such as the royal treasury and the palace, remain in the control of the future monarch. All of Talia's personal assets—including the estate on Pa Ferie—are to be divided equally between you, except for a handful of items that she left to others. I'll be in touch with them as soon as we're done here."

"What items?" Eldoris asks. "We'll gather them for you."

"A sword for Hershel, her diamond comb for her lady's maid—Anika—a first edition novel from the mortal realm for King Simi. And a few more; I'll give you the list."

We both nod. My hands are shaking at this point, even as my brother keeps hold of them.

"Now, let's discuss ascension to the throne." Her square chin lifts to me before she looks back at the paper, reading aloud. *"In regards to the future monarch of Summer Court—"*

By the goddess, I can't breathe.

"—I name my daughter, Devorah, as the next Queen of Summer Court."

"Oh, thank fuck," I exhale, and Eldoris envelops me in a bear hug that lifts me in the air. He swings me around before setting me back down, kissing my forehead, and hugging me again.

"However," Nava continues, and our mirth comes to a screeching halt.

"However?" I demand, my voice a touch shrill and brittle.

"There is a condition to your ascension."

"A condition."

"Is that even allowed?" Eldoris asks. "There's never been conditions before."

"Yes, well, there have never been twins next in line for the throne." She clears her throat. *"To ensure the strength of the court and the future of our royal line, Devorah can only take the throne upon her marriage to another of royal status."*

The room goes silent. Gone is the sound of the crashing waves, the squawking gulls. Even the chatter in the hallway seems to cease as all that remains are those words.

Marriage.

To someone of royal status.

Royal. Fucking. Status.

"She's also included a list of potential suitors," Nava says, taking a page from the file and putting it to the side. "Though any royal not in line for their own throne will do."

"No," I breathe, shaking my head wildly. No. Marriage is...marriage is impossible. Unthinkable. There's no way she can be allowed to do this.

"Yes, Your Highness."

"Nava," Eldoris says, wrapping his arm around my shoulder like he can keep me from breaking by sheer force of will. "If I tell you something about our mother, can I trust we'll have your discretion?"

"As her record keeper, I am prohibited from divulging any personal information about Queen Talia, even in her death."

He nods and looks to me for permission, but I'm too stunned to move.

Marriage.

Magically binding, eternal marriage.

To someone of royal blood.

Not someone who makes me happy. Someone who has *status*. I don't even need to look at that list to know Ari isn't on it. He's high up in our society, but he's not royalty.

Maybe this is retribution for asking Eldoris to marry for an alliance. And maybe it makes me a hypocrite—to resent marrying for my court when I asked him to do the same—but Eldoris had a choice. If he said no, I wouldn't have pushed. If he had feelings for someone else, I wouldn't have even suggested it.

I have no such option.

"Our mother was sick," Eldoris is saying somewhere beyond the words echoing in my brain. "She was fading. So, if this was dictated recently, I'm afraid she wasn't in her right mind, and it should be—"

"She included this clause right after you and Devorah emerged."

A strangled chuff emits from my throat.

I emerged almost five hundred mortal years ago. She had *five hundred years* to tell me of this caveat, to let me search for a suitable spouse. I worked with her every single day, dedicated my entire life to becoming her replacement. I sacrificed everything; personal relationships, days off, *my damn fire magic*, all so I could prepare to be queen.

And it still wasn't enough.

I can't lose it here. The fact that Eldoris hasn't run us both out of here tells me my façade is in place, even through my shock.

So, I do what I do best. I shove it all down, burying it so deep that it will never rise, not until I'm ready to deal with it. "Give me the list." My voice is cold and detached. It gives away none of my inner turmoil.

"Dev—"

"Give. Me. The. List," I order, leaving no room for further argument. The centaur extends the paper.

One glance at the scrawling script tells me my mother, in fact, did write this. And based on the multiple types of ink, she added to it over the years. I don't bother looking at the names, I need to do that in private, where I can throw things.

"One more thing, Your Highness." The paper crinkles as my hand clenches. Nava gives me a pitying look as she says, "You must be married within ninety days. Otherwise, Eldoris will be named king."

"Ninety days?" Eldoris demands. It doesn't take a lot to ruffle my brother, even less to get him to show it in public, but hurting me crosses that line. He's always been my protector.

"Yes."

"And if *I* don't get married?" he asks, a vein bulging in his forehead. "Then what? It reverts back to Devorah?"

"There's no marriage caveat on your rule."

I'd laugh if I weren't completely numb.

My mother, who insisted Eldoris couldn't rule because of his goddess-damned *ears*, said he could rule on his own, while I have to have a chaperone. She may have claimed it was *to continue the bloodline*, but if that was true, Eldoris would have to marry as well.

No. She never trusted me with this court.

I grab the pen designated for me and sign all my copies. Eldoris still seems prepped to rage at the centaur, but it isn't her fault. She's simply the messenger.

"Was there anything else?" I ask.

"This—" Nava extends another paper—"Names you the interim queen until you're married." I sign it. "At the end of the ninety days, if you're not married, I'll be back to name Eldoris as interim king until the coronation."

Eldoris scoffs, but finally signs all his paperwork.

"Thank you, Your Highnesses." Nava takes everything and doesn't wait for us to show her out.

Chapter Fifteen
Ari

I can't concentrate.

I've read this report from the Seelie Army base eight times. Every time I get to the bottom, I realize I didn't comprehend anything, and have to start again.

What could be taking so long?

Devorah asked me to wait in her office. I wanted to be in the meeting, but the centaur made it very clear that she would only meet with Devorah and Eldoris.

When I can't bear sitting any longer, I sort through the urgent missives, file away the older ones that no longer need to clutter her desk, and even check that the stash of potions hidden in the bookcase has been refilled.

Surely, these meetings shouldn't last this long. It should be simple; Devorah is named queen, the assets get divided evenly, and it's done.

But Devorah shared the necromancer's warning. So, no matter how much I assure myself everything will be fine, dread coils in my gut.

I'm behind the desk when the door finally opens. My heart flies into my throat as Eldoris holds it open, ushering Devorah inside. She moves as if in a fog, like she's a shell of the female who woke in my arms this morning. All that fire, all that bravado, it's been wiped out.

Eldoris, on the other hand, is steaming. The air around him ripples, and I'm worried for the state of all the valuable papers in this office.

I'm about to suggest moving this meeting elsewhere when Edina slips into the room. She takes one look at the fury etched on Eldoris' face before ice coats her arms, her sapphire eyes glowing in anticipation of using her power. Good. At least someone will be able to cool Eldoris off, both emotionally and magically. She's got a level head; she'll be able to diffuse this situation.

"Who do I need to kill?" she demands.

Maybe not.

"She's already dead," Eldoris seethes. Devorah meets my eyes for one second before looking down and walking around the other side of her desk. She registers the lack of mess—something which would normally get me a whole diatribe, or at least some playful banter—but says nothing.

"What happened?" I dare to ask. I take a step closer; Devorah shrinks away.

Eldoris flops down in one of the wingback chairs, tugging Edina into his lap and burying his head against her shoulder. The warmth of his skin hisses against hers, faint steam billowing between them. "My mother happened," he growls. Edina loops her arm around his neck and starts playing with his hair.

"Did she..." I swallow.

Devorah expressed her concern that Eldoris would be named king, and what that would mean for his relationship with Edina and the court's relationship with Winter Court. I assured her it would never happen. Queen Talia, in one of her lucid moments, agreed to the betrothal between Edina and Eldoris, encouraged the alliance they'd be forging. She wouldn't do that if she planned on giving Eldoris the throne.

No one answers, and for a moment we sit in a foreboding silence. "Oh, for the love of the goddess," Edina finally exclaims, escaping Eldoris' hold and pushing past me to get to Devorah. She hops on the desk directly before her and cups her cheeks. "Tell us. Whatever it is, we'll figure it out."

As if Edina pulled back the layers of shock surrounding her, Devorah blinks, and those ocean eyes grow stormy. Melancholy and rage, unlike anything I've seen from her, brew in those depths. Edina, to her credit, holds fast.

"To become the queen," Devorah says, shuddering in disgust. "I need to marry someone of royal blood. In the next ninety days."

I stagger back a step, hitting the bookshelf directly behind me. I don't even feel the wood jabbing into my spine, it's nothing compared to the impact of those words.

Devorah has to marry someone else.

It feels like someone ripped the rug out from under me.

I just got her, felt the rightness of falling asleep beside her, discovered the perfection of her taste, and now it's...over?

I should have known it was too good to be true. Nothing can be that easy.

Edina is shaking her head vehemently. "That's...Can she do that?"

"Apparently," Eldoris says, swiping a hand down his face. The record keepers know the laws better than any of us, and I'm sure, if there was a loophole, she would have informed Devorah of it. Marriage makes most

Fae balk; it's too final. Even the priestesses require long betrothal periods to ensure the couple understands what they're getting into.

To force someone to find a partner—someone they're binding themselves to in ninety days—that's something that would have been researched.

Devorah finally looks at me, a tear brimming in the corner of her eye. I want to brush it away, to tug her into me and hold her until I can find a way to make this better. But I know if I touch her, I'll never be able to let go.

She tosses a piece of paper on the desk beside Edina's thigh. "If I don't get married to someone on this list, then Eldoris becomes king."

Edina jumps away from the paper like it's contaminated. I watch as she puts all the pieces together. Devorah didn't discuss her fears with Eldoris, lest he be worried for no reason, but Edina figures it out quickly. And judging by the look on his face, Eldoris has, too.

"Well, that's fucking stupid," she declares.

"Thanks," Devorah deadpans, but there's a hint of a smile directed at her future sister. Edina drops into her lap, wrapping her arms around her torso, stroking her hair. Devorah leans into her, and I can tell she's trying not to cry.

I should be the one comforting her, but I can't move. I can only watch as every hope I had for the future slips through my fingers like sand on a beach.

"Have you looked at the list?" Edina asks, not-so-subtly looking at me like I might be on there. I'm not. My blood is anything but royal. I don't even know who my mother is; she dumped me on my father's doorstep without a word when I was born, and my father bedded too many females around that time to even narrow down the search. He hoped he'd have more of a clue when my magic manifested in full, but I have his fire.

"Just a glance," she says.

"I'll do it," I say, my voice shredded. Much like how I feel.

"Ari—" Devorah starts. Fuck, I've never hated the sound of my name so viscerally. I'd kill for her to call me Little Hershel right now, so I didn't have to hear that pity and sorrow lacing my name.

I try not to react as I take the paper off the desk and sit in the empty chair beside Eldoris.

"Nava said mother made the list right after we emerged," Eldoris tells us, and Edina gasps.

"When you emerged?" The sound is so high-pitched it hurts my ears. "She could have said something—"

"She didn't trust me," Devorah says dejectedly. All attention snaps to her, and she shrugs. "She had to name me heir because of those bullshit prejudices, but she never wanted to. She always wanted it to be Eldoris."

"Dev—" he says, but she holds up a hand to halt him in his tracks.

"Why else would she do this? This way, she gets to keep up appearances with the royals. 'I picked the child who looks more *Fae*,'" she spits the word like a curse. "'But she couldn't fulfil my wishes, so I guess it *has* to be the one who looks human.'"

"Careful," Edina warns.

"You weren't alive then," I say gently. "Elemental Fae—royals in particular—just started coupling with other races. It was still taboo for non-elementals to rule."

"King Oakley is a brownie," she argues.

"He was the pioneer, but he married into royalty, and became the sole king about a century after we all emerged, when..." No one talks about the Autumn Court queen or how she abandoned her husband, child, and title to live in the mortal realm, so I don't finish the story. "If Radley had taken after his father instead of his mother, it would have been hard for him as well."

Eldoris and Devorah are silent, but their eyes are locked on each other in a way that tells me they're having a mental conversation. Devorah sits up so abruptly, she bucks Edina off her lap. Eldoris breaks eye contact first with a growl of frustration.

"You've more than proved yourself," I say, stepping in once it's clear they're done speaking.

"And yet, she never changed the will," she laughs mirthlessly. "So, what does that say about her? About me?"

"It says nothing," I seethe, leaning forward so I can brace my hands against the edge of the desk. "You are a strong, capable leader who will be a fantastic queen, and if she didn't see that, then she was fucking blind."

"I agree," Eldoris says.

Devorah sighs. She clearly doesn't believe me. This has taken a huge chunk out of her self-confidence.

"Read the rest of the list," she says finally, pinching the bridge of her nose. Edina immediately goes to the false book on the shelf and pulls out a vial of her tonic. "Does everyone fucking know about this?"

"There's nothing wrong with taking a tonic. It's not like you're snorting Faerie dust."

Devorah grumbles, but downs the vial, and when she's done, I look back at the list of males who are *good enough* to marry *my* female.

In the sprawling script of the late queen is a written list of about ten names. "She added to this," I remark, noting the different ink colors. Some of the names are older—made around the time Devorah emerged—and the last name is only a few centuries old.

"The first name is Izar."

"Not Zahir?" Edina asks.

Devorah mutters, "Kill me," before explaining. "No one in line for their own throne is eligible. It's the same reason you wouldn't be allowed to marry El if he becomes king. If you only had one heir, either the courts would have to merge, or one would pass to a lesser bloodline."

"So fucking antiquated," she says. "Then there can't be more than ten names on that list."

"Close."

"Izar can be a good match," I say, steering the conversation back. "It would allow us to ally with the Night Court, and we could work in a clause that says you can take other lovers so he could be with his mate."

And Devorah could be with me.

"But if we tell them of that option and they say no, they'll know Devorah is only an interim monarch," Eldoris says. "Then we're left vulnerable."

"Who else?" Devorah asks.

I glance back at the paper. "There are a few werewolf alphas." Unlike the courts, packs change leadership all the time; so, if one were to wed Devorah, combining their pack with another wouldn't be an issue.

"Are they all from Unseelie Courts?" she asks. I nod. "That leaves us in a similar predicament of trusting them not to go to their monarchs."

"There's a siren elder. He's from Winter, so that's doable."

My mouth dries at the last name. He's young, but from our court, which would keep the terms of the agreement within our borders. He's unmated, unwed.

And he's good-looking. Overtly good-looking.

He's perfect.

I toss the paper back on the desk. "Kai," I say with a tight smile. "You should marry Kai."

"Shesha's son?" Edina asks.

"He's the second born, so he's not in line to lead the hoard," Eldoris nods.

The room goes silent as everyone in it realizes that I'm right. Devorah looks like I slapped her across the face. Unlike before, when she couldn't look at me, now she can't look away. Tears gather at the corners of her eyes, threatening to spill at any minute.

I need space. I need air so I can fucking breathe and not break down completely.

I'll take the night to compose myself, to shove aside all the feelings I have for Devorah so I can go back to being her advisor.

"Kai," Devorah agrees, her voice thick with emotion.

"You can still include a clause that will allow you to be with others," Edina says softly, her gaze ping-ponging between the two of us.

I shake my head. "You could try, but dragons don't share."

Devorah leans down, pressing the heels of her hands into her eye sockets.

"I'll go there in the morning," I say. "Ask them to come to the palace to discuss details."

"I can do it," Eldoris says. "Shesha and I are good friends. He'll say yes to me."

I nod again, feeling like a fucking bobblehead, but I have no words. This situation is so fucked up. "Is there anything else you need from me?"

"No," Devorah mutters. "I'll see you tomorrow."

I dip my head in supplication and leave the room as quickly as I can muster. Then I drink two-thirds of a bottle of magic-infused whiskey until I can no longer feel the gaping hole in my chest.

Chapter Sixteen
Devorah

Sleep is an impossibility. I've only spent a few days sharing my bed with Ari, but it already feels empty without him. The sheets are too cold, and his scent, which is normally comforting, makes me want to cry. His shocked face is seared in my brain, surfacing every time I close my eyes. In the silence, I hear his back hitting the bookshelf and the dejected way he said Kai's name when deciding who I should marry.

I almost went to his room a million times, getting as far as the door before I turned back. I might want to talk, but he clearly needed a minute to process everything, and I won't put my needs in front of his. Not when I'm the reason for all this fucking mess.

Part of me wishes that I had gotten my head out of my ass earlier so we could have had more time together. But I know it would have made things even harder. As it is, Ari breached every wall I erected; shattered it with his attentiveness, with his banter, with his kiss. It doesn't matter that we barely started this...whatever it is. It means something.

Meant something.

By the fucking goddess, how am I supposed to forget how he touched me? How he kissed me like I was his entire world. How he made me come so hard, I was convinced I'd shatter into a thousand pieces.

Somewhere around dawn, I give up on sleep and teleport to my favorite cove. Nestled between three walls of dense jungle, the beach is hidden from prying eyes. It's a quiet, secluded spot where I can escape for a while and think.

I plop down on the pink sand, close enough that my toes are in the water, and watch the sky turn with the rising sun. It colors the aquamarine water various shades of pink and gold, broken only by the sirens whose tails pop above the surface and create white caps.

A breeze brings forth a familiar scent—sandalwood and salt, the ocean personified. "You're up early," I remark as Eldoris takes a seat beside me. He's dressed in a white shirt that he's left unbuttoned and a pair of khaki linen pants, unlike me, still in my white nightgown.

He digs his fingers beneath the grains of sand, reaching for the cool beneath the surface. It's something he's done since we were kids. "I thought I'd find you here."

"Remember when we'd come here to escape Mom?" I ask, absently picking up a pearly shell and running my fingers over the grooves.

"And to escape all the fanfare around us being twins."

"*Are you sure they're twins, Talia?*" I say, mimicking a male voice. Because we look so different, no one thought we were twins. Although I have no idea why they thought my mother would lie.

"*Would you like the details of how they came out, effectively ruining my vagina even with the healer's intervention?*" Eldoris does an almost perfect impression of our mother's voice, low and sultry even as she sounded aghast.

"I was always so embarrassed when she'd say that," I chuckle. "Now I think it was badass."

"It was the only time she ever dropped her cool."

We fall into silence, both of us staring out at the water where her charred remains now lie.

If only I could bring her back to ask her what the fuck she was thinking. To tell her how she's made me feel completely inadequate.

To ask if she ever thought I'd be a good queen.

"How can I be so mad at her and still miss her?" I ask, tears once again gathering in my eyes. I've cried more often in the past few days than I have in my entire life, and I'm getting sick of it.

"I'm mad at her, too." When I turn to face him, he's already watching me. "Don't look so surprised. You know I'd fucking murder anyone who hurt you."

All our lives, we were set up to have a tenuous relationship. The entire realm was determined to pit us against each other, but we never fell into their trap. The pressure only made us closer, an unbreakable unit, even when things seemed ready to tear us apart.

"I'd say the same, but we both know I can't fight for shit."

He growls at me. Eldoris hates self-deprecating humor, even if the statement is completely true. "I could train you, you know. Or Ari could if you want to be inconspicuous."

"I'm pretty sure Ari doesn't want to be near me at all."

"That's a lie and you know it." I tilt my head to lean against his shoulder. "I'm sorry," he sighs.

"For?"

"Telling you to be happy." I bark a mirthless laugh. "That's not what I meant. I just meant..." He looks down at the sand, becoming very interested in the way it sifts through his fingers.

"It wouldn't have mattered. I'd be in the same situation, but I'd also regret missing my chance. At least we had something."

"I'll find a way to make it right, Dev. We'll talk to Shesha and Kai, but until you're married, I'll keep searching for a loophole."

I already know it'll be pointless, but Eldoris can be stubborn when it comes to the people he loves, so I nod.

"Where's Edina?" I ask, desperately needing a change of subject.

"She went back to Winter Court to tell her mother we need to slow down wedding plans." In case this falls through. He doesn't need to say it aloud; we're both thinking it.

We sit in silence until the sun is fully risen and the temperature ratchets up. The humidity of the jungle seeps toward us, battled only by the light, ocean breeze.

"You should go," I say. On some level, I need to get this over with. If Kai says no, then I'll need to find another suitor, and that will take time. If he says no, we'll have to be very careful with our next moves so that the news of my necessary marriage doesn't spread around.

Eldoris stands, shaking the sand from his clothes and slipping on sandals I didn't see him discard. "I'll be back in an hour." He teleports away.

I want to stay here for the rest of the day, but I need to make it look like all is well.

If my mother taught me anything, it's that my emotions and problems have to take a backseat to the court.

"COME IN," I CALL when there's a knock at my office door.

I'm expecting the palace event coordinator, who should be coming to plan my coronation.

Eldoris and I decided we'd keep everything surrounding the marriage a secret until we had confirmation from Kai and his father. As such, we're planning my coronation at the very end of the three-month deadline. Fae are notoriously unhurried with events—we're immortal, time isn't that important—so it won't be suspicious that we're taking time to arrange everything.

But it's not the palace event coordinator who enters.

It's Kai.

My potential future husband.

He's a very handsome male, almost painfully so. He has rich brown skin and a square, clean-shaven jaw. Dark hair hangs to broad shoulders, and his muscles are so defined I can see them through the fine material of his shirt. What I find amusing is the gold dripping from every inch of him. He has too many chains to count around his neck, earrings every few inches along the outer edge of his ear, and even a belt buckle that catches the low light in my office.

"Princess," he says, his smile wide and easy, like he's never had a hard day in his life. I find myself jealous of that unburdened attitude. Is this what I would have been like if I had remained the spare? Goddess knows I wouldn't have run the army like Eldoris does, so maybe I would have lived a life of luxury.

I stand and circle my desk. I'm not sure how to greet him exactly, if I should shake his hand or hug him, or kiss his cheek. What does one do when greeting their future husband whom they have no romantic feelings toward?

Kai is more comfortable in this situation than I am, because he bends low and kisses the back of my hand. His lips are soft and full against my skin, but it feels...wrong.

He stands and brushes his hair back, procuring a tie that's made of golden thread. Seriously, this male is ticking the box of every dragon stereotype.

"So, we're getting married." He's so loud that it takes me aback. I quickly erect a shield that will keep our conversation private since Kai, apparently, has never heard of an inside voice.

"Looks like it." I try to match his enthusiasm, but fail spectacularly. If he notices, he doesn't comment.

"My father sent me to talk about some logistics with you. Should we do that here or in our chambers?"

Our chambers.

Our.

He's already invited himself into my life.

The overwhelming urge to kick him in the shin arises. I know that's irrational, he's doing as he's told, but I didn't expect him to be so gung-ho about the situation. A little trepidation would be nice. A little reluctance in signing away our lives.

"Here is fine." I gesture to one of the seats, but instead of letting me retreat to the safety behind my desk, he takes my hand and guides me to the other wingback, turning both so they're facing each other. I bite my cheek, but sit across from him.

"Look," he sighs. "I know this isn't the way you pictured getting married."

"No. It's not."

"And I know you have a relationship with your advisor."

"I don't—" He arches his eyebrow. I'm not sure how he knows, but I should have guessed the news would spread. The pixies know everything and are terrible gossips.

"It's over," I settle on, and Kai nods.

"Then, I think we can make the best out of a bad situation." His smile returns. "And I think, in time, we may grow to be great friends—if not grow to love each other."

Love seems like a stretch, but he seems so earnest that I find myself agreeing.

"Eldoris mentioned we'd like to keep your situation a secret," he continues. Eldoris and I decided we'd tell Kai and his father the truth, but tell everyone else I'm marrying for a military alliance. It's an easy out. Ensuring the dragons will protect our mountain borders is something that will be expected, especially by someone like Zahir.

"And I'm more than fine with that. But I'd like to court you."

"Court me?" I can't hide my laugh. It's so fucking innocent. I knew Kai was young, but I didn't peg him for naïve.

"We have three months, right? I'd like to spend one month taking you on dates and attending public appearances on your arm. Then we take one month to plan our wedding, and you'll be coronated by the end of the third month, if not sooner."

I hate to admit it, but it makes a lot of sense. People will still think we're marrying for political gain, but it will lessen the urgency of our situation. The citizens may even romanticize it and think we're falling in love, which will give them a sense of security.

Another knock interrupts my thoughts before I can agree, and I drop the shield to tell them to enter. Again, it's not my event coordinator.

It's Ari.

"Oh." He looks between me and Kai, sitting facing each other with very little space between our knees.

He's paler than usual, and his eyes have dark circles beneath them. He immediately covers his shock with a false smile. "Glad to see you two getting acquainted."

Kai doesn't appear to hear the way his voice is tight or see the tic in his jaw at the words. "Actually," he gestures for Ari to enter and close the door. He does so with a glower. "We should run our plan by you, being the court advisor and all."

I don't miss his use of the word *court*, as opposed to my personal advisor. Kai is drawing a line in the sand. If we're to do this, I'm his. His treasure, his hoard. Ari is nothing more than an employee.

He was right; dragons don't share.

Kai tells him everything we discussed, and Ari listens attentively. When we're finished, he says, "That's a very sound plan. It also gives you time to discuss what conditions you'd like the priestess to include in your marriage agreement."

"Oh, just the typical ones," Kai says with a challenging smile. "Fidelity, loyalty, no other partners. That sort of thing."

"Eternity is a long time for such rigidity in your agreement," Ari counters, his shoulder squaring as he responds to that challenge.

"My parents have no issues."

"They're mates. It's not an arranged marriage."

"My mother also isn't half as beautiful as Devorah." His thumb caresses my knuckles in a way that should be sweet, but feels possessive.

"By the goddess," I breathe, and both males shift their attention from each other to me. "If you're done measuring your dicks, I have a court to run."

Kai's laughter is booming once again, but Ari grits his teeth.

"I'll take my leave of you, princess," Kai says, leaning over to kiss my cheek. "Would you like to join me for dinner tomorrow at the Seelie Army base? I hear there's a new Thai restaurant and the chef just returned from a mortal year studying in Thailand."

"You like Thai food?"

"I've never tried it," he smirks. "But Eldoris said it was delicious and that you'd love it."

That's sweet of him. Or my brother. Possibly both.

I agree to the date, and Kai goes, leaving me alone with my advisor.

Mine. Not the courts.

He'll always be mine, no matter what anyone else says.

Chapter Seventeen
Ari

THIS IS HELL.

No, it's worse than hell—the demon realm isn't that bad. This is akin to walking over hot coals, only to be stabbed repeatedly by iron spikes when you're finally on cool ground.

And worse, it's completely self-inflicted.

I don't need to sit at the bar while Devorah and Kai are on their *date*. The Seelie Army Base—while the size of a small city—is the safest place in the entire realm. No one would dare attack a compound of soldiers or their families. I could have sent her here on her own, in the capable hands of her betrothed.

But apparently, I'm a masochist.

The happy couple is outside in the restaurant's patio area. Located in the center of Day, Spring, and Summer Courts, the Seelie Army Base always has pleasant weather. The sky is always cloudless, the heat warm but dry. And because so many Fae live here, it has become a cultural hub. There's always a new restaurant popping up as Fae travel to the mortal realm and learn different cuisines, and there's just as much nightlife as the Underground—though it leans towards chic taverns and dance clubs versus strip and sex clubs.

Devorah giggles and playfully swats Kai's arm. I know they have to do a certain amount of pretending, but I also know Devorah enough to know that laugh was real.

"Another?" the male behind the bar asks, gesturing to my empty bottle. The Thai beer is imported directly from the mortal realm, though he definitely added some magic to make it more potent. There's no human alcohol that could get a Fae drunk, and I already feel this seeping into my bones.

I nod my thanks, and he uncaps the beer, placing it before me just as I hear her laugh again. I take a long swig, hoping it quells the jealousy churning in my gut.

Why am I here?

Do I have no sense of self-preservation?

"Well, well," Hades' cool voice eclipses instrumental music from the enchanted lute as she enters the restaurant with Queen Lysandra. I wobble a little as I stand from my teak stool—fuck, those drinks were stronger than I thought—and bow to them.

"Oh, you don't have to do that," Lysandra says, her body shaking with mirth. While I know she's as cutthroat as any of the Fae, she has a warmth to her that many don't. Maybe it's because she was raised in the mortal realm, or maybe it's her round face and plum hair that make her more approachable, I have no idea. But she's the type of Fae you want to be friends with.

"Have you eaten?" she asks.

"Oh, I uh..." I so eloquently respond, gesturing to the bottle on the wooden counter. "I'm not really—"

"Have dinner with us."

Oh, she knows exactly what she's doing. By phrasing it as a command, I can't possibly say no. I couldn't deny a queen unless I wanted to make trouble. Lysandra might be new to this realm, but she knows how to play the game.

Hades watches me put it together with a feline smile, offering no help. No way out.

"It would be my honor," I say with a tight smile, grabbing my beer and following them to a table the owner directs them to. Lysandra chats animatedly with him, but Hades' navy eyes are on me, head tilted to the side in curiosity. She often has that look about her, the one that feels like she's peering into your soul and determining if you're worthy.

I look anywhere but at her penetrating gaze, opting to stare at the jewel-toned walls, the shoots of bamboo that obstruct the entrance to the kitchen, the other patrons who are trying their damnedest not to look at the royalty in their midst.

Lysandra checks our preferences and tells the owner to make whatever dish he likes best. He's so excited to be serving a queen that he bows three times in quick succession before heading to the back, bumping a table in his haste.

"So!" Lysandra claps. I feel the kiss of magic, the scent of cherry blossoms telling me Lysandra was the one to put a shield around our table to hide our conversation. "Let's talk about how we're going to handle the Night Court and their plan to attack you."

In my slightly inebriated state, I'm unable to control my jaw from dropping open. Hades snorts into her glass of water.

"I'm sorry," Lysandra says with an innocent smile, even though she's anything but. "Would you rather talk about the fact that Devorah is dating someone other than you?"

"Goddess," I breathe, taking a large swing of my drink.

"Have I told you how glad I am that you're a queen?" Hades smirks, patting Lysandra's head like a dog. She playfully shakes off the touch and is still chuckling as the bartender brings drinks for the females and another for me. Though I should probably switch to water if I'm going to be having dinner with these vipers.

"So, Night Court." Lysandra takes a sip of her drink—something pink with chunks of fruit in it—and hums happily. "Hades told me she spoke with Devorah before the queen passed. I assume you haven't had time to discuss her offer."

No, we hadn't. Honestly, I assumed Devorah's conversation with the Princess of the Night Court was unimportant since she never brought it up.

I wait for Hades to say something, but she just sips her whiskey until Lysandra elbows her in the side. "Fine," she grunts, jabbing her elbow in her friend's ribs as well. It's an odd interaction to witness. I know the second generation is quite close, but I've never been privy to their private moments. Even when they're friendly in public settings, it's never as openly playful as these females are being. Especially Hades, who typically looks like she'd rather be anywhere but a royal function.

"My brother is going to attack," Hades says.

"Well, obviously, he knows that. I just told him as much," Lysandra scolds.

"*But*," she returns pointedly. "I can confirm that Izar will join the assault."

Fuck. I was afraid of that. Izar is in charge of Night Court's naval fleet and all that entails. The Night Court is ninety percent desert except for the one raging river that stems from the mountains of Day Court to the ocean. While they have a decent army of foot soldiers, the navy is their real powerhouse.

"Really?" Lysandra asks. "But Izar is so nice."

"You'd do well to remember he's Fae, and his loyalty is to our court, not his friends. If Zahir is hell bent on attacking Summer, then he'll be involved."

Lysandra looks a little spooked by that thought. I know she grew close to Izar too, and I doubt she's as practiced at separating friendship from politics as the rest of her peers. Night Court and Summer have been at war before—Eldoris and Izar have fought on opposite sides of the same battle—and yet they're able to put that aside when they're not on the battlefield.

"And you're not helping your brothers?" I ask.

Hades scoffs. "Would I be here if I were?"

"But what about *your* court loyalty?" Lysandra asks, her head tilting in the same way Hades does when she's observing someone.

"I've told them my views on this matter. Attacking Summer Court, when it's clear across the fucking realm, is stupid. Suppose they *could* conquer you, then what? Now they're stretched thin trying to keep control of a territory that's across a mountain range and between three of their allies' courts. We'd lose it before it was even under our control."

"Heartwarming," she deadpans. And while I agree that the reasoning isn't exactly warm and fuzzy, I appreciate that Hades is on our side.

Hades is content to ignore that comment. "As I told Devorah, you have full access to my resources, including use of the tunnels, which Zahir is banned from using."

"Puck and I have already signed off on your use of the Seelie Army," Lysandra adds. "I spoke with Larisa, and she said as soon as you ask her father, he'll agree as well. Though I'm sure he'll expect his borders to be protected in case The Night Court decides to go over the mountains, but I'll let you discuss those details."

"Thank you." While combining three courts' armies is helpful while dealing with a common foe, each monarch needs approval for moving and mobilizing troops. And since most Fae have no sense of urgency, it can be tedious. Having Lysandra at the helm of her court will certainly make things move faster since she still operates on mortal tendencies regarding time.

"One final thing, and then we can discuss that." Hades waves at the patio where Kai and Devorah have scooted closer to each other.

"The navy won't go up the Padauk," Hades says. I almost drop my bottle in my shock.

"They always have before."

"Which is why they won't do it now. They'll use the ocean and attack the beach. They may circle and enter the river from the west, but they won't cross through the Day Court. I think my brother is trying to curry favor with Simi."

This is invaluable information. We would have concentrated our efforts on the mountains and the river, leaving our beaches relatively unguarded. It's a brilliant move on Zahir's part; he would have caught us with our pants down and would have a direct line to the palace.

The news sobers me, my mind shaking loose the cobwebs caused by the beer, so I can make the most of this impromptu meeting. Hades is clearly willing to help, and I'm going to take advantage.

"They'll have to get past Winter Court that way," I say.

"They don't believe Gwyneira will help you." Hades gives me another of those feline smirks. "They think she'll allow them to pass and feign innocence."

"They should know better." Gwyneria is incredibly territorial, and her court is veritably impenetrable because of it. Even sailing past her court with malicious intent is suicide.

"This all came from one of my spies, in case you're worried that my brothers would lie to me," Hades says.

"Is the spy reliable?"

"Hasn't failed me yet."

"Do you know when this is happening?"

"No," she states. "But I'd be on my guard, especially before other alliances—" she jerks her head to the windows, "—are solidified."

I nod my thanks. It would be so easy to tell Devorah that we need to go to Eldoris and Edina's townhouse a few blocks away to discuss this intel. It's a legitimate excuse; it has nothing to do with the fact that she and Kai are once again laughing—honestly, no one is that funny.

As if the goddess knows my intentions, our dinner arrives. "Eat," Lysandra commands, and I have to fight back my growl of annoyance.

The food is delicious. Lysandra ordered me some sort of spicy noodle dish loaded with vegetables and seafood. At her insistence, I try her noodles, which are longer and thinner than mine, in a peanut sauce, and Hades' rice that came in half a coconut.

"Now," Lysandra says, dabbing the corner of her mouth with a napkin before taking another sip of her drink. "What the fuck is going on out there?"

I look over her shoulder. Kai has removed his jacket and slung it over Devorah's shoulders—even though we're between the warmest courts in the fucking realm and there's no way it's cold. He has his arm stretched on the back of her chair, and she's leaning in close.

"I don't know what you mean." The lie tastes like ash on my tongue, ruining the delicious meal to the point where I push the plate away.

"Is there a specific reason why Devorah is planning on marrying a dragon when she's infatuated with you?" Hades asks.

"Fuck, you two pull no punches." I swipe my hand down my face, but they wait patiently, eating their food in silence as they wait for me to answer. "We need the added protection."

"The dragons are members of your court," Lysandra counters.

"They're law unto themselves. It's an old treaty; we leave them to govern themselves, and they don't attack our court. They're under no obligation to help us in a conflict." It's a half-truth. The treaty exists, but the hoards that live in our court are irrefutably loyal and would help if we asked.

"And their price was marriage?" The females exchange a glance, before clearly deciding to drop it and nodding. "Fine, then. If that's what you say."

"It is what I say."

"Then we should start planning a bachelorette party for her," Lysandra says, and Hades waves her off with a look that says, 'Who do you think you're talking to?'

The thought of a bachelorette party makes rage bubble up in my throat. It's just another aspect of her life that will distance her from me.

They don't ask me anything else about Devorah, and when all is said and done, Lysandra drops a heavy bag of gold on the table for the owner to cover our bill. After a few final pleasantries, I watch them walk out.

Devorah and Kai are already gone.

Chapter Eighteen
Devorah

Kai is...lovely.

We've been 'dating' for about a month now, and each time he takes me out has been a lot of fun. He does all the right things. He sends me flowers or other little trinkets to let me know he's thinking about me, always opens doors, gets along with Eldoris and Edina, who are both hard to please.

He's kind. Thoughtful. Makes me laugh.

And I'm not attracted to him at all.

I wish I were. It would make this whole situation easier if there were a modicum of attraction, just one little spark. But there's nothing.

Tonight, he's going to propose.

I don't know when it's happening, or what he has planned, but I'm to meet him just after sunset on the beach outside the palace. He wants it to be a surprise. I'm not sure why he's so determined to put on a show for the court. Everyone knows this is a political engagement, but I don't have the energy to argue.

The one time I got frustrated and asked why he even needed to propose, why we couldn't just announce our engagement and be done with it, he gave me one of his wide, easy smiles and said, "Because we only get to do this once."

And then I felt like shit. I feel like I'm corrupting him, tarnishing his pure soul by dragging him into the murky world of politics. I never viewed myself as a bad Fae, but comparatively, my soul feels blackened.

Maybe I'm just jaded from the extra years I have on him. Maybe dragons are kinder than the Fae of the royal courts have been bred to be.

Or maybe I just resent the entire situation.

I brush my hair aside so Kalinda can fasten my necklace, a pendant made of pure stardust. It catches the sunlight, creating rainbow prisms against my skin that I hope distract from my pallid complexion. Even though the chain is long, hanging low enough that the pendant dips between my breasts, it feels like a noose. The white sundress, despite being too large, feels like a vice around my ribs.

My strap slips off my shoulder, and Kalinda makes a tsking sound before righting it and performing magic to alter the dress so it fits properly. "You had this made three days ago."

I nod. Weight has been falling off me. I haven't been able to eat between everything going on with the Night Court and this engagement.

And the fact that Ari is barely speaking to me.

He's all business, refusing to talk to me about anything but work and disappearing as soon as he's not needed. I get it, I do. But I miss him. In the short time since he took over for his father, he's become my best friend.

I could really use a friend right now.

I feel too guilty to talk to Eldoris about all this. How can I complain about my situation when I asked him to do the same thing? Radley would be my next go-to, but I can't tell him in case his father is allied with Zahir. Which leaves me alone, letting the dread eat away at me.

"You look beautiful."

I practically knock poor Kalinda over as I spin, finding Ari leaning in the doorway of my room. His hair is mussed from his fingers, his stubble has grown to a full beard, and the light in those purple eyes has dimmed. Even though he's smirking, it looks forced.

"Thanks," I rasp. His tongue pokes out to wet his lower lip. That simple motion has me feeling hotter than I have in three weeks of dates with Kai.

I clamp it down hard, shoving away the attraction like I'd done so many times before. But the problem is that before, we flirted. We flirted a lot. So even when we were staying away from each other, there was this easy banter. Now, it's just awkward and stilted. I'm not sure where we go from here.

My lady's maid excuses herself, leaving the two of us alone.

"Listen," we both say at once. His chuckle—while wry—is the first I've heard in weeks, and it eases something in my chest, lifting my hopes that we can find some semblance of friendship.

I motion for him to speak first. He clears his throat. "How long do you have before..."

Before I get betrothed.

"I have some time." The haunted look he's been carrying around lifts slightly as a smile graces his lips. "Why?"

"Would you like to go flying?"

Goddess, I can't even remember the last time I've taken to the skies just to feel the wind in my wings and the sun on my skin.

"Fuck, yeah I do," I exclaim, making him grin even wider as he opens the balcony doors for me. The scent of jasmine mixes with the salt of the ocean in the perfect combination, and I take a breath that feels like the first I've taken in months.

Releasing my wings feels like letting my hair down after a long day. I've kept them tucked away too often, even at night since I rarely sleep. The moment they stretch free, some of the tension in my shoulders melts, and I roll my neck with a sigh of relief.

"Beautiful," Ari murmurs so softly I'm not sure if I was meant to hear. I thank him anyway. I love my wings. They're sheer and iridescent, but when the light catches them, they change from orange to red, looking like living flames.

There's the briefest brush against the rounded edge; it makes me shiver. Ari meets my stare, but doesn't acknowledge the intimate touch as he stands beside me on the stone balcony.

By the goddess, he's shirtless. I forgot how many damn muscles he has, but there's even more definition to them now. Maybe that's why I've never run into him after hours—he's been living at the gym in the basement. I zero in on the tattoo of my crest inked above his heart, and I long to touch it.

"Do you make it a habit to fly around half-naked?" It's only after I say the quip that I realize it may be crossing a boundary. We used to tease each other like that, but it could be too much now. Especially since the last time I saw him naked was in the shower. My skin heats at the memory.

Luckily, Ari chuckles again. "Some of us don't wear backless dresses."

He rolls his shoulders, the sinew and tendons bulging with the motion, before his wings snap out, almost pushing me back from their span. They're round with very small indents on the edges that give them a webbed appearance. And they're solid—some kind of membrane—in a pale gray color with blue veins snaking in uneven horizontal lines. They remind me of something you'd see underwater rather than in the sky.

"I've never seen wings like this." I find myself reaching for them to see what the shiny material feels like beneath my fingers, but I stop inches away. Touching a Fae's wings is a very intimate thing. Brushing against them is nearly taboo, but a deliberate touch should only be done in private with explicit consent. No one has ever touched my wings in that way.

"Don't you worry, they fly just fine. I bet I can beat you to your house on Pa Ferie."

"On those clunky things?"

That glint returns to his eyes. "I'll even give you a head start."

I hum, tapping my finger against my chin. "What do I get if I win?"

"Bragging rights."

"I'm gonna need more incentive, Little Hershel." I walk over to the edge of the balcony and climb up on the smooth, beige railing, facing Ari so my back is to the ocean.

"I have an idea, but you only find out if you win." He sticks out his hand for me to shake. It should be something so innocent, something I've done hundreds of times with hundreds of Fae. But initiating that kind of deliberate contact...I'm not sure I'm ready for that.

"You have a deal." I tip over backward and free-fall as Ari rushes to the railing. I let myself simply fall, enjoying the rush of the air around me before I right myself and start flying toward the island off the coast.

The sun is high enough not to be glaring, but low enough that the rays illuminate the sea life swimming amidst the cerulean water. A large ray, with fins that are remarkably similar to Ari's wings, coasts along the bottom, kicking up sand that hides some of the smaller fish. A water sprite—a type of mer-Fae that has scales covering their entire body—glances up and waves at me, before she launches herself at an unsuspecting school of fish, tearing into them with her sharp teeth.

There's not much of a breeze, but flying this fast has my carefully styled hair whipping around my face. It's exhilarating, like being set free. I might feel inadequate on land, but in the sky, I'm perfect. I'm enough.

I chance a look over my shoulder to see how close Ari is, but I can't find him. I'm fast, but his wings are huge; there's no way he's far enough behind that I can't see him.

Shrugging, I turn back toward my destination when something appears right in my path. I shriek as Ari snatches me around the waist and tosses me up in the air. I tumble until I catch my bearings and float back down to him. The laugh he gives me is—fuck it's beautiful. It's full-bodied, and it crinkles his eyes, though his dimple is hidden by the beard.

"How did you catch up to me?" I demand. He's flipped over, his wings beating in long, powerful strokes beneath him.

"You're never going to beat me gliding like that." I don't get the chance to respond to that as he takes off for the island, covering space in an instant.

"Gliding my ass," I mutter. But my wings, with their fast-fluttering movements, struggle to catch him. He turns to a speck before I get a few paces forward, and I'm not ashamed to say I pout for the rest of the flight.

When I finally approach the black sands of the island, Ari has a shirt back on and his wings tucked away. He's sitting on a blanket, lazily leaning back on his forearms. The golden light seems to shine directly on him, casting him in a perfect, hazy glow.

"Cheater," I taunt as I land, slipping off my sandals to feel the warm sand beneath my toes. He barks a laugh and nods to the large blanket for me to sit. Between us is a picnic basket that's already opened.

"I figured you might be hungry," he says, scanning my body.

"I'm on a wedding diet." My attempt at levity falls flat, so I reach into the basket and pull out a sandwich wrapped in parchment paper. "You got these from Baxter?" Izar's mate is one of the best bakers in the realm, but he hasn't baked much since moving to the Night Court.

Ari shrugs. "He took pity on me. I may have begged."

I unwrap the sandwich with the enthusiasm of a child opening gifts on their birthday. Instead of bread, the sandwich is made of a flaky pastry that's not quite a croissant, but probably Baxter's take on one. The groan I let out is obscene as the flavors flood my taste buds. Salty ham mixes with gooey cheese, combined with the buttery pastry to create pure bliss.

"What's that flavor?" I ask, mouth full but not caring one bit. There's something different about the sandwich. Something sweet.

"Elderberry." He averts his gaze, looking down at his sandwich. "I've heard it helps with nausea."

My heart skips a little beat at the thought that went into this gesture. The amount of work that went into this, the level of preparation needed to do this for me. He didn't even know if I'd come.

I can't think about that too much. It's too confusing to ask those questions or delve into why he's doing this on the night when I'm going to agree to be someone's wife.

"You've been talking to my brother," I say instead. Eldoris found elderberries as a remedy for Edina when she was in so much pain that it caused her constant nausea.

"Yeah."

We fall into silence that's filled with many unsaid words. It's so nice to just be with Ari, to be able to joke and laugh with him. The flight, the picnic, it's all been amazing. But as his attention remains on his sandwich, the blanket, the ocean—anywhere but at me—my brain starts to run rampant. We've barely spoken in weeks. Why now? What does this mean?

My anxiety spikes. It starts slow, just a sinking in my gut. The longer we sit in silence, the worse the scenarios in my mind become, and suddenly, I can't get a good breath. My chest rises and falls in quick succession, but I clamp my jaw tight so he doesn't hear my rattling inhales.

A wave of dizziness overwhelms me, and I drop the remainder of my sandwich and the wrapper onto the blanket as I brace my hands by my sides. "Shit," Ari mutters, and in a flash he's in front of me, cupping my cheeks. "Beautiful, I need you to breathe."

But I can't. I'm spiraling, and when I start spiraling about one thing, everything else becomes fair game. It started with Ari and the reasons he could have invited me on this picnic, but it's branched out to every aspect of my life. I can hear all my mother's criticism; feel the crushing inadequacy I've experienced every day since we've read her will. I'm panicked over the expectations of my court, of what I'm being asked to do and to sacrifice.

It all seems impossible. I'm not sure how I'm expected to ever breathe again with all this on my shoulders.

"Tell me five things you can see," he says gently.

I blink rapidly, clearing tears that have formed a film over my vision. "Why?" I pant.

"Humor me."

I swallow. "I see...you." He nods, giving me an encouraging smile. "The picnic basket. The sun setting. The jetty. The...birds. Or are those pixies?"

"Either way. Can you tell me four things you can feel?"

"The blanket beneath my legs. My dress. The sand. And...you." I let go a watery laugh that has more air flooding my lungs.

"Three things you can hear," he prompts, his thumb running a line over my cheek. I lean into the touch.

"My breathing. You...again. And the waves crashing." My heart rate starts to slow.

"How about two things you can smell?"

I very well can't say him *again*. I can't admit that he's all I see when he's near me, or that his citrus scent is part of why I can breathe again. "The salt air and the ham from the sandwich."

"And one thing you can taste."

As the panic recedes, leaving only a buzzing, lightheaded feeling, I notice just how close he is. I wish I were tasting him instead of the salt from my tears.

"Are you leaving me?" I whisper, one more tear sliding down my cheek.

"What?" He brushes it away with incredible softness, and I close my eyes against the intensity. He pulls me closer and his lips brush against my forehead, before he envelops me in a hug so tight my ribs strain against him. It should be constraining, but it helps ease some of the lingering tension. "Never. I will never leave you."

"Then what is this about?"

He sighs, not letting me go. "I wanted to apologize for the idiot I've been this past month." I press my hands against his chest, and he backs up so I can meet his eyes.

"You have nothing to apologize for."

"I do." He sinks back on his heels. I instantly miss his warmth. "This is an impossible situation for you, and I've been behaving like a petulant child because I don't get to keep you."

There's so much to unpack in that sentence. I'm not sure I could begin to process it on a good day, but certainly not when my mind is still hazy from my panic attack.

"I wanted to show you that we can still be...us." He winces at the word. "You know what I mean. I want you to be able to come to me as a friend."

Ari leans over and reaches into the picnic basket and pulls out a package of those damn cookies from the mortal realm, pulling a chuckle from my lips. "A peace offering," he smirks.

"I didn't even know Edina went to the mortal realm." I take the package and hold one cookie out to him. We twist in tandem and pull away.

"She didn't," he says, popping his half in his mouth. "She was holding out on us."

"What?" I screech.

He shakes his head in disgust. "I know, I felt betrayed."

"You should. I do too."

This time when we laugh, it's genuine, and it makes my heart feel lighter.

"So, what do you think?" he asks, taking another cookie and shoving the whole thing into his mouth. "Can we try to go back to normal?"

Normal for me is wanting him so badly that I ache. But I suspect it's similar for him, so for the sake of any relationship we could have, I nod. Maybe one day the undercurrent of want will lessen.

"How did you learn the counting thing?" I ask, picking at another cookie. "It really helped."

"I asked a healer; made it seem like I was having panic attacks. He told me that's one way to ground yourself."

How is he so goddess-damned thoughtful? Not only did he find a way to help me with my anxiety, but he did it in a way that wouldn't make me seem weak. The healers don't talk about their patients, but things can still get out. He completely protected me.

"Thank you." I reach out and take his hand in mine. Little electrical currents flow between us, making my breath uneven for a whole other reason.

The sun gets closer and closer to the horizon, staining the sky and signaling my impending proposal, but I can't move, can't look away. He holds my gaze, the air between us once again going taut. "Devorah," he starts, his voice rough.

I'm not sure who moves first, but the two of us press up on our knees and our mouths crash together. He doesn't hesitate to draw me into his arms, meeting me stroke for stroke of our tongues. I groan at his taste, the faint taste of chocolate mixing with something that's all him.

For a moment, the world around us fades as our bodies mold together. My heart soars, everything falls into place, and all feels right.

Then he's breaking away, breathing raggedly, and I'm whimpering at the loss. "That's the last time that can happen," he says gruffly.

"I know."

And then he's kissing me again, and I'm sighing into him. We shift so I'm lying on the blanket with him hovering over me, one of his hands on the back of my head, protecting me from the ground. It's slower this time, both of us savoring the moment we know will be fleeting. Because this *is* the last time this can happen. Soon, I'll be betrothed to another, and even though we won't yet be bound by magic to be faithful, I wouldn't do that to Kai.

So, one last kiss.

One last moment to remember while I'm living the rest of my immortal life with another.

When we break apart this time, we don't go back. Ari helps me up, and I brush the crumbs and sand from my dress. He smooths the hair that he mussed behind my ear, his fingers brushing against the gentle points with exquisite care, and I straighten my dress and necklace at my throat.

We don't say another word, I just unfurl my wings and take off in the direction of the beach where I'm meeting Kai.

Chapter Nineteen
Devorah

I FLY TO THE small strip of beach outside the palace and find Kai waiting, hands shoved in the pockets of his linen pants and his shirt left open, highlighting all the jewelry he wears. I debate circling so it looks like I'm returning from the palace, but he zeroes in on me as I close the distance over the ocean.

"Sorry, am I late?" I land beside him and retract my wings. I'm obviously late, the sun has fully set now, the abundant stars making a mockery of my flimsy question.

The smile he typically gives me is absent, leaving only a hard jaw and a scowl. His nostrils flare as he inhales—probably scenting Ari all over me—and then releases his breath in a puff of smoke. "Kai—" I start.

"Is it over?" is all he asks. His pupils narrow to slits, and I know I've triggered the possessiveness of his dragon.

Part of me wants to scream that he has no claim over me, has no right to be territorial. But the sane part of me, the one that knows I need him more than he needs me, the same part that ended things with Ari moments ago, says, "Yes."

He releases another breath, smoke absent from this one, and the tension in his body eases. "Alright then. Shall we?"

"You're not upset?" I search his face for signs of that previous anger, but it's completely gone.

"I know you have a past, Devorah; I'm not going to fault you for it," he sighs, running his fingers through his dark hair. "But it needs to be over. It might be a fault of mine, but I'm not good at sharing."

I swallow thickly. "He's going to be my advisor. And my friend."

"Nothing more," Kai insists.

The words are hard to force out, but I agree, "Nothing more."

He holds out his arm in invitation, giving me a wide, easy smile. I take it and we meander down the beach. "Can I ask a favor?" Kai nods. "Can you tell me what to expect tonight? I know you want it to be a surprise, but..." I don't tell him I had a panic attack earlier, and my nerves are fried; part of me doesn't trust him enough to tell him about that, but Kai seems to understand.

"We're walking to the public section of the beach. It shouldn't be too crowded, but there will be enough Fae around to see me propose and spread the word that we're officially betrothed without it looking staged."

"Smart," I comment. It's remarkable how normal he sounds once again. I'm still a little thrown from our earlier interaction, but it seems like he truly put it behind him.

"But before we get there," he says, tugging me to a stop. "I need to know if it's okay to kiss you."

Shit.

I knew this was coming. I'm expected to bear Kai's heirs for fuck's sake, of course I'd need to kiss him. I just didn't expect it to be right now, while I can still taste Ari on my tongue.

But that can never happen again, so am I going to go my entire existence without intimacy? Without affection? I try to imagine a future where Kai and I might be happy—not in love, I'm not sure we'll ever get to that—but friends. Who kiss. And sleep together.

Fucking hell.

"Yes," I hear myself saying, my body going on autopilot, retreating to that place that always puts my duty to my court first.

"I'll let you control the pace," he says, squeezing my arm in reassurance. "If you change your mind, hug me instead. And maybe pretend like you're crying."

Not gonna be a problem. "Thank you."

We round the corner and into a section of the beach that's lit with magical fireballs that pulse in time with guitar music that someone is playing. One Fae child runs around, kicking up sand in his wake as he flits from group to group. Children are so precious in our realm that everyone takes turns playing with him before he runs squealing back to his parents.

"So," I start. Kai's attention is on the child with a wistful smile. *Well, it's good to know he wants children.* Though if he's this possessive of *me*, I can't imagine what he'll be like with a child. "Are you going to just drop down on one knee?"

"I figured we'd sit for a moment." He procures a blanket from thin air and lays it down close to the crowd, but far enough away that it looks like we want some privacy. By now, Fae have noticed we're here, and are leaning in, pointed ears pricking as they try to listen to us. Some pixies go as far as circling us like flies until Kai playfully bats them away.

"We should also talk for a bit," he adds once we're seated. "Make it look like any other date."

Luckily, talking comes easily. On all our dates, we've never once had an awkward silence or had to search for conversation topics. I can actually see Kai becoming a close friend. We just have no romantic chemistry. Even now, with him practically shirtless, every one of his large muscles on display, I feel nothing.

Kalinda thinks it will grow over time.

"Your room in my suite is ready," I tell him. We previously agreed that we should have our own space until we're more comfortable with each other. Sleeping beside a virtual stranger is too intimate, too vulnerable. "You can move in tonight, or tomorrow, if you'd like."

"Fuck that's weird," he chuckles.

"You don't have to—"

"No, it's not that." He reaches over and slings an arm around me. It should be comforting, but he's a little too warm, and we don't fit together seamlessly. "I've never lived anywhere but the hoard. Hell, I barely visited the other courts except when flying."

"That will change pretty quickly." I never really thought about the differences to his life, and how he's felt about them—which makes me a selfish bitch. He's just been so enthusiastic about our agreement that I assumed he was excited for the adventure.

"I've trained for life in court," he says, like that's the thing I was most nervous about. Which I should be, I suppose, but the Fae in court will know exactly the type of male he is—where he came from—so even though they'll judge, they won't be surprised if it takes him some time to acclimate. They certainly are used to it now that Edina and Lysandra have come to us from the mortal realm. It's a nice change of pace from their stunted immortal lives.

"But it's different learning about it than being a part of it," I finish for him, and he nods.

"Especially at such a high position."

He won't be a king, but as my husband, he'll be the second-highest-ranking member of our court, which means there are a lot of expectations.

"I know firsthand how crushing those expectations can be, so if you're ever feeling overwhelmed, please tell me."

"I will," he promises, and we share a commiserating smile. "And on that note, I think it's time. What do you say, princess?"

"Do you have a ring?"

"I do."

"Will you be able to part with it?" I tease, and he playfully nudges my shoulder. The two of us dissolve into easy laughter, which draws the attention of those around us.

"I guess we'll have to see."

He stands briefly, leaving me staring up as he's silhouetted by the light from Day Court in the distance. My mind takes that exact moment to remind me this is my last chance to run. Kai pauses, sensing my hesitation, but I lock it down and give him a nod to continue.

He reaches into his pocket, pulling out a simple silver band with a round diamond winking in the center before dropping to one knee.

The gasps from around us drown out the sounds of the crashing waves. Some Fae squeal, and I already hear the pixies buzzing with chatter as they prepare to spread the news. At this rate, it will circle the length of the realm by the time Kai finishes his proposal.

"Devorah of Summer Court," he says, his voice booming as per usual. "Would you do me the honor of being my wife?"

I can already tell what the Fae will say about this moment. The romantics of the realm will spin the narrative to say that, even though we're marrying to strengthen the court, Kai and I fell in love.

They'll say my hand flew to my mouth in shock, not because I wanted to hide my trembling lip. They'll say the lone tear that spills down my cheek is because I was overcome with happiness, not because I was hoping the male before me was someone else. And when I drop the hand covering my mouth, they won't be able to tell my smile doesn't reach my eyes. When I nod emphatically, they won't know it's because I can't speak around the lump in my throat.

No one will know except Kai, which is why the smile doesn't reach his eyes either.

I let him slip the ring on my pointer finger and fling myself awkwardly into his arms, burying my face in his neck. The cheers and applause are ear-splitting, the enthusiasm veracious that they got to see such an important moment for our court.

When they start clambering for a kiss, I pull back, moving so Kai and I are nose to nose. "You good?" he whispers, his breath fanning out across my lips. I nod, focusing on the flecks of pale green in his gold irises. I delay as long as I can, resting our foreheads against each other before it's clear I can't put it off anymore.

He pushes a piece of hair behind my ear. I cup his cheek. We both lean forward.

And then everything goes dark.

Chapter Twenty
Devorah

"WHAT IS THIS?" KAI murmurs.

It's pitch black, as if someone draped the beach in a heavy blanket. The constant sunlight from the Day Court is gone, the magical lights and fires snuffed out, and even the stars and moon are swallowed by the overwhelming darkness. I try to conjure a magical light, but the moment it appears, ebony tendrils wrap around it, snuffing it out.

"Shadows," I gasp.

The Night Court is here.

They've breached our wards. Judging by the lack of sunlight, I'd say they came through the Day Court mountains.

Blindly, I crawl on the sand in the direction of the child and his parents, following the sound of his wails until I bump into a feminine shoulder. The female yelps.

"It's alright, it's Devorah," I soothe, and I feel her relax. "Do you know where the wards to the palace are?"

"Yes," she whispers.

I drop my voice so low it's barely audible. "Teleport there and tell them Princess Devorah said the word *cantaloupe*. They'll give you sanctuary until you can get home."

"I'll stay," the child's father says. Then, he addresses the crowd, "We won't run from some shadows."

A chorus of cheers goes up, magical lights flickering in and out as Fae try and fail to light them. We should all be running the fuck away and notifying the army, but I can't help but admire their guts.

"Go, please," I assure the mother. "The code word will alert the army to trouble." She agrees, and after I let go of her arm, disappears from the beach in a cloud of earth-scented magic.

"Anyone who can fight, come to me," Kai says, his voice booming and authoritative. An ultraviolet flame flares to life in his hand, briefly cutting through the darkness before it fades. He repeats the motion, again and again, creating a flare that guides the Fae, allowing them to fly or scramble across the sand toward him. They gather together, instinctively taking up defensive positions as if they're not ordinary citizens, but battle-hardened veterans who've fought in formations their entire lives.

"Devorah?" Kai asks, abandoning the group that is now taking turns calling fire magic for the brief illumination it provides. With as much dignity as I can muster, I crawl to him, stopping only when his strong arms gently lift me to my feet. "You should get out of here," he whispers.

"What?"

"Go to the palace, get the guards."

"I asked that female to—"

He ignores my protest. "Your safety is more important than—"

"I will not leave civilians of my court to fend for themselves," I hiss.

"You should—"

The darkness is sucked from the air, leaving me momentarily blinded by the harsh sunlight of the Day Court. Kai's pupils—so round they almost eclipsed his irises—momentarily shrink to slits before evening out. I spin around, searching for the source of the darkness and the sudden absence of it.

Then they appear.

Even with the restored light, it's hard to see the Night Court soldiers between the shadows they command and the black tunics they wear, but they lash out from the edge of the jungle. Ropes of shadow wrap around arms and legs, taking the Fae to the ground. The group of civilians counters with fireballs, which collide harmlessly against the shields.

Pixies—vicious things despite their small size—dive bomb the small battalion. But the Night Court has brought their own pixies, and they attack with equal ferocity.

I call upon my fire, but my magic is weak on a good day, and when I'm flustered, it's barely competent. My blasts fizzle out quickly, not anywhere near strong enough to breach the enemy shields, let alone do any damage.

"You won't leave?" Kai asks. I shake my head. "Okay, hold this." He strips off his many gold adornments and gives them to me.

"Just put them down, I need my hands."

He looks scandalized that I'd even suggest such a thing, and keeps loading me up with jewelry, although he does switch to putting them on me rather than piling them in my arms. I'm so weighted down by the heavy chains and cuffs that I can barely move, let alone muster the energy to fight.

"I'll protect us," he says, undressing and shifting into his dragon form. He's fucking massive—his head reaches some of the tallest trees. His black scales blend seamlessly into the darkness, camouflaging him among the shifting shadows on the beach. The only sign of his presence is the slick sheen that glimmers in the firelight.

He pumps large, membranous wings, stirring the sand into a whirl-wind that has friend and foe covering their eyes and shielding themselves from the grains rather than fighting the Fae before them. Then he opens his giant maw and sprays ultraviolet fire at the line of Night Court Fae. Some shriek and scatter—clearly not expecting an attack from a dragon—and some turn their attention to face the beast. It doesn't make a difference; there are enough soldiers to continue fighting the citizens.

Laden with jewelry and armed with nothing more than a flickering ember, I've never felt more useless. None of the Fae around me seem concerned by my lack of involvement, but their opinions don't matter. What matters is that I'm utterly powerless to protect my court.

I shriek as a figure materializes beside me, shooting flames so hot they're almost blue at the line of our enemies. "Sorry," Eldoris says, aiming at the jungle behind us, where a line of Fae was attempting a sneak attack. "Had to teleport directly to you since I didn't know where you were. Edina will be here in a second—"

A blast of ice hits the closest trees, freezing Fae in their tracks. Coming from the direction of the palace, Edina floats down the beach surrounded by a shield that's...is that a bubble?

"It's good to see me, isn't it?" Edina asks with a smirk before she unleashes a torrent of water at the trees, extinguishing the flames caused by misaligned attacks.

"Yes, thank you for coming."

She goes still for a moment, blinks, then rolls her eyes. "That was pop culture gold, Devorah, and it was completely wasted on you." She angrily pops the shield-bubble and returns to the sky, chasing down the Fae who start running away at the sight of her and my brother. They scream as she freezes their escape route, causing them to slip and slide. Eldoris runs forward, putting himself between the Night Court soldiers and the civilians on the beach.

Hands wrap around my waist so tightly that they squeeze the breath from my lungs. I'm overwhelmed with the coppery scent of blood that emits on a stream of hot breath near my ear. "Sorry, princess. You're coming with me."

I shift enough to get a look at my captor. He's tall, with skin so pale it's almost translucent and black hair that hangs in loose, greasy strings. He flashes me a smile, bearing his fangs.

Vampyre.

Inhaling sharply, I have just enough time to scream before he throws me over his shoulder and we move. Part of a Vampyre's magic is the speed at which they move, and this one is faster than most. The battle becomes nothing more than a blur of shadow and fire, of ice and sand. Tauntingly, the vampyre slows enough so I can see him zip around Kai's four legs, but my betrothed doesn't notice; he's too focused on wildly spraying his dragon fire at the border between Day and Summer Court to cage in the remaining Night Court soldiers.

For a second, I hope Kai's blaze will keep me and the vampyre in as well, but my captor speeds up again, and the world turns green as he runs us into the jungle before anyone even knows I'm gone. I do everything I can, punching and kicking, trying to summon my magic to add extra power to my strikes, but he laughs as though I'm a kitten swatting at a mountain lion.

The vampyre has no care for the branches and vines that scrape my arms, barely slowing as the vegetation clogs his path. Something slices into my calf and tears. White-hot pain sears up my leg, making me go limp, and my stomach roils. "Shit," he hisses. He stops, leaning against a tree. He inhales deeply, my body bobbing as his shoulders rise.

Then there's the feel of a rough tongue dragging up the gash in my leg.

I scream.

The vampyre shifts me so the wound is closer to his mouth and there's a faint sucking sound that makes me gag. I writhe, trying desperately to get him to drop me, but his grip is vice-like. "If you don't stop moving I can't get the damn poison out of your leg. I'm not being paid to deliver a dead princess."

Every one of my instincts is to keep thrashing, but I force myself to hold still. It's not like it was doing anything anyway.

The vampyre spits, and the wad of what I assume is my poisoned blood hits the ground with a sizzle. "Fucking snakes," he shudders. Then his tongue is back on my leg again. "Interesting."

I go back to wriggling, trying to keep him from chowing down on my leg any further, but he doesn't seem to be drinking, just...tasting.

"You taste like a wildfire," he says, unworried by my escape attempts.

"I have fire magic," I deadpan.

His thumb brushes against the wound, and it's like a balm has been poured over it. Coolness soothes the agony. He must have used his blood to heal it for me.

He drops me down his shoulder and scans my face. His eyes are dark, black with the tiniest hint of red like glittering rubies. "You taste more powerful than that pathetic showing back there. Are you hiding something, princess?"

The curious part of me wants to ask what he means; if he can really sense my power level from a sip of my blood. The practical part of me realizes it doesn't matter. I might not be strong magically, but I know an opportunity when I see one.

I knee him in the balls.

He wheezes and doubles over. I use his temporary incapacitation to bolt around him and run back toward the dying sounds of the battle.

El! I call down our mental connection, frustrated that I didn't think to use it earlier. My leg, while mostly healed from the vampyre's blood, is still tender, and after a few precarious steps into the underbrush, I realize I'm not getting very far. I unfurl my wings instead. The trees are close together here, so I'll have to go high if I want to put any distance between myself and the vampyre.

I send a visual of my location and my intention to fly to Eldoris. I bend my knees in preparation. I jump off the ground. My wings beat. My fingers touch the lowest leaves.

Then a hand clamps around my injured leg.

Sharp nails dig into the newly-healed flesh, and I howl. My wings flutter furiously as I try to flee, but he's heavier than I am and drags me down like a stone.

"Little bitch," the vampyre says and throws me over his shoulder once again. We take off so quickly that I banish my wings to keep them from getting sliced open by the vegetation. It doesn't stop me from thumping on his back, aiming for the sensitive bit at the base of his spine.

The jungle flies by until the sunlight from The Day Court breaks through the leaves. The vampyre winces, but unlike vampires in the mortal realm, the sunlight won't hurt him. I brace for the feeling of the barrier as the trees thin, the prickly sensation that comes when crossing our wards.

But he doesn't cross into the Day Court. He runs alongside the barrier.

He's heading to the portal.

No, no, no.

He'll have me in the Night Court in seconds. I'll be completely at Zahir's mercy.

Eldoris—

My mental cry is abruptly cut off as a blast of power strikes the vampyre, sending us flying backward. He cushions my fall, and I scramble off him, running toward the jungle. I'm snagged around the waist again, but this time it's by arms I know. A scent I recognize better than my own floods my nose, and I blink away the panic enough to see Ari—his eyes glowing electric as his power thrums through him. He steps in front of me, shielding me with his giant wings.

The vampyre chuckles as he stands, blood trickling from his nose and the top of his head, marring his moonlit skin.

Ari growls, a fireball expanding in his hand. "The damage is already done," the vampyre snickers. "You've lost this battle. By now, everyone will know—"

He doesn't get to finish. Ari incinerates him where he stands.

Chapter Twenty-One

Ari

"Are you hurt? Did he bite you?" I grab Devorah's shoulders, needing physical confirmation that she's unharmed. That she's here and alive.

It was a stroke of luck that I found her when I did.

I was sitting on the beach, feeling sorry for myself, when a female with her child appeared and said the code word: cantaloupe. Such a stupid word to signal the sky is falling, but it's effective. After ushering them into the safety of the palace, I found Edina and Eldoris. Eldoris gave me instructions for the soldiers and palace guards, and then they went directly to the battle, leaving me to sound the alarm.

Once everything was set in motion, I led a small group to the border between Day and Summer Courts to intercept retreaters. We were fighting a few Fae at the edge of the jungle when I saw the blur of the vampyre and heard Devorah's screams.

Devorah shifts her weight under the intensity of my gaze and winces, drawing my attention to rivulets of blood trickling down her calf. "I was bitten by a snake and the vampyre sucked out the venom," she says offhandedly, as if sounding cavalier will lessen my distress. "But this is from when he grabbed me when I tried to fly away."

I growl, the thought of someone's hands on her, digging into her flesh, makes fire burn my throat. "Where's Kai?" I ask, noticing the stacks of jewelry layered on her neck and wrists. If she wasn't laden down with all that gold, would she have been able to run faster? Would this not have happened?

"He went to help. It's better to have him fighting as a dragon than playing babysitter."

"Wrong." Devorah is the only thing he should be concerned about—not running off to play hero. Her safety comes above all else. He and I are going to have a very long conversation about what's expected of him as her new betrothed.

"I need to get you out of here," I spit through gritted teeth, but I don't trust myself to open my mouth further or I'll start screaming—and Devorah is not the subject of my ire.

"The safe house," she insists. "Eldoris will meet us there."

"I need to get you to a healer."

"I'm fine. There are tonics in the safe house." I know her well enough to see she's not fine, but a jungle with a battle raging nearby isn't the place for this conversation.

I wrap my arms around her to teleport us, and we appear in the heart of the jungle beside the largest tree in the entire court. Its trunk looks like many woven together in an intricate tapestry and is so wide that five Fae with fingertips outstretched wouldn't encircle the whole thing. Romantics say it's the soul of the jungle—that it spawned the rest of the trees and other vegetation. The reality is that one of the previous advisors grew it to conceal the bunker hiding within.

I help Devorah over the uneven roots. As I hold aside a branch full of hunter-green leaves, she places her palm on a pockmark in the bark, activating the magical sensor. A hidden door pops open, a blast of stale air accompanying it. We enter into darkness, the door shutting behind us with a heavy *thunk.* Inside, Devorah dutifully waits on a landing while I call forth a magical light and scout ahead.

The safe house is a simple stone structure whose stairs descend several stories into the ground before opening to a room with moderate-sized ceilings. Over the ages, the monarchs have added furniture, none of which matches. There are two very uncomfortable-looking, floral up-holstered couches, an animal-skin throw rug, and a bookshelf painted bright teal. One wall is dedicated to metal shelves that hold stores of dried, packaged food that have long since been covered in dust, and the other houses a small cot and a whole pile of bedrolls.

"All clear." I don't call forth more light, opting to make the one I already have brighter. Using magic in the safe house is discouraged since particularly powerful Fae can sense magical signatures, even through the strong wards surrounding the tree.

Devorah doesn't say a word as she enters the room and starts method-ically pulling off one piece of jewelry at a time, setting them on a small mahogany end table. My rage is still simmering under the surface, but I try to keep it at bay by busying myself looking through the shelves until I find a generic vial of healing tonic that should fix her leg.

When everything except the new betrothal ring and her stardust pen-dant is off, she finally looks at me. "Eldoris said the Fae are mostly gone. Dead or escaped."

I nod and gesture for her to sit, and she flops on the couch, a puff of dust expelling into the air. She props up her leg, giving me a better view of the gauge marks. The skin around them is pink like it's been recently healed, which is why they're so deep, as opposed to her other leg, which only has slight indents.

"Would you like to talk about what happened?"

"What's there to talk about?" She takes the vial of tonic from me and downs the contents in one gulp. Her skin immediately starts knitting itself back together. "Should we talk about the fact that my citizens—those who have never fought or served in the army—were attacked because of me? Or the fact that I'm so inept I couldn't protect them?"

"You're not inept."

"You may be the only one who thinks that."

"Not true."

She's saved from responding as the doorway to the bunker creaks open. I turn, braced for a fight, but Eldoris appears at the base of the stairs, retracting his long, curved horns so he can fit in the low space. He jerks his head in greeting before pushing past me and sitting beside his sister, lifting her legs so they rest in his lap. He inspects them silently. After a moment, there's a scoff of derision from Devorah and an angry exhale from her brother that tells me they're speaking mentally.

"I shouldn't have to remind you about the use of magic down here," I drawl. "Even mental magic." Their identical eyes lift in an identical glare.

"Fine," Devorah says. "What do we know so far?"

"The vampyre said they accomplished their goal," I say, recalling his words before I killed him. In hindsight, I should have let him talk, but I wasn't exactly rational at that moment.

"They were probably testing us," Eldoris says. He rolls his shoulders, and it's like watching him become an entirely different male. He's no longer Devorah's twin, but the general of the Seelie Army talking to his queen. "Sussing out our weaknesses, seeing how long it took us to respond to a threat. Which was too long, by the way."

"You were there in minutes," Devorah says.

"*I* was, but the soldiers didn't get to us until the battle was mostly over. I'll start working on rapid response drills right away so this doesn't happen again. I don't want one battalion left on their own when the Night Court sends a larger force."

"And we need to secure the portals," I add. "That's where the vampyre was taking you, right, Devorah?"

"Yes," she whispers. "But what do we do? We can't possibly station soldiers at every portal entrance and all four borders. We'll be stretched too thin."

"We can't. But..." Eldoris drifts off and gives her a meaningful look.

Her mouth pops open. "You want to close off *all* the portals?"

"All but one. We can afford to keep guards stationed outside of one."

"That will only scare everyone."

"And having Night Court Fae infiltrate us won't have them scared?"

"A compromise," I interrupt, holding up my hands in a placating gesture. "We close the portals and then reopen them with stricter regulations. Right now, everyone can use any portal to enter our court, but we can modify the wards within them so that only Summer Court citizens can come and go."

"And when we have to host my betrothal ball?" Devorah asks.

"We'll keep one portal open, the one in the heart of the jungle, and we'll keep it surrounded by soldiers." It's taking a page out of Queen Gwyneira's playbook. There are two portals in her court; only one is open for Seelie Fae to enter, and it's in the middle of the harshest terrain in the court. The other—the one for her Unseelie allies—is in a tavern whose owner is not-so-secretly part of her army.

"They'll hate that." The suggestion brings a true smile to Devorah's face. "Let's do it. Inform the citizens that the portals will be closed for maintenance."

"I want the wards surrounding the palace strengthened as well," Eldoris says. "No teleporting. For anyone."

"Not even us?" Devorah asks, affronted.

"No. If someone captures one of us—"

"Me, you mean," Devorah grumbles.

He ignores her. "—I don't want them forcing us to teleport into the palace. We lock it down completely."

"Agreed," I say.

Devorah rolls her eyes, but eventually nods. Her gaze lingers on mine briefly before turning back to her brother. "What of our border defenses?"

"The wards are solid, but we've been concentrating our soldiers on the river and the oceans," he says. "Winter Court reinforcements should be here in a few days, and I'll station them before the Orasite Mountains.

"As far as the Underground..." He drifts off. So far, Hades has been adamant that she's on our side, but the Underground entrance is close to where the Night Court Fae emerged. "I don't want to piss Hades off by stationing guards at the entrance. She hasn't given us a reason not to trust her, and I don't want to risk that alliance if we can avoid it."

"Set up a meeting," Devorah says to me. "I'll talk to her, that way she's warned, but I want to be extra vigilant. I'm sure she'll understand."

"Hopefully," I say.

Devorah groans. "I wish we had more information."

"You're in luck," Eldoris says with a smirk. "What kind of general would I be if I didn't take at least one hostage?"

"Really?"

"Edina encased him in ice so we could transport him. He's in the dungeon at the palace."

"And I suppose I need to deal with that tonight?"

Eldoris shrugs. "Ari and I can handle it."

"No, I'll do it," she sighs heavily. "Do you think the palace is safe to return to?"

"I'll leave first and confirm, but it should be fine." With that, he moves Devorah's legs off him and exits the bunker, leaving us alone together.

The silence is deafening. It was only a few hours ago since we said goodbye on the beach, but it feels like it's been months. There's an ocean between us. It's too far and not far enough all at the same time.

"The vampyre said something to me," she says softly, picking at the hem of her dress. "After he removed the snake venom, he tasted my blood. And he said..." She shakes her head. "It's probably nothing."

"Tell me anyway." I perch on the arm of the couch, far enough away to keep some semblance of personal space, but close enough to reach out and touch her if she needs comfort. Not that I should be physically comforting her at all. Fuck. I hate this.

"He said that...that there was power in my blood." She seems skeptical, but there's a profound level of hope laced in her words. "He accused me of holding back during the battle."

"He thought there was more inside you than you were showing."

It's not a question, but she nods anyway. "There's no way that's real. I've tried—"

"It could be real." She lifts those gorgeous ocean eyes to me, open and pleading.

Devorah comes from a family with formidable elemental magic. Her mother and aunt were powerful enough to topple the realm if left unchecked, and even her brother, a half-human, is terrifyingly strong. She may have more magic than she's currently accessing.

Magic—elemental or raw magic, specifically—like any muscle, needs to be exercised. Devorah has spent so much of her life ignoring that side of herself, focusing on her mind and not training her power.

It will be hard work to get her into fighting shape. But if that means I can spend extra time with her, I'd train her indefinitely.

I offer her a smile. "Meet me outside your suite at sunrise tomorrow."

"Sunrise?" she says, wrinkling her nose. "Why in all the realms would I do that?"

"I'll make it worth your while," I wink. Shit, that probably sounded suggestive. I can't say those kinds of things, can't flirt with her like that anymore.

Her lips purse, and I know she's trying to hold back a laugh. "Fine. There better be coffee."

"Deal."

Her stare goes vacant for a moment before she sighs and says, "Eldoris says it's safe to go back to the palace."

I don't want to. I'd rather stay here, alone with Devorah. But I motion for her to follow me out of the safehouse and teleport us back to the palace.

Chapter Twenty-Two
Devorah

I RARELY COME DOWN to the lower levels of the palace. Over half of it is used for storage, but the side closest to the jungle is comprised of training rooms for the guards stationed here. Even at this late hour, the sounds of magic being cast, steel clashing, and bodies hitting the soft mats filter into the hallway. The area smells like embers and sweat, though it isn't entirely unpleasant.

And then there are the dungeons.

The hall, while remaining the same beige stones, turns dark under the dim, magical lights. The scent shifts to that of damp earth as water from the wet jungle floor drips through the cracks. Large, black insects with squishy bodies and too many legs crawl up the wall, scattering when Eldoris increases the brightness of the lights.

But—unlike some of the dungeons in other courts—it's typically warm, so it's not the worst place to be locked up.

Except for today.

Today, the humid air is replaced by frigid temperatures. Ice clings to the iron bars and slowly creeps over the floors and up the ceiling, turning to stalagmites that hang dangerously close to the one prisoner housed here. He's huddled under a threadbare blanket, his body convulsing as he shivers.

"Is this him?"

"No, he's a thief we apprehended this morning. He's awaiting a trial," Ari says.

"Give him a coat," I order. My advisor summons a thick fur coat from thin air and, without getting too close to the iron, tosses it inside. Then he procures one for me and slips it over my shoulders. I won't comment on the fact that neither he nor Eldoris are wearing a coat. Their fire magic is strong enough to keep them warm.

It's because you're wearing a sundress, Eldoris says telepathically. I'm not sure if he read my mind or saw it on my face, but either way, I'm not in the mood for his placations.

"Thank you, Your Highness," the prisoner says through chattering teeth.

"What did you steal?" I ask, and the tips of his pointed ears turn even pinker than they were from the cold.

"Oh...it was..."

"He was caught sneaking into Princess Larisa's guest room, trying to steal her underwear," Ari says.

I grimace. "Maybe I didn't need to know that."

Eldoris shakes his head, his shoulders bouncing in silent laughter, as he takes the lead to the end of the hall. He procures a leather glove before grasping the handle of a thick, iron door and yanking it open. "Careful," he says, and I sidestep the opening, even though it's large enough to fit three Fae across.

The room—an interrogation room, I assume—is made entirely of iron walls with no windows, and only one door. Like outside, the room is coated in ice, but a path clears as we enter.

Edina sits in a chair, one leg crossed over the other. She looks completely calm, not an ounce of the power that's turned the basement into a tundra showing on her gorgeous features, save the glow of her sapphire eyes.

"Welcome to the party," she says cheerily, throwing her arms out wide.

In the center of the room, suspended by iron chains, is a male with fiery red skin and stubby black horns jutting out from long, moon-white locks. He lifts his head with a snarl, revealing pointed incisors. Not a full-blooded vampyre—he lacks the sharpness of their features—but maybe the product of a vampyre and an elemental Fae.

But the most terrifying thing in the whole room is the shards of ice pointed at every vital organ in the male, each one thin and scalpel-sharp. The red skin blurs the line between blood and tissue, but a pool of blood collects at his feet. The iron chains—and a collar around his throat—keep him from using magic to escape or heal himself from the pain Edina is inflicting.

"We were just discussing his position," Edina says, one of the thin, needle-like icicles inching toward the male's forearm. "I've already learned he's not a part of the greater Unseelie Army but rather works in a regiment in the Night Court's personal forces. And they came through the portal closest to the dragon hoard."

"Nicely done," Eldoris says, crossing the room and bending to kiss his betrothed in a way that's entirely too sweet given the circumstances. Mentally, he says, *I'll set up a meeting with Shesha to find out why he didn't see them and alert us.*

"How did you learn to do this?" Ari asks Edina, reaching out and touching the edge of one of the icicles. He withdraws with the slightest pinprick on his fingertip. I tamp down the irrational urge to banish the ice for hurting him.

"Queen training," Edina answers. When we all turn to her, eyes wide, she scoffs. "I have seven fathers. One teaches me history, one teaches etiquette, and one teaches me torture techniques. Really, did you expect anything different from my mother?"

Both males then turn to me. "I never had torture lessons."

"Good," they growl in tandem.

"Males," Edina mutters under her breath. "I can teach you, Devorah. It's all about blending actual pain with the anticipation of pain." On cue, the shards inch closer to the prisoner. One barely touches his neck, and his jaw goes so tight a vein bulges in his forehead. Edina laughs and runs a hand through her long, blonde locks like this is a day at the beach and not an interrogation.

"Mind if I take over the questioning?" Ari asks. She waves him on. He approaches the male, getting as close as he can without being impaled. "How did you blot out the sun?"

The male spits on his shoe.

"That's why I'm sitting over here," Edina jokes.

The ice closest to the male's forearm inches forward, but instead of a direct jab, it slides under the skin. He grunts in pain as it continues embedding itself until it releases, shaving a chunk of red skin off with it. I gag at the sight of muscle and sinew revealed, and the blood that gushes from the wound.

"Want to try that again?" Ari asks.

"Fuck you."

"So predictable," he tuts, and motions for Edina to continue while walking over to me. He stands in my line of sight so that I can't see the male, but I can hear his screams and...is that the smell of burning flesh? One glance at my brother tells me he did indeed join in on the ministrations.

"You good?" Ari asks, hands twitching like he wants to reach out and touch me, but doesn't.

"Fine." Just trying not to breathe through my nose.

He nods once, and then the prisoner screams, "Someone modified the wards." Ari spins, and I glimpse the icicle pointed at the prisoner's eye. The male is sobbing, all traces of confidence from moments ago washed away by the tears and snot dripping and mixing with the blood.

"Someone in the government?" Ari presses.

"I don't know." Edina inches an icicle closer, this one right above his dick. "I swear it, please. That's above my pay grade. They only told us the plan was to blot out the sun, then cause mayhem and grab the princess."

"Why kidnap her?"

"To prove she's weak."

It's like being punched in the stomach. Eldoris was so convinced this was about testing our defenses that I began to believe him, but deep down, I knew it had something to do with me. It's my biggest insecurity, my biggest fear, and The Night Court not only knew that but tried to use it to poison my court against me.

"They wanted to show everyone they'd be better off with a strong king," the male is saying, twisting the knife in deeper. Eldoris glances at me, but I'm as still as a statue. I refuse to give this male the satisfaction of knowing his words hurt me.

"Which makes no sense," Edina rolls her eyes. "The citizens would prefer El to Zahir."

"I told them that." He smiles as if being on common ground with us will get him out of his predicament. "But next time, they won't just come here to prove a point. Next time, they'll come for blood. They're coming to take over."

"Do you know specifics?" Eldoris asks.

"No," he whimpers.

Ari nods, before looking to Edina, then Eldoris, and finally me. "Any other questions?" he drawls, and we all shake our heads. The doors open again, and a necromancer enters, bringing with him the stench of decay.

"Wait," the male starts scrambling. "Wait, you can use me. I'll—"

Ice jabs directly into the base of his skull, the light draining from his eyes instantly. The ice melts to water, cleaning the room before Edina banishes it.

"Let us know if he has any secrets," Eldoris orders.

The necromancer steps closer to the limp body. "I'll be done by the morning, General."

With a hand on the small of my back, Ari ushers me from the room into the now-damp hallway, Eldoris and Edina following closely behind as we leave the necromancer to do his magic.

ARI INSISTS ON WALKING me back to my room. It doesn't matter that Edina and Eldoris are walking my way, or that Eldoris promised to check my room for threats before he dropped me off; it's as if Ari can't stand to let me out of his sight until he knows for certain I'm safe. He's been on edge all night—and I'm not sure if it's because I was captured, or because we officially ended things. Goddess, how was that only tonight? It feels like I've lived centuries since we kissed on the beach.

We leave Edina and Eldoris at their door with the promise that—should any threat arise—I will use my mental connection to call my brother immediately. He already gave me an earful about not using it sooner tonight. It's not like I've been in an active battle before, and when I reminded Eldoris of that fact, he huffed out a non-committal sound and said, "Next time, remember."

The second their door closes, Ari grabs my arm and pulls me in the opposite direction of my suite. "What—" he presses the wall, opening a hidden door and pulling me inside. It's tight in here, and I bump my elbow against something round and wooden before casting a magical light to illuminate the space.

"Why are we in a closet?" I ask. The small space has room for approximately two bodies in between the stacked chairs and the shelves crammed with excess decorations. I glare at the chair leg that's slightly askew, which is clearly what I bumped into.

Ari closes the door behind us, and I spin to face him. We're close enough that I can feel the heat radiating off his body. If we take a deep breath at the same time, our chests will touch. I look up at him through my lashes, meeting his violet gaze. His citrus scent overwhelms me, wrapping around me like a caress, and it takes everything in me not to sink into his strong arms.

Ari's jaw feathers; his fists clench. When I lick my lips, he tracks the movement.

I don't know what I'm doing. I'm the one who broke things off with him. I'm the one getting married—the one who's now wearing a betrothal ring on my pointer. But after today...fuck, I need him to kiss me. Logically, I know it would make things harder. The romantic in me wants him to do it anyway.

In the end, Ari is the stronger one. He steps back until he's against the door, and I try not to deflate at the sliver of cool air that fills the space where his body was moments ago.

"Are you alright?" he asks, his body practically vibrating his muscles are so taut.

No. "I'm fine." He arches an eyebrow. I sigh, "You've asked me this about a hundred times since—"

"Because I don't believe you."

"I'm as fine as I can be," I settle on, biting my lower lip to keep it from wobbling.

His brow furrows. "Tell me what's wrong. What you're feeling."

What's wrong is that I miss you even though we're two inches apart. What's wrong is that I need you, but I can't have you. What's wrong is that the only person I can talk to about this is standing in front of me, hurting as badly as I am.

I don't say any of that.

Tilting my head back to the ceiling, I let out a drawn-out sigh. "They did this to prove I'm weak." My voice feels small, nothing like the commanding tone I use when I'm in charge and nothing like the carefree, sarcastic one I reserve for my friends. But with Ari, I can be honest.

"I know," he responds.

"Not the court. *Me.* Do you know how that feels? I've spent my entire life preparing to lead this court. I've sacrificed everything I've ever wanted, all for it to be erased by one attack."

"Your subjects won't turn on you because you were caught off guard. They adore you."

I hear him, but I can't take his platitudes. "Even my mother didn't think I could rule alone. If it wasn't for my brother—" I pinch the bridge of my nose. "If it wouldn't destroy his happiness, I'd be done. I'd let him take the throne, I don't even want it anymore."

"You don't mean that."

"No, but I should."

Ari chuckles lightly, and it breaks my spiral. I meet his gaze again. I'm not sure what I expect to see, maybe some kind of pity or gentility, but I don't expect the challenge I see in his gaze. "So, what are you going to do about it, beautiful?"

That nickname is going to be my undoing.

"Are you going to roll over and take it?" he continues. "Run away? You know I'll support you no matter what—say the word and we'll go straight to the portal and hide in the mortal realm. I have friends there, it'd be easy."

"You know I'm not going to run away."

He beams with pride. "Then what's next?"

I release a heavy breath. "Next...I'm going to meet you outside my suite at sunrise."

"Good girl." The phrase makes my stomach tumble; pixies flap their wings and do somersaults in my damn gut. I roll my eyes in an attempt to keep my dignity. "Off to bed then. You'll need your rest for tomorrow."

As SOON AS I get to my suite, the day's events catch up with me. Exhaustion crashes into me like a tsunami, making me sway on my feet. Leaning against the door, I hear Ari's whispered goodnight. I close my heavy lids, letting the silence of being alone swallow me up.

"Hey, betrothed."

So not totally alone.

Kai is leaning in the doorway of my guest room—his room now, I suppose. Kalinda must have brought him here after the battle. He's only wearing a pair of black sweatpants slung low on his hips, and something about seeing him so informal unsettles me. With no chains obstructing his muscles, I can see a tattoo of four dragons that starts at the hollow of his throat and moves in a vertical line to right under his breastbone.

"I'm so relieved you're alright, I was worried." Even though his words are light and easy, he's frantically scanning me, roving over every inch of my body.

"Yep. All good," I say. There's a moment of awkward silence where neither of us moves. "Thanks for your help tonight."

Kai makes a strangled sound that I don't know how to interpret. His jaw is clenched and his fists keep balling and flexing, and...is that sweat by his temple?

"Oh, your gold is safe," I offer.

"Thank the goddess." His whole body relaxes on an exhale. I can't control the giggle that escapes my lips. Maybe it's slightly hysterical on my part, but it feels good to feel anything other than confusion or worry. "You laugh, but you have no idea what it's like. It's like being separated from my child."

"It's in the safe house. I'll send someone to get it for you tomorrow."

"I can go," he pleads, but I shake my head.

"You don't have that kind of clearance."

"Please. I'm dying here, Devorah." He drops to his knees in front of me, and this time my laughter is unrestrained. "Take pity on me." He pouts—making his bottom lip quiver and everything.

"I'm not sending someone out this late to get your gold." Instead, I take my necklace off and extend it to him. His eyes go wide as saucers, and I'm pretty sure he drools. "Think of it as a security blanket."

"I'm not sure I'll be able to give it back once I take it," he warns.

I shrug. "Fae notice when I wear jewelry more than once, and the last thing I need is for them to think our coffers are low and I can't afford new pieces. It's all yours."

"You're the best betrothed ever." He stands and plops the necklace in his pocket before scooping me in his arms and spinning me around. He does that a lot.

When he sets me down, he stays close, his hands remaining on my hips. "Okay, I'm off to bed." I gesture to my room in the opposite direction from the one he emerged from. "I have to be up early."

I turn to go, but he holds me still. "I was thinking," he says. "We never got our betrothal kiss."

My throat works. "No, I suppose we didn't."

"Would you like to?" His tongue peeks out to wet his lips. "I figured we might want to try it in private first. That way, if it's awkward, we won't look bad."

He makes a good point, we should practice. But tonight, I broke up with a male who may have been the love of my life, got betrothed, was in a battle, was captured, and saw someone being tortured.

I've hit my limit.

"Not tonight."

To his credit, Kai releases me and grins like it is of no consequence to him. "Then goodnight, Devorah." He removes the necklace from his pocket, lovingly stroking the stardust gem in the center, and retreats to his room.

Chapter Twenty-Three
Ari

I'M A HYPOCRITE. I practically ordered Devorah to go straight to bed, but rather than sleep myself, I went to my office and got to work. Most of what needed to be done was to arrange meetings. I sent couriers to our Seelie Court allies, asking for a meeting at the Army Base. Someone high up in the Day Court sabotaged their wards, and we need to discern if King Simi was involved, or if he can be trusted. Then, I sent a message to the citizens who helped defend during the attack, offering them a reward, as well as our invitation to all of the betrothal events—a high honor that's rarely offered. For the two families who lost someone, we covered all their expenses for the foreseeable future and arranged a soldier's burial for their loved one. It's not enough, but it's something.

When I still couldn't sleep, I went back to the safe house to retrieve the dragon's jewelry. Some dragon shifters place enchantments on their treasure so they can always find them. I'm not sure if Kai is skilled enough in magic—he's very young—but I can't take any chances that he'll learn the location of the safe house. I don't trust him.

Especially after he left Devorah.

I still see red when I think about it. Devorah tried to convince me that Kai meant well, but if it was up to me, I'd rip his head off for abandoning her. Eldoris assured me he'd handle it, and the way flames danced in his eyes when he said the word *handle,* I knew Kai was in for a world of hurt.

Leaning against the wall across from Devorah's suite, I wait until the sun rises. She's nothing if not punctual, so she steps into the hall as the rays trickle through the colored-glass windows. Her hair is tied in a messy bun atop her head, and the bags under her eyes are twins to mine. Even so, she looks radiant.

"I assume this is appropriate?" she says, gesturing to her body. The shirt she's wearing is tied in a knot, leaving a peek of creamy skin showing above her leggings—which are so damn tight I can see the line of her thong beneath.

Torture. This is going to be actual torture, the likes of which make Edina's ministrations last night look like child's play.

"You're perfect," I choke. She blinks up at me; I shake my head like it can erase the comment. "The outfit. The outfit is perfect."

Her smile is soft and sad. We're just two Fae, doing our best to pretend we're just friends. An employer and employee. An advisor and his queen.

I extend the cup of espresso I brought for her, and then the sad smile turns mega-watt. "Bless you." She snatches the drink from me and drinks it all before banishing the porcelain mug into thin air. "Now where the fuck are we going this early?"

I chuckle, grateful that the tense moment has passed us, and beckon her to follow. We cross the length of the palace, enter the wing that borders the jungle, and descend the stairs to the basement. "Tell me you don't have another prisoner to interrogate," she pleads.

"Nothing like that." I lead her into an empty training room and illuminate the space with several balls of magical light. I watch as she drinks in the sparse area. It's empty, save for a few fireproof dummies and the scorch marks that mar the sandy-brown, misshapen stones of the walls and floor.

"Every morning at sunrise, we'll meet here and we'll work on your raw magic so that you can use your fire to defend yourself," I say. "We'll also work on physical defense, so if—goddess forbid—your magic fails you, you can punch your way out of a situation." I give her a cheeky smile that I hope will lighten the mood.

Despite her resolve to get stronger last night, I can see the trepidation, the fear, the doubt creeping in. "Ari..."

"You wanted to know if the vampyre was telling the truth." I cross the room to her and take her hands in mine, unable to help myself. "This will tell us."

She sighs. "I don't want anyone else to know. If I can't—if it doesn't work..."

"This is just between us. I reserved the room for the morning so no one will interrupt us."

I drag her to the center of the room and point to a target on the back wall. "I want to test your range first, so don't worry about aim. We're going for distance."

She swallows and calls a flame to her palm. It starts as an ember, no larger than the flame atop a candle, but slowly grows to a medium-sized ball. She holds her breath, and her shoulders creep up to her ears.

"Wait," I say before she launches it. "Take a deep breath. You need to relax, or it's going to fight against you."

"What the fuck does that mean?" she grits.

"Fire is an...obstinate element. It's not like water, air, and earth want to be commanded, to be molded and shaped. It has a mind of its own, its own agenda. If you're going to bend it to your will, you need to trust it."

"You talk about it like it's alive."

"It is," I shrug, and call a fireball into my hand. As I relax and it grows and it begins to dance. "Fire is life. Creation. If you treat it as something to be feared, it will never work properly."

"I'm not afraid of it," she says, but even as she speaks the words, I hear her realize the lie in them. She's scared of her magic—not because of what it can do, but because she's afraid it won't do anything.

I banish my flame and take a step behind her. "Can I touch you?" I ask, and she nods. She tenses when I touch her shoulders, but slowly melts as I knead the muscles with my thumbs. "Imagine the fire growing. Breathe."

It jumps so abruptly that she banishes it. I laugh, pulling her back against my chest in a hug. "Now do it again."

She does, not moving out of my embrace, controlling the growth this time. Without prompting, she launches it at the target and hits a perfect bullseye. "Now we'll step back."

The farther we step back, the worse her aim gets, and when we reach the doorway, the flame falls flat altogether, but it's a lot better than I thought it would be. "Don't worry, the more you work with it, the easier it'll get."

"Newly emerged Fae have better control than I do," she grumbles, retreating into that place of insecurity. "How is that possible?"

"When was the last time you used your raw magic, other than last night?" I ask, and her cheeks turn bright red. "It's nothing to be ashamed of. You emerged, and then your mother dragged you into thousands of lessons that kept you from practicing."

She groans. "What's next?"

We work for a while longer, testing her accuracy, seeing how large she can grow the fire, and finally, how hot she can make it. She surprises both of us when her flame turns from red to blue without much of a thought, which proves my original theory. The power she's inherited from her family is within her. Her magic is vast, it just needs to be stretched and exercised.

At one point, Devorah sheds her shirt, leaving her in only a sports bra. The effort it takes to focus on her hands and not her exposed skin should make me a goddess-damned priestess.

When she's panting and sweaty from exertion, I call it a day. "Now the day really begins," she deadpans, and I nod. "What do you have for me?"

"We have a meeting with your other advisors this morning, one with King Simi this afternoon, and tonight, you and Kai are meeting with the priestesses to discuss the parameters you'd like to set up for your marriage."

Fae marriages are magically binding. The couple decides in advance what they're comfortable with in regards to children, fidelity, and such, and then tells the priestess so that she can weave those desires into the magic of the ceremony.

She sighs heavily. "And preparations for the betrothal events?"

"All taken care of, according to your event planner. There are a few things for you to sign off on; they're on your desk. Alongside Kai's jewelry." I mime gagging.

"Thank you for dealing with that," she chuckles.

I shrug, downplaying how that sound makes my chest feel lighter. It doesn't matter that we can't be together; I would do anything to make her happy, to make her life easier. I suppose I'll have to grow out of that, but right now...

Right now, it's the only thing I can do to be a part of her orbit.

THE MEETINGS GO EXACTLY as expected. Devorah is firm but assuring and somehow convinces her other advisors that we've solved a problem that arose the night before. No one disputes her sound suggestions, and by the end of the morning, security within the court is significantly enhanced. Any damage that was done from her capture was effectively erased by her decisiveness and fast action.

I'm not the only one in awe of her. Every servant and guard in the palace, every Fae I run into in the army base are all talking about how amazing she is, how wonderful of a queen she'll be. She doesn't see it; she's still terrified that they think she's too weak to rule. I hope our lessons will give her more confidence because she deserves to feel as wonderful as she truly is.

By the next day, everyone has moved on to preparing for Devorah and Kai's betrothal celebration. There are three events; the first is a 'small' affair for the royalty, advisors, and other high-ranking members of society. Then there's a luncheon for the citizens of Summer Court, and finally, a ball for any Fae who wish to congratulate the happy couple.

It's the last event that has me on edge. Because we can't look weak to the other courts, we have to adhere to the tradition of inviting all citizens from all courts, but no one is happy about it.

"Please," Eldoris begs his sister as the three of us sit in her office. She stopped listening a long time ago, tuning out her twin like only a sibling can do. She signs a few papers, orders extra guards to be stationed in the palace. "Dev, this is a terrible idea. We can cancel the last ball."

"The strongest Fae in the realm will be in the room with us," she says, and then addresses me, pointing to the paper on top of her pile. "This is for?"

"Soldiers to be stationed outside each guest room."

"Even the Seelie Fae?"

"Unless you want to look like you're singling out the Night Court."

Eldoris pounds his fist on the desk. "Devorah Talia—"

"Don't you dare," she snaps. She turns to her brother with wrath etched on her face, the fire we've been so carefully cultivating the past two days flickering across her eyes.

Fucking hell. Names in Faerie—full names at least—are never spoken. They have power, power that can be catastrophic if it gets out. I don't even know my father's full name. It's why most are referred to by a first name and a court, never a last name.

For Eldoris to slip like that—in front of someone who isn't family—means he's at his wits' end. His jaw tics; he must know he's in the wrong, but is still unable to let go of his frustration. Literal smoke comes out of his ears.

"I need you to take this seriously," he grits through his teeth. "I won't lose you because you want to keep up appearances."

Devorah softens a fraction. "I know this is hard for you, especially because it's The Night Court."

"Don't make this about Arella," Eldoris says, referencing his deceased mate. "It's not about her. It's about you. I can't lose *you*."

Devorah reaches across her desk to take his hand. "What will it take for you to be okay with this? Cancelling isn't an option."

He swipes his hand down his face. "You'll have guards around you at all times."

"That'll be hard."

"It can be us," I say, finally comfortable inserting myself after that personal moment. "Eldoris and I can find excuses to be near you. Edina, too."

"You know I'm betrothed to an actual dragon, right?"

"He already abandoned you once," Eldoris growls.

Devorah chuckles. "What did you say to him, by the way? He was still quaking when we went to meet with the priestess yesterday."

"I simply told him I'd scatter his treasure across the mortal realm," Eldoris smirks. "Ari's the one who scared him. Threatened to melt everything down into...how did you put it?"

"An unrecognizable puddle of ore."

Devorah grins. "Diabolical."

I tip an imaginary hat, thrilled that I get to be the one who makes her smile.

Chapter Twenty-Four
Devorah

THE FIRST TWO BETROTHAL events were uneventful.

The first was spent in a receiving line, and every well-to-do member of society came to congratulate us. Normally, pasting on a smile and dealing with ass-kissing Fae is just another day in the office, but with all that's weighing on my mind, it's been difficult. Every time someone spoke too loudly or someone dropped a glass, I'd tense. But nothing happened. When everyone wished us well, Kai and I had one dance and then retired for the evening without an incident.

The second event was even better. Held during the day, it's more like a lively brunch than a ball. Every Fae of Summer Court is invited, and I much preferred speaking with my citizens than the same droll Fae at every event. Kai's hoard—while invited to all events—chose to attend the brunch. Getting to know them was fantastic. Dragons get the reputation of being surly, but they all had wonderful senses of humor and infectious laughter. They didn't hesitate to make fun of themselves or tell embarrassing stories about Kai when he was a hatchling.

Kai has taken to court life surprisingly well. His friendly demeanor and larger-than-life personality set the stuffy courtiers and royals at ease, and even our rival courts took a liking to him. Even if I hate the circumstances, I can't deny that he'll be an asset as a consort.

Zahir barely spoke to us at either event, other than the obligatory greeting at the first ball. But every time I looked at him, he was staring intently. There was something about his gaze that felt...off. It wasn't predatory like it was at my mother's funeral, but I couldn't discern the emotion. When I mentioned it to Ari, he grumbled something about melting Zahir's eyes for looking at me at all.

As well as the first two events went, tonight is the real test. The night every citizen of every court is invited. Security has been high all week, but tonight it's off the charts. In addition to the palace guards, Summer Court soldiers—plucked straight from the Seelie Army—are stationed every few feet in every hallway. There are also guards in the jungle trees, on every trellis and balcony, and on the rooftops. That's not to mention the soldiers stationed along our borders, and those guarding the path from the portal to the palace.

Our court is a verifiable fortress.

Personally, I think Night Court citizens aren't going to come at all. I think they'll opt to insult us rather than attack, but Eldoris and Ari aren't convinced, and I promised they could stay at my side the entire night.

The dress Melia made for me is a statement piece. It's completely encrusted in black gems that taper off into the train, and the underlying material starts off midnight blue and fades gradually into a brilliant teal. The strapless bodice is fitted before gently flowing out, the folds of the skirt barely concealing the slit at my thigh. My makeup is smokey and dark, making my eyes look like they're glowing. Even though it's stunning, everything about my look—from my tied-back hair, to my flat shoes, to the movable material of the dress—is ready for battle.

"Wow," Ari gasps from the doorway. I spin, and the material of the dress flutters around me. "You look..."

"Ravishing?" I tease. Things between us have been better in the past few days. I'm not sure if it's the early morning training sessions or because our days have been crammed with events, but the awkwardness between us has dissipated. We're more or less back to the way things were before, back when we were both ignoring our feelings and pretending to be friends.

I think this is going to be as good as it gets.

Ari looks entirely too good in his black-on-black tuxedo that's fitted to accentuate his thick muscles and broad shoulders. His teal tie perfectly matches my dress, which I'm sure Melia did on purpose—meddlesome brownie.

"I mean, yes. But you look like a warrior." Emotion clogs my throat as I struggle to put words to my gratitude. That simple statement has more weight than any other compliment he could have given me. "I have a present for you."

He withdraws a rectangular box from his jacket pocket. Our fingers brush as I take it from him, and my traitorous heart gives a little flutter. That part hasn't changed. Every time Ari touches me, there's a zing of awareness that I dutifully ignore.

Pulling off the lid. I find a small silver dagger with an aquamarine gem in the hilt. I gently trace the flames etched into the silver. "The blade is iron," he says, slipping a leather sheath around the deadly metal.

"Where did you find an iron blade?" They're not exactly sold in the villages; some courts have outlawed their making entirely.

"The Underground."

"Of course," I chuckle.

"It's not much," he says, handing it back to me. "But I wanted you to have an extra layer of security tonight."

"Thank you," I breathe. "But where am I supposed to put it?"

"Ah." He withdraws something else from his pocket and drops to his knees. I hold back a groan. Why does the goddess feel the need to torture me with the sight of this male kneeling before me? My restraint is only so great.

My breath catches. As if he realizes the position he's in, Ari swears. Voice gritty, he says, "Lift your leg, Your Highness."

I'm powerless when he uses that rough tone. Steadying myself on his shoulders, I lift my leg, allowing him to slide the cool leather up my calf. His knuckles graze my skin, sending a shiver of goosebumps in their wake. That fleeting touch, so light, makes it hard to breathe.

His eyes lock on mine. Their intensity is terrifying and dangerous. When he reaches my thigh, a whimper escapes my lips. He slides the holster into place but doesn't remove his hand, his fingers toying with the sensitive skin there.

"Ari," I warn. The sound of my voice snaps him out of his trance. He shoots to his feet so abruptly that it sends me stumbling backward.

"Sorry," he says, grabbing me around the waist to stabilize me. I find myself laughing as I secure the dagger to my thigh.

"What's so funny?" Kai asks, trying to fasten his cufflinks as he walks into the sitting room.

We jump apart.

"I was just being clumsy," I say in what I hope is a breezy tone. "Look what Ari got for me." I flash Kai my upper thigh, hoping the jewel will distract him.

"Thoughtful." He steps up beside me and extends his wrist so I can help with the cufflinks. As soon as I'm done, Kai wraps a possessive arm around my waist. "But aren't you supposed to get a gift for the couple?"

"I'd think Devorah's safety *is* a gift for you both." The look Ari is giving Kai could melt glass, but either my betrothed doesn't care or doesn't acknowledge it.

Instead, Kai tilts my face to his. "Of course." He leans in. For a second, I think he's about to kiss me, and I completely freeze. Instead, he brushes his nose against mine before kissing the tip. His thumb tenderly strokes my cheek. "But I'll never let anything happen to my betrothed."

It's all very calculated. The words, the acts of affection, the casual moments of domesticity. On their own, they're harmless. But directed at Ari, it's a challenge. Staking of a claim.

I hate the male posturing. I think I'd prefer if he peed in a circle around me than this bullshit.

That might be an over-exaggeration, but I really fucking hate it.

A knock on the door startles all of us from the tense situation. "Oh great, Edina and Eldoris are here." I slip out of Kai's hold and past Ari to open the door. "Hi, great. Ready?"

Edina and Eldoris exchange a confused glance as I grab my brother's arm and tow him down the hall. At the last second, he grabs hold of Edina, and she trails behind us like the tail of a kite.

What did we walk into? Eldoris asks.

I have no words.

When we reach the main hallway—and Kai and Ari catch up to us—I take my betrothed's hand and prepare for our entrance to the ballroom. Ari steps in front of us, and Edina and Eldoris line up directly behind, sandwiching me in a protective bubble.

The sound from the ballroom abruptly quiets, and a musical chime plays before the guard at the door introduces us.

"Announcing Princess Devorah of the Summer Court and her betrothed, Kai of the Thisavroús Dragon Hoard. Along with Prince Eldoris of the Summer Court and Princess Edina of the Winter Court."

We chose to go light on decoration for this event. "Less places to hide behind and fewer things to use as weapons," Ari said. And while I scoffed at the time, the simple white silk cascading from the ceiling, fastened with gold clasps in the shape of clam shells, is elegant. The gold filigree on the walls is enchanted so that sparkles float around their waves like the shimmer of the ocean.

Fae of all races crowd the ballroom, a line already forming to greet us as we enter from the back door. Pixies buzz about on their tiny wings, tossing flower petals and confetti. The way Ari tenses, you'd think they were throwing exploding powder. The right wall, which is all windows, has been opened to accommodate two large tanks, one for the selkies and one for the water sprites. They wave webbed hands or press scaled-covered faces against the glass. Larger Fae, like the centaurs and trolls, stand at the back, clapping and stomping hooves loud enough to rattle the chandeliers.

The royals and their families are clustered on a large dais that spans the length of one wall. Gwyneira, who is speaking with Oakley and Zahir, gives me a nod of solidarity. If anything happens tonight, I think we'll find Zahir with an icicle jabbed in his temple.

"This receiving line business is getting tedious," Kai says softly for him, but loud enough that both Ari and Eldoris hear.

"You better get used to it," Eldoris grumbles.

"Oh, don't act like *you* enjoy it," Edina teases.

With that, we take our place and prepare to greet the citizens of the realm.

We're not one hour into greeting guests before someone calls, "Devorah!"

Eldoris swears as the King of the Night Court approaches. Ari takes a step closer, and Kai tenses, grabbing my hand, ready to spirit me away.

The Fae in line scamper back a few steps with hasty bows as Zahir steps directly in front of me, ignoring Kai completely. "I think it's time for a dance," he says, offering me his large hand.

His disposition is different tonight. His cheeks are pink, his nose a ruddy sort of red that leaves me wondering if he's been indulging in something stronger than faerie wine. The longer he stands with his hand outstretched, the more he wobbles as if the floor is rolling beneath him.

"I'm sorry, Your Majesty," I say coolly, glancing down at his hand before meeting his ice-blue eyes once more. "I'm previously occupied with the fair Fae of the realm, who I so appreciate coming out tonight to greet me and my new betrothed. But I'll be happy to save you a dance once we're finished here." *If he's still standing by then.*

Something dark morphs his expression, and his skin flushes further. "I'm sure they won't mind one little dance, would you folks?" He turns to the crowd who simper and shake their heads, bowing further under the weight of his gaze. "It's settled then."

This time, he doesn't wait for me to take his hand, grabbing mine roughly and pulling so hard my arm almost flies out of its socket.

"Get your hands off her," Ari growls, but I give him a look that I hope conveys I'm okay. I don't think Zahir would try to hurt me in a room full of royals, and something in my gut tells me this conversation will be advantageous. Zahir is rarely this indisposed. There's no telling what kind of things I can pry from him in his inebriated state, especially if he thinks he has the advantage and that I'm intimidated by him.

He snaps his fingers at my orchestra, who look aghast until I nod for them to begin playing. Though their choice isn't what I would have picked. It's a slow, sensual kind of dance that relies heavily on power dynamics.

Zahir takes my waist. I place one hand on his shoulder. Our free hands clasp, and then we're off.

Oddly, the position isn't unfamiliar. Zahir was once a part of our friend group, and he and I had common ground since we were the only future heirs to also have siblings. However, I would have gladly passed my responsibility to Eldoris, and he was terrified Izar or Hades—especially Hades—would challenge him for his place.

"I'm surprised, Dev," he says. The nickname on his tongue sends shivers down my spine, leaving me feeling slimy.

"Of what, Your Majesty?"

His chuckle is deep. "Come now, you don't have to use my honorific. You never used to."

"We were friends then."

"And we're not now?" The steps switch. He drags me in closer, slotting his thigh through my legs, and dips me back and to the side. He moves remarkably well for someone who looked ready to faceplant moments ago.

With my sweetest smile for all the onlookers, I say, "Friends don't try to abduct you." It's a gamble, bringing it up, but if I'm going to get any information out of him, I need to lead the conversation in that direction.

His laugh echoes across the ballroom. It's too loud, not the way Kai's is loud because he's a loud person. This is forced merriment and has an undertone of violence. "It's nothing personal, you know. You're untested. New. And I've grown bored with the desert."

It takes all my composure to keep my smile in place. "You understand my court has some of the most unforgiving terrain in the realm."

He shrugs. "I debated going after Spring Court, but then Lysandra added Puck to the monarchy and made it more difficult. Plus, you've been floundering for ages, what with that nasty skirmish a while back and your mother's decreasing involvement in social events.

"Tell me, princess—" he licks his lips, "—was she sick before she passed? We never did find out, but my gold is on the fact that she was fading."

Luckily, the dance requires me to kick between Zahir's legs at that moment, and while you're supposed to keep the kick below the knee, I aim high. He swerves right before I connect with his balls.

"So sorry, I don't seem to know my strength," I giggle, offering a passing nod to some of the couples who have joined us on the dance floor. I'm not sure if Zahir realizes, but Edina is dancing with Puck right behind us, completely ignoring him as she watches me. Ari is with a courtier to my right, and Eldoris, while further away, is dancing with Gwyneira. On the outside, it looks completely normal, royal Fae pairing off at random, but I know better. They're circling vultures lying in wait.

"There is a way we could make this all go away," Zahir says. He pulls me flush against his body, and when he does, I feel a rock-hard erection against my belly. Bile rises in my throat. I try to pull away, but he holds me fast.

"Ditch the dragon. Marry me."

Chapter Twenty-Five
Devorah

My mouth pops open. Never, in my entire life, have I been struck this speechless.

Marry me.

Has he lost his damn mind?

Ari dissolves into a coughing fit. Puck and Edina give up all pretense of dancing to stop and stare. Eldoris deposits Gwyneira into the arms of one of her husbands and takes a menacing step closer. If Lysandra hadn't swooped in and pulled him into a dance, I'm sure he would have thrown Zahir across the dance floor.

"Marry me," Zahir repeats. "We'll unite our courts. We can put this ugly war business past us."

He *has* lost his mind.

Slowly, the shock ebbs, and I regain my faculties enough to say, "You're married."

He shrugs nonchalantly. "Accidents happen."

Edina gasps, but when Zahir turns, Puck dips her so low she almost falls flat on her back. He returns her to standing, and she giggles, smacking him playfully. Puck meets my eyes, and I widen mine imperceptibly in thanks for his quick thinking.

"You'll think about it?" Zahir asks. He brushes a finger along my cheek in a far too intimate gesture. "We used to have fun, once upon a time."

You slept with Zahir? Eldoris screams in my mind.

It was before he was a self-important asshole. And I was drunk.

I'm going to be sick.

Zahir interprets my small smile at Eldoris' reaction as curiosity and leans in to whisper in my ear. His breath smells rancid, a mix of whiskey and something acrid that's definitely from some sort of drug. Before he can say anything, a cool voice says, "May I cut in?"

Vladimir Orlov—a vampire from the mortal realm—appears over Zahir's shoulder. Unlike vampryes in Faerie, Vlad was once a human who was turned into a vampire; with his immortality came an aversion to sunlight and a diet consisting exclusively of human blood. He's been alive longer than most of the Fae in this room, and even though he only visits once in a while, everyone knows him.

Vlad straightens the jacket of his dark blue tuxedo before adjusting the aquamarine tie. His blonde hair is perfectly styled, and his lips are turned up in a sardonic sneer.

"We're in the middle of something," Zahir snaps.

"I see that." Vlad clucks his tongue. "Consider this cashing in on one of the many favors you owe me."

Vlad has a habit of collecting favors from Fae and cashing them in at the most inopportune times. It's very interesting that Zahir has racked up a debt to the vampire. One look over Zahir's shoulder tells me Edina heard that as well, and she nods, confirming she's tucked that piece of information away for later.

Zahir's grip tightens around my hand, the pressure so intense it borders on pain. Just as I'm about to scream from the bone-crushing force, he lets go, his smirk dripping with smugness. "She's all yours."

He backs away, and Vlad takes his place. My shoulders come down from my ears, and my body relaxes into his hold the slightest amount. "You're welcome," he says, his smile going wide enough to show off the sharpened points of his fangs.

"I didn't say thank you," I tease, slipping into the easy banter like a comfortable sweater. For as calculating as Vlad can be, I consider him a good friend.

"You can thank me without me asking for a favor." Another one of those toothy grins has me laughing. When it dies down, he says, "You have quite the entourage."

"Noticed them, did you?"

Eldoris and Edina are now dancing together, and Puck and Lysandra are still on the floor, seemingly awaiting orders. Ari has switched partners but also remains close, and Kai has joined in as well, dancing with Larisa of the Day Court.

"Only an idiot would be dumb enough not to see the group orbiting you. And yes, that's a dig at the honorable King of the Night Court."

I let out a heavy sigh. "How much of that conversation did you hear?"

"Enough," he says, tilting my chin so I'm forced to look into his ice-blue eyes. "I trust you read between the lines of that proposition."

"Yes."

"Because, while I agree that you're a wonderful lay—"

"Is everyone determined to bring up my drunken sexual endeavors tonight?"

"—That's not a reason to propose matricide, especially when Haiza is so beloved."

"I know." As twisted as it is, Zahir's proposal was a good thing. He showed his hand, revealed his thoughts on the upcoming war.

He's worried he'll lose.

"Good girl." He chuckles when I purse my lips. "Do you not enjoy praise anymore? I seem to remember—"

"Change the subject," I command, and he howls. There are times when Vlad carries the weight of all his years, but when he laughs, it's easy to see the young man who was turned. It brightens his face and makes his eyes twinkle mischievously.

"I haven't congratulated you on your betrothal," he says, mirth still coating his words.

I hum. "I assume you know everything about this situation." I'm not sure how he does it, but Vlad always knows all the goings on in our realm. Everyone knows he has spies, but no one has ever been able to find them, so we've all given up.

"More than you think." He leans in to whisper in my ear. "I know the contents of your mother's will." I jerk back. "School your features, princess," he croons and tugs me in close again. I release a breath that flutters his blonde hair.

"How?" Is all I can think to ask.

"She told me. She knew you'd have questions and would need to ask someone."

One glance around the dance floor shows other couples have drifted closer, despite the group still surrounding us. "We shouldn't talk about this here," I murmur. Not only do I not want others to hear, but I need time to process. There's a very high probability that the information Vlad has will make me cry, and that can't happen in this room. Not with these vipers.

"We shouldn't talk about it *at all*. Not yet."

If I thought punching him in the face would be helpful, I'd do it. But Vlad would use his superior speed to outmaneuver me before my fist connected. "When?"

"On the evening before your wedding. Your mother was very clear." I huff out a frustrated breath but nod. "Can I offer some unsolicited advice?"

"Will it cost me anything?" I deadpan.

"On the house." He leans close again. "There's a better answer than marrying the dragon. You just need to look for it."

And with that cryptic as fuck message, he kisses my cheek, congratulates me again, and leaves to wrangle Edina into a dance. While I can't hear them, I can tell she's pestering him to know what we talked about.

Eldoris swoops in and begins dancing with me. "Tell me," he commands.

"He knows everything," I admit.

Eldoris scoffs. "Of course he does. What else?"

"Later," I promise him, and while I can tell he wants to argue, he nods.

There's a better way than marrying the dragon.

What in the goddess's name could that possibly mean? My mother's directive was clear—marry someone of royal blood within three months or I can't be crowned queen. I know there are other options, but of the list she gave me, Kai was the least offensive option. He'd be an *attractive* option if I weren't infatuated with someone else.

So, what could that possibly mean?

I lose track of time as I get passed from partner to partner, the well-wishers congratulating me and Kai on the dancefloor rather than in a receiving line. I'm so lost in my head that I don't even realize when I land in the arms of Izar.

"You've been avoiding me," he says. He's usually easygoing and quick to smile, but today there's nothing but hard lines. It's like he and his brother flipped personalities.

Once again, my crowd closes ranks around us.

"You can call off your dogs," he jokes, but it falls flat. "You know I wouldn't hurt you."

"Do I know that?" My hand shifts on his shoulder. It's bonier than normal; he's lost weight in the days I haven't seen him. Now that he's close, I can see the dull sheen to his gray eyes, and the slightly haphazard strands of black hair tugged out of place.

I lower my voice to barely a whisper. "What I do know is that your court has attacked mine twice—once when our parents were still alive and once the other day—and you don't have plans to stop."

He swallows. "I'm saying *I* wouldn't hurt you."

"Because we're in the second generation?" I scoff. "We both know those friendships only go so far. We're wonderful in times of peace, but outside it, it's every Fae for themselves."

"That's how you feel then?"

"How am I supposed to feel?" I hiss. "If I ask what your navy is doing right now, would you tell me honestly? Or would you lie and say they're docked when I know for a fact that they're on the move?"

His mouth pops open.

Oh shit.

I was calling his bluff. I had no idea the armada was on the move; they would have blindsided us.

Alert our navy right away, I order Eldoris. *I want ships on every body of water ready for an attack. Do not let them get on land.*

In my peripheral vision, I see Eldoris murmur something to Edina. She gives him a sultry look and grips the lapels of his jacket, tugging him off the dance floor. Just two lovers sneaking away for a rendezvous.

"It's nothing personal," Izar says. I return my full focus to him, ready to play my role once again and mine for more information. I may not be the best soldier, but at this, I'm an expert.

"It feels personal," I murmur, trying to sound helpless like there's no way in all the realms that I'll be able to stop him.

"I'm only following orders. I'm not Hades. I can't oppose my brother at every turn and get away with it. Especially now that—"

I follow his gaze to where his mate is sitting beside a male I've never seen before. He's dressed as a commoner, but the rigid set of his shoulders tells me he's a guard.

I gasp. Some things in Faerie are sacred. Fated mates are one of them. You don't touch a person's fated mate, partly because the other would go feral and tear the attacker to pieces. But mostly because mates are a gift from the goddess, and are meant to be regarded in the highest manner.

"If Zahir is threatening Baxter, you need to tell someone. Oakley—"

Izar shakes his head sadly. "He's chosen his side."

Damn it. Autumn Court is working with Night Court.

I wasn't certain, and I hoped Gwyneira's alliance with us would spook Oakley into behaving, but it looks like it had the opposite effect. If they enlist the werewolf packs in their court to fight, we'll be in a world of hurt.

I send the message to Eldoris and receive his confirmation before I close our mental channel.

"You see my problem," he continues.

"Did you know your brother wants to marry me?" I ask.

Izar's mouth pops open again. "He's already married."

"That's what I said."

The music is coming to an end, but I have too much to learn from him, and there's no way we'll be able to talk openly again, not with Zahir keeping his mate as collateral.

"He's always had a thing for you," he mutters under his breath. As if I'll ever believe that's the reason he proposed marriage. "Not that it will mean anything. He's a misogynistic asshole who will never be happy because he's unhappy with himself."

"Is that your professional opinion?" I tease, and Izar relaxes enough to give me a small smile.

"Hypothetically," I begin carefully, "if Edina were to invite Baxter for dinner in her and Eldoris' townhouse in the Seelie Army Base. And he was, hypothetically, permitted to stay there so someone in the Unseelie Courts couldn't reach him. Hypothetically, what could you do for me?"

I open my mental channel with Eldoris just enough that he can hear me ask the question and will be able to hear Izar's answer. It's tricky since I know Izar can shatter my mental shield and peer at my thoughts with little to no effort, but I'm also dangling a carrot in front of him, so he may be more inclined to leave it alone.

"The navy is loyal to me, not Zahir," he says. "If I ordered them to drop anchor in the ocean, they would listen."

"And, if that were to happen tonight, where would they be dropping anchor?"

"At the mouth of the Shab River. Or just beyond it, not to raise suspicion."

So, they haven't left The Night Court yet. If they're not planning an ambush tonight, they must be planning one for my wedding. It's the right amount of time for them to skirt around the Winter Court's domain of the sea and return to land.

Received, Eldoris says. *Close the channel for now and keep me posted.*

"Then he should join us for dinner tomorrow evening." I lean in closer. "And if you're screwing with me, Izar, I will not hesitate to end you. Not your mate, I'm not a monster. I will end you. I recently had a very informative lesson in torture from my future sister-in-law, so believe me when I say that I would make it hurt."

"I understand," he whispers, and then louder. "You should consider my brother's offer. It would be beneficial for all of us."

The music ends; he bows, and I curtsy. As soon as he's gone, I release a long, heavy breath, closing my eyes until someone else steps into my space. The familiar citrus scent overwhelms me, and I want to collapse into Ari's arms.

"May I?" His grip on my waist is firm, pulling me in close as we sway to the melody, not saying a thing. I feel myself recharging simply by being in his presence. "Anyone else you need to charm into giving up state secrets?" he murmurs.

I grin. "I'm quite good at subterfuge, don't you think?"

"Brilliant." He says it with such sincerity that it makes me want to cry. The praise lights me up from the inside, and my magic jumps in my chest, little embers crackling and spreading through my limbs.

Damn, Vlad was right; I do have a praise kink.

"It will be a cold day in hell when I let you marry Zahir." His fingers absently brush the tendril of hair at the base of my spine.

"I won't have to." I glance at my betrothed, who speaks with King Oakley. Kai may pretend not to know politics, but I've seen him working over the members of opposing courts. He catches me watching and winks.

"Goddess," Ari grumbles. "Under other circumstances, I think I'd like the dragon." It startles a snort out of me. Then we're both cackling in the middle of a sensual dance that has many of the partners groping each other in public. "Why did Eldoris leave?" he asks. "Something Izar said?"

"Yes."

"I thought it might be something Vlad said." The vampire is currently swaying with Lysandra, speaking about something that has her cooing. "Speaking of you and Vlad—"

"Don't even start." He releases another one of those laughs I haven't heard in too long. "It was right after I was named heir apparent."

That sobers us both. If Ari hadn't left, we would have been together.

How different could my life have been if we had gotten together then? Would we have stayed together? Gotten married?

Would my mother have forced me to marry someone if she knew I was in love with Ari?

"Did Vlad say anything of use?" Ari asks. I push my musings aside; it won't do any good to dwell on what-could-have-beens.

"That's a whole can of worms I'm not prepared to open."

He nods. "Tomorrow, then."

I take one last look into Ari's eyes as the music comes to an end. "Tomorrow."

Chapter Twenty-Six
Ari

I CIRCLE PA FERIE, waiting for the sun to set so I can meet my contact at the island's far end, and mull over the information Devorah obtained at the ball. It's remarkable how much she was able to pry from Zahir and Izar. In just a few minutes, she learned of The Night Court's alliance with Autumn, their battle strategy, and the location of their naval fleet.

And, most promising, she learned Zahir is nervous. Devorah did such a good job in the aftermath of the battle, shoring up our defenses and convincing our court of her ability to lead, that his easiest strategies won't work. To reach us, he'll now have to bypass Winter Court's oceans or Day Court's mountains. Simi may play the part of an old bumbling grandfather, but he's as sharp as a spear. He told Devorah he had already narrowed down the pool of suspects for who could have altered his wards to go dark during the attack. And Gwyneira—he'd be a fool not to be afraid of her power.

As promised, Baxter is safely sequestered in the Seelie Army base, and the Night Court's armada hasn't moved yet. But it's only been a few days. It's hard to trust Izar explicitly, to believe he still isn't under Zahir's thumb.

Which is why I'm taking precautions.

I take another lap around the island as the sun dallies toward the horizon. For some reason, my contact was adamant we not rendezvous before sundown, but I needed to get out of the palace. Devorah and Kai are planning their reception, and no matter where I went, I couldn't escape her voice, her laugh, and my spiraling thoughts that it should be me beside her. Flying for hours seemed like a much more attractive option.

Devorah only shared one detail about the wedding: the ceremony will be small. Only royals, their partners, and Kai's family will be allowed inside the chapel. No courtiers. No advisors.

"I would never make you watch me marry another male," she said when I asked if she was sure that was the right move.

I didn't argue.

Finally, the last hints of orange and pink sky fade into indigo and purple, and the waning crescent of the moon replaces the sun. I bank right and head to the part of the island that's ignored by society members, the section where the sirens have their vacation homes. Sirens typically live in the Winter Court, preferring the perilous waters, but even the cold-blooded merfolk crave the warmth occasionally.

Which is why I'm here, descending in altitude toward a cove where a female waits, dangling her feet off the edge of a cliff. Sirens have three forms. One is an elemental Fae-like form where they have legs, one where their torsos resemble Fae but have beautifully scaled tails. The third is the thing nightmares are made of. They completely transform. Their skin turns leathery, their fingers turn webbed with black-barbed nails that can take away a Fae's magic, and their teeth turn razor sharp.

The female I'm meeting tonight is in her Fae form, her long purple hair with a natural wave that looks like she just emerged from the ocean. Her lavender skin reflects the moonlight, shining with luminescence. She wears nothing but a flimsy silk robe.

Celesta is a siren elder, one of the highest-ranking members of their underwater society. I've met her dozens of times, mostly in the Winter Court, though occasionally she'll pop up at other courts or in the Underground. Most recently, she was one of the judges in the competition that decided the Spring Court's monarch.

I land on the lush green grass that leads to the cliffside. Without turning to me, Celesta says, "Interesting wings." Her voice is a symphony, the melody and cadence impossible to recreate. I retract my wings and put on the shirt I stashed in the back pocket of my jeans. "Have you ever used them in the water?"

"Why would I do that?" I sit beside her and stare into the pitch-black sea.

"They remind me of a stingray." She turns to me. Her purple eyes shine as though they're permanently teary. She appears innocent, stunning. But the smile she has for me isn't one of flirtation; it's a predator's smile.

"I was surprised to receive your summons," she continues, leaving no room for me to process her odd observation. Where before she ignored my presence, now she's locked onto me, her gaze encapsulating and refusing to let me look anywhere else. "To what do I owe the pleasure?"

I don't bother with pleasantries. "I need a favor."

That takes her aback. Her flawless features shudder before they shift back into place. "You should know better than to say those words without qualifying them. Has your father taught you nothing?"

I'm not sure if I imagine the edge in her voice when mentioning my father, but I ignore it just the same. "This is worth it."

She clucks her tongue and pats my cheek like I'm a child. "So admirable, selling your soul to a siren to protect the female you love."

Hearing her say the word *love* so plainly, as if it's obvious, does things to me. It makes my stomach turn over; it makes my heart beat wildly in my chest like it can escape its confines.

I'm not in love. I care for Devorah in unspeakable ways, and I want to ensure her safety. But no, I can't be in love with her.

She places her hand atop mine. "I can feel your denial, but know that I don't use that word lightly or as a taunt. It's simply a fact.

"Now!" She claps, once again moving on with a speed that makes my head spin. As if she didn't just make me question my entire world. "I'm in a fairly amenable mood, and won't hold you to that simply asinine request. Tell me what you want and we'll negotiate."

I pack away her words, returning to my job. "I want an alliance," I answer. "The same one you have with Winter Court."

She purses her lips. "That's a big ask."

"You're an elder. You can make it happen."

"True."

"I want the sea protected from the tip of the Winter Court to the edge of ours. I want your help convincing the kelpies to protect the Padauk River."

At the mention of their sister species, Celesta sighs. "I can't agree to that, and you know it. Vicious little creatures. They're spoiling for a war so they can eat the flesh of those who die." As opposed to the sirens who kill for sport rather than sustenance. I keep that thought to myself.

"But," Celesta continues, "My school will align with you with the caveat that, should Gwyneira remove her support from Summer Court, so will the sirens. I won't go against her—it would be suicide."

I release a breath and roll my shoulders, which have crept up to my ears. It's not exactly what I want, but I don't anticipate Gwyneira withdrawing her alliance anytime soon.

"And in return?" I ask.

She doesn't hesitate. "I'd like a meeting with your father. Tonight."

"My father?" She nods, her features unreadable. "You know he's no longer the advisor."

"I'm aware."

"I'm not sure I can find him. We haven't spoken much since I took his position." He wasn't mad at me, quite the opposite, but he made it very clear that my job was to serve Devorah, that I should put her first. And she's kept me busy.

"Lucky for you, he's at your home on the island."

It makes sense that he would retire to our vacation home. Queen Talia purchased it as a gift for his many years of service. It's right beside her estate, so that when she, Devorah, and Eldoris vacationed here, we could be close by while also enjoying the beach.

"That's it?" I ask warily. "One meeting."

She turns her attention to the water. "Deliver him here before sunrise, and you'll have your alliance."

That seems entirely too simple.

I stand, still wondering what the hell she could want with my father as I remove my shirt, extend my wings, and take to the sky, returning to the wealthiest section of the island.

Compared to the mansions next door, the house is small, but it's cozy, and right on the water. But the house is dark; I hope Celesta's intel was correct, and I won't have to spend the night on a wild goose chase.

I land in front of the white, wooden steps that lead to a blue shingled house. Even though I haven't been here in a while, I know exactly how the grooves of the banister will feel, and the sound the third step makes when it supports my weight.

"Shouldn't you be guarding the princess?"

My father sits at the corner of the porch closest to the royals' summer house. Cloaked in darkness, I only make out his features when he lights some sort of cigarette. By the smell of the smoke, it's Taggu, a mild drug that grows in the Autumn Court and is typically used to relax. I conjure a magical light, keeping it dim.

His chocolate hair has grown out a bit, though it's still far shorter than most Fae wear, but he's shaved his beard completely. It makes him look younger—I actually look older than him right now—and the perpetual crease between his brows has softened. While I'm sure he's bored out of his mind, he can't dispute that retirement has done wonders for him.

"She has guards," I answer.

He scoffs and nods to the rocking chair beside his. I sit, and for a second, the only sound is the creak of our chairs, the crash of the surf, the crackle of fire, and subsequent inhale as he puffs from his blunt.

"Having trouble sleeping?" I ask, referencing the table between us, where there's a stack of pre-rolled paper cigarettes and an amber decanter that glows slightly from magic infusing the whiskey. I summon a glass and pour myself a measure.

"Always have. It's hard to turn your brain off when you've spent your life ready to defend." I take a sip and sputter as the whiskey burns my throat. Fuck this is strong. My father's eyes, so different from mine in their light brown, twinkle in the magical light. "Take that slow if you have work to do tonight."

"Could have used that warning a minute ago," I chuckle, and set the glass down. "Where'd you get that?"

"It was a retirement gift from Hades." I arch an eyebrow. "Your generation likes to think she only deals with you, but she and I have had a working relationship since she took over Summer Court's Underground. Still do. Her pixies are how I hear most of my gossip."

"That so?"

"Speaking of. There's a nasty little rumor about you and the princess, you know."

"Is there?"

He places his blunt on the edge of an ashtray and takes a sip of his whiskey. "Want to confirm it for your dear old dad?"

There's no way in fuck I'd tell my father anything about me and Devorah. Keeping boundaries was something he drilled into my head from the moment I emerged. If he knew how much I crossed that line, he'd probably kill me.

"You've always carried a torch for her," he chuffs.

"I have not."

"Since you emerged." He dares me to deny it.

"Do you know the number of females I've bedded since I emerged?"

"Which is how I know the signs." That feels so weighted, I'm surprised the porch doesn't cave in and deposit us on the beach within a tangle of splinters. He shakes his head absently. "Like father, like son."

I decide not to ask who his unrequited love was—even if it is killing me to know—because I don't want him to ask about Devorah.

That's twice tonight someone has implied I'm in love with Devorah. I've always found her attractive, and when we were younger—before I entered her family's employ—I would have done something about it.

But love? And long-lasting, unrequited love, at that.

That seems...tragic.

It wasn't like I was waiting for her. I meant what I said to my father, I'd been with plenty of females. But nothing ever felt right. Even when I was in a relationship, something was missing.

Fucking hell, maybe I *was* subconsciously waiting for her.

It doesn't matter. If I had realized my feelings and told her earlier, all that would have accomplished is worse heartbreak. She'd still be marrying Kai, he'd still be possessive, and we'd still have to stop seeing each other. All that would be different is that I'd have had her for longer. I could have had years instead of moments.

Like the mature adult I am, I avoid the topic in favor of picking up my glass again. "I have a favor to ask."

"'Course you do. Why else would you be here amidst all the threats to the princess?" His eyes meet mine. "Is it for the crown?"

"In a roundabout way. I need the help of the sirens."

"To keep an eye on the Night Court Armada?"

"We have a tentative solution," I weigh how much to tell him, and decide he doesn't need to know about our involvement with Izar. It's not that I don't trust him—my father would rather die than betray his court, even if Devorah fired him—but the less Fae that know about it, the better. "But I need the sirens to monitor it."

"And to be the first line of defense in case your solution isn't solid," he surmises. In tandem, we take a long drink of the whiskey, and I wince at the burn as it scorches a line of fire down my throat and warms my belly. "What did they want in return?"

"A meeting with you. Tonight."

His mouth flattens into a line. "Which elder?"

"Celesta."

My father, the most composed male I've ever met in my life, chokes on his whiskey. I stand, preparing to help, but he waves me off and gets it under control. "Celesta," he repeats, his voice strained.

"I assume you know what it's in reference to?"

"I have an idea." He puts his glass down and stands. "Let's go then."

"That's it?" I ask as he brushes past me to the end of the porch.

"You think I'd give up your chance at an alliance with the sirens over a conversation? I may be forcibly retired, but Devorah is like a daughter to me. I'm not going to let someone walk in and take her."

Something about that warms my heart, though maybe it's the whiskey. I took two sips and I feel like I'm about to keel over. Shaking loose the brain fog, I walk up behind my father. He doesn't have wings, so I'll have to fly him to the other side of the island. But before we go, I pause. "Do you know anything about Queen Talia's final will? About her orders for her succession?"

"No. I offered to help her with the record keeper, but she was adamant about handling it on her own."

It was a long shot, but I figured I'd ask.

I wrap my arms around his waist as I spring into the sky. "Goddess," he grumbles as I ascend. "I fucking hate flying." I laugh the rest of the way until we're back on the cove and I deposit him at the cliffside. Celesta is sitting exactly where she was when I left, bare feet dangling over the edge and purple hair floating around her in a halo as she stares out at the ocean.

"Well done," she purrs without looking at either of us. "I'd like to speak to Hershel alone, please."

"And?"

"You have our alliance. If Night Court ships move past their territory, we'll sink as many as we can."

I sigh in relief. "Thank you."

"Off you go," she waves me off, and turns to my father, who trudges over and sits fairly close beside her.

"I'll walk home," he assures me, so I nod and head into the sky.

Hopefully, Devorah and Kai are done with their wedding plans for the evening.

Chapter Twenty-Seven
Devorah

THREE MORE DAYS AND I'll officially be queen. Three fucking days. It can't come soon enough.

Of course, that means I'll be married in two days, but I choose to ignore that.

Over the past few weeks, I delegated most of the plans to my event planner and Kai. I claimed to have too much to do running the court and organizing the coronation, and while that's not a lie, the truth is that planning gives me a headache that no amount of tonic can sate.

Zahir has been quiet these past few weeks. Eldoris has spies and sentries monitoring things, but it seems like everything has come to a standstill. I'm not sure if the armada's stasis has thrown a wrench in his plan or if there's something worse coming.

The words on the contract in front of me start to blur, and I press my hands to my eye sockets to give them a short respite. It's late to be in my office, and I haven't been sleeping much between the stress and the early morning training sessions with Ari. I should take a break. Kai mentioned getting dinner—I should probably take him up on it. I'm not sure the last time I ate.

"Come in," I call when there's a knock on my office door.

Edina flounces into the room wearing a tight-black dress that's just a scrap of fabric. It has a thin strap that starts at one shoulder, crosses her breasts, and snakes back across her stomach before it widens into a short skirt. No one else could pull off that dress. She claims it's because she has no boobs and barely an ass, but I think it's because she has a ridiculous amount of confidence.

Behind her, Lysandra, wearing an off-the-shoulder ruffled top and dark denim jeans that are molded to her generous curves, and Larisa, who's wearing a sparkly mini-dress, enter my office.

"Why aren't you dressed?" Edina demands without greeting.

"For?"

She whirls to the other two, her blonde hair fluttering dramatically. "You didn't tell her?"

"Hades was supposed to," Lysandra shrugs.

"Tell me what?"

"Tonight is your bachelorette party!"

Bachelorette party?

No. Nope. Absolutely not.

I don't want to spend an evening that reminds me of my looming wedding. I'd rather stick my head in a vat of acid.

"Don't even think about saying no," Edina says, grabbing my arm and tugging me out of my desk chair.

"How are you this strong?" I ask, stumbling after her.

"You're not allowed to back out of this. Hades and I have been working on it for ages—"

"Days," Lysandra corrects.

"—and we're not taking no for an answer." She pulls me out of the office, and Lysandra and Larisa fall in line behind us, boxing me in.

"It'll be super low key," Edina continues. "Just some of the second generation."

"E—"

She lowers her voice so only I can hear. "Let us take your mind off everything for a few hours."

I meet her sapphire eyes, annoyingly full of sympathy and understanding. She's genuinely trying to be helpful. And maybe I do need a night out.

With a long, drawn-out sigh, I say, "Eldoris better not be there."

"Why would I invite your brother?" She grimaces. "Although the last time I threw a bachelorette party, I *did* accidentally invite the future mother-in-law, but she was awesome. She took a shot out of a penis ice-luge."

"You're not instilling confidence here," Larisa says.

Edina shoots her a glare. "Anyway, no partners of any kind."

I nod. "We're going to Tartarus?" Hades' night club would be the obvious choice for a party. Though I'm not sure I'll ever be able to go in there without thinking of Ari and the last time we were there.

"We're going to Styx," Lysandra announces.

I stop so abruptly, Lysandra and Larisa bump into me. "The strip club?" I take a step back so I can see all three of them. "A 'low-key night with the second generation' is at a *strip club*?"

"It's not like we're going to the sex club," Edina mutters.

"I talked her out of that," Larisa says. "You're welcome."

"Do you know the field day the gossips would have if they caught me in a strip club?" I ask. "I'm about to be a queen—"

In sync, Edina and Larisa point to Lysandra, who raises her hand high in the air. "I'm already a queen, and I'm going."

"Any other excuses?" Edina asks.

The three of them smile devilishly.

"I swear it'll be fun," Edina promises, and continues to guide me down the hall. I'm so stunned that I let her.

I guess I'm going to a strip club tonight.

We burst through the doors of my suite and find Kai sitting on my circular chair that overlooks the ocean. There's a breakfast tray balanced on his lap, and he's using tweezers to place little gems onto a canvas. "Is that a diamond painting?" Edina exclaims, running over and dropping beside him. Impressively, she does so without flashing any of us.

"Yes," he answers with as much enthusiasm. "My brother brought it back from the mortal realm." Edina squeals and starts chatting with him animatedly.

"The future Queen of the Winter Court. Distracted by shiny objects," I mutter. Without missing a beat in her conversation, Edina flips me off.

Chuckling, Lysandra and Larisa usher me into my bedroom. "Edina had Melia make you a dress," Larisa says, walking straight to my closet.

"Please, make yourself at home," I deadpan.

Lysandra smacks me lightly on the arm. "Play nice." And then, dropping her voice lower, "She's been trying to be a better friend to all of you. I don't know why you don't get along, but I swear she's nice."

I hold back a scoff. Larisa always had a superiority complex—and she's been an asshole to a lot of the second generation because we're not purely elemental Fae. Radley laughed it off, my brother ignored her completely, but I took it personally.

However, Lysandra is also half-human. If she has a positive view of Larisa, maybe she's changed. Her boyfriend might be a good influence. I grew up with Behar, and he's a good male.

Or maybe she just matured.

I give Larisa what I hope is a decent smile. I can try. I won't trust her, but I can be nice.

She passes me a white dress with two thin straps connecting to a sweetheart neckline. I put it on and cross to the full-length mirror. Three diamond cutouts descend my sternum. "Wow." The ruching in the front complements my figure, and it's short enough to be sexy without feeling like I'm going to expose myself.

Lysandra pushes me into the chair in front of my vanity and tousles my hair into sexy waves. Simultaneously, Larisa sweeps makeup over my eyes.

"You look hot," Edina says, leaning in the doorway. The girls move away, giving me a glimpse of myself in the mirror, and she's right. I do look hot. And somehow, I look like myself, or the version of myself before I took over the court. Back when I was unburdened and fun.

"Are you ready? We're meeting Hades and Radley there."

"Isn't a bachelorette party supposed to be all females?" Larisa asks as we follow Edina out of the palace.

She shrugs. "He heard us planning and told me if he didn't get an invite, he would just crash it."

"No Izar?" Lysandra asks carefully, regarding me cautiously.

"Hades doesn't allow her brothers in the Underground."

As soon as we breach the wards, I teleport us to the Summer Court's entrance to the Underground. It appears to be a normal tree—if you ignore the two sentries stationed on either side and the handful of archers in the canopy, bows pointed at the tree roots. We walk up to the base of the trunk and take a step down. The magic that camouflages the tree dissipates, revealing a dark stairwell.

"Why are the entrances to the Underground so theatrical?" Edina asks.

"Have you met Hades?" I quip.

The staircase is lit with flickering torches, and the earthen stone walls make it feel like entering a tomb. Vines snake up the walls; actual snakes slither and hiss and twine around the railings.

"Why is it always fucking snakes?" Lysandra shivers.

When we reach the bottom, the creepy torchlight turns into soft candlelight, and the earthen walls and floors are replaced by terracotta tiles and light blue paint. Paved tributaries branch off the main path, leading to the far reaches of our court.

The Underground extends beneath every inch of Faerie—except Winter Court—and each court is home to its own vice. Our section mostly houses restaurants and bars that appear normal until you see what's on the menu. As we pass a window, a server places a plate of pasta with a large kraken tentacle wiggling on top. The female being served—a harpy, with her wings retracted but beak on full display—claps excitedly, grabs it with both hands, and takes a large bite.

All three of Hades' clubs are beneath Night Court. Since it's three courts away and there are strict wards permitting teleportation, the fastest way is to take a shuttle. The shuttle is a large contraption that looks like a boat on wheels, with a giant propeller at the back. An elemental Fae with dark blue skin offers her hand to assist us up the ramp. When we're situated, she walks to the back of the boat and casts air into the propeller, shooting us down the hallway at impressive speed.

We cross into Day Court. Because of the height provided by the mountain range, this section of the Underground is reminiscent of a city.

Each floor of the tall buildings has a different business. There are signs advertising everything from fortune-telling seers to multilevel brothels, but the largest building with the brightest lights is a casino. It spans almost the entire main pathway between Summer and Night Courts.

As we leave Day Court behind, the walls shift from red clay to matte-black stones. The sound of gamblers' revelry is replaced by the thud of bass, and the sign for Styx flashes neon red.

After tipping the shuttle driver, we disembark and walk straight to the front door, bypassing the line of Fae, and push aside the black curtain that leads to the club.

In the center of the club is a catwalk made of clear glass blocks that have magical lights that pulse in time to the beat of the music. A siren's voice is weaving a melody that instantly makes my muscles relax and my center start to throb. On the stage, there's a trio of females doing a choreographed dance. Every time they turn, one piece of clothing disappears into thin air. At the same time, muscular males in nothing but sparkly boxer-briefs spin on poles.

Edina maneuvers us through tables where Fae of all races give lap dances. I can't help but grin when I see a pixie grinding on a troll.

We reach a table in front of the catwalk where Hades is speaking with Radley. He's sitting with his legs spread and fingers interlaced behind his head, and when he sees us, the biggest smile breaks out on his bearded face.

"Ladies," he yells over the music, abandoning Hades and crossing straight to me. He envelops me in a bear hug. Radley isn't much taller than me, but he still makes me feel small and fragile in his large arms.

He smacks a wet kiss on my cheek. I groan and shove him off. "Ahh, so it's you this time," he says, and pulls me onto his lap. "Not that I would mind cuddling up to your advisor, but I want to know what I'm getting into."

"It's me," I chuckle, flicking his nose. I try to get up, but he holds me fast.

"Stay," he whines. "I've missed you. We never hang out anymore."

"I've been busy." *And your father is in an alliance with my enemy.*

"I've been hiding in Spring Court," he says pointedly, picking up on my unsaid thoughts. "Puck and Lysandra are letting me stay in my suite in the palace until my dad stops being a douche."

I look into his deep brown eyes, and I know that even if his father is working against me, Radley disagrees.

It's a huge weight off my shoulders.

"Is he still on your dick about getting married?" I tease, changing the subject.

He laughs so hard it bounces me on his leg. Radley's dad has been bothering him for ages to get married and start popping out heirs. Because he's half brownie, he shouldn't have as many fertility issues as those who are pure elemental Fae, and his dad wants grandbabies.

"Maybe I should bite the bullet so he'll abdicate the throne." He tugs me closer and tries to lean his head against my boob. I push it to my shoulder. "It'll be different when we're in charge."

"You think?"

"Look at Lysandra and Puck. They're already bucking the norm." He waves it off. "Too serious a conversation to be having when a male's balls are inches from your face."

"What?" I turn forward and shriek when I find there is indeed a male at the edge of the catwalk rolling his hips in front of us.

We descend into giggles, and then Radley shoves me off his lap. "Time to go," he declares. "Unless you want to give me a dance." He waggles his eyebrows, and I smack him across the back of the head.

"Come here," Edina pats a chair between her and Hades. Lysandra is next to her, bopping in her chair, hands raised in the air.

I sit, and Hades motions to a server who brings over a tray of shots that have smoke billowing out of the top. "No," I groan. Magic-infused drinks are always strong, but when you mix liquors to make something smoke, it's bound to be a disaster.

"Yes!" Edina gives me a shot glass, passing them all around but leaving hers on the table in front of me. "And since I don't drink, you have to do mine too."

"Can't let it go to waste," Hades agrees, raising her glass. "To Devorah! And her loss of freedom."

"Don't be depressing," Radley yells. He clinks his shot glass with Larisa's and they both down the liquid, shuddering when it's down.

Maybe I do need a drink. If this is the last time I'll truly be single and the last night I won't have to worry about my image as a queen, I deserve to get fucked up. But I don't take both. Instead, I crook my finger at a female dancer and offer her the shot. She looks sidelong at Hades, who gives her a curt nod, then taps her glass with mine.

The dancer sits on my lap; the server brings over another tray.

"It's gonna be a good night!" Edina declares.

Chapter Twenty-Eight
Devorah

Fuck, I'm drunk.

Hah, that rhymes.

"No, it doesn't," Larisa laughs.

Guess I said that out loud.

I don't remember ever being this drunk. I feel fucking *amazing*. I'm not sure if it's the siren's song or the drinks I've happily started chugging, but I feel better than I ever have in my life.

Or maybe it's the female in my lap.

I've never particularly liked females—I've always preferred males—but she's very pretty, and a great dancer.

"Oh my god," Edina breathes. I turn and find a female straddling her, whispering something in her ear.

"Goddess," Hades amends. Edina is always slipping into her mortal colloquialisms, and it's become a running joke to correct her.

She doesn't even acknowledge it; she's too busy responding to whatever the dancer said. I can't hear over the music, but the female's wings pop out, and she blinks rapidly while Edina smirks. What the hell did Edina say to fluster a stripper?

Hades procures a skeleton key. "Eldoris told me to give you this. Private room twenty. He's waiting." Then, to the dancer, "Go play."

They practically upend the chair as they flee the table, leaving me gaping after them. "I'm going to pretend I didn't see that." I definitely don't need the mental image of my brother having a threesome.

"Probably smart," Hades says, sipping a whiskey.

"Am I supposed to tip them or something?" Lysandra asks as her male dancer returns to the catwalk.

"We're not in the mortal realm," Hades answers. "I pay them well."

"She does," the female still on my lap purrs. I honestly forgot she was there. Huh. My lap must be numb. Hades reaches over and smacks her ass before she runs off and cartwheels onto the stage.

A female in a smart suit appears at the table, leaning over and whispering something to Hades. Her long brown hair falls over her shoulder, obscuring her from view, so I go back to sipping on my drink and watching the show.

"Thanks, pet," Hades coos before pulling the female into a kiss that's hotter than the strip show, and then sends the female stumbling off with weak knees.

"Did Minthe want to join us?" Lysandra asks. Minthe, right. Minthe is Hades' assistant—and her submissive—but I think there's much more going on there. "I know we said no partners, but she's welcome—"

"We can't both take the night off," she says, righting her smeared lipstick and staring after Minthe. Lysandra shrugs and heads to the dance floor with Larisa, leaving me alone at the table with Hades.

"Is Minthe coming to the wedding?" I try unsuccessfully to get my straw in my mouth. It circles the drink three times before I give up and tip the drink into my mouth, plucking the straw from my cleavage when it finally reveals itself.

"I don't know," Hades responds, and then she blushes. Stone cold, immovable, never-shows-an-emotion-other-than-snark Hades *blushes.* "I think I'm in love with her."

I squeal and launch myself at her. She stiffens so much it's like hugging a board.

"I'm not sure that's what this is." She smacks me away until I sit back down. "It's intense. And it's more than sex. I...like being with her."

My thoughts turn to Ari, but I quickly banish them and say, "That's great."

"No, it's not. If my brother finds out, he'll use it against me. He's been trying to bend me to his will for ages, and I swear to the goddess if he hurts her, I would fucking tear the realm apart with my bare hands."

"Damn that's hot," Radley says, appearing between our shoulders. I have no idea what he did or where he went, but there's lipstick smeared all over his mouth, and glitter in his beard. He circles and drapes himself over Hades, sitting in her lap. Hades is tiny, barely five feet tall and thin. So, when Radley sits on her, she lets out an *oomph*. "Oh, please," he scoffs. "Don't act like you haven't had bigger males on top of you."

"I'm the top, darling."

Radley and I cackle, and he abandons Hades to sit on my other side. "So, Devorah—" he draws out my name for about ten syllables, "—how is sex with the dragon?"

I snag a drink from a passing server and chug the whole thing. Hades whistles long and low. "That bad?"

"I wouldn't know."

"No wonder you're wound so tight," Radley says. "You need to get laid."

I wave the hand with my betrothal ring in his face. "Off the market."

"Not for two days," Hades says with a sly smile.

But it would be cruel to sleep with someone when the only Fae I want, I can't have.

A MINUTE OR AN hour later, a male dancer appears in front of me. "I've been instructed to give the bride-to-be a private dance." He's remarkably attractive—blonde shaggy hair, green eyes so arresting they appear to glow, and a body that could have been cut from marble. He extends a hand, waiting for my permission.

"By who?" I ask, my words a little fuzzy.

"Me," Radley and Hades say in unison.

"Trust me," Hades says with a wink.

"Famous last words," I grumble. I eye the male in front of me warily. "I'm not looking for sex—"

His chuckle is a low, deep sound that I'm sure makes Fae trip over themselves. "Just a dance, Princess."

I'm not sure why this dance has to be in private—it's not like I haven't had Fae grinding on me all evening—but I reach for his hand. Then, I reach for it again once it has the decency to stop doubling until my hand connects with warm flesh. I wobble like a baby centaur, and the dancer wraps an arm around my waist and guides me toward the back of the club.

We go down a short hallway comprised of alcoves covered with thick curtains. It's much quieter back here, and some of the lust from the siren's song has dissipated. But, since I'm still properly smashed, the entire hall spins and warps.

The male opens one of the red curtains, and I stumble inside, right onto a leather couch. The alcove walls are matte black, lit with the soft, red glow of magical lights. It's barely enough to see the small polished table with a bottle of sparkling Faerie wine.

Before I can get settled, he leans over me, tipping my chin up and staring into my eyes. They search for a moment before he smirks. "I'll be right back," he says, and disappears behind the curtain.

I manage to drag myself upright and scoot to the center of the sectional, wincing as the leather sticks to my sweaty thighs. Relaxing back into the cushions, I let my eyes drift closed, allowing myself to soak up the relative quiet and cool temperature that comes from being away from the main club.

My thoughts drift back to what Radley and Hades said earlier. I have two days until I marry Kai, two days until I'm locked with him forever, and I haven't even kissed him yet. I could be in for a lifetime of sloppy kisses, bland sex and zero passion. Maybe I should have one last hurrah.

Soft music with a throbbing beat begins playing, pulling me out of my head. I drag my heavy lids open as the curtain is pulled back.

My breath catches.

The room simultaneously spins and stills.

The air gets thick.

"What are you doing here?" I whisper as Ari slips into the room. Did Hades send for him? Is this why she wanted me to go to a private room? Or did I summon him by the sheer power of my thoughts?

His smile turns devilish, and he presses a finger to his lips. The music grows louder and Ari's hips roll, stealing all questions from my alcohol addled brain.

He prowls around the table, stopping to grab the bottle of Faerie wine and uncorking it with a loud pop. Frothy bubbles cascade down the neck of the bottle until Ari tilts it over my mouth. I dutifully open, and he pours a measure down my throat. His purple eyes never leave mine as he pauses for me to swallow. I smirk and open my mouth again. He chuckles, dark and sensual, but there's something...

The thought is like water through my fingertips, and I lose hold of it as soon as Ari takes a swig from the bottle. I watch his throat bob as he swallows, and my throat dries. Sensing my attention, he places the bottle back down and places his hands on either side of the couch behind me. My hands lift to run along his chest, but he slides back just out of reach and shakes his head.

"No touching?" I ask, and he nods. And I suppose that's for the best. If we never touch, it's completely innocent.

Once again, his strong arms brace beside my head, and he begins rolling his hips in time to the music. His powerful muscles flex and contract, showing just enough through his shirt that it's a total tease. Ari moves like he's been doing this for his entire life. I really should have fucked him when I had the chance.

He stands, his eyes never leaving mine as he slowly peels his shirt from his body. He's oiled up, and I giggle at his commitment to the part. My head is swimming, so much so that I can barely see Ari's tattoo over his heart—it looks more like a black blob than the Summer Court crest.

"Eyes on me," Ari says, and I blink through the haze to find him. His voice is guttural, and while the words are stern, there's still amusement on his features. He banishes the table and summons a chair in its place.

I take it at his urging, but my posture is rigid, my legs clamped together like my life depends on it.

He saunters to me, placing one leg on the seat beside me and leaning down so he's speaking in my ear. "Let yourself enjoy this."

Before I can answer, he's rolling his hips, his bulge so close to my face that I giggle once again. I give myself over to the dance, letting Ari perform for me as he moves from simple thrusting to more complicated moves—one of which has him tipping the chair back and landing on top of me with a full body roll.

The chair disappears, and Ari flips me over even though he barely touches me. "Fuck," I breathe as his hands brace around my throat and pull me up so my back is bowed.

"You like that, Princess?" he asks, grinding into my ass.

"I—" Wait.

That's not right.

Ari doesn't call me Princess. And the voice...it's off slightly.

He flips me over so our faces are inches apart. My eyes flit down to his chest once again. His tattoo. It wasn't my eyes or the alcohol. It's not a crest at all, just a circle.

I break the rule and touch the man above me. Magic sparks and his visage flickers briefly, purple eyes turning to green before they turn back again. I scuttle away, and the male wearing Ari's face lets me go, sitting back on his heels and holding his hands up in supplication.

"Remove the glamour," I command.

"Your Highness—"

"Now."

The male sighs and drops it, revealing the blonde dancer who brought me back to the room. I feel like I'm going to hurl. I press the back of my hand to my mouth to keep the night's drinks from reappearing. "Explain."

"It's a service we offer," he says. "I use mental magic to see who you fantasize about and become that for you. The boss—and Prince Radley—requested it for you; they thought you'd enjoy it. I assumed you knew."

The fun buzz I had going is completely gone, leaving only the kind of drunk that makes me want to cry.

I reach for the couch behind me, grasping it to help me stand. The male offers his help, but I can't touch him. Not when I was that vulnerable around him. Not when he looked into my head.

"I'm magically bound to secrecy," he swears.

"I believe you," I say listlessly, and exit the alcove alone. My vision is swimming, so I'm not sure how, but I make it back to the main room and the table. Edina and Eldoris are standing by Hades, emphatically telling a story. Radley is nowhere to be seen.

"You're a real bitch, you know that?" I say to Hades, interrupting my future sister.

"What?" It takes her a minute to realize I'm speaking to her, and for that minute, her typically impassive expression slips into utter confusion.

"Did you think that was funny?" My voice is cold, not revealing the tempest of emotions I'm suppressing. "Or were you trying to fuck with my head?"

"I wasn't—"

"Because that—" I gesture to the back, "—pretending to be my friend and then screwing with me is worse than anything your brother has done. Or maybe that's the point. Maybe you're actually working with him and this has all been a crock of shit."

"What?" Eldoris demands.

Hades stands so abruptly that it makes me stagger backward. "I might be a bitch," she says measuredly, "but I don't lie. If I wanted you dead, I'd look you in the eyes while I did it."

"Hades," Edina warns. I'm not sure when, but she wound up behind me, directly over my shoulder. Judging by the way the temperature has dipped, her magic is brewing right under the surface.

"Don't threaten me in my own club, Edina," Hades snaps back, shadows pooling in her hands.

"What's going on?" Lysandra steps between me and Hades, pushing us both back a step.

"Just a misunderstanding," Hades responds, not taking her eyes off me and Edina. "I got Devorah a present, and it wasn't received well."

"A present?!" I shriek.

"It was," Radley appears behind Hades, hands up in supplication. "We thought you'd like it. I swear. No bad intentions."

I can sense the truth in their words, but I'm furious and sad and *really fucking drunk.*

A lump rises in my throat, and I can't say another word. So, I just shake my head and walk away, leaving the club.

I don't look back, but I feel Eldoris and Edina following me, on the shuttle, up the stairs, and back to the palace. They stay five steps behind me until I slam the door of my suite in their faces and run into my bathroom to throw up.

Chapter Twenty-Nine
Devorah

"WHY ARE PRIESTESSES ALWAYS late?" Edina grumbles. Despite her agitation, she looks bright and peppy. Unlike me. The only reason I don't look like I got hit by a boulder is because Kalinda worked some magic to even out my green complexion and erase the bags under my eyes. That's what happens when you drink a troll's weight in magically infused alcohol.

Today is the wedding rehearsal. Sunlight streams through the clear ceiling of the small chapel, playing off the blue stones so it feels like we're underwater. The pews have been polished so they gleam in preparation for tomorrow, and, as we speak, earth elementals weave elaborate arrangements of jasmine and calla lilies for the rose quartz altar. It's all a little too bright and cheery for my current disposition, but it's beautiful.

Kai huffs in agreement, also looking a little worse for wear. After we left for the club, his brother—Ormr—kidnapped him for the dragon equivalent of a bachelor party. I didn't ask what it entailed, but he stumbled into the suite around dawn, soaking wet and wearing a golden crown on top of his head.

Most of the small group here to witness the rehearsal have long since given up standing while we wait for the priestesses. Kai's parents, decorated in their gold finery, are sitting in the first pew, where they'll sit tomorrow. Edina and Eldoris have taken to lounging on the altar, Edina between my brother's legs as he runs his fingers through her hair. Kai and his brother have taken spots nearest the open door—even though there's no breeze coming in from the jungle. He's tried multiple times to get me to sit with him, but despite being nauseous and exhausted, I can't sit still, pacing back and forth up the aisle.

"Let's go over the processional," Narolie, our event planner says. When no one immediately moves, she claps her hands in clear command and everyone snaps to attention. Kai's parents don't move—since they're already in their seats—but they sit up straighter. Edina takes her spot in the first pew on the opposite side of the aisle.

Kai and Ormr follow Narolie to their places at the altar, Kai on the top step with his brother flanking him. They face toward the door, where Eldoris and I will enter.

"Right," Narolie says, scurrying down the aisle to us. It doesn't matter that she's almost a foot shorter than my brother, she moves him to my right side with ease, and maneuvers our arms so his is linked in mine. "You'll be holding a bouquet...." She snaps her fingers and one of the earth elementals creates a small bunch of flowers and tosses it to her. She wraps my fingers around it and pushes my hand down to where she wants me to hold it.

"And we're walking on one, two, three—" she counts, walking backward in front of us at a snail's pace. "This is the speed. Do. Not. Go. Faster."

I had no idea Narolie was such a drill sergeant, Eldoris says through our mental channel, as she barks at us to move even slower.

This is mild; she's been worse.

Would you be mad if I hire her for the army?

We reach the end of the aisle, and Narolie instructs Kai to descend the steps, shake Eldoris' hand and then take mine and help me up the stairs. My brother takes his spot to my left, the mirror of Kai's brother.

"Then, we'll start the ceremony."

We all pause, looking at the side door that leads to the priestesses' residence. It's traditional for three priestesses to bless a marriage, amplifying the magic of the binding. We've only met the head priestess, today we'll meet the other two.

Narolie taps her foot impatiently. Between the dinner tonight, the wedding reception, and the coronation in two days, I know she's stressed out. I tried to assure her that we didn't need her for today's rehearsal, but she just pursed her lips at me and led us down the path to the chapel.

"A Goddess blessed afternoon to all."

The priestess flits into the room without a care in the world—seemingly unaware that she's kept us all waiting for the better part of the day. Most Fae lack urgency, but that typically refers to the number of days it takes to do something, not hours. The head priestess is the same who performed my mother's burial, and—after being magically sworn to secrecy—will be the same priestess who performs my coronation.

She pats Kai on the cheek with her tiny hand before kissing mine. It's like being brushed by a butterfly. "Are you ready for tomorrow?" she asks excitedly, and then doesn't wait for a response before continuing. "My sisters—" which is the honorific all priestesses call each other "—will be here momentarily, but I wanted a moment with both of you to confirm what we discussed. This is the last chance you'll have to change the magic of your binding ceremony, so I want to be clear."

She casts a shield around us so no one else can hear before extracting a small notebook from thin air. "As per our discussion the other day, you would like your marriage to only include the two of you, no other partners under any circumstances?"

"Correct," Kai says, and I nod stiffly.

"This includes emotional and physical affairs." Again we nod. "A physical affair includes anything intimate—including, kissing, oral sex, traditional sex, anal sex, and use of toys or any appendages with another who is not your spouse."

"Yes."

"This does not include masturbation, but does include any instance of voyeurism—including strip clubs or sex shows—when your spouse isn't present."

"Yep," I grit through my teeth. Though I have no desire to return to any of Hades' clubs after last night, it's still annoying that I'm unable to without Kai accompanying me. But he insisted.

"Both parties are held to the same standard, and should the magic regarding fidelity be broken in any way, the penalty will be death."

I pinch the bridge of my nose against the headache brewing, but I nod. The death clause is a barbaric standard to all marriage contracts. It's part of the reason so few Fae get married.

"There is just one final question that we didn't answer." She summons a pen, prepared to jot down our answer. "Neither of you has met your fated mate. In that situation, what would you like to happen?"

I didn't even think about that.

Because Fae are immortal, a fated mate can be revealed at any point in one's life, and some never meet their mates simply due to timing. One female I knew was centuries old when her mate emerged and the bond snapped into place. Others—like my brother—grew up with their mates.

As such, fated mates are typically regarded as the exception to all rules when it comes to marriage contracts.

"If one of us meets our mate, we'll remain married, but all rules of fidelity are null and void when it comes to the mate," I assert before Kai can open his mouth. I won't give up my one chance at true, goddess-blessed love.

"I don't share," Kai growls, and I jerk my hand from his grip. Even the priestess looks shocked.

There have only been three documented times where a Fae rejected their mate. In the first two cases, both Fae involved killed themselves shortly after. The third...

My eyes lift to find Edina. She can't hear us, but from the rigid set of her jaw I know she suspects something is wrong and is ready to go to war for me. She knows first-hand what being rejected by a mate does to a Fae.

For me to inflict that pain on someone else, I wouldn't survive it.

The priestess does all she can to convince Kai. She insists that a mating bond is a gift, a blessing. But I can tell by the set of his shoulders that he won't budge on this. He won't falter, won't change his mind.

I look between Edina and my brother, two Fae who—despite tragedy surrounding their mates—found each other and fell madly in love. They're the ones who will suffer if this marriage doesn't go through. I can make one more sacrifice to ensure they get their happy ending.

"It's fine," I cut the priestess off. Her tiny features fall. Kai's gaze settles on mine. I know he was thinking he'd get more of a fight from me, but I'm so fucking tired of fighting. I just want to get this over with so I can be coronated and start focusing on my court.

The priestess goes over a few other details, mostly expectations for Kai regarding his title. He won't be king, he'll be a consort. I won't have anyone think he's above me even for one second.

Those terms he agrees to easily.

I disassociate as she finishes, snapping back into myself only when the shield around us drops and the priestess calls for her sisters.

The side door creaks open and a brownie walks in, her mahogany skin-tone rich and warm against the starkness of her pressed white robes. She crosses the space surprisingly fast for someone with such short legs, and bows deeply to me before shaking Kai's hand. He has to practically kneel to reach her.

Following a moment behind is a beautiful female with pale pink skin and magenta freckles spotted over the bridge of her nose matching her short hair. The second she walks through the door she freezes, her eyes connecting with Kai, who rises from his crouched position as if in a trance.

The air in the chapel crackles and—though invisible—I can practically see the shimmering golden thread between them go taut. It's an intense magic, filling the room with a lightness that I've seen only a handful of times.

"Oh fuck," Edina breathes, shattering the silence. No one else speaks. How could we?

What words are there to possibly say as I witness my betrothed meet his fated mate?

"I…" the female looks to the pixie priestess before looking at me, and ultimately back at Kai who is rooted to the spot.

He swallows and opens his mouth. Oh, shit. Kai just insisted we be monogamous.

He's going to reject her.

"Wait," I say hurriedly, an idea taking shape. The pixie hasn't performed the binding ceremony; we change the rules of the marriage. Kai and I can be together in name only, he and his mate can live in the palace in their own suite.

And I can have Ari.

I take both of Kai's hands, stealing his attention from the priestess, who growls slightly as I make him face me. "We'll make it work. We can have an open marriage."

"I don't share, Devorah." A puff of smoke releases from his nostrils. "And I have no desire to be shared. I couldn't be your husband in public while also having a mate. I'd feel unfaithful. And that wouldn't be fair to her."

"It wouldn't have to be hidden," I press, knowing I sound a little hysterical. "Everyone will understand. It's not like it hasn't happened before. Gwyneira is married to her mate and six others for goddess' sake."

He shakes his head, closing off again. Fucking dragons and their stubborn streak.

I brace myself to hear the words that Kai will speak to reject his mate. I've heard them before; I know what it sounds like, know how the breaking of that magic affects everyone in the vicinity, as if we're forced to share their pain. Stealing one last look at the female priestess—I'm not sure I'll be able to face her once this all happens—I try to offer her condolences with just my eyes, but she's still locked on Kai.

A large hand on my cheek pulls me back to my betrothed. The earlier anger has morphed into sadness and regret. "I'm sorry, Devorah," he says.

I'm not sure I hear him. No, I can't be hearing him correctly at all. Did he just apologize to me?

"I can't marry you."

My brain goes blank. No matter how hard I try to comprehend those words, they won't sink in. My mouth opens, then closes, then opens again.

What. The. Actual. Fuck?

"Excuse me?" Eldoris says for me. I sense rather than see him step up behind me, Edina flanking my other side as the three of us stare down my betrothed. "You gave your word."

"That was before..." he tries to peek back around at the priestess, but the three of us shift to block his view.

My face goes hot, my fire magic rushing to the surface with an intensity I've never felt before. "You just..." I blow out a breath; it comes out as steam. "You just made this big fucking deal about fated mates interfering in our marriage. How you don't share."

"We're not married, Devorah."

"You made a commitment all the same."

"And I hate that I can't honor it. But you can't expect me to give up my fated mate for a loveless marriage."

No, that's just what he wanted *me* to do. He insisted it be just the two of us, assured me we'd grow to love each other in time.

He asked me to give up everything.

And I agreed. I could have gone to one of the other options, but I swallowed it all down, because marrying Kai was the lesser of all the other evils. He didn't demand anything other than my exclusivity, and I could have handled that. But when I ask him to bend, just a little...

"Devorah, I'm so sorry," he repeats, reaching for me. He pulls his hand back with a hiss of pain, and I am vaguely aware that the fingertips that touched my skin are charred.

I want to scream. I want to tear Kai's fucking head off. But his parents are there, I can't afford to alienate Shesha.

"I'll step in," Ormr says, putting himself between me and Kai. "You can marry me."

"No," Shesha says. "You're the future ruler of the dragon hoard. You're ineligible." Ormr swears.

With Herculean effort, I swallow down my anger and turn to Shesha. "I want your undying loyalty, and I want use of your sentries on my side in every skirmish, battle or infighting. From now until the end of fucking time, you'll serve the Summer Court."

Shesha growls softly at the restrictions I'm imposing, but his mate places her hand on his shoulder to hold him back. She knows that the second I become queen, I could order Kai's execution for his betrayal. They live in *my* borders. We've let the dragons govern themselves out of mutual respect, but no fucking more. They owe me. Now I need to quickly find another husband before I assume the throne. The other monarchs aren't stupid; they'll figure out that marrying is a stipulation of my ascension, and we'll be vulnerable to attacks.

Shesha looks at the door like he's considering bolting with Kai and his mate. There's a flash of movement, and the door shuts with a resounding clang. The temperature dips, and ice creeps along the windows as Edina effectively seals everyone inside.

With a resolute nod, Shesha stands and extends his hand. "I agree to your demands." His magic—like smoke and brimstone—wraps around us, sealing the deal as I place my hand in his and the agreement between us solidifies.

The ice evaporates completely as I turn on my heel. I don't look back at Kai as I walk straight down the aisle and out of the chapel, but I feel the ripple of magic as he and his priestess accept their mate bond.

"Dev—" Eldoris starts as we exit into the thick of the jungle. I don't turn around, don't acknowledge him as I walk straight toward the beach, willing the tears not to fall.

He murmurs something to Edina, and she jogs up beside me. When her cold hand touches mine, steam expels into the air. "Your magic is still too close to the surface," she says softly. "Let me help."

I ignore her and keep walking toward our private cove. As soon as I reach the pink sand, I kick off my shoes and run straight for the sparkling water. The waves reach for me, knowing what I need as I charge ahead, water splashing around my ankles and kicking up white froth until I reach the shelf where it drops off.

Plunging under the water, I swim further out, seeking cooler temperatures. Steam is billowing off me, but nothing cold enough to soothe the inferno raging inside me.

I pop up for a moment, gulping down air, before sinking straight down and letting the water muffle my savage scream.

Chapter Thirty
Ari

THE PALACE TREMBLES.

I look up from the mountain of paperwork I've been working through these past few weeks. It's been the only way to avoid all the wedding bliss that coats the palace halls. Currently, I'm trading missives back and forth with Hades to ensure her argument with Devorah doesn't spark a war with The Underground. Eldoris didn't tell me what the fight was about—I'm not sure he even knew—but he impressed the importance of smoothing things over.

Thankfully, Hades' last message just said:

Devorah owes me one.

Not ideal, but not the worst thing that could happen.

Another shockwave rocks the foundation, the glass windows clinking in their metal frames. Books shift on my shelves, a wooden clock falls to the floor, emitting a final squealing tick as it smashes into shards.

I throw open the door of my office. Chaos. Pure and utter chaos.

Even though the tremor has subsided, Fae are screaming and crying. Palace guards, servants, and the guests who have already begun arriving for the rehearsal dinner rush to the closest windows. "What's happened?" I demand, snagging a guard by the collar of his tunic.

"We don't know, sir," he says, his eyes a little wild. "There's—"

"Look!" someone shouts, pointing out the window in the direction of the ocean. I push my way through the crowd, elbowing a male out of the way when he doesn't give me a clear path.

In the center of the ocean is a plume of thick, white smoke. It writhes in the air, snaking its way through the cloudless blue sky. Little flames arc over the tops of the trees before plunging back into the water. "What in the goddess' name—" I murmur.

A gigantic explosion of ruby red flames replaces the smoke, shooting straight into the sky. It looks like liquid magma, and if I didn't know better, I'd say a volcano erupted. The air ripples as heat stretches out in a bulbous wave. Fae scream and duck as it smacks into the palace. Rock shivers. Glass shatters.

A tsunami-sized wave swallows the fire with a thunderous hiss before the water rushes away from the shore.

Away from the shore?

"Are we under attack?" someone asks. I shake my head. There are only two Fae with water magic powerful enough to make a wave that large, and both are our allies.

It has to be Edina.

But who made the fire?

"Ari," a voice calls. Narolie flies over the heads of the Fae, low enough that she kicks a centaur in the head. Her hair is askew, her smart blazer shredded from her wings, and her usually confident expression has given way to a mixture of rage and panic.

She lands in front of me and her magic wraps around us, a shield sliding into place that will keep our conversation private. "Eldoris told me to come straight to get you," she says, her eyes briefly looking at the window, where the smoke is rising again.

"What's happening?"

"It's Devorah."

It's like she tore the rug out from under me. Devorah is making that fire. Devorah is...exploding.

What the fuck happened?

"Eldoris said you'd know where to find them—"

I shatter her shield, shouting to the guards to keep everyone in the palace until Devorah, Eldoris, or I return. With a blast of fire, I punch through the glass window and dive through, extending my wings just before I reach the tops of the trees.

I land on the pink sand of the cove beside Eldoris, who's watching as the smoke turns from white to black. Glaciers form and break apart in a dizzying dance of ice and fire.

A blonde head surfaces near the worst of the smoke, panting. In synchronicity, Eldoris and I take a step into the shallow water. Edina's sapphire eyes turn to both of us, her mouth in a hard line before she gulps in air and dives down again.

A sonic boom rocks the beach as more fire explodes—this time going wide as well as straight into the air. Eldoris and I drop to the ground, landing in shallow water. I expect to smell the burning of foliage as the fire hits the jungle trees surrounding the cove, but it runs into a shield and gets absorbed by the sand.

"Smart thinking," I mutter. Eldoris and I rise, adding more magic to the shield in case Devorah's magic weakened it.

"I knew you were training my sister," he says, almost to himself. "And I knew she had to be stronger than she gave herself credit for, but I didn't know it'd be like this."

Even in our sessions, she's been controlled, almost reserved. But this... This is undiluted, unrestrained power.

"What happened at the rehearsal?" I demand. Because for Devorah to lose control like this means something terrible happened. My mind spirals, conjuring worst case scenarios.

His ocean eyes—mirrors to his sister's—turn to me. They're filled with sadness and worry. "One of the priestesses who was performing the wedding is Kai's mate. She walked in and the bond activated."

"By the goddess," I breathe. And then, "Did you say she *was* performing the wedding?"

Eldoris' voice goes thick. "Kai backed out. Dev was... Her skin was so hot it burned his hand when he tried to touch her."

"She burned a dragon?" I gasp. That's not an easy feat; most of us with fire magic have a high heat tolerance.

"I could practically see her shoving down her magic, and even through all that, she made Shesha pledge his hoard's allegiance."

Of course she did. I'd expect nothing less.

"Then she walked straight into the water and..." He gestures to the ocean as if to say, 'you see what's happened.'

And with good reason.

We have two days before the coronation. Devorah needs to find a new husband without alerting the other courts.

But that's a problem for later. Right now, we need to figure out how to get her out of the water without her setting the entire court alight.

Edina resurfaces, and this time she looks pissed. "This isn't gonna be pretty," she yells, before she dives again. Almost instantly, water smothers the flames and the smoke dissipates. An iceberg floats up from the depths of the ocean, bobbing on top of the surface before Edina appears beside it. With a burst of frigid magic, Edina pushes the ice to shore.

Without thinking, I charge into the sea, water flooding my shoes and climbing up my pants. When they reach the shelf, Edina shakes the water from her hair like a dog.

Inside the crystalline ice, Devorah is trapped with her arms outstretched, her mouth open wide toward the sky in a silent scream. Her hair fans out around her like strands of seaweed caught in turbulent tides and the white dress she wore to her rehearsal is singed into a mottled mix of brown and black.

"Kitten," Eldoris barks, clearly triggered by the sight of his twin submerged in ice.

She whirls on him. "Anytime I got close to her she burned me," she snaps, matching his tone. "I did what I had to do to get her out of the water. And before you *growl* at me again, the only reason she didn't drown out there is because I kept the water away from her nose and mouth."

Eldoris sighs. "I'm sorry," he murmurs, chastised. Edina winces as he lifts her hand to inspect the reddened skin of her palm. He presses a gentle kiss to it before drawing her into his arms.

"Can she still breathe?" I ask, and Edina nods. Devorah's eyes are wild and unfocused, lost as the magic courses through her, trying to escape the ice prison. "How do we get her out?"

"We need to calm her down first," Eldoris answers. "Then Edina can melt the ice."

"If she doesn't beat me to it," Edina adds. As she says it, Devorah's skin glows orange and the layer of ice closest to her bubbles and melts.

I take one step forward and her eyes snap to mine. She's not in her right mind right now, drunk on power, a slave to her despair and anger. Every emotion is etched on her face, but mostly, I sense her fear.

"Beautiful," I breathe, and the primal set of her eyes softens slightly. "I'm so proud of you." Her brow creases and a huffed breath makes the water around her nose melt before Edina hardens it again to keep her from inhaling.

"No one can ever call you weak again, Devorah. No one would dare face the wrath of your magic.

"But I need you to let it go." As if spooked, her fire flares. Spider-webbed fissures breach the outer layer, and Edina pours more magic into it. "It's okay. No one will hurt you. Everything will be okay."

She seems skeptical, so I inch closer and place my hand on the ice, right beside where her face is, as if I can reach inside and stroke her cheek. "I want to hold you while we figure this out. Please, let me in."

I can almost see the tears in the water. The anger from before is gone, leaving only crushing defeat. "Let her go," I order. When Edina doesn't immediately react, I whirl on her. "I said, melt the goddess-damned ice."

"It's okay," Eldoris reassures. Edina angles herself in front of him, as if she needs to protect him from his twin. Very slowly, the ice around Devorah begins to melt, first around her face, then it creeps down her body until her hands are free, then her torso, and finally her legs.

When she's completely released, she collapses forward, but I'm there, wrapping my arms around her as we sink into the shallow water. The waves lap around us, coming up to my waist as I tuck Devorah into my chest and kiss her temple.

"My beautiful queen," I murmur, stroking her back as she sobs into me. When her breaths get choppy and uneven, and her skin starts to heat again, I whisper, "Give me five things you can see."

She shakes her head against my chest. "Nothing, Ari. I can't..." She shudders and pulls back. Her eyes are red rimmed, but somehow the glassy sheen of tears makes her even more stunning than usual. I cup her cheek in my hand, the ocean water from my skin dripping down her chin and neck. "I'm out of moves."

"We'll find one together," I assure her. "I have you."

"Everyone will know by now." Her eyes get that unfocused look again so I pull her even closer, resting my forehead on hers. "We can't fight a war on all sides."

"We won't."

"You can't promise me that." She starts to pull away, closing her eyes, so I thread my fingers through her hair and pull her back in.

"Devorah," I whisper, my breath fanning over her lips. "There is nothing we can't do together. Nothing we can't accomplish. I will not stop until we have a solution, do you understand?"

She nods slightly. My eyes drift to her lips on their own accord and her tongue pokes out to wet them.

I don't know how long we sit there like that, just gazing at each other while the ocean rushes around us, but eventually Devorah murmurs, "My brother is gone."

Looking over my shoulder, I indeed find that he and Edina have retreated, probably to seek a healer for Edina. "Seems so." Her hand is back to its normal temperature when she runs fingers over my jaw. "Is there a reason you mentioned that fact?"

"Because I'm not betrothed anymore," she rasps. I hadn't allowed myself to think of that little fact, to celebrate that she was free again. Free to be mine. She was in crisis, and if I let myself think of that, I wouldn't have been able to help myself.

But self-control is an illusion when it comes to her. So, when Devorah leans in to place a kiss on the corner of my mouth, I tug her closer and she submits to me. I kiss her cheeks, tasting the salt on her skin—from the sea or her tears, I'm not sure. She moans softly as I move down the slope of her neck to its hollow, and I can feel the vibration on my lips. "What do you need from me?"

"You," she says, and I ascend, halting inches from her lips.

"You need me to distract you?" And as much as it would kill me if she said this is just as a distraction, I can settle for that. I'll settle for any piece of her that I can get.

"No." It's her turn to lean in and kiss my jaw. "I need the safety I feel with you." A kiss just below my ear. "I need the way you make me feel cherished but strong." A kiss on my pulse point. "I need the way you make me feel lighter, like you're stealing some of the crushing weight from my chest."

I miss the heat from her lips as she pulls away to look me in the eye, so I see the sincerity in each of these words.

"I need all of you. I need you more than I need fucking air."

Chapter Thirty-One
Devorah

ARI AND I CRASH together like the surf that meets the shore around us. His lips claim mine, and we both moan as our tongues find each other's, stroking with fevered movements. His hand braces against my throat. Not choking, just a possessive hold that promises he'll never let me go again. The other fumbles for the hem of my dress, which is trapped between us.

"For fuck's sake," he grumbles against my lips, standing and hauling me up with him before depositing me in the thigh-deep water. He grasps part of the singed material at my neckline and rips until the dress unravels, leaving me only in my lace panties.

My fingers claw at his belt, the button, and the zipper of his pants as he tears his shirt off over his head. His cock springs free as soon as I push his pants down to his knees, and I whimper. I can't wait to know what his piercing feels like inside me. Between that and the size of him, I'm positive I'll be sore tomorrow.

"Keep looking at me like that, beautiful, and I'll come before we even get started." I kiss his chest, right over his tattoo, as my fingers trail down his length before rolling over the metal stud. "Shit," he swears, his head tilting back as I pump him, the soft skin of his hard cock wet from the ocean water. "Fuck, Devorah, just like that."

Watching this male fall apart from only my hand has me so fucking wet I can barely stand it. I squeeze my thighs together, seeking friction. As if he senses my need for something, Ari grabs my throat again and uses the grip to tilt my head the way he wants. His soft groans mix with my own as he sucks on my tongue and nips my bottom lip.

"I need you to stop," he growls, putting his hand atop mine and holding it still at the base of his cock. "I need to be inside you."

"We should go somewhere private."

"Now you're modest?" he chuckles, gripping my ass hard enough that the lace from my panties digs into my skin. It's something that shouldn't be so fucking hot, but combined with the really deep kiss he gives me, has me ready to melt.

"I don't want to get interrupted again." I gasp as there's a sharp tug, and the material of my panties falls away, lost to the ocean.

"I'll murder anyone who tries," he growls. He cups my pussy possessively, and a finger slides inside me while the heel of his hand grinds against my clit. I cry out at the sudden onslaught of pleasure.

"No need for murder," I pant. My magic flares out as I send a shield around the entire cove so no one can see or hear us.

The smile he gives me at that use of simple magic does things to my insides. It's one of pure pride and admiration. "Look at you, showing off," he teases, and I laugh lightly until his finger flicks that spot inside me that makes me see stars.

"Just like that." He does it again. And again. "I love your hands," I sigh.

He hums and starts pumping them in faster, hitting my G-spot every time. The pleasure builds, stealing my breath until my head feels ready to float away from my body. "You're squeezing the fuck out of my fingers, beautiful," he murmurs, suckling on a spot on my neck that has my toes curling. "You're going to feel so good wrapped around my cock."

"Then give it to me."

His chuckle is dark and full of promise. "Oh, trust me, I will. But I want to watch you come like this first." I groan, long and loud, tilting my head back to the sky. "Can you do that, Devorah? Can you be a good fucking girl and come for me?"

The dam inside me breaks and I explode.

Literally.

My entire body erupts in flames that surround me and Ari in a blazing inferno. I gasp, trying to get it to halt, to recede, but Ari keeps pumping his fingers in and out of me. "Don't worry," he murmurs in my ear before sucking the lobe into his mouth. "You're not going to burn me." The combination of his words and his fingers keeps my orgasm rolling on. As it ebbs and Ari slowly brings me back down, and as the fire slowly recedes. "See?"

"I can't light on fire every time you make me come." I mean it seriously, but it comes out on a breathy giggle.

"Why not? It's so fucking sexy."

"I can hurt you."

He clucks his tongue. "I don't think for a minute you'd hurt me." His kiss turns soft, reverent, before he hoists me into his arms and jogs a few steps into shallower water before lowering me to the sand. Warm waves caress my body, making my hair float around me like a dark halo.

"By the goddess, you're stunning," he breathes. It's like a prayer, made even more significant when he drops to his knees. I open my legs for him to crawl between. It's like he's made to be nestled between my thighs.

His mouth lowers and he sucks my nipple into his mouth, making me arch into him. I blindly reach for his cock, but he thrusts up so my hand is trapped beneath us. His dick glides along my wet center, the warmth of his skin contrasting with the bite of his cold metal piercing in an explosion for my senses that makes me a whimpering, thrashing mess.

He finally releases my nipple with one final swirl of his tongue. "Please, Ari." He braces the head of his cock at my entrance and pauses. "Please, fuck me."

I pull him down for a kiss and just as our mouths connect, the head of his cock slips inside me. I groan and drop my hands to his shoulders, clawing at him, needing him to go faster, but he takes his time. Inch by glorious inch, he enters me so I feel every bit of him. It feels so good that even as I writhe to get more, I'm completely blissed out.

When he's finally seated completely inside me, he lets out a low hiss. "Fuck, beautiful." His voice is more of a growl than actual speech, and his muscles start to shake where they brace by my head. "You feel better than I ever imagined."

"You imagined it then?" I tease.

"Every night as I stroked my cock," he says like it's the most natural thing in the world. He slides out only to slam back into me, and my eyes roll to the back of my head. "You've been my dream for as long as I can remember."

He starts to move quicker, pumping his hips so fast I can barely keep track of his thrusts. My nails dig into his shoulders, but that only spurs him on. "That's right, mark me," he growls. "Let the whole realm know exactly who I belong to."

I scrape my nails down his back, hard enough to draw blood, and he groans. "Such a good girl," he pants.

I'm vibrating with the need to come, and my feet press into his ass and forcing him deeper. The water starts to sizzle as I build higher and higher, but it's extinguished before it can ever ignite. With the reassurance that I won't hurt him, I relax as Ari fucks me so hard I sink into the sand.

"Too good," he pants. "I'm not going to be able to last much longer." His hand slips between us, stroking my clit in fast circles.

"I'm close."

"Come with me," he begs, his jaw ticking as he holds himself back.

"Kiss me." He obliges and it's enough to send me straight over the edge. I scream Ari's name loud enough to be heard in the Winter Court, and his thrusts get impossibly harder and deeper.

"Oh shit, Devorah," Ari's eyes are dark with lust as he stares into my eyes as I keep coming. "You're gripping me so tight. You're going to make me come."

"Please," I scream, still in the throes of my orgasm. It's as if he needed my permission. Ari's head tilts back and he roars out his release. The feel of his cum inside me is enough to have my inner walls spasming again in a mini-orgasm, aftershocks ripping through me like small little sparklers surrounding the larger fireworks.

When he's spent, Ari collapses on top of me. I welcome his weight, clinging to him and holding him close as he whispers my name over and over while placing kisses along every inch of skin he can reach. It's like I can breathe for the first time in my entire life. Like the realms have finally aligned with Ari in my arms like this.

"Fuck," he finally breathes, taking his weight back onto his forearms. "I don't think I can ever go back to a realm where we don't do that."

"Same," I pant.

This kiss is slow and sweet, and full of all the words we've left unspoken. It's a promise, a vow more significant than any marriage vow could ever be. It's us, together, against the realm.

I don't know what comes next, what will happen when we leave this cove and have to face reality, but for the first time in my life, I don't care. I refuse to focus on the future while Ari is in my arms, kissing me like I'm the most precious thing he's ever held.

And when he hardens inside me again, I give him a devious smile. "Think we can fuck in deeper water? So I can get some of the sand out of...everywhere?" The smile he gives me in return has me clenching around him.

Then he fucks me standing amongst the waves until the sun finally dips below the horizon.

"WHAT MADE YOU GET your dick pierced?" I ask, snuggling as far into Ari as I can get.

We haven't made it out of the cove. Eldoris popped into my mind briefly to let me know he'd make an official announcement about the engagement at the rehearsal dinner, so we decided to stay as long as we could. I know logically we'll need to head back soon to talk to Eldoris and

Edina, but right now I want to stay here, curled up in a blanket with Ari as my only heat source and the moon and stars as our only companions.

"Are you complaining?" he asks wryly.

"Nope," I say with a pop of the 'p'. I can't help but shiver as my mind conjures the memory of the metal brushing along my inner walls. I wasn't prepared for how much sensation it would add. "Just curious."

Ari toys with the ends of my damp hair. "I lost a bet."

"What?" I prop myself up on my hands. The stars glimmer in his purple irises, creating galaxies all of their own.

"I lived in the mortal realm—New York City—in the 1980s," he says, mirth coating his words.

My brow furrows. Unlike many of the Seelie Fae, I never spent time in the mortal realm. My mother always said there would be time, but there never was. The only things I know about New York are from the stories Edina shares of her youth growing up there. And I have no idea what the relevance of the 1980s means.

Ari continues. "I found a little community of vampires living in an area of the city that was...let's call it edgy. The king—that's the title vampires who run a territory are called—owned a night club. He was conducting an experiment to gauge mortals' reactions to vampires. And it was a convenient hunting ground."

"They told them vampires existed?" I ask. Non-magical humans—mortals, as they call them—are judgmental and quick to persecute. The magical community has remained hidden for so long for a reason. The vampires going against that mandate seems reckless.

He nods. "And then they'd use mental magic to erase their memories."

"Ah."

"So, one night, the owner claimed that anytime he told a woman he was a vampire, she would beg him to bite her. I made him a bet. He would tell five women he was a vampire and if three believed him and asked to be bitten without any kind of mental manipulation, he'd win. Anything less, I'd win.

"I stayed close to make sure he didn't cheat, and still, all five women believed him and asked to be bitten. By the end of the night he had a fucking pot belly, he was so full."

I laugh. "Do you ever regret making the bet?" My hand slowly trails down his abs, hovering around his pubic bone. His breath hitches and I move lower, running my fingers gently along the soft skin of his cock as it hardens under my touch. I don't stop until I reach the piercing in question, and run my thumb over the head. I lightly drag my nails back to the base before gripping it tightly and slowly pumping his length. His head tilts back, the blanket shifting down so his hair is in the pink sand.

I kiss down the path I took with my fingers. "I think I need a closer look." My tongue lingers over the V of his hips, and I shift so I'm situated between Ari's legs.

"Is that so?" he pants. I flick the piercing with the tip of my tongue. I hum, and suck him into my mouth until the cold metal hits the back of my throat and makes me gag.

I work Ari's cock with my mouth and hand in tandem. He swears and moans, spurring me on as I increase my pace. I love being able to give this to him, to be able to take care of him after he's taken care of me consistently.

"Beautiful, I'm gonna come if you don't stop," he says.

I keep pumping his length as I say, "Like that's going to make me stop." My cheeks hollow out as I take him into my mouth once again, and his hands shoot out, gripping my hair and guiding my pace. A few more pumps and Ari groans, long and low as his release coats my tongue. I swallow every drop of his cum, keeping him buried in the back of my throat as his cock twitches and starts to soften. I release him with a pop and one final swirl of my tongue against his piercing.

"To answer your question," Ari says, breathlessly. "No. I don't regret the bet."

I cackle and slide back into the cocoon of his arms, but not before he kisses me slowly, like we have nowhere else in the realm we need to be.

Chapter Thirty-Two
Devorah

ARI AND I FLY back to my suite, avoiding the throng of people celebrating my failed marriage attempt. After a quick shower, we curl up on the couch and wait for my brother to return from dinner. Ari sprawls his long legs across the cushions with me between them, the back of my head resting on his bare stomach. I'm practically purring as he runs his fingers through my damp hair.

I don't want to leave this moment—our little utopia where our responsibilities can't catch up with us—but the farther removed from the ocean we are, the more reality sets in. Kai and I wasted so much time 'selling' the courtship. Now, I'm boxed in, back against a wall.

"I can feel you thinking," Ari says. I flip over, resting my hands under my chin while I gaze up at him. Goddess, he's beautiful like this. The ever-present crinkle in his brow is smoothed, his lips—typically in a hard line or a wicked grin—are relaxed, easy. His hair is still wet from the shower, and adorably tousled.

"I'm always thinking," I sigh and close my eyes, not wanting him to see the storm building.

"Hey," he whispers, gripping my chin and tilting it up so I'm forced to look at him. "Together, remember? We figure this out together."

I nod as much as I can in his hold. He lets me go, and I flop on his chest, his arms folding around me like he's trying to fuse our bodies.

Together.

I let the word sink beneath my skin to the hardened shell of my heart.

I've never had a true partner before. Eldoris has always been there for me, but he had a mate, then a career in the army, and now Edina. So, while I rely on him as a confidant—and as my best friend— he was never available to completely help with my burden, and I never felt comfortable putting that pressure on him.

In the short time he's been my advisor, Ari has become my rock, my damn lifeline sometimes. He's been beside me through every lie, every secret, every sacrifice, and he's never wavered.

Even though he technically works for me, he's my partner in every way. I love him.

I keep the thought to myself, knowing it would be cruel to say those words when I'm still bound to marry someone else. Yet, I can't deny the depth of my feelings for him. Today only made that clearer. He reached me when no one else could, offering calm in the midst of the hardest storm I've ever endured.

"What am I going to do about my magic?" I ask. Compared to all the other things I need to worry about, this feels the most manageable. "I never thought being too powerful would be a problem."

"I did." I can hear the smirk in his voice. "I just thought we had more time. You're so composed that I didn't expect your emotions to trigger your magic so violently."

"Until I literally exploded."

"It's a simple enough fix. If left to its own devices, your magic will react when you're upset or angry—it's our bodies' way of protecting itself. You just need to show it who's boss; you're the ruler of your magic, not your emotions." He smooths down my hair. "Everyone goes through it."

Now that he says it, I vaguely remember Eldoris setting part of The Autumn Court on fire when someone said something about his ears. And when Edina came to Faerie, she was constantly accidentally freezing things she touched. It makes me feel better.

"What did it look like?" I ask. The question is vulnerable, unsure. Ari said the magic was strong, but I was so lost in it that I didn't know.

"It was breathtaking," he says reverently. "Awe-inducing. Terrifying."

"Terrifying?" I ask, sitting up again so I can look at him.

"Yes. At first glance, you looked like your aunt."

I gape at him. My aunt was evil. No matter how powerful she was, her magic was twisted. She's the last person I want to emulate or be compared to.

"I mean—" Ari rushes in, "—that the level of raw power you displayed was on par with what she could do. But it didn't feel tainted. It wasn't like the fires of hell—it felt like the sun."

My instinct is to run from that comparison, to vow never to use my magic to the extent that I can be lumped in with my aunt. But then, an idea starts to take shape. It's just an outline, not the full picture, but the more he tells me about the fire and what I looked like while trapped in the ice, the more it crystallizes.

Before I can ask Ari if my idea has merit, there's a knock at the door, and my brother pokes his head in, a hand covering his eyes. "Is it safe to come in?"

"Now he's a comedian," I tease, letting the idea go for now. There will be time to discuss it later.

Eldoris walks in, yanking off his tie and throwing it on the floor with a sigh. Edina enters close behind him, shutting the door behind her, but not locking it. I shift just enough to face them, but I don't leave the comfort of Ari's arms. "How was the dinner?"

"Oh, just delightful," Edina deadpans. The two of them take a seat on one armchair, Edina perching on the arm before my brother tugs her into his lap.

"How bad?" Ari asks, his hold on me tightening.

"Zahir was smug, but he didn't declare war, so it could have been worse," my brother says. "But..." he swallows, and my heart leaps into my throat. Ari and I move as one, sitting up as if the change in position will soften the blow.

"We did something," Edina adds, her usually smile-lit face concerned. "We're not sure you're going to agree with the decision, but it's done now."

"Okay..." I wait for them to continue, but then the door opens.

I'm not sure who I expect to walk in, but it's not Radley charging toward me with the force of a bull and crushing me in a hug. When he releases me, I find Larisa summoning chairs for her and Behar and another sofa for Lysandra and Puck, who enter last.

"We told them everything," Edina supplies.

"You what?" Ari asks.

"The four of us have exhausted our resources. We need help navigating the next steps. We need fresh sets of eyes."

Lysandra ignores the sofa summoned for her and sits beside me, wrapping her arm around my shoulders. "We want to help," she says, squeezing me in a one-armed hug.

"You're the monarchs of another court," I say cautiously, looking between her and Puck, who runs a hand through his auburn hair.

"So you're kicking us out of the second generation?" he quips, his emerald eyes sparkling with challenge.

"We'll all be monarchs one day," Larisa adds, taking Behar's hand in hers. "Standing beside each other now will make our realm that much stronger when we rule."

I try to swallow the rising wave of emotions, but I can't help my lip from quivering. When my mother got sick, I retreated into myself. Even when I was with my friends, I always held myself apart. I kept things light; I never discussed problems or fears because it could be used against me.

How have I ignored the depths of their friendship? Overlook what was right in front of me?

"It was a good decision," I say to Edina and Eldoris. I didn't notice the tension they were holding until their shoulders relaxed, and they both gave me wide smiles. I'm so grateful for seeing what I was blind to.

"Hades and Izar know too," Eldoris says. "But we agreed they should lie low for the time being."

All of them. Every single one of my friends is willing to step up to help. The bands that constantly constrict my chest loosen. A tear slips down my cheek, and Ari wipes it away.

"Thank you," I whisper, looking at every one of them, but lingering on Larisa the longest. She's the one who owes me the least, and yet, she didn't hesitate.

She nods curtly, understanding the weight of my gaze without needing me to say anything more. "So," she claps her hands before summoning an ancient book from thin air. "Behar and I skipped dinner and looked up laws regarding ascension to the throne, and whether a previous monarch can add stipulations."

"And?"

"Unfortunately, they can," Behar says. I swear under my breath.

"Thank the goddess your mother never learned of that," Puck murmurs to Lysandra, who nods vigorously.

"However," Larisa says, putting the book on her lap and pushing her honey-blonde hair behind her ear, giving us a view of the golden butterfly tattoo on her temple. She points at one paragraph as if we can read it across the room. "According to the same law, the ascending monarch has three hundred days to complete the stipulations of their ascension before forfeiting the crown."

"We showed this to the record keeper," Behar adds. "And she agreed the law trumps your mother's wishes."

"So, I have more time, but I still need to marry a royal," I confirm. It's a start, but it still leaves me in the same position. I have to marry someone when I'm in love with another.

"I volunteer as tribute!" Radley says, sticking his hand in the air. Edina and Lysandra both laugh, but the rest of us stare in confusion. "It's from *The Hunger Games*." More blank looks. "Did none of you watch a single movie when we were in the mortal realm?"

"We were fighting in a war," Eldoris deadpans.

"We had downtime."

"Can you explain the reference for those of us who don't watch television whenever we're in the mortal realm?" Puck drawls. Radley gives him a particularly crude gesture from the mortal realm that Edina taught us.

"It means..." he draws out the word dramatically while dropping to his knees and crawling on the floor until he's in front of me. "Devorah of the Summer Court, will you marry me?"

I flick him in the forehead.

Ari bursts out in laughter that's quickly joined by the rest of the group. "No, seriously," Radley pouts, rubbing the red spot on his head. "We can live our own lives, see other people. We just need to bang one out every once in a while so you can get pregnant. My dad wants grandbabies."

"How romantic," Edina pretends to swoon.

"Isn't that what you want?" he asks, looking between me and Ari. "We'd be married in name only—you two could be together in every way that matters."

"As beautiful as that proposal was," I say, taking Radley's outstretched hands. "You're in line for a throne. You can't marry me."

"Oh, right." He shuffles back to his chair, still on his knees.

"Izar would be an option," Larisa says. "It would be a similar situation, where you would both stay with your respective partners."

Ari shakes his head. "He'd need permission from Zahir for that kind of political marriage."

"And then they'll know something is wrong," I say with a sigh. "If I search for another husband so soon after Kai, then everyone will know something is keeping me from taking my throne."

Everyone goes silent. Lysandra abandons my couch in favor of sitting beside Puck, who kisses her on the temple. Radley drags his hand down his face. Larisa pulls another book from the air and starts frantically scanning and flipping pages.

"There is another way," Edina interrupts. She and Eldoris exchange a loaded look that sobers us all. "We spoke with my mother. She's agreed to honor our alliance as long as Eldoris and I stay together."

"We don't have to get married," Eldoris says mournfully. "I can take the throne; you and Ari can be happy."

A frozen tear drips from Edina's lashes onto my brother's lap. He whispers something too low for us to hear and she kisses him softly. By the time they turn back to us, with determined looks on their faces, half the room is crying. Radley sniffles so loudly that Larisa summons a handkerchief for him.

"No," I rasp, wiping away a tear. "I won't let you do that."

"You two are meant to be together," Puck says, and I know the rest of us wholeheartedly agree.

"Marriage doesn't mean we're not together." But even though he says it, Eldoris' hand shakes. "We're in love, that's all that matters."

"I never wanted to get married anyway." Edina is going for flippant, but it's tinged in sadness.

"We can call that plan B," Ari offers gently. "If at the end of the remaining three hundred days we're in the same situation, we'll take you up on that offer."

They glance at each other before nodding. I can't help but notice the relief on their faces.

No, I'll never let them sacrifice a marriage for me. I'll figure something else out.

The glimmer of hope I had when seeing my friends vanishes. The situation is still impossible, there's still no positive outcome. I flop back against the couch, and Ari wraps his arm around me.

"It's like a funeral in here." The voice from the door has all of us gasping as Vlad—the vampire from the mortal realm—swaggers in. He's impeccably dressed as usual, his blue tie bringing out the ice color of his eyes.

Whatever emotion Edina was feeling breaks as she sees her friend, and she runs across the room and launches herself into his arms. "Fuck, Tinker Bell. I didn't know you'd miss me so much." She playfully shoves at him, and he joins our little circle, shaking hands with everyone and handing out hugs like he's a celebrity before sitting beside me on the couch.

"So," he drawls, crossing one leg over the other. "Catch me up."

"You probably know more than we do," Lysandra scoffs.

He flashes her a fang-filled smile. "I like hearing information from the source. Who knows how gossip gets distorted? For example, am I really to believe that Devorah turned herself into an underwater volcano?"

Well, that's certainly one way to describe it.

I catch Vlad up on everything that's happened since we saw him at my betrothal ball, and he nods thoughtfully—even though it's clear he *does* know it all. When I get to the part about my magic, he says, "Badass," before letting me finish the story.

"So, you still didn't figure out my message?" he smirks.

Honestly, I got so wrapped up in everything going on that I forgot about his message. Training my magic and getting through my betrothal took precedence over an 'easier way' to get out of this.

He sighs and dramatically rolls his eyes. "You need to marry someone of royal blood, yes?" I nod. "Could there...hypothetically...be someone with royal blood that you've overlooked?"

"If you're suggesting I marry you—"

"I'm an elected official in the mortal realm, not royalty. And I'm spoken for." His smile turns momentarily wistful before it snaps back into its usual sarcastic smirk. "Come now, some of the most brilliant minds in the realm are in this room. Certainly, one of you can figure this out."

Everyone glances around, like somehow we'll find the answer sitting in the middle of the room. "Someone in the mortal realm?" Lyandra asks, looking at Edina. Both of them were princesses living in the mortal realm until recently, so it's plausible that someone else is there.

Vlad makes a sound like a buzzer. "Valiant effort, darling, but incorrect."

"Can't you just tell us?" Edina asks.

"I could, but where would be the fun in that?"

Larisa gasps, looking up from the book. Looking straight at the three of us on the couch.

"Care to venture a guess, Larisa?" Vlad asks.

"Ari," she whispers, hand floating to her mouth. "Who is your mother?"

Chapter Thirty-Three
Ari

"WHO IS YOUR MOTHER?" Larisa asks.

Every eye in the room is on me, waiting with bated breath for the answer to a question I've asked myself countless times.

"I don't know," I reply. "I've looked for information on her for ages, but never found anything. Not even my father knows. She dropped me at his doorstep and left without a note."

"Are you sure he *still* doesn't know?" Vlad asks.

I think back on our recent conversations, but there was no inkling that he might have had new information. I don't believe he'd lie or hide that from me. He knows how hard I've looked; how much I've longed to know where I come from. Devorah squeezes my hand, drawing my attention. Her brow is creased with worry, but there's hope in her eyes, hope that this is the answer to all our problems. But no, that can't be possible. My father would have considered a relationship with a royal to be treason.

As much as I want to join Devorah in her optimism, I have to keep a level head. It doesn't matter that my heart is hammering against my ribcage, and my stomach has lodged itself in my throat. I need to remain realistic.

"What do you know?" I ask Vlad, shifting forward so I can see him on the other end of the couch.

He gives me an inscrutable look and a one-armed shrug. "If I were you, I'd be on my way to Pa Ferie right now."

I abandon all pretense of composure and leap to my feet, stalking out of the circle of second-generation members and throwing open the balcony's double doors.

"Wait," Devorah calls, running after me, her wings already unfurled. "I'm coming with you."

I pull her into a kiss that's long and deep enough to have her whimpering against me. "Stay here, please," I whisper against her lips. "Zahir is still a wildcard, there's no reason to take unnecessary risks."

She sighs, placing her hands on my bare chest and rubbing soothing lines over the muscles. "Okay. Come straight back."

"Promise." I seal it with another kiss, pulling away when an obnoxious chorus of *awws* shatters the moment. I mock salute them all before walking onto the balcony, unfurling my wings, and diving into the air.

I MAKE GOOD TIME to Pa Ferie, flying harder and faster than I've ever flown before, and soon I'm landing on the black sand beach before my shore house. My father is sitting on the top step of the porch, elbows braced on his knees, his head hanging forward and cradled between his hands.

"It's about time you showed up," he says, gruffly. When he finally looks at me, his eyes are weary, his hair—which has grown out in his retirement—looks like he's been running his fingers through it.

"Was I supposed to?" I ask carefully. I don't know what could have my father looking so distraught, but it can't be anything good.

"I sent you letters." He reaches behind him, extracting a bottle of whiskey and taking a swig from the neck. "And I came by the palace, but you've always been out."

"I've made myself scarce. I didn't want to be around all the wedding stuff." My father nods and takes another drink. "But that doesn't matter anymore." I stand at the railing, leaning against the sturdy wood. "The wedding is off. One of the priestesses was Kai's mate. He backed out of the agreement."

His eyes go wide, but some of the tension in his face softens in relief.

I try not to read too much into it and fail miserably.

He hands me the bottle of whiskey, but I wave it away. "I take it the plume of smoke was from you or Eldoris when you heard the news," he says.

"Devorah." I smile like a fucking fool, because no matter how danger-ous that display was, I'm so proud that she let go of everything holding her back.

"She needs to learn control."

"I've got it." I climb the stairs and sit beside him, staring out at the ocean. The stars reflect in the water, disrupted only by the gentle current.

I don't know why, but I can't seem to find the words to ask my father what he knows. Everything that pops into my mind sounds accusatory or desperate, and I don't want to sound like either.

"How bad is the situation?" he asks softly.

"We have some time to react." I haven't told him the details of why Devorah needs to be married, but he knew Queen Talia completely—the same way I know Devorah. I'm sure he has some inkling of her directive. "But the slower we do, the longer the rest of the realm has to react, too."

"Devorah needs to be coronated as soon as possible."

"The plan was..." I trail off, and my father raises an eyebrow. I quickly throw up a shield before admitting anything further. "We were going to have the coronation the day after tomorrow."

"After she got married." I nod. "To someone of royal blood." It's not a question, but I nod again.

"Which brings me to the reason I'm here." I clear my throat. "Vladimir Orlov told me to find you."

"Meddlesome oaf," my father grumbles, suddenly refusing to meet my eyes. His hand clenches around the whisky, and the liquid starts to smoke as the control of his magic slips.

That can't be good.

He sets the bottle aside, summoning one that's not flambeed and taking several gulps before speaking. "First things first," he says gruffly. "Everything I told you about your mother was true. She dropped you off at my doorstep without as much as a magical signature to track her with. And at the time, I'd been with so many females—honestly, I didn't even remember half of them—"

"Dad," I clip.

"Right," he sighs. "I just found out. It's why I sent all those messages. I could have tried harder, stayed in my room in the palace until you returned, but I didn't want to dangle this information in front of you if it didn't change anything."

I can barely breathe. This moment is one I've waited for my entire life. I grew to believe this would never happen—that this was destined to be my great unanswered question. And now I get to know, and while part of me is relieved, the other part of me is terrified.

"Who?" I ask, my voice barely audible over the crash of the waves behind us. "Who is my mother?"

"Celesta."

Celesta.

The female I met with a few weeks ago. The female who granted me an underwater army for the price of a conversation.

My mother is a siren. I'm part siren.

It all begins to make sense. Half-siren children are born without the ability to breathe in the water, which is why she left me on land until I emerged. Now that I think of it, Celesta arrived at the palace when I emerged, but when she saw me use my magic, she just smiled and disappeared. I thought it was odd at the time, but I quickly forgot about it.

"Why didn't she say anything?" I ask. It's not like children between elemental Fae and sirens are taboo. It may have been once upon a time, but not in ages. Most of the second generation are mixed heritage for goddess' sake.

"That's something you'll need to ask her," my father says. "But the reason she didn't tell you the other day was that she wanted to tell me first. She decided I was owed the courtesy of finding out from her."

"Why now?" This is all a total mindfuck, and I can barely wrap my head around it.

"She said, 'because he deserves to be with the female he loves,'" he says, his brown eyes meeting mine. "She must have figured out the princess' predicament, and she wanted you to have a chance to marry her."

The world spins.

In the utter shock from finding out Celesta is my mother, I forgot who she is. She isn't just a siren.

She's a siren *elder*.

She isn't a royal in the elemental Fae sense, but she's a highly regarded member of society. She's a monarch—the same way Shesha is a monarch.

Which means I have royal blood.

And I can marry Devorah.

"Yes," my father gives me a small smile, and I realize I must have voiced that last bit out loud. "Though ethically, you should resign as her advisor."

The laugh that bubbles from my throat is unrestrained. I can marry the female I love. She can be mine, all fucking mine, for the rest of eternity.

I wrap my arms around my father, smacking a kiss on his cheek. He chuckles, losing a battle to remain stoic as he breaks into a wide smile. "We'll do it tomorrow," I announce.

"Tomorrow?"

I nod. I know the odds are against us, but Devorah and I can make it happen. "We need Devorah crowned as soon as possible." And selfishly, I don't want to spend one more minute of my life without her. Knowing she could be my wife...it gives me more hope than I've ever dared to want.

My father must realize this, because he says, "You need to take your mother to the record keeper to confirm your status. She's been in the Winter Court, watching the Night Court's armada."

"I'll go now."

"I'll take a boat to the palace, tell the princess to get ready, and summon the priestesses."

"When you get to the palace, talk to Gwyneira's advisor. She'll pass along the information to the pixies, and everyone will know about the wedding in seconds."

My father chuckles. "You act like I wasn't the one who taught you everything you know." He shoves me forward a step. "Go on then. If you plan on marrying Devorah tomorrow afternoon, you better hurry."

I pat him on the shoulder before releasing my wings again and jumping straight into the air with a whoop. I make it halfway across the ocean when I catch sight of the light in Devorah's room.

Fuck, I need to ask her first.

While we were on the beach earlier, Devorah confessed that she wished we could get married, but I still need to ask her. Before any plans are made, I need to hear it from her lips that she wants this as badly as I do.

And I need to tell her I love her.

She can't hear this news from my father.

I change my trajectory, deviating from my path to the Winter Court and heading toward that light. Suddenly, I'm nervous. My stomach ties itself in knots at the thought that she'll say no. Even if I do technically have royal blood, I'm still her employee. Fae will gossip, and there may be some backlash. The part of my brain that's Devorah's advisor insists she consider the implications.

I shake loose the thought. She's never had a problem with my role before. It will be fine. She'll say yes.

I wish I had a ring.

No time. Maybe Celesta will have something I can use.

The light draws closer and closer until I can make out the shadows within the room, all sitting around in a circle. The second generation, it seems, hasn't left Devorah alone. I'll have an audience when I propose, but that's fine.

I'm inches from the balcony when something punches through my wing. Pain lances through me, worse than anything I've ever felt. It makes me heave, even as I start to spiral into the trees.

Something hits my other wing, but this time, it doesn't go clean through. I get the barest glimpse of a metal bolt as I careen toward the beach. No, not metal. Iron.

I try calling my magic to slow my fall, or fight whoever is sending these bolts at me, but the iron has neutralized me. I keep falling, smacking into palm fronds that slip through my fingers when I try to grab them.

The last thing I see before I crash into the ground is a circle of black cloaked figures holding iron chains.

Chapter Thirty-Four
Devorah

"Stop pacing," Edina says gently.

Vlad refused to say anything else about Ari's potential parentage, which means my mind has been running a mile a minute since Ari left. My friends have stayed, but I can't concentrate on their conversations when the answer to all my prayers may be across the ocean.

Ari might be royal. I may be able to marry the male I love *and* become queen.

This beautiful, dream-like future is so close I can taste it. But fate hasn't exactly been kind to me, especially when it comes to matters of the heart, so it's hard to believe I could get this lucky.

Edina takes my hands in hers, the cool temperature of her skin a welcome reprieve to my sweaty palms. She takes a large inhale through her nose, and I mimic her, releasing the breath only when my lungs feel full enough to pop. My heart rate slows, the pounding in my head subsides, and the room focuses.

"Shouldn't he be back by now?" I mutter, and though it's a hypothetical question, Edina squeezes my hand and says, "In my experience, meeting a biological family can take some time."

"Facts," Lysandra adds.

"So come sit and let's talk about something else." She gently tugs me toward the couch. I'm hesitant to take my eyes off the ocean for even a minute, but she's right. Worrying myself sick isn't helping anyone.

Eldoris takes Vlad's seat so I can sit between him and Edina on the couch. I rest my head on her shoulder, and Eldoris wraps his arms around my shoulder. I'm truly grateful the goddess brought Edina into our lives and the small family we've formed.

"I have a gift for you," Vlad says, with a mischievous grin. He reaches into his suit jacket and withdraws an envelope that's worn and slightly discolored with age. Before it's even fully out of his pocket, I recognize the aquamarine wax seal.

"I said I had something from your mother," he says.

I gingerly take the letter, my hands shaking. "I thought I couldn't open this until the night before I get married," I murmur, tracing the scrawled script on the envelope.

"Technically," Vlad draws the word out dramatically, "your mother said to give it to you the night before your wedding. She never said the wedding couldn't be cancelled."

Across the room, Behar chuckles. I didn't realize how quiet the group had become until I heard that infinitesimal sound. My eyes dart around. I could go to my bedroom, but part of me wants to be surrounded by friends while I read this letter. But I also don't want them staring at me.

Radley loudly clears his throat. "My father has decided I need to be married," he announces, using the full extent of his booming voice.

"How is that news?" Larisa teases.

He flicks a small gust of air at her; it puffs her hair into a frizzy mess. "He's serious this time. He's ready to step down, but he won't do it until I have an heir. And for some reason I don't understand, he's insisting on marriage."

"Our parents had that in common, apparently," Eldoris mutters.

The group descends into conversation again, and Radley winks at me. I mouth my thanks for the distraction and gently remove the wax seal from the envelope. Compared to its outer wrapping, the paper inside is crisp and white.

I won't read if you don't want me to, Eldoris says, tightening his hold on me.

I'm just gonna tell you everything anyway, I shrug.

With one final breath, I open the letter.

My dearest Devorah,

If you are reading this, then congratulations on your upcoming wedding. It is with great sadness that I will not be there for you tomorrow, but I am sure it will be a wonderful affair.

I know you have many questions, all of which I will try to answer. Please know, despite what you may think, I have your best interests at heart.

Like you, I never planned on being queen.

"Seriously?" I unmeaningly ask aloud.

I knew that, like me, my mother was the second-born and was never raised to take the throne, but I always believed she wanted to challenge her sister. The stories said she trained extensively in her youth, which caused her sister to become paranoid enough to seek terrible ways to increase her strength, corrupting her magic in a way that ultimately led to her demise.

I turn to Vlad, who arches an eyebrow in silent command for me to continue reading.

Your Aunt Tamara told the world I was conspiring against her, but the truth is that I loved my sister enough to never challenge her, even if I was more powerful. When she twisted her magic, I lost not only my freedom, but my best friend.

In the years after she died and I became queen, I grew accustomed to being alone. I spent all my time dedicated to our court, reestablishing relationships that were damaged under Tamara's reign, persecuting her followers, and the hundred day-to-day operations that come with running a kingdom. I had my advisors—Hershel, in particular, became more like a brother to me than an advisor—and a handful of friends, but I was always careful around them, never sure who I could trust explicitly.

It was not until I met your father that I understood how important it is to have a partner.

As you know, at the urging of my advisors, I went to the mortal realm to conceive a child. Your father was the equivalent of royalty amongst his tribe, and while our relationship started as transactional, we grew to understand each other in a way I have never felt with another. I loved him, yes, but it was more than that. Having someone I could rely on, someone I could confide in who understood my problems, took a monumental weight off my shoulders.

I know the stipulation to your ascension may seem as though I find you ill-equipped to rule, but that simply is not true. You, dearest, are going to make a fantastic queen. Far better than I was ever able to be.

However, I worry that once you are crowned, you will disappear into your work, until all that you are is a queen. My hope in forcing you to marry another royal is that you will find a partner, someone you can rely on to take the weight from your shoulders after a long day.

I love you and your brother very much. You both are, and always will be, the best thing I have ever done with my life.

My eternal love,
Mother

I swipe away the tears that trickle down my cheeks. My emotions are a tangled mess, each one fighting for supremacy until they're so knotted up that I can't think straight.

My mother trusted me, thought I'd make a good queen. I didn't think I needed her validation, but I did. It's such a relief to know she believed in me. On the other hand, I'm still furious at her for forcing me into a corner. And I also feel guilty for that anger because, though her approach was terrible, she wanted the best for me.

I slump against Eldoris, and he envelops me in a hug. *I don't know how to feel,* I tell him.

I think that's okay. He kisses the top of my head. *It's a lot to take in. You can sit with your feelings.*

I've never been good at that, so I read the letter again. And again. And when the fourth read still doesn't quiet my mind, I abandon the paper and return to worrying about Ari, and what's taking so goddess damned long for him to return.

WHEN THE FIRST RAYS of the sun break through the night sky, Vlad bids us good day and goes to the suite we have for him in the basement. Everyone but Larisa has fallen asleep. Lysandra and Puck are curled into each other on their loveseat, and Behar is sitting with his head resting forward on his chest. Edina and Eldoris have sprawled on the couch, and Radley has taken a spot on the floor, snoring softly and muttering something unintelligible every few minutes.

I abandoned the couch hours ago for my round seat in the bay window, alternating between staring outside and sketching portraits of my friends. "If it was good news, he'd be back by now," I mutter under my breath.

As much as Vlad can be a dick, I don't think he'd send Ari on a goose chase for nothing, Eldoris says in our mental connection, startling me so much that I throw my pencil out the open window. Larisa arches an eyebrow, but goes back to reading her book without comment.

If he went to find his mother, he continues, *the wards won't make things easy. It'll take time.*

What if it's someone in The Night Court? It's a thought that's been bothering me all night. What if he needed to go into enemy territory? What if something's happened?

I think it's more likely to be a werewolf alpha. There are so many of them. And Ari can certainly be territorial.

So, he'd be in Autumn Court? That's not much better.

"If you share with the rest of the class, we may be able to help," Edina snips.

"Is anyone else awake?" I ask, a little more edge to my words than I mean.

Wordlessly, Eldoris summons Edina a cup of coffee—at least I think there's coffee under all that whipped cream—and summons a cup of espresso for me.

As Eldoris tells Larisa and Edina of our conversation, I walk onto the balcony, letting the early morning air off the ocean wake me up. I find myself staring toward Pa Ferie, and the spot where Hershel's house is.

There's no sign of anything amiss, but my gut is screaming at me to move, to go there myself and make sure everything is okay.

A glint of something on one of the palm trees outside the window catches my attention. I blink, willing my eyes to focus, but I can't identify it. "El?" I call, and he comes running over, bracing himself on the stone railing and following my gaze. "What's that, on the palm frond?"

"Looks like some kind of creature."

"It's not moving. And look," I point to the tree right above it, "that's bent."

He leans forward, muscles straining as he peers closer. "The one just beyond it, too," he mutters, turning back to me with worry creasing his brow. I unfurl my wings, but he grabs onto my wrist and shakes his head. "Edina?" he calls, and she appears a moment later, Larisa right behind her. "Could one of you fly down to that tree and get whatever that splotch is?"

Edina and Larisa exchange a glance. "My wings are smaller," Edina says, stripping off her shirt so she's just in a sports bra and extending her iridescent wings, a gentle swirling snowflake pattern glittering silver and blue in the morning light.

"I'll cover you," Larisa says, her wings—white feathered monstrosities that dwarf her slim frame—extending from slits in her sweater.

Edina dives into the foliage, and Larisa flies above the tree line for surveillance. They return a moment later, a piece of something blue and fleshy in Edina's hand. Something about the pattern niggles at my brain. Those ridges, the way the gray lines ripple across the blue, are so familiar, but I can't place them.

"It's an odd texture," Edina says, wrinkling her nose. "It reminds me of the time I pet a stingray when I was on vacation in the Caribbean."

I'm about to reach for it when there's a loud knock on the door of my suite. The entire second generation jumps up, shouting a battle cry and summoning their perspective elements like we're being attacked. I slip from Eldoris' hold and run from the balcony to the door, my heart leaping in anticipation.

"Hershel?" I ask. He gives me a warm smile as I usher him inside. Right behind him is the pixie priestess who was supposed to marry me. "What's going on? Where's Ari?"

"He isn't back yet?" His brow furrows. "He was going to find his mother and go straight to the record keeper."

"Who's his mother?" I ask at the same time as Eldoris says, "The record keeper?"

"My question first," I insist. My hand flies to my chest, scrubbing at the skin there as I try to tell my stupid heart to calm down and hear the male's answer.

"His mother is Celesta," he answers.

"The siren elder?" Lysandra asks, and Hershel—realizing a queen is in the room—bows deeply.

"His purple eyes," I whisper. How have we never realized? I worked side by side with Celesta during the Monarchy Trials, and I never put together that her rich, purple eyes were the same as my advisor's.

Hershel gestures to the priestess. "When Ari left, he told me to summon the other monarchs back and get the priestesses ready. Not the one mated to your former betrothed, of course, but the others."

"Why?"

Hershel runs his fingers through his hair, the same way Ari does when he's nervous. "He should be the one to tell you..."

"Don't make me pull rank here," I deadpan.

He chuckles and takes my hand. "He wants to marry you. Today." My stupid heart starts rattling my ribcage like it wants to fly free and leave my body behind. "So that you can continue with your coronation plans. That's why he went straight to the record keeper to legitimize his royal status."

"Damn," Edina breathes, stepping forward and grabbing my brother's hand in her own. "That's so thoughtful."

"Romantic," Radley sighs.

"That's Ari," I breathe, tears brimming in my eyelashes. He's so aware of exactly what I need, what I want, and he'll spend the entire night flying between the Winter Court and Day Court to make this all happen for me. "So, I'm getting married this afternoon?"

"We moved the ceremony to sunset so you have a few extra hours to sleep and get ready," the priestess says. "Plus, we need to discuss your binding spell—I assume it will be vastly different from the one you had with the dragon." The way she says *dragon* clearly shows how she felt about the entire situation with Kai. Priestesses are easily angered when someone goes against the goddess, and outright dismissing a fated mate will have Kai on her shit list for a long, long time.

"When do you think he'll be back?" I ask.

Hershel's mouth tightens into a hard line. "Even if it took him a long time to find Celesta—and it shouldn't have—he should have been back by now. It's been hours since he left the beach house."

Another knock has everyone bracing themselves for battle once again. Eldoris takes a protective step in front of me while Hershel answers the door, blocking it with his body.

I recognize the voice instantly.

"Let her in," I say. He scowls at me, but steps aside for Hades to enter.

I've never seen Hades like this before. She's typically polished, impeccably dressed, never a hair out of place. But today, her hair is in frizzy waves rather than straight, clean lines. She's wearing a baggy sweater, leggings, and *sneakers*. She looks so small, nothing like the imposing figure I've come to know.

"I can't stay long," she says, chewing on her bare lower lip. "But I had to give you a heads up."

Just like the night my mother died, I suddenly know exactly what's going to happen. It plays out in my mind in slow motion. It's like someone sucked all the oxygen from my lungs and replaced it with lead. My previously light and fluttering heart has its wings clipped.

Pieces of the puzzle slot together. I know where I've seen the blue and gray pattern of that chunk of flesh.

It's a piece of Ari's wing.

Combined with the broken palms fronds, the fact that Ari should have been back hours ago. It means—

"My brother has Ari."

Chapter Thirty-Five
Devorah

ZAHIR HAS ARI.

He was inches from me, just outside the balcony, and he was taken. Shot down from the sky—if the chunk of wing in Edina's hand is any indication. If I had stayed by the window, would I have seen him? Would I have been able to react before Zahir dragged him off to goddess knows where to do goddess knows what?

The heaviness filling my lungs seeps to the rest of my body, making it impossible to remain on my feet. Hands reach for me. I hear my friends calling my name, trying to console me, trying to get me to act, but I can't move. Ari's my protector, not the one who needs protecting. I should have sent someone with him to Pa Ferie; he should have had backup. But I always thought of him as indestructible, and now he's in the hands of my worst enemy—an erratic megalomaniac who won't hesitate to kill him to destroy me.

"Princess." A hand on my cheek has my eyes opening—*when did they close?*—and blinking away the tears that have formed a sheen over my irises. In the hazy moment before my vision clears, Hershel looks so much like his son that I startle.

"It's alright," he says soothingly, and lifts his hands to where I can see them. I lean back, knowing instinctively that my twin is behind me, and I steal his strength to bolster my own.

"I have to go," Hades says. "He has Minthe too, and—" Our eyes meet, and all the animosity from the bachelorette party evaporates. We're in this awful situation together.

"If you find—" she starts again, before looking up at the ceiling and blinking away tears. "If you rescue Ari and find Minthe with him—"

"We've got her," Edina says.

"Any ideas where they could be?" Eldoris asks.

Hades shakes her head. "I checked all of the places I can think of, and I have spies searching, but—" Another shake of her head. "If I don't do what he wants, if I disobey his *orders*—" she spits the word between her teeth.

"Go," I insist. "Don't get caught here."

She nods gratefully and disappears down the hallway. The pixie priestess excuses herself, telling us to call on her once things "work themselves out."

"What do I do?" I whisper, more to myself than to the room. Eldoris' chin rests atop my head.

Hershel clears his throat. He hasn't moved from my eyeline, remaining on the floor with me and my brother. "I know the last time I was your advisor was contentious."

"You told her to kill our mother," Eldoris retorts.

"Not my finest hour. But I served your mother—and you, Devorah—for a long time. You know I only want what's best for this court.

So, if you can trust me for the time being, I'd like to resume my role until we get my son back. Allow me to advise you again. Can you do that?"

I search his face, the strong cut of his jaw hidden, his tired eyes, and I find no trace of deception. No matter how we left things, I believe Hershel wants to get Ari back as much as I do. I nod and release a shaky breath.

"Do you want everyone here?" he asks. My friends all turn to me, the same question echoing in their eyes. All signs of the exhaustion that plagued them moments ago are gone, most likely due to the abundance of espresso cups and vials of energizing tonics that now litter my coffee table.

"Yes," I say, sounding much more assured than I feel. "We'll need them." I move to the couch and am once again flanked by my brother and Edina, the three of us forming an unbreakable wall. I don't acknowledge their support with words, but I do take their hands and squeeze them tightly. Edina pumps cooling energy into me, lowering my body temperature before I realize it was simmering.

"How did they get to Ari?" I mutter. "We screened everyone who came into the court for the wedding extensively. The Night Court was allowed the bare minimum of guests; we would have noticed if they brought in a group of soldiers."

"Glamour?" Edina asks. "They could have made themselves look like pieces of luggage or something."

"That would take sophisticated magic," Radley says.

"They have the best mind magic users in the realm," Larisa says. "They could have tricked the soldiers."

"I knew inviting them was stupid," Eldoris huffs. I shoot him a glare. Now is not the time for told-you-so's, it's the time to find the male I love.

"Do you know where he could be?" I ask Hershel.

"I have a few ideas." There's no hint of hesitation in his voice, no emotion making it waver. He's slipped fully into his role as my advisor once again, helping me through a hostage situation, not the capture of his son.

I gesture for him to continue. "Zahir won't kill him yet. He wants to humiliate you, corner you into surrendering your court. He'll announce Ari's capture somewhere public where everyone can witness it."

"Did you summon him back with the rest of the monarchs?" Eldoris asks. Hershel nods. "Did you tell them about another wedding?"

"No. I said our court wanted to host a luncheon. I didn't give a reason, and no one questioned me."

"Of course they didn't," Lysandra scoffs. "Any reason to party."

"And to see Devorah squirm," Puck adds. "They'll be desperate to see how she's handling the cancelled engagement."

"Which makes the luncheon the perfect place for Zahir to make his statement," Hershel says. "'Look how easily I captured your most trusted advisor. If you can't protect him, how can you protect an entire court?' It will make your foes salivate and your allies question their allegiance."

"Not us," Lysandra says.

"Or my mother," Edina says. "Probably."

Behar clears his throat, his brown eyes focused on me as he silently asks to speak. I nod, interested to hear what he has to say. "Even if it doesn't affect your alliances, it could make your soldiers question your rule. They would still serve you, but disgruntled soldiers are never a good thing."

Eldoris denies that, but I hear the truth in Behar's words. Eldoris may lead the army, but Behar is *in* it.

"We have to rescue Ari—and possibly Minthe—before Zahir can make a move," I say. "But we can't use our troops for this. Or, at least, not a lot of them." Hershel raises an eyebrow, so I continue. "We need to handle this quietly."

"You can use me," Behar offers, and I thank him. As a high-ranking member of the army, he's a perfect option to help—lending us the muscle and experience we need while still being discreet.

"And I'll go," Eldoris says.

"No," I say firmly. "Everyone will expect you and Edina to host. You need to be obnoxiously visible all day." I brace myself for this next part because Eldoris is not going to like it. "I'll go."

He rears back. "You want to go in there by yourself?"

"With a small contingent of guards. You can pick which ones."

There's a moment where everyone starts talking over each other, each expressing their visions of what needs to happen. I hold up a hand, and they instantly fall silent. "How many places could Ari be in?" I ask Hershel.

"Two that I know of."

"Then you'll lead one small group of guards, and I'll go with the other."

"Are you out of your fucking mind, Dev?" Eldoris' eyes flicker, flames dancing across them. "You expect me to let you slink off into enemy territory without me?"

I sigh and take his hand. "I'm not asking. Everyone will expect me to be hiding in my room all day. I'm the obvious choice to lead." He opens his mouth to protest, but I keep going. "I'll wear a glamour so no one recognizes me."

"I should go with you," Radley says, surprising all of us. "The portals are monitored, but my father made the barrier between us and Night thinner. As long as you have an Unseelie Fae with you—" he sketches a bow, "—it shouldn't be hard to cross."

"And if it is?" Eldoris asks, and Radley flashes him a smile.

"Then it's a good thing there's an Underground entrance right by the border, and the wards don't exist down there."

I go over a few more details with the others, specifically where I need them to be for the rest of the day, and they eagerly agree. We discuss the pitfalls and come up with contingencies and escape routes in case things go sideways. Throughout it all, I manage to suppress my debilitating fear for Ari, lending all my concentration to this plan. I can compartmentalize for now and worry later.

When there's nothing more to say, Hershel says, "It's a sound plan."

"It is," Eldoris sighs. Then, privately to me, he says, *I wish you'd stay here, but I know you can do this.*

I know I don't need his approval, but the fact that I have his support means everything. It bolsters my confidence and steels my resolve.

With one final smile at my brother, I square my shoulders and say, "Let's do it."

Chapter Thirty-Six
Ari

EVERY INCH OF MY being hurts. It's not enough that Zahir and his cronies have me in a cell with iron bars, but they have me shackled to the wall with iron cuffs, and they left the iron bolts through my wings. That last bit felt personal. You don't touch a male's wings—it's a cheap shot, like a kick to the groin.

I'm not sure how long I've been here, and the details of my journey are a blur. I remember stepping through the portal, the cool mist brushing against my face, and the tight sensation of teleporting, but beyond that, everything is hazy.

There's a very small window in my cell, not large enough to fit through, but it lets sand seep through and blow around the floor. The air is the kind of dry that saps every bit of moisture from your body. When I strain, I can hear the faint sound of rushing water, which makes me believe I'm not in the palace dungeon, which is in the dead center of the Dorchas Desert, but somewhere close to the Allagi River.

I do my best not to think of the pain from the iron, the way it burns my flesh whenever I so much as shift my position. My wrists are already rubbed raw where they're suspended above my head, and I can feel the shredding of the membrane of my wings. But I can endure this.

What I can't endure is being used as a trap for Devorah.

As far as I can tell, there are two ways Zahir can play this. He can essentially ransom me, using my well-being as a way to ensure Devorah's compliance. Or he could use this as a way to lure her here, forcing her to start the war on his soil. It would make it harder for our allies to help, and they may even hesitate if they believe she's the one provoking the situation.

Fuck, I hope she's okay. By now, she would have noticed my disappearance, and if I know her, she'll be worrying incessantly. But I trust her and her ability to let reason outweigh emotion, and my father will have gone to her. The two of them can put together a plan, not to save me necessarily, but for how to handle Zahir.

A door creaks open, emitting the barest bit of moonlight before slamming shut and plunging the cell into darkness once again. I hold my breath, listening to every scuff of boots against the stone, waiting for clues. The footsteps are even, and it doesn't sound like they're descending, which means I'm above ground. Each one echoes off the stone like a bomb in the otherwise silent chamber, and I count them. Just twenty. They've kept me twenty feet from the exit. They're that sure I'll never get out of the iron chains.

A burly figure walks in, but my eyes haven't adjusted enough to the darkness to make out any discernible features in the silhouette. The Fae is tall and broad, and holds their head aloft. When they stop inches from the bars, I catch the glint of white hair and the curve of ram-like horns.

Zahir.

"I didn't expect you to do your torturing," I say, my voice raw and gritty from the lack of water.

The Night Court King chuckles, his blue eyes catching the one ray of moonlight before his shadow magic conceals him in darkness once again. "Who said anything about torture?" he purrs. My eyes flick up to the shackles, and once again, he lets loose a low laugh. "How are your wings feeling?"

I resist the urge to snarl.

"No, I think we're torturing you enough as it is," he continues, crossing his arms over his chest. "We won't hurt you…unlike the treatment you gave our soldier."

"He attacked our princess." I shrug, my wrists and wings screaming in protest at the casual gesture. "An act of war deserves that, wouldn't you say?"

Zahir waves away my concern, like that little battle was nothing of consequence. For him, it might not have been. But for me? For my court? It was enough to make us realize how vulnerable we were. It took a lot of maneuvering to make that blow over.

"I suppose we'll see."

"See?"

"How your princess responds to your capture." His smile is feral, fucking evil. "If she cooperates, you'll be released and taken to a healer—no harm, no foul. If she doesn't…" He leaves the implication hanging. He'll send me back in pieces until Devorah cracks and agrees to his demands.

"She won't come for me." I try to infuse my voice with the barest hint of resentment, with a dash of hopelessness. Maybe if he thinks Devorah won't be bothered, he'll be forced to switch tactics, and that will buy her some extra time.

"I'm not so sure," he muses. "Maybe you've been blind to it, but the rest of us see how you look at each other. She cares for you—maybe even loves you." He sneers the word like it's a curse. "And love makes Fae weak."

"Some would say it makes you stronger."

Zahir barks a laugh so loud it echoes. "Those Fae are fools. Love is a liability. Just look at my siblings. Hades has always been a royal pain in my ass, but the second she fell in love with that gutter whore, she lost her edge. And from there it was only a matter of time before I could exploit that to my advantage."

Well shit. Zahir having Minthe complicates things. That will put the Underground out of commission. I hope Hades found a way to let Devorah know that little fact; otherwise, she really could be walking straight into a trap.

Fuck, I hate being stuck down here and unable to help her.

"Well, I should be off," Zahir says. "Someone called all the monarchs back to Summer Court for a little luncheon. I think that will be a great time to inform our beautiful Devorah of my prize." I bare my teeth at the sound of my nickname for her rolling off his tongue. "Or maybe I'll tell her you're dead and be there to pick up the pieces."

"You don't deserve to breathe the same air as her," I seethe.

He ignores me. "I just need something to seal the deal."

The iron bars swing open, and his shadow magic slips inside, reaching straight for my wings. I hiss and thrash as the smoke thins into a blade and slices off a piece from the edge. The agony is instant and everywhere. It's like he drilled into all my bones, stuck pins in my muscles, and peeled the nails from my fingers and toes all in one little slice. I roar, unable to keep my composure as his magic takes the flesh of my wing out of the cell and the bars slam shut again.

"Have a good day, Ari. I know I will."

I grit my teeth, trying to ignore the pain in favor of listening to his retreat, hoping I'll catch a comment or two between him and the guards so I can see how many there are. But just as the light from the door streams in, my hearing grows muddled and my head swims.

When I blink, a familiar face approaches the cell. "Hey, Ari," Tarek says.

I'm still panting, trying not to vomit from the pain. "Hello, friend," I deadpan, letting my head loll forward so I don't have to bother to look at him. "I guess it's too much to hope that you're here to let me go."

The bars swing open once more, and he approaches with a cup of water. I glare incredulously. "It's not poisoned." He takes a sip to prove his point before holding it to my lips. I drink greedily, but it still doesn't help the sand coating my throat.

"Why is an advisor delegated to guarding a prisoner?" I ask.

"You know better than to think I'm your guard."

The silence that follows speaks louder than words ever could. I stare in shock. We may be on opposing sides, and intellectually I know Tarek and I are more enemies than friends, but I never expected to be tortured by his hand. Questioned? Sure. Tricked and manipulated into giving information? Absolutely. But not torture.

"What would you do if you were me?" he asks softly. "You know the training, the oath we take. He's my king. I serve him above all else."

"I thought you served your queen."

It's a low blow, and one I expect to get me a kick to the balls, but he grits his teeth and hisses, "You would do the exact same thing if your queen demanded it."

"That's the difference. Devorah would never put me in the position of choosing between her and a friend."

"I never took you as naive." He rolls up his sleeves. Dark magic begins to coil around him. "Zahir isn't a bad king, you know? He keeps things running smoothly and has strengthened our relationship with the other Unseelie Courts. I won't sit here and tell you he doesn't want more territory, something more fruitful. That doesn't make him a bad king."

"He's never heard of trade agreements?"

Tarek sighs heavily and turns back to me. The magic has completely coated his skin now, serving both as an intimidation tactic and a shield. He and I trained together, so I know exactly what's coming, but that doesn't make it any easier. I grit my teeth, preparing myself for the onslaught of pain.

"Just make this easier and answer the questions," he pleads.

"You know I'd rather die."

He nods pensively. Then, in a magically amplified voice, he asks, "Why hasn't Devorah ascended to the throne?"

I give him a frosty stare. Magic crackles in the air. I hold my breath.

My scream echoes off the stones, reverberating so loudly the structure seems to quiver, but I haven't made a sound. My eyes, which have closed at some point, open to find Tarek screaming in my voice. He used a glamour to sound like me.

He drops the glamour and the amplifying spell and whispers, "We both know you won't break. Why would I hurt my friend so pointlessly?"

I regard him warily. I don't think that just because he spared me some pain, it means he won't try to gain information from me in other ways. But...it's something.

The next hour is more of the same, but now that Tarek understands, I'll play along; he amplifies my voice so I can provide the fake screaming, though my creative use of name-calling is all real.

"Will she come for you?" he asks softly, between faux torture sessions.

"I hope not," I admit, willing to give him that one piece of information.

"Me too," he sighs. "I can protect you this way, but if she tries to break you out—"

His hands will be tied. I understand, even if I hate it.

He leaves the cell and sits in a chair outside the door. "Do you know what he's planning at the luncheon?" I ask. He raises one eyebrow as if to say, 'Do you expect me to answer that?' "Will he hurt her?" I clarify.

"Not unless he has to."

Fucking hell.

I wish there was a way to warn Devorah so she's not blindsided, so that she doesn't need to decide on the fly without me there to help her. Not that she needs my help, or that she won't have her other advisors. But I want to be the one who helps her, not the one who makes her life more difficult.

Stay safe, beautiful, I mentally send into the ether, knowing with all the iron around me it won't get anywhere, but hoping against all odds, that it does.

Chapter Thirty-Seven
Devorah

I HATE THIS FUCKING court.

As Radley predicted, we were able to cross the border with his help, but Zahir modified the restrictions surrounding teleportation. And of course, the two prisons that Ari could be in are far from the Autumn Court border, which means we need to trek across the desert to get there.

I pull the scarf tighter around my face to block the blowing sand. It's not too hot, thankfully, since it's always night here, but the sand still clings to my eyes and makes it hard to see.

We reach the center of the court, where we can see the white stone of the palace reflecting the moonlight, and pause. This is where our party needs to separate. Hershel and Behar will take their small contingent of soldiers to the east, toward the ocean, and Radley and I will go west toward the border with Day Court.

"Remember," Hershel says right before he leaves, "if Ari isn't there, you leave right away. Don't linger; don't wait for me to join you. Head for the Day Court."

We go our separate ways, leaving me and Radley with a handful of soldiers to assist us on our journey. "You have your gloves?" he asks. I flex my fingers in response. Ari will be held in irons, so gloves that are resistant to the metal are crucial. As is the glamour we've cast; to everyone else, Radley and I look like Hades and Izar. With luck, the disguises will buy us time before a fight breaks out.

The trek seems endless. Between the darkness and the sand, everything looks the same. It's a tricky path to navigate. We can't get too close to the river to make it easier on our legs—the vampyres there won't hesitate to rat us out—and we need to skirt the palace, adding an extra half-hour of walking.

When my calves burn from the slipping sand and my back is screaming, sunlight crests the dunes. Day Court. We're getting close.

There are several small towns on this side of the court—a few of the citizens prefer to live in a section with a slight amount of daylight—but we won't find the prison amongst them. No matter how much of an asshole Zahir is, he won't risk civilian lives by stationing dangerous criminals there.

Between the first and second towns is a squat, unassuming building surrounded by sand on all sides. From here, it looks like an outpost for travelers coming in from the heat of the Day Court. But I can taste the iron surrounding it, coating my tongue and making me gag.

I keep quiet as we approach the prison door. "Odd," I murmur. There are no guards stationed outside, and no wards surrounding the perimeter.

Two of my soldiers push me back, taking the lead in case of hidden traps, but they make it to the door without incident.

"I don't like this," Radley says. I have to agree. Either there's an army waiting for us inside, or Ari isn't here.

No, he's here. He has to be.

"Stay by the door unless you hear a commotion," I instruct the soldiers. They nod, bowing slightly. One wraps his hand around the handle and waits for my signal.

"Let's get your boy." Radley smirks, and the guard yanks the door open.

As much as I want to go in a blaze of glory, confrontation isn't the best option here. It doesn't matter that my entire body is vibrating with adrenaline and unspent magic; I have to keep the element of surprise.

Once inside, I banish my cloak and scarf and brush the sand that clings to my fitted suit. It's a look I've seen Hades wear a hundred times, one that screams *I'm in charge of a fucking underground empire*, and I have to admit, I may need to steal the fashion choice for less formal events. I summon a pair of heels to complete the look. Radley, having taken the disguise of Izar, complete with a dark shirt and black fitted pants, nods and gestures for me to lead.

We walk down a surprisingly short hallway—there's not even a set of stairs; it's just a straight shot to the door. And there's not a guard in sight.

What the hell do they do to their prisoners that makes them so confident they won't escape?

Fortunately, I don't have much time to ponder as we enter the room with the cells lined with iron bars. Thick gray stones separate each cell from the next, blocking my view past the first few cells. Every one of them is empty. Radley and I exchange a look. Hershel was under the assumption that these prisons were always full.

"Could be a glamour," he mutters. I don't know what would inspire the Night Court to glamour their cells to appear empty, but it's plausible.

Just before the very last cell, Tarek—Zahir's advisor—sits in a wooden chair, staring straight at us.

"Your Highnesses," he says, jumping up and bowing deeply. Channeling Hades, I don't bother with a greeting, though Radley says hello. "I thought you were attending the luncheon in Summer Court."

Radley shrugs in a perfect imitation of Izar.

Tarek fidgets. "King Zahir said—"

"Do I look like a lapdog to you? Like Zahir can make me heel?" I ask, keeping my voice cool and dispassionate the way Hades does right before she's about to blow shit up. "He's taken what's mine."

"Minthe isn't here."

"I'll verify that for myself."

Tarek looks like he wants to protest, but decides against it. He resumes his seat and gestures to the cell, making no move to unlock it, but I'll deal with that later. Radley lets me take the lead, and I finally allow myself to look into the cell.

Radley swears when he catches sight of Ari. His hands are shackled above his head—his shoulders look moments from popping out of their sockets—and his legs are spread-eagled and secured about an inch above the ground.

But that's not what makes me sick, and not what made Radley swear. Ari's wings are mutilated. They're pinned to the wall, little spider web fissure spreading from the large iron bolts. There's one gaping hole that matches the shape of the flesh we found outside my room, and there's one surgically precise slice missing from the edge of the other, which is still bleeding.

I want to scream. I want to burn the entire place to the ground, killing Tarek and anyone else who may have had a hand in Ari's treatment. My body goes hot; my blood boils.

"Easy," Radley whispers. A cool breeze, courtesy of his air magic, washes over me, making it marginally easier to think.

Ari lifts his head. His complexion is pallid, like he's been here for months rather than hours. A side effect of the iron. His eyes, those gorgeous purple eyes that made me fall in love with him, are dull and tired. I can sense the pain radiating off him in waves.

"Good to see you, Hades," he drawls. Thank the goddess his spirit isn't broken yet. "Thanks for the alliance, by the way. That worked out well."

I ignore that. There's no good answer that won't end up biting Hades or me in the ass later.

"Open the bars," I order Tarek, deviating from the plan. I was supposed to subdue the guard before I got Ari out, but I need to be in there. I need to make sure he's alright.

Tarek doesn't move, he simply arches an eyebrow. "King Zahir said—"

"Does it look like I give two shits what Zahir said?" I ask. Beside me, I can feel Radley tensing, getting ready to attack in case this part doesn't go to plan. "Open the damn bars or I'll tell Zahir exactly what goes on in the Underground between you and a certain married female."

Ari told me about Tarek and the queen one night when I needed something to take my mind off all the shit I was going through, but it was a total guess that Hades knows anything about it. Luckily, Tarek pales so badly I think he's about to pass out. "You wouldn't," he breathes.

"Try me."

He eyes me skeptically for a moment before the door clangs open. After a wordless exchange, I enter the cell while Radley waits in the hall with Tarek, ready to incapacitate him when needed.

Walking into the cell feels like a centaur just dropped onto my chest. At least the iron isn't touching my skin, which means I can still use my magic.

I throw up a shield to silence our conversation and prowl closer to Ari. "If you think I'm going to tell you anything about her—" he starts.

"It's me," I breathe, letting the glamour around my voice drop. "Don't react."

Ari, thankfully, grimaces like he's still dealing with Hades. "What are you doing here, beautiful?"

"I'm here to save you, obviously." I turn and walk a pace away, affecting Hades' signature smirk before turning back to Ari. "Have you seen any other guards besides Tarek?"

"None," he says, keeping very still. "But you need to go."

"I will. Once I figure out how to get you down from there." His tongue pokes out of his mouth to wet his lower lip. I take that as acquiescence. "Will you be able to run once we get you out of here? We're not far from the border."

"Will we be able to cross the border?"

"I think so. Zahir has been working with someone in the Day Court, so I think the wards will be weak. If not, we have to make it to the Underground."

He slumps down even further. "I still think you should get back to safety."

"Not without you. Are you ready?" I ask.

"Ready."

I put my hand at the small of my back and form a circle, giving Radley our signal. Coughing fills the chamber, and I spin in time to see Tarek grappling at his throat as Radley uses his air magic to suck the oxygen from his lungs. He lashes out with his shadow magic, but I'm ready, smothering it with a blast of hot flame.

"Go down, you little shit," Radley grits—still using Izar's voice. "I'm not trying to kill you. Just pass out already." Tarek's magic lashes out again, but instead of attacking me or Radley, this time it flicks the stone wall behind him.

"Shit," Ari swears. "That was a panic button. We're about to have company."

Tarek passes out just as ten soldiers appear from within the shadows of the cells, banging open all the doors and using their dark magic to plunge the prison into total darkness. Even the ball of light I conjure isn't enough to combat it.

"Use your fire," Ari gasps.

I call fire to my hands, and it pierces the shadows just enough for me to see Ari. Radley lets loose a sharp whistle. The footsteps of our guards running into the prison is a precursor to a torrent of fire that explodes down the prison hall, making it harder for the Night Court Fae to hide within the shadows. They start attacking each other, fire and darkness colliding in a shower of sparks.

Radley joins me in the cell, glamour still in place. They may know we're not Hades and Izar now, but it would be a stretch for them to assume a prince and princess would be here.

"Hey, buddy," Radley says, letting his vocal glamour drop enough for Ari to realize who's helping him, before he withdraws a key and starts working on the shackles. "Got this off Tarek. Figured it'd be faster than trying to pick the locks."

"Smart," I praise him.

"See? I'm so much more than a pretty face."

As Radley works on Ari's hands, I reach for the bolts in his wings. "This isn't how I imagined you first touching my wings." Ari's laugh turns to a groan as Radley gets his arms free. Behind us, the sounds of battle rage on.

I take hold of the bolt, the iron so thick it almost burns straight through my gloves. I get a good grip and lay my other hand on his wing to hold it steady. "Just do it," he says. Without taking my eyes off his, I yank it out. He screams. His dislodged wing droops, almost touching the floor.

"I'm so sorry," I whisper, running my fingers over the hole.

"We gotta hurry," Radley says, switching sides with me so he can get the final shackle around Ari's ankle.

"One more, Little Hershel," I say, and the use of the nickname makes him chuckle enough that when I pull the last bolt through, he doesn't see it coming. It doesn't stop the slew of curses that spill from his lips or the way his whole body collapses against us as we finally get him free.

"We have to move fast," Radley says, summoning a pair of boots for Ari and gently putting them on his battered feet. "We need to get to an experienced healer if he ever wants to fly again."

"I can run," he promises, but he can barely stand. Getting over the sand is going to be really fucking hard.

"Can you support half his weight if we fly?" Radley asks me.

"I'll figure it out." I'll do whatever I have to do to get Ari the fuck out of this court. "Let's go."

Our guards spot us and immediately push back the Night Court soldiers, clearing a path. As much as I hate abandoning them, I know they'll follow as soon as we're in the clear; we chose them specifically because they all have wings.

When we're two feet from the door, Tarek appears in front of us. "You won't make it," he says, his voice still raw from Radley's earlier asphyxiation.

"Move or I will burn you alive," I say, my voice still disguised as Hades'.

He shakes his head, but steps aside. Radley and I monitor him warily as we pass. "Hang on," Ari says, panting from the exertion. He motions for Tarek to come forward and grabs him around the back of the neck.

"Thanks, brother," he says. And then head butts him so hard that Tarek crumples.

"What in the goddess's name were you thinking?" I ask as Ari sways.

"He was supposed to torture me and didn't." His eyes are glazed and not quite focused, but his speech is clear, and he doesn't sound confused. "Least I could do was knock him out so he can't be held accountable for our escape."

"Feel free to never help me. With anything," Radley laughs.

The second we're outside, we unfurl our wings, the material of my suit shredding as they pop loose. We take to the sky, Ari hanging between us. His wings flutter, but the air passes through the holes and makes it impossible to help.

The sunlight gets brighter and brighter. We're so close I can practically taste the heated sand of the desert. I can see the shimmering of the wards. "Here's hoping our guess was right," Radley calls as we approach the boundary.

"Shit," Ari swears, turning to me in panic. "Look down."

Radley swears and pulls hard enough that we come to a stop in the air, hovering right before the Day Court border, where an entire legion of Night Court soldiers awaits.

"Well, fuck."

Chapter Thirty-Eight
Ari

"Well fuck," Devorah breathes, a bit more cavalier than I expect, but maybe that's shock. The soldiers—what has to be two-thirds of their army—stretch from this side of the border and well into the sun-drenched desert of the Day Court.

Hands raise and shadows coalesce, growing so thick they blanket the sand. With preternatural strength, a legion of vampyres drags catapults loaded with iron bolts to the front of their lines. They draw them back until the strings whine, waiting for a signal to launch.

"That about sums it up," Radley mutters. He and Devorah haven't dropped their disguises, but everyone will know they're not Hades and Izar—neither have wings. It will be bad enough when they discover it's Devorah here, but if they realize the Prince of the Autumn Court is aiding her, it could plunge the entire realm into war.

We need to get the fuck out of here.

I try to think of a strategy, but my mind is sluggish from the iron and all the blood loss. Even if I were in top form, I'm not sure I could find a way out of this situation. One look at Radley's tightened jaw and resigned expression tells me he feels the same. Not Devorah, though. Her eyes dart from the border to the army and back again so quickly it makes me dizzy.

After a moment, she nods, satisfied with her plan. "Radley, can you take Ari by yourself?"

"Absolutely not," I snap at the same time as Radley says, "Without you?"

"You're going to take on an entire army by yourself?" he continues.

The Night Court won't aim to capture this time—we attacked their soldiers, broke out of their prison, and are on their soil. They'll aim to kill. And if Devorah is by herself...

"Beautiful," I plead. "You both need to go. Leave me. If they discover it's you—"

She ignores me. "I'm going to distract them while you get out of here."

"You'll die," Radley says, not bothering to sugarcoat it.

She smirks, a devilish, beautiful thing. "I've got this." Her eyes meet mine, a thousand words brimming in their ocean depths, but she doesn't voice any of them. "Go." She retracts her wings and plummets out of my grasp. I reach for her, toppling me and Radley.

"We just have to trust her," he grits through his teeth, flapping his wings until he can right us. "And if you ever want to fly again, you need a healer." His brown eyes meet mine imploringly. "I'll come back for her. I promise."

I don't stop thrashing. I need to help her, to stand at her side. It doesn't matter that I'm barely conscious. If I die, at least I'll be with her. Protecting her.

"Do not make me knock you out," he snaps when I almost slip free of his grasp. He tightens his hold until I can barely breathe. The sounds of battle drift to us: war cries, explosions, and the twang of catapults being fired. I beg—actually beg—for Radley to let me go, but it falls on deaf ears. Later, I may be impressed that Devorah got him to obey her plan so thoroughly, but right now, all reasoning has abandoned me.

Radley zooms toward the shimmering boundary between Day and Night Courts at warp speed. The stars blur until they're nothing more than streaks of white against a sky that turns from navy to cornflower blue.

"Should we slow down?" I ask. This time, my concern has nothing to do with the female I love, and everything to do with the fact that Radley is going headfirst into an unknown magical shield. They may have made it solid, restricted the passage to Night and Day Court soldiers only.

At this speed, we'd break most of the bones in our bodies. And that's the best-case scenario.

Radley doesn't slow down. "Gird your loins!" he shouts, followed by a high-pitched shriek.

We sail through the ward seamlessly.

In the bright sunlight of Day Court, there's no hiding the blush that rises in Radley's cheeks as his shriek dies out. "Well," he clears his throat. "That was embarrassing. Maybe don't mention that to anyone, yeah?"

Absolutely no chance of that.

"Let me go back to her, and I promise I'll never mention your banshee scream to anyone."

"Nah. I'm more afraid of Dev than you, especially while you're all weak and pathetic."

"Thanks."

"But bright side—" he gestures to the sand below us. "There's no army." I frantically scan the landscape. He's right. They must have crafted an illusion and built it into the shield.

"There are still too many for her to fight on her own," I say.

He nods, but keeps flying toward the foot of the Orasite Mountains toward a cluster of birds.

No, not birds.

Dragons.

There seem to be six of them, their large lizard-like bodies huddled together in the shadow of the red-rock mountain, seeking refuge from the harshest rays of the sun. In the center is a male in his Fae form, naked but draped in gold.

Radley descends, landing a few paces from Shesha and the members of his hoard. At our presence, two female dragons—Shesha's mate and one I don't recognize—shift and rush forward, bracing me on either side. "Oh my," she whispers, looking at the state of my wings.

"Those assholes," Shesha growls, smoke escaping flared nostrils. "We will make them pay."

"Shesha, please. Devorah—"

"We ran into a bit of trouble at the border," Radley interrupts. "She stayed behind to let us get out."

Shesha spits a curse in an old Fae language before whistling sharply. Dozens of dragons emerge, popping out from behind trees, standing where they crouched behind other dragons, and cresting some of the smaller hills. Some are as large as a mountain, some as small as a lion; they come in every color from ruby red to pitch black. There are so many, I can't count them all.

This isn't just Shesha's hoard.

He brought all the hoards from Summer and Day Court. Every single one.

At my expression, he smirks. "We'll take care of our future queen."

Hearing the dragon refer to Devorah as her queen is mind-blowing; they've never recognized the monarchy's rule. Only Devorah could convince this terrifying group to abandon their feelings on elemental rulers and unite them on her behalf.

He begins removing his gold, handing it to his mate, who secures it in a pouch at her feet. "You—" he points to Radley, "—go with the advisor and my mate to the healer."

"I promised Ari—" Radley starts, but Shesha's face elongates, navy blue scales extending over his body. We both jump backward as he grows into a mammoth monster.

"Don't be daft." His voice is so deep that it sounds like it comes from the mountain itself. "You know what will happen if they see someone using air magic."

Radley mutters something under his breath about already using his magic in the Night Court, but doesn't protest further. Honestly, I don't blame him. I wouldn't argue with a being that could eat me without even having to chew.

Without another word, Shesha flies off, releasing a plume of ultraviolet fire that ripples the already heated air. The dragons follow, roaring a chorus that's more terrifying than any war drum.

"Come," Shesha's mate says. "Your Highness, please help Ari onto my back. It seems he may need help staying in his seat."

"I can't leave without her," I rasp. Knowing Devorah has allies headed her way makes me feel slightly better, but it's not enough. I need to see her, to know she makes it out of this alive.

"Our orders were to get you to a healer and then back to the palace. I won't risk our newfound alliance and my family's safety by going against my queen."

She transforms into a sleek, emerald green dragon, and Radley grabs me beneath the arms and flies me up to her back. He wraps his arms around my waist, setting us both into a seat along her spine, and I grip a spike at the base of her neck. "Here we go, lover," Radley chuckles, leaning close enough that his bushy beard scrapes against my shoulder. I go to bat him away, but think better of it as the dragon launches into the sky, opting to hold on. Radley whoops. I do my best not to lose the contents of my stomach.

I expect to be taken to the palace or the healer's compound nestled in the mountains, but we fly straight past them, all the way to the border between Day and Summer Court. My head is pounding from the relentless sun, and my already parched mouth is dry as the desert below us.

We slow, descending near a small inn with blue siding and white trim that seems strangely out of place against the barren mountain landscape. As soon as we land, a brownie steps out the door and waves us in. "Upstairs, second door on the right," she orders in a no-nonsense voice.

Radley helps me down, and Shesha's mate shifts so they can both drag me inside. They move fast enough that I don't have the time to take a look at the quaint sitting room and kitchen downstairs. I'm hustled upstairs, entering a room where Larisa is sitting on the edge of the bed. She stands as we enter.

"On the bed, face down," she dictates.

"How come you never talk to me like that?" Radley teases. She shoots him a withering glare.

"Get back to the palace," she snaps. "Make your presence known. The story is that you snuck off with a harpy late last night."

"Fuck yeah I did," he winks. After depositing me onto the bed, he pats me on the shoulder and murmurs, "Heal fast," then disappears with a salute to Larisa, Shesha's mate on his heels.

"What are you doing here?" I ask.

She scoops her honey-blonde hair into a ponytail and calls white light to her hands. "I'm one of the best healers in the realm." She isn't bragging, she just recites the statement like a fact. "This is going to hurt."

The light around her hands flares brightly, the white splitting into silver and gold sparkles as they connect with my wings. I bury my face in the mattress, biting down on the comforter to stifle the screams. "Sorry," Larisa says, though she doesn't sound it. "Normally, I'd give you a tonic to knock you out, but we need you awake for this next bit."

I can actually feel her magic knitting my skin, pulling both sides together until new skin grows over the hole. It's painful enough to make me black out all on my own, tonics be damned.

"Next bit?" I ask when I can finally take a full breath.

"Devorah has a plan for Zahir, but you need to be whole and unharmed for that to work."

"She does too," I grumble. My thoughts stray back to the moment she slipped from my grasp, the way her sleek brown hair billowed around her before she allowed her wings to slow her fall. I know I would have been useless in a fight, but I hate that I'm so far away from her now.

"Tell me what happened." I know she's trying to distract me, but I need it, so I humor her. I tell her of my capture, of the holding cell, and everything that's happened since our escape.

When I'm done, the magic fades long enough for me to look over my shoulder to see Larisa flexing her hands and cracking her neck. "Holes are patched," she says. "Now I need to deal with the slice." She lowers her hand close to the edge of my wing, but doesn't touch it. This entire time, she's been very respectful, not touching my wings once, even as her magic batters away at them.

"This is the one Zahir did?"

I nod. "He wanted something to show Devorah. To prove he had me."

"Dickbag," she swears. "Maybe someone will kill him."

I scoff. As much as I'd love that, I don't think anyone strong enough to rival him would take that shot. The other monarchs—King Simi and Queen Gwyneira, especially—may hate what he's doing, but they're used to infighting amongst courts. An abducted advisor isn't enough for them to kill a king.

Just before Larisa's magic flares again, there's the sound of a door bursting open downstairs, followed by shouts and the scuffle of feet coming toward us. Larisa positions herself between me and the door, her magic ready to use in defense. I prop myself up, determined to help even though the raw skin from the iron shackles protests the motion.

"Larisa," my father's voice calls, and she sags in relief when he opens the door. The figure in his arms is thin as a rail, and wearing what looks like a tattered pantsuit. She lifts her head, brown hair falling back just enough that I can see it's Minthe—Hades' girlfriend.

There's a moment of pure relief when he sees me, followed by a flash of horror as he takes in the state of my body.

"Is she alright?" Larisa asks, dragging his attention back to the female in his arms. He brings Minthe into the room, laying her on the other side of the mattress.

"Just dehydrated, I think. She's lethargic and hasn't been able to answer questions."

Larisa nods and places a glowing white hand atop Minthe's head. At once, she shrieks and bolts upright. "They drugged her," Larisa says, as Minthe's eyes search the room wildly, her breath coming in faster and faster. Tears stream down her cheeks.

"No, no, no," she whimpers. "I'm—I was sober." Tears streak down her cheeks.

Larisa makes a sound low in her throat that sounds remarkably close to a growl. Then, she releases a slow, measured breath and says, "Don't worry. When I'm done with Ari, I can take it from your system. Do you know what they gave you?" Minthe shakes her head, her body wracked with tremors. "That's okay. I've got you.

"Hershel, there are four vials in my bag. Give two to Minthe and two to Ari. Minthe, I need you to take them, okay?"

"No—" she sobs.

"I promise they're non-habit forming. They'll rehydrate you and replace any blood loss. Ari can take them first, if you'd like."

She nods, lip trembling.

My father hands me a vial and I down its contents in one gulp, instantly feeling better. When I give Minthe a nod, she takes it as well and settles back down on the pillows. He climbs in beside her, smoothing her hair and shushing her softly as she curls into his chest.

Larisa releases another shaky breath. I can feel the anger radiating off her. When she catches me glancing at her, she lowers her voice and says, "There are lines you don't cross, even in war. You don't threaten someone's mate, and you don't drug a recovering addict."

I agree wholeheartedly.

Larisa finishes quickly, healing my wing, my wrists, and finally my ankles. Her healing, combined with the tonic, makes me feel as good as new, better even. I feel like I could fly across the entire realm. Which is exactly what I plan to do.

With a word of thanks, I spring up and turn to leave.

"Don't even think about it," my father barks, suddenly blocking the door with his arms crossed.

"What?"

"We're going back to the palace, right now."

"Devorah—"

"Was very clear with her instructions." I growl at my father, but he remains an immovable wall between me and the love of my life. "Don't make me knock you out and drag you back to the palace."

Why do people keep threatening to do that?

Then, softer, he leans in and says, "She needs you at the palace."

It's like she popped a hole in me and deflated all the air in my chest. I can't deny Devorah anything, even if it means leaving her when every instinct screams to return to her.

I nod, and he smiles. "We can't cross the border, so we'll have to take the portal. There's one not far, deep in the mountains."

I know the one he's speaking of, and nod again. Turning to thank Larisa again, I find her already working on Minthe. She has a shield around them both, I assume because Minthe's mouth is open on a silent scream as she thrashes and tears apart the bedding.

"Can you at least tell me what this plan is?" I ask my father, once we're out of the inn and he's in my arms, as I fly to the portal.

"Why would I spoil the surprise?"

Chapter Thirty-Nine
Devorah

FREE-FALLING THROUGH THE SKY isn't the most tactful way I've ended an argument, but it's certainly effective.

I know Ari is upset, but I can't stand the thought of him being hurt further because he's trying to protect me. For once, I'm in a position where *I* can protect *him*.

And I have the perfect idea for a distraction.

I drop like a stone, and it surprises the army enough that they halt. At this point, they know I'm not Hades, but they still can't find out it's me. Not only would it be a major issue if a princess were found staging a jail break, but I don't want the realm to know how much power I've amassed. I want to keep the element of surprise.

So, as I fall, I create a glamour. I got the idea from something Ari said after my fire exploded. He said I looked like one of the most feared Fae in history.

So, that's who I'll be.

When my wings snap out, they don't look like my own. They're black, closer to the shape of a bat's wings, and decorated with silver swirls. My skin goes alabaster pale, but my eyes remain the same. Whispers start immediately, the soldiers recognizing my alias.

Queen Tamara. My aunt.

A nightmare given flesh.

It doesn't matter that she's been dead for centuries. It doesn't matter that many of the soldiers on this field watched her die at the hands of Gwyneira. And it doesn't matter that my glamour isn't one hundred percent accurate since I never met her in person, and am basing my glamour on renderings. Reason flees the soldiers in the face of this abject horror, taking with it any semblance of control or order. Whole groups scatter, their ranks breaking as they hightail it for the safety of the dunes. Those who stay are visibly shaken.

The second I land, fire pools in both of my hands. I glamour that too, making it appear white instead of orange and blue. More abandon ranks—their fear of my aunt's deadly fire overriding logic. I use the advantage, aiming an attack at the mechanisms launching the iron bolts. The blast itself is sloppy; it's too wide and too tall, not concentrated like it should be—but my aim is true.

The catapult detonates.

I aim at the second, but the soldiers catch on to my plan and charge, abandoning the catapult in favor of attacking me with magic. Black shadows stream toward me from all directions, blotting out the stars and the faint sunlight from Day Court. It's disorienting and makes it too hard to execute targeted strikes. I get a few lucky shots in, soldiers going down as they collide with one of my fireballs, but as soon as one goes down, they're replaced by another.

My mind conjures images of last night, where my fire exploded so violently that it churned the sea. Can I tap into that power again?

Yes.

But without Ari to anchor me, to pull me back from that vast power, I could decimate the entire area. There's a town not too far from here. I can't be certain they'll be exempt from the blast, and even though these Fae aren't mine, I can't justify innocent casualties.

I switch to defense, concentrating my energy on keeping the army at bay. Flames encase every inch of my body, so I wear them like a second skin. The brightness of the fire makes some of the soldiers wince, and I use their distraction to carve a path toward the border. One glance at the sky tells me Radley and Ari are gone, and all I can do is hope the army on the other side didn't give them too much trouble.

I make it a few more steps, penetrating the army's ranks, when the ground vibrates. A sound like thunder rolls over the sand, starting quietly before growing to a deafening roar. The grains shift beneath my feet, sucking me down to my ankles.

The soldiers pause. Half of them pivot toward the Day Court, where a large cloud blots out the sunlight. "What is that?" someone asks as the roar repeats.

"My backup," I say on a sigh of relief.

The cloud separates, revealing the silhouetted shape of wings. A plume of ultraviolet dragon fire rips through the ward between Day and Night Court, which shimmers futilely before winking out of existence, taking half the army's ranks along with it. They must have created an illusion to make me think they had more numbers than they did. Clever.

Leading the charge is a navy-blue dragon. From this distance, Shesha looks long and serpentine, but the closer he gets, the more his bulk becomes apparent. Behind him are dozens of the beautiful beasts, the darkness of the court muting their brilliant-colored scales, but making them no less impressive. As one, they roar again; a battle cry and a warning.

Sensing a new threat, the soldiers turn to target the hoard.

Huge mistake.

Controlling my breathing, I allow the power to build within me. My skin heats, my blood boils. Just when I'm sure I'll burn alive with the sheer heat of my magic, I release it in a wave, rolling through the soldiers closest to me. At the same time, Shesha and his dragons attack the far ranks, starting from the edge of the wards. Our fire collides in an explosion of light. Sand turns to glass, and bodies disintegrate, their charred remains smoking as they fall.

As they get closer, the dragons dive bomb the soldiers, spraying their fire or crushing them in their maws. One beast picks up a horned male and soars straight into the sky before letting him plummet to his death. Their attacks are vicious. It's thrilling, yet also a little disturbing, to watch.

A dragon lands before me, crushing an entire circle of soldiers beneath its considerable weight. Black scales that shine like an oil spill cover his body. He rests his head on the sand, and a familiar pair of green eyes blink at me.

"Kai?" A puff of smoke is my answer. "What are you doing here?"

His bones pop and rearrange until he's shrinking into his Fae form. I summon a robe, and he takes it with a tentative smile. His sunshine demeanor has dimmed, and his shoulders curve in on themselves, as if he's trying to make himself as small as possible. "I know I'm not who you want to see right now—"

I throw myself into his arms, wrapping him in a big hug. He stiffens momentarily before embracing me in earnest, picking me up and swinging me around in typical Kai fashion.

"You don't hate me?" he asks, vulnerability cracking his voice.

I pull away and pat him on the shoulder. "I was frustrated. And terrified. And maybe a little pissed because you insisted on total fidelity and then bailed the minute you found your mate." He has the decency to look rueful, rubbing the back of his neck and hanging his head. "But no. I don't hate you."

"So...we can be friends?" He perks up, looking like a puppy who was told he's going on a walk.

A blast of dragon fire lands beside us, making me jump. "Maybe let's discuss this when we're not in the middle of a war zone."

"Right. I'm actually supposed to escort you to the nearest portal." I arch an eyebrow. He shivers. "Fuck, that's terrifying with the glamour. You need to change that."

A horn blares, signaling the surrender of the army around us. The dragons chuff in frustration, but then lower to the sand, encircling the army and cutting them off from escape.

"Did you see Ari?" I ask.

"He went with my mother and Prince Radley to the healer. His wings were fucked, but he was okay when I saw him."

My shoulders come down a bit at that news, and I stretch my wings. They're still disguised and sit oddly on my shoulder blades. "I have guards back that way." I gesture toward the prison. Kai jerks his head at the closest dragon, and she nods, taking off to check on them.

"She'll make sure they get back safely. Now, on to the portal!" Kai shifts and roars. "Let me take you on a ride, princess."

I roll my eyes, but don't hide the smile tugging my lips. The dragons have successfully subdued the army, and I trust Shesha will take them as war prisoners...not barbeque them all. So I fly onto his back, and Kai leaps into the sky.

We sail over the barrier and into the Orasite Mountains. The sun is blinding here, the heat oppressive compared to the cool darkness of the Night Court.

Part of me still wants to beg Kai to bring me to Ari, but I know I can't. I need to get back to the palace to enact the next phase of the plan.

We land just before an old log cabin that's tucked into the red-rock mountainside. Kai shifts and ushers me inside. The exterior is run down, the brittle wooden walls bleached by the unrelenting sun, but inside is immaculate. It's a simple space with a few rocking chairs and a plush area rug surrounding a door in the center of the room.

He opens the door, revealing the swirling mist of the portal. "Off you go," he says, pulling me in for a quick hug. "And Devorah?" I pause. "Thank you. For asking me to marry you. And for...not actually marrying me."

I laugh and shake my head. "When things get settled, you and your mate will have to come over for dinner."

"I'd like that."

With a final wave, I step onto the ley line, hurtling toward the palace. I change my glamour again so that this time I look like Kalinda, who promised to remain in my suite until I returned. Before long, I leap off the moving walkway, landing on soft feet in the sandstone palace hallway.

Everything appears normal, quiet even. There are no whispers of an attack in the Night Court, no frantic guards worried about the missing princess. The only brief snippets of conversations I hear are about the luncheon today, and what could be happening that the monarchs needed to return after such *a scandalous evening.*

Moving with purpose, I knock on the door to my suite once, as Kalinda usually does, before slipping inside the room. The second the lock clicks, I release an exaggerated groan and drop my glamour, relieved to be back in my skin once again.

"It's the funniest thing..."

I shriek and whirl around. The cool voice who interrupted my silent celebration of a job well done belongs to Gwyneira, who is sitting in my window seat, thumbing through some of my old sketchbooks. She's dressed in fighting leathers and a dark blue tunic with a silver snowflake embroidered on the breast, and her hair, which is usually elaborate and curled, is in a tight bun.

Kalinda is sitting stiffly in an armchair. She gives me an apologetic smile with wide eyes that screams *she just showed up and I had no idea what to do.* I nod, dismissing her, and—though she remains stoic—her shoulders deflate in relief. She bows to both Gwyneira and me before hastily retreating into my bedroom.

Gwyneira doesn't take her ice blue eyes off me, but waits until Kalinda exits before continuing. "My spies reported an odd sighting today."

I do my best not to fidget like a child under her gaze. By tomorrow, she'll be my equal, and I need to treat her as such. Even if she does scare me shitless. "Oh?"

"They claimed they saw a hellfire attack in the Night Court."

"We eradicated all the Fae who used—"

"They also claimed to see someone I killed."

The temperature in the suite dips, making my breath visible and goosebumps rise on my skin. "Odd," I say impassively, and let my fire magic surge just enough to counteract the arctic air.

Gwyneira arches one eyebrow at my unspoken challenge. "Indeed." Her stony expression cracks slightly, giving me the tiniest hint of a smirk. "I trust she won't make another appearance."

It's a warning, a not-so-thinly veiled threat. *Don't pretend to be the undisputed most evil Fae in existence, and we can continue to be allies.*

"I'm sure it was a one-time thing," I reply, straightening my clothes.

She nods once, gracefully stands, and crosses the sitting room. "I look forward to your luncheon, Devorah." And without another word, she leaves my suite.

My body buckles with relief, and I swipe my hand across my forehead. That could have been so bad. I should have thought through the repercussions of pretending to be my aunt, but I was acting on impulse. It was a good idea when it came to getting everyone out of the ambush safely, but it could have had a major pushback. Thank the goddess Gwyneira was in an accommodating mood. Finishing one war only to start another would be one hell of a way to start my reign—and not one I think I could get out of easily.

"You handled her beautifully," Kalinda says, reappearing in the doorway to my bedroom. "I'm sorry, I should have kept her out of your rooms, but—"

"She's terrifying," I chuckle. The remainder of the tension surrounding Kalinda slips away. She appraises me. I can't even imagine what I look like. The seams of the pencil skirt I was wearing as Hades ripped when I transformed into Tamara, and the fabric loosely clings to my hips. There's hair stuck to my neck with adhesive-like sweat, and the bit of skin I can see is dusted with sand and soot.

"Let's get you ready," Kalinda sighs. "You've got work to do yet, Your Majesty."

I'm not sure if it's a slip on her part, but the use of *Your Majesty* instead of *Your Highness* sends a rush of warmth through me.

It's a title I'm ready to claim.

Chapter Forty
Devorah

THE LUNCHEON IS HELD on a patio that overlooks the jungle. Thick trees lean over the terracotta stones, shading the area and giving the illusion of privacy even though palace guards are perched within the branches. Faerie lights magically dangle in long, swooping strands. Small tables with hibiscus centerpieces are clustered around one long, banquet table, which is set with enough places for the royals—spouses and the second generation included.

At my behest, everyone is dressed casually. Most of the females opt for breezy sundresses, and the males wear loose-fitting, floral, button-down shirts and linen pants. It does nothing to cool them against the heat. The humidity weighs down their elaborate hairstyles despite the magic keeping them in place, and sweat slicks their skin and makes those flowy garments cling in unattractive places. More than one Fae has procured a fan, which does little but move around the heavy, jungle air.

Was it petty to choose a location that I knew would be hotter than the depths of the demon realm?

A little, but there is a reason for it. I want everyone on edge, easily agitated. Ready to jump at the slightest provocation.

And there's nothing quite like oppressive heat to elevate emotions.

My dress is white—a nod to my would-be wedding day—and the lace hugs every inch of me, starting at the base of my neck and ending just below my knee. I've swept up my hair so that only a few tendrils float down around my face.

Most everyone is here when I arrive, and all heads swivel to me as I enter. I take a glass from a female Fae at the entrance, ignoring everyone's attention while I take a delicate sip. It's one of my favorite drinks—a clear liquid that fizzes on your tongue and tastes of mint and lime, as well as the earthy zing of magic. When everyone realizes I won't be making an announcement at the start of the event, they go back to their conversations.

Before I can take a step, a Fae steps in my path. A far cry from this morning, Hades is impeccably dressed in a cream silk shift-dress, and her makeup and hair are flawless. Despite the hard edge to her jaw, when her eyes meet mine, there's nothing but softness.

"I spoke with Larisa," she says, glancing back at the Day Court princess, who is on the arm of her boyfriend. "She told me your..." Hades clears her throat. "Larisa healed someone important to me today. Someone who was found in the desert."

Minthe.

Kalinda told me Hershel and his entire crew returned, but I haven't had the chance to meet with him to see what he found in that other prison. I suppose I have my answer. Hershel found Minthe, and she was in bad enough condition that he felt the need to bring her to Larsia. Knowing what Zahir did to Ari, I can't imagine what he had in store for Hades' lover.

"I hope she's well," I say carefully.

Hades' expression is unreadable, which I take as a sign that she's feeling too much to let any emotion show. She nods once, then leans in just close enough for me to catch the faint scent of black cherries. "And for that, consider us even."

As she says the words, there's a subtle caress of magic. "I—" I stammer. It may be unrecognized, but Hades is essentially the seventh monarch, her court being the entire Underground. When Ari told me I owed her a favor after my bachelorette party, I was dreading it. And now it's wiped out. It's a huge weight lifted off my shoulders.

I can barely manage a 'thank you' before Hades melts back into the crowd as if she were never there. Taking a page from her book, I slip through the small gathering toward my brother. He has his arm casually draped around Edina's shoulders. The two of them seem calm, just a pair of betrothed Fae enjoying time together amidst a party, but I know my twin. I see the way his shoulders are bunched and how his hand flexes toward me as I sidle up beside them.

See? I'm in one piece, I say through our mental channel. *You don't have to worry about me.*

"I don't care that you're about to be queen," he says softly, no doubt speaking aloud for Edina's benefit. "I'm your older brother—"

"By like two minutes."

"—and I'm always going to worry about you; to want to protect you." Then, in my head, *Don't think that'll go away just because you can overpower me now.*

I bark a laugh. Edina steps back so that Eldoris can embrace me, and I sink into the comfort of my twin's arms for just a moment, letting myself revel in the fact that I'm alive and well and things are going to plan for once.

Radley breezes out onto the patio—quite literally using his air magic to billow his long hair around his shoulders—as he walks toward us. "It's hotter than a witch's tit out here," he says, slinging his arm around Edina.

"That's not the expression."

"That's rich, coming from you," he deadpans. She rolls her eyes, but loses the fight with her amusement and smiles. Radley, satisfied his joke had its intended effect, turns his brown eyes to me. "The eagle is in the nest."

"I thought we agreed not to use code words."

"Come on, you can't have a heist without code words!"

"Would we call this a heist?" Edina asks, her head tilting to the side. "Seems like the heist-y part of the day is over. This is more like a confrontation...maybe a squabble."

"Fine." His expression goes flat, and his tone is robotic when he says, "We're ready when you are, princess." The act is negated by the flamboyant turn he executes as he flounces away.

Not dramatic at all.

"Ready?" Edina asks.

I meet Eldoris' ocean blue eyes, and he gives me a reassuring nod.

"Let's do this."

I gesture to one of the servants, and he starts ushering Fae to their seats as I make my way to the head of the long table. It's a similar setup to that of my mother's funeral, except this time Edina and Eldoris are directly to my right and left, surrounding me in a show of support, but also a protective bubble. Gwyneira is at the other end of the table, her husbands surrounding her, which puts the rest of the monarchs in the middle. I spoke with King Simi, Lysandra, and Puck about the arrangements—about how I needed them close to Zahir and Oakley—and they all agreed wholeheartedly.

When everyone is seated, I clear my throat lightly. Despite the low hum of chatter and the buzz of insects, they hear me and go silent. Fae at the smaller tables, mostly advisors and some influential courtiers, position their chairs so they can see me, and those at my table shift so that they're all in my eyeline.

I pause for dramatic effect. This part of my speech needs a bit of pageantry. I need Zahir to think I'm nervous, shaken, so that he's comfortable enough to confront me. It's a multifaceted approach: pretending to be a broken female who is trying to keep it together, all while I really want to scream at Zahir and crucify him for what he's done.

But this is a dance I excel in.

"As you all undoubtedly know," I begin slowly, swallowing like it's hard for me to voice the words. Even though I can feel Zahir's piercing stare boring a hole in my skull, I keep my attention averted in feigned embarrassment. "My betrothed, Kai of the Thisavroús Dragon Hoard, has met his fated mate."

There's some murmuring, my audience putting on their own performances as though they didn't hear the news within minutes of it happening.

"As such, we will no longer be married," I glance to the table to the side, the one where Shesha and his mate sit and raise a gold-studded glass to me. After they returned from the battlefield, I insisted they be present, hoping to give them a bit of an alibi after their earlier help. "But I look forward to continuing the friendship we have forged.

"You may be wondering why I called you all back to our court..." I trail off, my eyes lifting to the doorway and the hint of a shadow that lies beyond. "Tomorrow morning, just after sunrise on the beach, I will accept my crown and be coronated as Queen of the Summer Court."

The typically tactful crowd erupts in a chorus of shocked whispers. Several advisors stand, bowing to their monarchs and wishing me well as they leave to get the news to the citizens of their court. Coronations are events that happen rarely due to Fae lifespan, so the entire realm—regardless of court, alliance, or rank—comes to witness the swearing in of a new ruler. There are usually weeks to prepare travel arrangements; I've just given them a ton of work to do before sunrise.

Despite the surprise, there's an undercurrent of excitement, especially from the Summer Court courtiers, who feared living in a court with no queen, even if they never said it aloud.

"Your Highness," Zahir's voice cuts through the din. He pushes away from the table with enough force that the delicate stemware clinks together. With the swagger of a conqueror, he meanders over to me. "There are some matters I wish to discuss before you ascend the throne."

"Well," I stammer, like he caught me off guard, but I'm trying to compose myself. "After lunch, I'd be happy to—"

Zahir closes the distance between us. Beneath the table, Edina conjures an icicle the size of a small spear. "You see," Zahir says, his voice magically amplified. *The prick.* "I have something that may change your mind about merging with my court."

"Merging?" The question comes from Oakley, and I have to bite down on the inside of my cheek to keep from smiling at how this is panning out. I don't know what Oakley and Zahir agreed upon, but it certainly wasn't a merger between Summer and Night Courts.

"Not an alliance?" I ask.

"No," he asserts, coming up beside me at the head of the table. "You see, last night, my soldiers captured something of value in your court.

From right under your nose. And—if you'd like it back—then I suggest you reconsider my offer."

The murmurs increase in volume, most disbelieving. With the level of security surrounding the palace, how in the goddess' name could Zahir take something? He would never be able to get close.

I assumed I'd need to prompt this next part, but Zahir just continues talking. "You see, a trusted member of the Seelie Court aided us."

"From my court?" I ask, incredulous.

"No," Zahir says with a wave of his hand, like he's swatting away a bothersome gnat. "This Fae realized the need for strong leadership, the likes of which are not present in the Seelie Courts, and left his court to join our side."

Bullseye.

Now, everyone knows someone flipped, and since they're all smart enough to realize Day Court's wards were disrupted, they know it's someone there. It absolves Lysandra and Puck from blame, and, as I discovered earlier, Simi already knows who the culprit is and is planning on apprehending him after my little show today.

"What did you take?" Eldoris snaps, his hands gripping the arms of his chair so tightly they turn white. Everyone is playing their part in this plan so perfectly.

Zahir reaches into the pocket of his linen pants and withdraws a piece of Ari's wing. Seeing the flesh makes me want to vomit. I saw what was done to Ari's wings, but seeing this clump of it, dried from lack of blood and rough care, infuriates me.

But simply tilt my head to the side and part my lips in confusion.

"What is it? What did he take?" Fae from the farther tables ask, craning their necks or even standing on chairs to see what Zahir holds before me.

"I took her advisor."

All pretense of politeness is gone. The courtiers are shouting over each other to find out what's happened. There are some truly terrible sentiments—"I knew she wasn't ready to rule "—but most are downright appalled.

"Is that part of his *wing*?" Oakley gasps. One of Gwyneira's husbands snarls.

Zahir smiles smugly. "So you see, my dear Devorah, it is in your best interest to bow to me." He says it casually, but I see the glint in his eye. He's practically foaming at the mouth to see me on my knees before him.

Everyone on the patio is silent—even the bugs have stopped their incessant buzzing as they seem to lean in to see what will happen next.

"No," I say simply.

"What?" The word is little more than a growl.

"You didn't take my advisor." I laugh like it's the most preposterous thing in the world. On cue, Hershel walks outside, nodding to Zahir before standing directly in front of the doors, arms crossed over his chest.

"Not that one," Zahir chuckles. "The new one."

Ari strides onto the patio in a shirt that clings to his muscles and has two strategically placed slits that allow his wings to be completely unfurled—showing no trace of a scar, let alone a wound.

We haven't seen each other since he got back—there was too much to do.

But he's here. He's well.

He's all fucking mine.

I don't bother hiding the lovestruck expression on my face as he crosses the patio, withdrawing his wings once he's sure everyone has gotten a good look at them. He steps in beside me, wrapping his arm around my waist and kissing my temple.

All I can do is smile.

Chapter Forty-One
Ari

My beautiful, brilliant queen.

I want to pull her into my arms, steal her away from all these prying eyes, and drop to my knees before her in eternal worship.

She looks fucking stunning, her turquoise eyes glowing in the slanted light beneath the jungle canopy, staring down her toppled opponent. Not only has Devorah bested Zahir's forces, but she outmaneuvered him. She put him in the worst position. He can double down and insist he breached our defenses, only for me to escape, or, if he says nothing, look like he got caught in a bluff. Neither option is favorable.

Both make him look like an ass.

On top of that, Devorah got him to admit that he conspired with a Seelie Fae *and* that he deceived his only ally. He's lost any credibility he gained over the past few months.

The patio is in utter chaos. Courtiers twitter in excitement. Radley is physically restraining his father, who looks thirty seconds away from vaulting over the banquet table—place setting be damned—to strangle Zahir with his bare hands. Zahir's face is purple, his blue eyes swirling with his shadow magic. Ayelet, the Day Court advisor and a truly despicable excuse for a Fae, has been restrained by his own soldiers. He must have been the turncoat.

Devorah keeps her cool, smiling sweetly despite the bedlam raging around us. She leans into my side, wrapping her arm around my waist. It's such a small gesture, something that's sure to be overlooked amidst the chaos, but it makes my heart swell. She's claiming me in front of all these Fae.

We stay like that, waiting for Zahir's reaction, determined not to let him slip away without acknowledging his defeat. I'm on the metaphorical edge of my seat, giddy with anticipation, hoping he'll somehow manage to dig himself into an even deeper hole.

With force of will, Zahir smiles—a fake, sickly-sweet thing that fools no one. "I—"

Unfortunately, Gwyneira interrupts. "I believe—" Even though she doesn't raise her voice, it's enough to have everyone take their seats once again and regain some semblance of decorum. "—we've had enough excitement for one afternoon, and should return to lunch."

I understand why she steps in. At the end of the day, the Night Court is still an Unseelie Court, and still her ally. It makes sense that she would come to Zahir's aid; appearances are important. I'm still disappointed we don't get to see him stammer through an apology.

"I, for one, would like to eat or get out of this goddess-damned heat!" Oakley grits through his teeth. Radley tentatively removes his hand from his father's shoulder. The king flops back in his seat and downs an entire glass of wine in a few, hearty gulps.

Just before Zahir is about to sit, Devorah leans in and whispers, "I'd reconsider this silly notion of attacking my court. If you speak with your advisors, I believe they'll have some horror stories to tell you. Talk of ghosts come back to life. Ghosts wielding *hellfire*."

Zahir's face goes as white as his hair. "Understood," he seethes. He abandons his attempt at diplomacy and walks away without looking back. The second he clears the doors, light laughter fills the outdoor space, amplified by an unnatural wind that has the prince of the Autumn Court's magical signature.

"Now," Devorah says on a light chuckle. "There's something I need to tell you about my coronation—"

"It will be an affair to remember," I say, cutting her off. She looks up at me in confusion. I take a step away from her, shifting from holding her waist to holding both her hands in mine.

"However," I continue, shooting a smirk at the crowd. "I hope it won't be the only event for you to look forward to."

I turn back to Devorah and sink to my knees.

"Ari," she gasps, her hands tightening in mine. "You don't have to do this now. We can wait..."

"Devorah, I have been in love with you for longer than I can remember," I say. Her lower lip trembles, and a little puff of air escapes her mouth. "Marry me? Tonight, at sunset. I don't want to waste another minute of this life without you by my side, without the realm knowing I am wholly, unequivocally yours."

And, unlike any queen before her, Devorah drops to her knees in front of me so that we're even. Equals. Partners.

"Yes," she whispers.

It feels like my heart has ignited, lighting up my entire body at those three little letters. I'm surprised I'm not glowing. I pull Devorah into my arms and kiss her. She laughs against my lips, her hand cupping my cheek while mine tangles at the base of her hair.

"I love you," she whispers.

"I love you so goddess-damned much, beautiful."

Everyone erupts in cheers.

We get it together enough to stand, neither of us bothering to hide the happy tears flowing from our eyes. "Well," Devorah says, clutching her chest as if her heart may spring free. "Enjoy lunch. We uh...have some preparations to make."

"Is that what the kids are calling it these days?" Edina teases. Eldoris wrinkles his nose at her. The two of us laugh, and I let Devorah take my hand and drag me into the cool air of the palace.

THE SECOND WE ENTER Devorah's suite, she pushes me up against the door, her lips capturing mine in a searing kiss. It's been less than a day, but my body missed hers like it'd been years. I'll never get enough of this, of her demanding mouth drawing out our passion as she sets the cadence of the kiss. Of the way her body fits against mine so perfectly.

"I need to hear everything," she murmurs between soft brushes of our lips. As utterly tempting as she is, there's so much we need to discuss. Fuck, I just proposed and she doesn't even know about my parentage. I assume my father told her, but I'd still like her to hear it from me.

I bury my face in her throat, luxuriating in her scent, the intoxicating mix of jasmine and something uniquely *her*. She hums contentedly, playing with my hair and lightly dragging her nails along my scalp. I could stay here forever, hovering in the entryway to her suite with her wrapped in my arms.

"I'm technically royalty," I say, smirking into her skin. Pulling away, I cup her face in my hands. She leans into my touch, eyes drifting closed momentarily. When she opens them, the ocean blue of her irises shimmers with a layer of unshed tears. "Did my father tell you?"

"He did, but it wouldn't have mattered. I would have married you anyway." Her hands land on my chest, right above my pounding heart, where my tattoo of the court's crest lies.

"I wouldn't have let you—"

"Ari, you don't *let* me do anything," she says sternly. "Besides, I'm pretty sure I have a trump card that even the record keeper can't ignore."

She slips from my grasp, going to her bay window and pulling a piece of paper out from the back of her sketch book. "It's a letter from my mother." She hands it to me, pausing to let me read the scrawling script before continuing. "All my mother wanted for me was a partner who could understand the stresses of my job—who could be a sounding board when I needed one most." Her smile is slow and sexy. "Who better than my advisor to help me navigate my reign?"

"And you were planning on showing this to the record keeper?"

She takes the letter back and magically returns it to its place.

"Larisa and Vlad were pretty sure I could use it as a loophole. But then your dad came and told me everything." She drapes her arms around my neck. "How are you feeling about it all?"

I haven't had time to process the fact that I now know who my mother is, or that my father knew for a while and never told me. I shoved all that into a small box in the back of my mind when I found out I was eligible to marry Devorah—and then I was kidnapped and had other things on my mind.

I'm sure most of it will come to a head when I see Celesta—she's coming to the palace to meet with us and the record keeper—but for now, I'm content to focus on the good things. Like the beautiful female in my arms. The way that white dress clings to her body.

And the fact that I get to keep her for all eternity.

"I feel like the luckiest male in the world." I tuck a piece of her coffee-colored hair behind her delicately pointed ear. She shivers as I thread my hands through her hair and grasp it at the base of her neck. She inhales sharply as I use my grip to tug her head back so I can kiss her deeply. It's a kiss that stokes the fire within me, illuminating all the darkest parts of my soul.

"That's one way to change the subject," she chuckles. Her lips are pink and swollen, and it makes me ravenous. That chuckle turns to a whimper as I tug her head to the side and trail kisses past her jaw and down the slope of her neck. There's this primal part of me that needs to claim her wholly, to imprint myself on every inch of her, and I lean headfirst into the urge. "Ari—"

"Keep saying my name like that and we'll never make it to our ceremony."

I spin us so that she's braced against the door and rock my erection against her core. She moans into my mouth, all protests disappearing. "I need you," she says, grappling for my belt, then the buttons of my pants. "Need you inside me."

"Me too," I say, tugging her skirt up and shoving her panties aside before dipping my fingers into her wet heat. "You're so fucking wet for me, beautiful." It unleashes me. I step out of my pants and hoist her into my arms. Her legs wind around me like it's the most natural thing in the world for her to cling to me like this. And it is. She's made for me. My gift from the goddess.

"We should probably have sex on a bed, just once," I say, and Devorah tilts her head back and laughs. It's a gorgeous, musical sound that makes me want to pull it out of her over and over again. And when I notch the head of my cock at her entrance, and that laugh turns to a moan, I decide I'll spend the rest of my life making her make both of these sounds.

"Next time," she says, pushing down onto my cock just as I thrust up, the result is that I slide into her in one fluid motion, completely sinking to the hilt.

"Fuck," I swear. My wings snap out at the intensity of the feeling. Her eyes go wide at their appearance, of all that says. It says that I trust her wholly, that she's the only one for me.

Her hand raises cautiously, slow enough that I can tell her to stop, but I don't. Her fingers skate over the newly grown skin on the edge of my wing. White-hot pleasure, unlike anything I've ever known sears through me, tightening my balls and making my dick throb.

"Devorah," I gasp as she traces the horizontal ridges that ripple inward toward my back.

I want to draw out this moment, but the sensation of her hands on my wings is too good. I start pumping into her, trying to keep my strokes slow and languid but failing desperately. My fingers dig into her hips, and she screams as I hit that spot inside her that makes her see stars.

Her wings unfurl, shredding her dress. "Touch me," she pleads. I shift so she's braced fully against the door and skim my hand up her waist, bunching the remaining material. My fingers graze the bottom edge of her wing, and at the same time, I lean down so that my nose grazes the bit over her shoulder. They're so delicate, and they shimmer red and orange in the sunlight streaming through the windows of the suite.

With a cry, she digs her heels into my ass, urging me faster. "Just like that. Don't stop."

OF FIRE AND SACRIFICE

I couldn't stop if a fucking centaur burst in and trampled us both.

We're a panting mess of sensation—fingers against wings, lips against skin, our bodies crashing together over and over again.

"I'm close," I grunt.

"Me too. Ari...I fuck—" Devorah's head tilts back, smacking against the door as she comes with a scream. Her pussy clenches around me, pulling my orgasm from me and I bellow my release into her shoulder. It goes on and on, my cock spasming inside her, marking her as mine.

"All fucking mine."

"Yours," she murmurs.

We stand like that for a while, coming down from our mutual orgasms with panting breaths and cooling skin. When I finally slip out of her, our combined release follows. I groan at the sight, my cock already hardening again.

"Save that for tonight," she says, waving a hand to clean both of us up. I put my pants back on and perform a spell to even out the wrinkles in my shirt and jacket, which never quite made it off. "The record keeper and priestess should be here soon. And your mom."

My mom. "Fuck, that's weird." Devorah chuckles as she banishes the ruined dress and summons a silk robe.

"I can't believe I didn't see it," she says, but I'm transfixed by the way the silk cradles her breasts above the tie. Her eyes heat when she notices my stare. "Later."

"I hope you don't have any delusions of attending our reception." I prowl toward her and haul her against me, kissing her until she's breathless, only stopping because of the knock on the door. Tucking a piece of hair behind her ear, I say, "A few more hours."

"And then I'll be your wife."

That may be the best sentence I've ever heard.

Chapter Forty-Two
Ari

CELESTA FIDGETS IN THE robe Devorah made her wear for the meeting with the priestess and the record keeper. With the assurance that she's my mother, the record keeper easily agreed that we were eligible to marry and that Devorah can be coronated tomorrow.

The meeting with the priestess went just as seamlessly. It wasn't a surprise that Devorah and I easily agreed to the terms of our marriage. We agreed to be faithful to each other, but if either of us should meet our mate, we would open our marriage to include the other Fae. Simple. Uncomplicated. Traditional.

This meeting, on the other hand...

I knew my first conversation with Celesta as my mother would be awkward, but this feels almost unbearable. I'm at a loss for words. I have so many questions, some so vulnerable that I'm not sure I'll ever have the courage to ask them aloud.

We're sitting in Devorah's office, the large, cluttered desk between us. Devorah offered to be here with me, but I need to have this conversation alone. Being in her office, the room coated in her scent, the room where we've had so many wonderful memories, is enough to lend me some strength.

"I'm sure you know this," she begins slowly, her purple eyes—fuck how didn't I ever see that we have the same eyes?—lifting to mine. "But half-siren children can't breathe underwater. At the time, I had some enemies, and was worried that if I kept you on the shoreline that they would lure you to the ocean and drown you."

"They would drown a child?" I ask incredulously.

"We're not exactly known for our compassion." The words are defensive, her skin flushing a leathery green before reverting to its normal lavender. "It may not have been the best course of action, but I believed it was the right thing to do at the time. Then you emerged and didn't have any of the siren traits, and I knew you were better off here."

"You could have—" I clear my throat around the lump that's lodged there.

Celesta's face softens, not needing to hear the end of my statement. "I was going to tell you," she whispers. The usual magic in her voice drops, leaving only a rough, scratchy timbre that cuts through the walls surrounding my heart. I don't know why, but I know instinctively that the lack of melody in her voice means she's being honest. As if she shucked off all her outer layers and is letting me peer behind the curtain.

"There was one time I planned to tell you and your father, but you had just left for the mortal realm. By the time you returned, I had lost my nerve. I was ashamed." She averts her gaze, looking down at the hands she's wringing together. It's such an odd look on a woman whom I've only ever seen as immensely powerful.

I don't know how to respond to this. I understand it, but that doesn't make it okay. I may not have actively missed a mother, nor did I ever think my life was worse without one, but her abandonment still hurts.

"I just hope," she clears her throat. "I hope, one day, you'll allow me to be a part of your life. However big or small that part is."

That's the question. Do I want her in my life even though she left me? Can I forgive her?

"I'm grateful you told me now," I say slowly. "But I think I'll need time."

She nods in understanding. "I can wait. We have time; we're immortal."

A clock chimes in the corner, a reminder that I need to get ready. Again, without prompting, Celesta stands and hugs her waist.

"I'll just—" she starts just as I say, "Would you—"

We both chuckle awkwardly. She motions for me to speak first. "Would you like to come to the wedding?"

A squawk escapes her, and it's such an unsiren-like sound that it startles a full-bodied laugh out of me. Her cheeks darken to a pretty mauve color, but she joins me in my laughter. "I would love to. May I bring some of my school? They're technically your family, and they've been desperate to meet you since they learned of your existence."

I find myself nodding. "As long as you all wear clothing."

She smiles widely. "Deal."

THE SMALL CHAPEL IS stunning. The glass ceiling is stained in the sherbert colors of the sunset, casting the room in a hazy glow. Small bunches of white calla lilies and jasmine are the only decorations, letting the beauty of the blue stone floors and the gleaming polish of the rose quartz altar shine.

The guest list for the ceremony is sparse, just the monarchs and their families, my father, and Celesta and the school of sirens, which is much more than I anticipated, but still not enough to fill all the seats. The reception tonight will be larger, but we wanted this to be intimate.

I stand on the altar, my father beside me, and three priestesses standing behind us. I'm oddly nervous. The temptation to bounce on the balls of my feet is strong, but I remain still with my hands clasped in front of me.

"You ready?" my father whispers. He wears a black tuxedo with a teal pocket square in honor of Queen Talia, who used to insist everyone wear some scrap of the color at all formal events.

I'm about to answer, to tell him I've never been more ready for anything in my entire life, when the door opens, sunlight backlighting Devorah and Eldoris as they enter.

My breath catches in my throat.

She's the most stunning creature I've ever seen.

She wears a simple dress, some sort of ivory silk. It has thick straps that plunge into a deep-V, and it hugs her body to her knees before flaring out into a modest train. She doesn't wear a veil; instead, a turquoise flower is pinned amongst the curls that are artfully styled into a low bun at the side of her neck. Her bouquet is a myriad of turquoise, aquamarine, and lapis flowers that make it look like she's holding the very ocean itself.

Her smile illuminates the room, brighter than the sun, brighter than any star. I'm vaguely aware of Eldoris smiling at me, but I can't take my eyes off my future wife.

When they reach the end of the aisle, he kisses her cheek and takes her bouquet, before walking to the side of the altar and leaving Devorah to take my arm. "Goddess," I breathe. I want to scoop her in my arms and kiss her—or throw her over my shoulder and run off with her.

"You can't call me that here, we're in a chapel," she teases.

"I only speak the truth."

She playfully rolls her eyes. We turn to face each other fully, clasping our hands as the head priestess begins the ceremony. I stare into Devorah's eyes, the endless ocean depths pulling me under.

I only understand every other word in the Old Fae language, but I know deep in my bones what they mean. Mentally, I make my own vows to Devorah.

I promise to be the one you can turn to on the hard days.

I promise to be your best friend.

I promise to cherish every moment we spend together.

I promise to always lift you up, never tear you down.

I promise to never take you for granted.

I promise to love you eternally.

To my surprise, Devorah's eyes fill with tears. Her voice fills my head as she mentally repeats my vows to me.

When she's finished, and tears are unabashedly streaming down my cheeks, she adds, *You opened a mental channel. But you didn't exactly shield it.* She casually looks out at the pews, and everyone is teary-eyed. My father loudly blows his nose, making us both breathe a laugh.

As all three priestesses join in a chant, iridescent magic wraps around us, binding us together with the power of the ceremony. Slowly, it grows darker, to a pearlescent ivory before fading entirely, sinking into our skin, our bones, our very souls.

"I now pronounce you husband and wife," the head priestess announces.

Devorah doesn't wait for permission. She loops her arms around my neck and kisses me. I pull her into me, keeping her as close as I can so that our bodies are fused just as our souls have.

"I love you, beautiful," I say.

"I love you, Little Hershel."

I thank the goddess for every hardship, every heartache, and every sacrifice. It was all worth it because it led to this moment.

To the moment where I can hold this beautiful creation in my arms and know she's mine.

For eternity.

Devorah

A Little Way Down the Road

"I'M SORRY. CAN YOU run that by me one more time?" I ask, staring Hershel down from across my desk.

I opted to keep my office instead of moving to my mother's—mainly because it would have been too much of a pain in the ass to find everything once I moved it, but also because I feel comfortable here. Despite its small size, this space is mine.

When Ari and I got married, I asked Hershel to step in as my personal advisor. He agreed to be an interim advisor until I could find someone who wasn't family. I've lost track of how long ago that was. We both know I never really looked for his replacement.

Since that fateful day when he suggested I kill my mother, he hasn't made a bad call.

Until now, apparently.

"I think it's great," Hershel says, running his hand across his jaw. "Her-see-ellie." He accentuates each syllable, drawing it out.

"Adding an accent doesn't change the fact that you want us to name our unborn daughter Hershel."

"I don't know, I kind of like it," Ari says from his place over my shoulder. "We could call her Little Hershel." I glare. He barks a laugh, which causes his father to break and laugh as well. I hold out as long as I can before my stony façade breaks and I join in.

"I still think Celestina is pretty," Celesta says with a shrug of her bare shoulder, where the robe she's donned has slipped down. I'm lucky she's wearing anything at all—it's been a long battle to keep her from running around the palace nude. I understand it's a quirk of the sirens, and it mostly doesn't bother me, but she's my damn mother-in-law, and that makes it weird.

I place a hand on my stomach, the tiny Fae princess inside jumping in reaction to my laughter. Ari drops to his knees beside my chair and lays his hand beside mine, and our little girl kicks right at the spot where his hand is. "I don't think she likes Celestina," he says.

"Are we talking baby names?" The door opens, and Edina pops her head inside before she and Eldoris both squeeze themselves inside the small office.

"It's all we talk about lately," I say.

"In the mortal realm," Edina says, "celebrities sometimes name their children wild, unconventional names. You could name her Blossom or Meatloaf."

"Or Oreo," Eldoris adds.

"Are those the cookies Devorah likes?" Hershel asks.

Just the mention of them makes my mouth water. "Please tell me you're going back to the mortal realm to get some soon."

"About that," Edina bites her lip. A package of deliciousness appears in her hand. "It's been a really long time since I've gotten them from the mortal realm. I've just been summoning them."

"You mean to tell me I could have had these cookies every single day of my pregnancy?" I shriek, my voice getting louder with each word.

Edina shrugs. "I mean, they're super processed, so they're not really good for you—"

Ari rounds the desk and snatches the package, shooting her a frosty glare before opening them and handing me one. I take a pointed chomp of the cookie, exaggerating my frustration. My act dissipates as soon as the chocolate hits my taste buds.

Everyone is quiet for precisely one second, letting me finish my first cookie before Eldoris says, "Would you name her after Mom?"

"No, she needs to have her own identity," Celesta says.

"And Celestina or Hershell lets her have her own identity?" Edina deadpans.

They begin bickering amongst themselves, spouting baby names and looking at my swollen belly like my daughter will somehow agree with them.

Ari leans in, kissing my temple and stealing a cookie. "Should we tell them we've already decided?"

"And miss all the fun?" We both turn as Edina stops naming foods and moves on to types of weapons—"Rapier would be adorable!"—and laugh at their expense.

I lean into my husband's embrace, resting my hands on my stomach. "Just a few more days, and then we get to meet you, Jasmine," I murmur, soft enough for only Ari to hear. In the past, being due any day would have made me anxious, even panicked.

But with Ari by my side, and my crazy family surrounding us, I know there's nothing we won't be able to face.

The End

Thank you so much for reading Of Fire and Sacrifice: Book Three of the Fae Romance Series!
Reviews are so important to indie authors. If you enjoyed the book, I would be very grateful if you would leave a review on
GoodReadsAmazon
or anywhere you review books!

Enjoy FREE Bonus Epilogue about Devorah and Ari's wedding night. All bonus material can be found at linktr.ee/marianneascott.

Want to see how Edina and Eldoris got together? Head back to the first book:

Of Ice and Heartbreak

A rejected mates, arranged marriage, fake dating romance
The following is a special sneak peek of the first chapter...

Of Ice and Heartbreak
Excerpt

Edina

"FUCK ME, IT'S COLD."

The winter wind threw the door open, rattling the bell above it as I stumbled inside *The Cracked Chalice*, a dive bar down the road from my school and the only place I could conceivably get to in this weather. Though, in hindsight, I should have changed into jeans rather than the mini-dress I wore. Even with the thigh-high boots I chose for the weather, I still had a lot of skin showing. Skin that was now all pink and wind burnt.

It took me shoving my weight into the door to get it to shut again, and when I turned back to the interior of the bar, the patrons, all three of them, were staring. "Hey, boys," I wiggled my fingers in their direction while I knocked the toe of my boots against the floor to clear the excess snow that accumulated. I shucked off my puffy coat and hood, and shook out my hair, running fingers through my long blonde waves to untangle the knots. The scarf came next as I shoved it in my jacket pocket and hung it all on a coat rack in the corner beside the door.

"Didn't think you'd make it." I looked up across the dimly lit space and found Joe, the owner and bartender, lounging on a lawn chair behind the bar. He was a middle-aged man who had lost most of his brown hair, though he tried to make up for it with the scraggly graying beard he rocked. I grinned when I saw him wearing the flannel I'd bought him for

Christmas last year, the red marginally less faded than the ones he usually wore.

"Don't lie. I'm the whole reason you opened tonight," I laughed, making my way through empty wooden tables and approaching the bar. The other customers went back to whatever game they were watching, the lights of the flatscreen competing with a few neon signs that showcased the beer and liquor offerings alongside a large, red neon sign that read *BAR* directly over the liquor.

Joe shook his head and stood, making me a drink before I even got to the forest-green leather stools. I loved this place. I loved the worn wooden floors that always had a fine coating of peanut shells, even on slow nights. I loved that I could still spot the abnormally large scuff on one of the tables from when my best friend and I discovered tequila and table dancing. And I loved that it was just clean enough that I wasn't afraid to put my head down on the shiny varnished bar top.

Joe set my vodka soda on the bar by my preferred stool, tossing in an extra lime with a wink before logging the drink into the computer. I left my parents' black card here years ago. It was easier, and I trusted Joe. I checked the statement once and found out he wasn't leaving himself tips on the tab. When I asked him about it, he said, "You're not supposed to tip the owner." So, I started bringing cash.

I sipped my drink and sighed. The bitterness from the soda cut the citrus of the lime so perfectly that I took another large gulp. I didn't even taste the vodka tonight, which usually spelled trouble, but felt fantastic.

"Long week?" Joe asked, sitting back in his chair with a little grunt as he sank.

"Finals," I said around the straw, taking another gulp.

"Should I just leave you the bottle?" he chuckled. Without taking my eyes off him, I abandoned my straw and chugged the rest of my drink.

When I slammed the glass back on the counter, he was belly-laughing as he put another drink in front of me. "I was gonna drink this one but looks like you need it more than me."

"You're too good to me." I slid him the empty glass.

"Which final was it today?" he asked, and I noticed he kept the bottle within arm's reach that time.

"Battle Magic."

That was one of the other reasons I liked it here. Joe, like me, was a witch. As were most of the regulars. I know, witches in Salem, Massachusetts. Stereotypical. But sometimes myths were born from just enough reality that they're conceivable. Salem happened to be a major hub of witches in the Kingdom of Magic since one of the best magical academies and a magical military base were here. Not that any of the mortals— non-magic-using folk— knew we existed, living right alongside them. They explained away the extraordinary, and we did our best to keep our magic hidden. It's why places like *The Cracked Chalice* were so great. We were able to let ourselves relax.

"Any more?" Joe asked, and I shook my head. My Battle Magic final was my last one, which meant I had only one semester left at Salem Academy of Magical Arts. *Thank fucking god.* I got it, witches needed to learn to control their magic so we could blend into the mortal world, but I've had a pretty solid handle on my magic for years. I just wanted to be done and move to London to be near my best friend and set up a wedding planning business that used actual magic to make mortal weddings...well magical.

"Headed to the island for the break?" Joe asked as I stirred my drink. My parents...owned an island, which I didn't tell many people because they automatically assumed things, only some of which were true.

"Nah, London," I beamed, and Joe instantly caught my meaning.

"How is Katie? I miss her."

"Promoted again." I bragged like it was my accomplishment. My best friend was an overachiever like that. "In another high-profile relationship. Overall, killing it."

Joe laughed heartily. He got a kick out of our dating lives, mainly because I think it reminded him of the glory days. "I almost forgot," he said and pointed to something over the cash register covered in brown paper. "Wanna see your birthday present?"

"Is this what I think it is?" I squealed, standing on the footrest of my stool and leaning as far over the bar as I could. He got up and ripped the paper down, revealing a picture of me, Joe, and Katie from my eighteenth birthday. We'd had another blizzard like this, so we couldn't go into the city. Katie and I talked to Joe until he finally kicked us out, but not before I forced him to take the picture and promised I'd be his favorite customer one day. "*Joe!*"

"It's an incentive to keep drinking here even though you can be served anywhere now," he said, rubbing the back of his neck. I beckoned him closer and pulled him into a half hug over the bar. When Katie left for London, Joe sort of became my best friend here.

"It's cute that you think I don't get served everywhere," I whispered, and when he pulled away, I gave him a flirty wink and a shrug of my shoulder. His laugh boomed through the empty space.

My phone buzzed in my bra, and I turned away to fish it out to spare poor Joe like he didn't accidentally witness my nip slip a year ago. My good mood deflated when I saw Mia's name on my screen.

Mia

> Heyyyyyy. Soooo, Brett just texted and asked if I was going to Mikayla's party...and he seemed so sad when I said I wasn't.

I scoffed. Brett was her on-again-off-again situationship.

Mia

So, I'm gonna go there. Are you mad?

Mia

Don't be mad.

"Get stood up?" Joe asked. I rolled my eyes.

"It's impossible to find a decent wing-woman, Joe." I texted Mia back and told her to stop being a whipped little bitch. The three dots appeared and disappeared about five times before I gave in and told her it was okay.

"I don't think you'll have much luck in here tonight," Joe said, setting a fresh drink in front of me. I groaned and flopped dramatically on the bar. I really needed to blow off some steam and was hoping I could find someone to do that with.

I bailed on Mikayla's party because I'd already slept with the people I found attractive from my school. And I didn't do repeats.

My phone buzzed again.

Mia

So I just walked in...

Damn, that girl worked fast.

Mia

And Mark is asking for you. Laura too. And she's super drunk...Cinco de Mayo in Cabo, drunk. She keeps screaming that she wants to make out with a girl before we leave school.

I was not in the mood to be someone's first tonight, but Mark was promising. He wasn't really my type, he had the whole cute-nerdy thing going on, but I'd heard he at least knew how to find a clit. One more drink, two max. Then I'd be drunk enough to have some bad sex with a college student. That was the problem, once you started fucking people in their late twenties/early thirties. Anyone younger just...lacked.

The bell on the door tinkled as I shelled a peanut and discarded the remnants on the floor. "Maybe not," Joe muttered under his breath, as he stood and straightened his flannel. I popped another peanut into my mouth as the stool next to mine slid back.

"Scotch, neat," the voice next to me said to Joe. His voice wasn't deep, per se, but it had a faint accent that was intriguing. Not quite British, but close...like maybe he lived there for a bit.

I could feel his eyes on me, but instead, I made eye contact with Joe, who nodded, telling me the guy next to me was worth my time. I chuckled into my drink. *Maybe Joe is the wing-woman I've been searching for.* I turned over my shoulder slightly and scanned the body of the man beside me.

He was wearing dark denim, and a black button-down shirt rolled up to his elbows, exposing pale skin. He didn't look super muscular, but that slim kind of toned. Finally, I looked at his face and my mouth parted. His hair was brownish red, and he had a smattering of freckles over the bridge of his nose, but his eyes were what kept me captivated. They were so green it was almost otherworldly. He definitely had some kind of magic; I could practically feel it wafting off him.

His stare was intent, not even the slightest bit ashamed that I caught him looking at me as much as I was looking at him. "Do you come here often?" he asked, and I scoffed.

"*That's* your opening line?" I asked, unable to keep myself from laughing.

His flirty smile was crooked and all kinds of disarming. "Yeah, I fucked that up," he laughed.

"You wanna give it another go?"

Joe set his drink down. The man picked it up and downed the contents in one gulp. He cleared his throat, and in the most serious voice said, "What's your sign?" I cackled, the earlier drinks making my laugh easy and loud, and he lit up at the sound. "I'm Puck," he said, sticking out his hand.

"As in hockey?"

"As in Shakespeare. My mother was a tad obsessed with *A Midsummer Night's Dream*." I placed my hand in his. His grip was tight, but his skin was soft, so definitely not someone who worked with his hands. His thumb brushed against my palm in a way that made my core tighten.

"I'm Edina."

"Can I buy you a drink, Edina?" The sound of my name in his accent had my stomach flipping. I bit my lower lip and watched as he tracked the movement.

"Hmm." I playfully tapped my finger on my chin. "I'm not sure you moved past the first round. Those opening lines..." I clucked my tongue.

Somehow, I ended up spinning toward him, which wasn't noticeable until he placed one foot between mine on the footrest and his thigh brushed against mine. He leaned forward, and I fought the urge to mimic his movements. In a low, rough voice he murmured, "Don't worry. I *excel* at the next part."

A slow smirk spread across my face. "Prove it."

About the Author

Marianne A. Scott has been writing since she was a kid. When she was always singing, those stories appeared in song form, when she majored in acting, they appeared as screenplays, but novels and short stories were what she returned to when inspiration struck. Each and every story was driven by characters and love, and, most of the time, the hope that there was something fantastical about this world that we humans just haven't discovered yet.

When not writing, you can find her with her Kindle and a latte, sitting opposite her husband in their New Jersey home. In her other life, she teaches tiny humans how to sing, passing along her love of musical theater to the next generation.

Want first dibs on all future ARCs, special sneak peeks, and more? Join my Reader's Group or sign up for my Email List.

All links can be found at linktr.ee/marianneascott

Also by Marianne A. Scott

The Made from Magic Series
An Urban Fantasy Trilogy
Made from Magic
Made to Conquer
Made to Rule
A Court Where I'm Freezing My A** Off (Made from Magic #2.5)

The Fae Romance Series
A Series of Contemporary Romantasy Standalones
Of Ice and Heartbreak
Of Vines and Rivals
Of Fire and Sacrifice

Acknowledgements

First and foremost, I'd like to thank all of you who have made it this far. Thank you for helping me realize this dream.

This book was the hardest book I've ever written. When I finished the first draft, I was so excited, and planned on having the book out within a couple months. Then, I had surgery, and everything went tits up. I couldn't look at a computer for the better part of six months, so it felt like I was editing forever.

I was moments before throwing the entire book away when I decided instead to send it to a friend. She gave me the confidence, and some amazing advice, that I needed to fall in love with the story again. So, thank you Cortney. This book wouldn't have been possible without you. And to the rest of my beta readers who lifted me up during a time when I was still unsure about the reception of this story. Cara, Ariana, Shayla, Miranda, Sarah, Hannah, Samantha and Hanah—thank you from the bottom of my heart.

To the best husband in the entire universe of the world, thank you for always supporting me, and for always comforting me when the imposter syndrome hits. Thank you for being a sounding board when I need to talk through plot points, even when I don't listen and just need to talk at you. Thank you for taking care of all the behind-the-scenes things I wasn't prepared for when I went into self-publishing. And especially, thank you for not getting too frustrated when I watch you while reading the book. In my defense...if you're going to laugh, I'm going to ask what part you're on. Love you, pants.

To my amazing parents, thank you for being excited every time I tell you page read numbers and Amazon rankings. You're my biggest cheerleaders and I thank you so much for your never-ending support. And for John, thank you for reading and providing me with up-to-date texts to let me know what you think.

To all those who have helped me along the way, including my amazing editors Roxana Coumans who didn't hesitate to help me edit a chapter I forgot to send her in my original submission, Cassidy at Moonlit Town End Art & Design for listening to my ramblings about the cover and turning it into something truly stunning, Amanda at Eternal Geekery for taking a potato of a map and turning it into a real-life world.

When I began writing this series, I found myself suddenly needing names for landmarks. As someone who typically writes Urban Fantasy, I was overwhelmed. Thank you to everyone who offered amazing names for forests and rivers and everything in between on my Instagram and Facebook posts, but a super SUPER special thank you to the following for helping me bring this world to life: Samantha Newsome (Padauk River), Carol Bennett (Etherealia Meadow), Rachel Betancourt (Varesen Forest), Elizabeth Grimme (Dorchas Desert), Pradhyutha (Atavi Forest), Sarena (Allagi River), Kelsey Lynn (Oraiste Mountains), Sara Marney (the town of Blath), and Jillian Melko (Immutavi Ocean).

Thank you to my family who are literally the most supportive people in the entire universe. I'm seriously so lucky to have you all rooting for me. I hope you know how invaluable your support has been.

Last but not least, thank you to the amazing readers who have taken a moment to reach out and tell me how much you love these books and characters. You have no idea how much your comments, messages, and posts brighten my days and keep me going through the worst of the imposter syndrome. A huge mega shoutout to the readers in GrossBooks 2.0, for your overall positivity and willingness to talk about all things book-related!

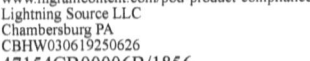